Soviet Literary Culture
in the 1970s

Soviet Literary Culture in the 1970s

_____ The Politics of Irony

_____

_____

_____

ANATOLY VISHEVSKY

With an Anthology of Ironic Prose Translated by
Michael Biggins and Anatoly Vishevsky

University Press of Florida
Gainesville Tallahassee Tampa Boca Raton
Pensacola Orlando Miami Jacksonville

The stories "One, Two, Three . . . " and "A Ruble Sixty Isn't Much," by Viktoria Tokareva, were first printed between 1960 and 1970 in Russian newspapers. Copyright 1991 by Diogenes Verlag AG, Zurich. All rights reserved.

Library of Congress Cataloging-in-Publication Data

Vishevskiĭ, Anatoliĭ.
Soviet literary culture in the 1970s: the politics of irony /
Anatoly Vishevsky; with an anthology of ironic prose translated by
Michael Biggins and Anatoly Vishevsky.
p. cm.
Includes bibliographical references and index.
ISBN 0-8130-1225-2. — ISBN 0-8130-1226-0 (pbk.)
1. Short stories, Russian—History and criticism. 2. Russian
fiction—20th century—History and criticism. 3. Irony in
literature. 4. Short stories, Russian—Translations into English.
5. Soviet Union—Popular culture. I. Title.
PG3097.V57 1993
891.73'010918—dc20   93-1259
                                                            CIP

The University Press of Florida is the scholarly publishing agency for the State University System of Florida, comprised of Florida A & M University, Florida Atlantic University, Florida International University, Florida State University, University of Central Florida, University of Florida, University of North Florida, University of South Florida, and University of West Florida.

University Press of Florida
15 Northwest 15th Street
Gainesville, FL 32611

CONTENTS

PREFACE

In this book I investigate ironic discourse as representative of a world-view shared by a wide intellectual community in the Soviet Union in the 1970s. (By the 1970s is meant the broader span of time beginning in the late, and in a few cases mid, 1960s and extending through the end of the decade of the 1970s.) This phenomenon, which can be called the popular culture of the intellectual, consists of a variety of particular literary and cinematographic movements, stand-up comedy, chansons, and short humorous stories in the media. An anthology of the last of these genres and forms appears in English translation for the first time in Part 2 of this book, which is intended for students of contemporary Soviet culture and literature.

The transliteration of Russian into English follows that of the Library of Congress; exceptions are made for Russian proper and family names in the text and explanatory notes, but not in the bibliographical entries. When one Russian vowel is represented in the Library of Congress system by *ia, iu, ë*, we generally use *ya, yu, yo*, as in Lyudmila, Baranovskaya (but Sergachev). In exceptional cases, for ease of reading, *e* is rendered as *ye*: Soyev. *I-kratkoe* and *i i-kratkoe* at the end of the names are transliterated by *y*: Anatoly, Kurlyandsky, Zhvanetsky. *Iia* at the end of names is rendered as *ia*: Viktoria, Yulia, Danelia. Most names that have an exact English counterpart are anglicized: Alexander, Felix, Maxim, Herbert, Herman (but Eduard, Pyotr). Soft signs in names are omitted. When a writer uses a particular spelling of his or her name in English, it is preserved: Vassily Aksyonov. Names of Russian cities are given in the Library of Congress transliteration, except for Moscow; the same is true for the titles of Soviet periodicals. An exception is made here for *Literaturnaia gazeta*, which is referred to as *Literary Gazette*. Translations in Part 1 of the book are mine, except for passages quoted from stories in the anthology, which were translated in collaboration with Michael Biggins.

I would like to thank all of my teachers, peers, friends, and students who in some way or another helped this book to appear: Vassily Aksyonov, Milica Banjanin, David Bethea, Thomas Beyer, Michael Biggins, Boris Briker, Michael Finke, Vladimir Frumkin, Marina Jones,

Dodona Kiziria, Nicole Klungle, Lev Loseff, William Matheson, Mikhail Palatnik, Stephen Parker, Erik and Natalia Pervukhin, Elena Sedletskaya, Munir Sendich, Ilya Suslov, Ania Wertz. The research for this book was aided by a Washington University Summer Research Grant.

PART 1

_____

_____

_____

_____

Irony as the Leading Mode
in Soviet Literature and
Culture of the 1970s

Introduction

―――――――――

―――――――――

―――――――――

―――――――――

The events culminating in the disintegration of the Soviet Union have focused the world's attention on the current political and cultural atmosphere of that country. The policy of "openness" (*glasnost*) has made it possible for a number of works of literature, mostly of past decades, to appear in the press, on stage, and on the screen. Anthologies of contemporary literature include young authors whose major works have come to light only with the opening up of the Soviet press. Established writers have been reexamined and reevaluated according to their "new" works—written years ago but first published in the Soviet Union only after 1985.

The epoch immediately preceding Gorbachev's reforms has been called the "period of stagnation" (период застоя); this term has been also picked up by scholars of culture and literature, whose attention has shifted to the time of glasnost. This natural reaction—heightened interest in new and exciting events and a tendency to forget the preceding, presumably dull and uneventful period—ignores an important epoch in the cultural history of the country, an epoch that is essential for understanding not only the political but also the cultural and literary atmosphere of the country as it is today. The policy of "openness" and the other changes initiated at the end of the 1980s created a clear-cut line between the old and the new country, the old and the new individual. If this border allows us to look at the 1970s as a self-contained and finite period, it also provides our view with a perspective and a possibility to relate this period to the present.

The predominant worldview of Soviet writers in the 1970s was irony. The ironic mood was the result of the collapse of dreams and hopes for a better and freer society brought on by the temporary liberalization of the country's political atmosphere after Stalin's death. The ideals of the late 1950s were no longer valid, the values no longer unshakable, and the belief that it was possible to change society was finally abandoned. The brief thaw after Stalin's death had ended and a new epoch had begun, characterized by the strengthening of the bureaucratic apparatus and by a dull and eventless routine in art and everyday life. In the words of Maurice Friedberg, "The first post-Stalinist decade was, in essence, one of euphoria, social muckraking, and clamor of reforms, albeit within the limits of the Soviet idea and of Soviet institutions. The second, by contrast, saw the dashing of these hopes."[1]

The beginning of this process can be seen in the literary movement of the late 1950s and early 1960s called "Young prose" («Молодая проза»).[2] The period of the thaw brought new techniques of writing. Alongside literature that tried to comprehend the meaning and nature of the events of Stalinism, a new current appeared. Young writers grouped around the journal *Iunost'* (*Youth*), founded in 1955 by Valentin Kataev. They turned to new themes—the new horizons in life opened for the young with the death of Stalin and the fall of Stalinism. In the words of a critic, the new prose "signaled a change from the usual relationship of writer/Party/reader, to that of writer/reader."[3]

The Young prose movement is generally associated with its three major representatives: Vassily Aksyonov, Anatoly Gladilin, and Vladimir Voinovich. Their early works—*Colleagues* (*Коллеги*), *Starry Ticket* (*Звездный билет*), and the collection of stories *Halfway to the Moon* (*На полпути к луне*) by Aksyonov; *We Live Here* (*Мы здесь живем*) by Voinovich; and *The First Day of the New Year* (*Первый день Нового года*) by Gladilin—acquired considerable popularity, particularly among the youth. The prose writers Andrey Bitov, Vasily Kazakov, Fazil Iskander, and Yury Nagibin and the poets Evgeny Evtushenko, Andrey Voznesensky, and Bella Akhmadulina were also part of the movement. Besides treating unconventional themes, the writers experimented with style in their novellas and short stories. In general, their style was light, in contrast to the "heavy" novels of the Stalinist epoch. One of their objectives was, in fact, to break with literary convention. Aksyonov and Gladilin, for example, often parodied literary stereotypes in their works (Aksyonov's *Starry Ticket* , Gladilin's *Smoke in Your Eyes* [*Дым в глаза*] and *Eternal Business Trip* [*Вечная командировка*]). Irony in the works of the Young prose writers was thus restricted to narrative style.

By the late 1960s the Young prose movement had died out. Works written in its characteristic ironic tone continued to be produced, but they were quickly becoming an anachronism. In 1967 critics wrote: "The followers of the 'new' movement do not notice that that humorous, ironic, and parodic style, so pervasive in the literature, acts now as a signal of something new only by force of tradition. For a long time now it has represented only its own canons, its own inertia of mind and style. It turned into a mere sign of the truth, which is offered to the reader by the old memory of the truth itself."[4] The Young prose had an optimistic outlook based on the hope for social and cultural reform and for the return of the still-cherished values and ideals of the early postrevolutionary years, and the movement's deterioration was a sign of devaluation of those ideals and values.

A collapse of hopes and loss of faith brought the turn to irony in the literature of the 1970s. The Soviet invasion of Czechoslovakia was a major impetus for the appearance of irony as a dominant mode on the literary and cultural scene. Society could not be changed, and the interest of writers shifted to the inner world of man and woman. The subject was not a "Soviet citizen" but rather a generalized portrait of an Earth inhabitant—a detached and nonjudgmental picture. Abram Terts (Andrey Sinyavsky), in his pamphlet "What Is Socialist Realism" («Что такое социалистический реализм»), analyzes irony in the works of the Russian symbolists, but his definition fits the works written in the "ironic mode" in the 1970s as well. "Irony . . . is the laughter of a superfluous man at himself and at everything that is sacred in the world. Irony is an unfailing companion of the lack of faith and doubt."[5]

Irony in the literary culture of the 1970s was above all a product of this disillusionment and despair. Anatoly Bocharov ties the irony of this period to the attempt to compare a real person with the ideal individual. It is a reaction to the imperfection of reality as compared with the ideal. Bocharov sees "binary opposition," whether good versus evil, dream versus reality, static versus dynamic, comic versus dramatic, or logical versus absurd, as a main characteristic of irony. The critic explains the nature of irony metaphorically, claiming that it originates in the incongruity of art and life. "Nobody, probably, will say categorically that art is a game. But everyone already knows that art is not life itself and one cannot mechanically apply a copy to the original or the original to a copy. Irony penetrates into the clearing, the crack, that results from such an attempt."[6] Bocharov cites several factors influencing the rise of irony in contemporary prose. The first is the enormous popularity of Bulgakov and Platonov, with their ironic view of the world, coupled with the discovery of Brecht and Salinger and their respective "socially active" and "detached humanitarian" types of irony. (To these names we can add a number of others, such as Camus, Sartre, Kafka, Hemingway, Faulkner, Vonnegut, Saroyan, and Tennessee Williams.) The second is the rise of "intellectual" prose, which approached reality without the preformed vision of what reality is supposed to look like. Third, irony in prose is closely connected to the mythological and parabolic prose that developed at the same time. Finally, Bocharov connects irony with the high level of self-awareness present in the society of the 1970s.

The question of irony and its audience in the literary-cultural scene of the 1970s leads us to approach the problem from the viewpoint of the reader's response, which seems appropriate because of the special bond between an audience and the subject of its attention. In the words of Hans Robert Jauss, such an approach is based on the notion of literary history as "a process of aesthetic reception and production which takes place in realization of literary texts on the part of the receptive reader, the reflective critic and the author in his continued creativity." Specific sociopolitical processes create a dominant taste, a special approach to literary and cultural texts, a "horizon of expectations." The perception of a newly created text is connected to such a horizon: "The new text evokes for the reader (listener) the horizon of expectations and rules familiar from earlier texts, which are then varied, corrected, changed, or just reproduced."[7] In the time of disillusionment and despair of the 1970s, people were especially attuned to irony, which they found in Siberian prose and in Georgian film. If we accept that a text contains a multitude of different interpretations for different readers (the idea of the "implied reader"),[8] then our "real" reader reads this text as an ironic message, assuming a stance vis-à-vis the author. Specific atmosphere in the society that creates specific taste, however, in addition to providing a unified reading of a text, may produce texts geared especially to satisfying these tastes. Susan R. Suleiman poses the important question of "how changes in the composition (and consequently in the ideology and taste) of a national reading public have contributed to the emergence of new literary forms."[9]

This is exactly the case with the stories in the ironic prose genre that appeared in Soviet periodicals of the 1970s, in the monologues of the stand-up comedian Mikhail Zhvanetsky, and partially in the songs of the bards (especially in the case of Bulat Okudzhava and minor bards). Their texts came as a direct response to the public's taste; they were in fact created by this taste. In this way the distance between the horizon of expectations and the works was nonexistent—the texts made no demands on the receiving consciousness to make a change on the horizon of unknown experience. The situation thus created "demands no horizon change but actually fulfills expectations, which are prescribed by a predominant taste, by satisfying the demand for the reproduction of familiar beauty, confirming familiar sentiments, encouraging dreams, making unusual experiences palatable as 'sensations' or even raising moral problems, but only to be able to 'solve' them in an edifying manner when the solution is already obvious."[10] Jauss suggests that the smaller the distance between the horizon of expectation and the work, "the closer the work comes to the realm of 'culinary' or light reading."[11] In such a case, since the distance between the horizon of expectation and the works mentioned is almost nonexistent, these works should be labeled "pure culinary reading." (It is ironic that these works—stories, songs, or stand-up comedy—were as a rule discussed among friends in the kitchen, where most heated debates usually took place in the Soviet Union; there is even a term for it in the contemporary cultural slang: «кухонные разговоры» [kitchen talks]).

This takes us to the question of the identity of the reader. We would describe the reader as a Soviet urban intellectual and the culture that this person consumes as well as generates—even though it sounds like an oxymoron—can be called popular intellectual culture. This ironic culture is not acceptable to everyone. Wayne C. Booth offers five handicaps impeding the perception of irony: ignorance, inability to pay attention, prejudice, lack of practice, and emotional inadequacy.[12] Irony (unlike romance, detective stories, or travelogues) did not become a household idea, and the ironic worldview never turned out to be a nationwide ideology. That is why a majority of the cultural events discussed here (for example, G. Shengelaya's film *Pirosmani* [*Пиросмани*]) did not appeal to a wide audience yet became successful with a limited one. "As a box-office hit *Pirosmani* was a failure, but as a work of art it was a complete success with the lovers and connoisseurs of the art of cinematography. The theaters were half-empty while it was playing in many, and the theater was full for many days in a row [a special repertoire theater] when it started playing in one. People would go there to see this particular film, and not movies in general."[13]

The meaning of the popular culture of the intellectual is not much different from general popular culture—it, too, is a kind of escapism and entertainment, yet its form is more sophisticated. Instead of Indian and Arabic movies, the intellectuals watched Georgian and, on occasion, Italian films; instead of Georgy Markov's *Siberia* (*Сибирь*), they read stories of the Siberian Vasily Shukshin and watched plays of another Siberian, Alexander Vampilov; instead of pop bands they listened to the songs of the bards; instead of feuilletons (фельетоны) in the party-line *Pravda*, *Izvestiia*, and *Krokodil*, they read ironic prose on the "liberal" sixteenth page of *Literaturnaia gazeta* (hereafter *Literary Gazette*); instead of the slapstick comedians Shtepsel and Tarapunka, they enjoyed listening to the subtle ironic monologues of Mikhail Zhvanetsky. Such cultural events as Georgian film, the works of Siberian writers, and some of the songs of the bards—especially Vysotsky, whose popularity extended beyond the narrow circle of the intellectuals—cannot be exhaustively described as part of the popular culture of the intellectuals, yet all these works, because of their ironic elements, entered and conveniently satisfied the horizon of expectations of this circle. The same point can be made for some Moscow and Leningrad theater performances (especially of the Taganka Theater, Bolshoi Drama Theater, Contemporary Theater, and Theater of Satire), for literature of the 1920s that was "rehabilitated" in the 1960s, for translations of Western writers, and for works of the writers from Soviet republics appearing in Russian in the national journals or in book form.[14]

Irony is a major component of many works of leading writers of the 1970s, yet in this study I will concentrate on short literary forms in which ironic themes dominate. Skepticism, pessimism, lack of belief in humankind, and disillusionment in human potential could not become central themes of a major work published in the Soviet Union at the time. Yet such themes found their way into short stories, chansons, films, stand-up comedians' routines, and, finally, humorous short stories that began appearing in periodicals at the end of the 1960s. The goal of this text is not to cite an array of examples of the ironic mode in literary and cultural media but rather to establish a pattern and to demonstrate that this mode was the leading one in the cultural atmosphere of the time.

Part 1 of the book deals with ironic applications in literary and cultural texts. As examples of irony in literature in Chapter 1 I chose a number of short stories by Siberian writers. Generally, the works dealt with here were published in Soviet periodicals and are recognizable to an average Russian reader. The stories of Evgeny Popov are an exception; although largely published abroad, these stories (some of which did appear in the Soviet press) are part of the same tradition. Furthermore, juxtaposing Popov's stories published abroad with the stories of Popov and other Siberian writers that appeared in Soviet periodicals exposes irony as their underlying mode.

As examples of irony found in literary-cultural texts, in Chapter 2 I chose the Georgian cinema, the chansons, and the stand-up comedy of Mikhail Zhvanetsky. My intention is not to give an exhaustive analysis of these complex and multifaceted phenomena but to consider the texts from the point of view of the subject. Therefore my analysis does not claim to be comprehensive; rather, this section of the book is to be approached as a description of a leading cultural mood of the time. Zhvanetsky's monologues are most homogeneous; from the Georgian cinema and chansons I selected examples in which irony appears as a prevailing element. To say that all of the Georgian cinema is dominated by the ironic view of the world would be facile, since the films, although ironic in tone, are often optimistic in their outlook, perhaps reflecting a Georgian national trait. Yet in a number of films mentioned here, an ironic view is prevalent. (It is interesting to note the 1979 film *Autumn Marathon* [*Осенний марафон*], based on a play by the Russian playwright Alexander Volodin and directed by the Georgian director Georgy Danelia, which in tone resembles Georgian films while it tells the story of a Russian man of the "lost generation" of the 1960s.) The same is true of the Russian chansons of Vysotsky, Okudzhava, and Galich. Even though the notion of irony does not exhaust the thematic range of their songs, it serves as a common denominator and helps in understanding the immense popularity of the genre.

Chapter 3 of Part 1 is devoted to a description of ironic prose, a subgenre of the humorous short story that began appearing at the end of the 1960s and enjoyed unparalleled popularity. Since most of these stories never appeared in books and were buried in the humor pages at the end of periodicals, this body of writing is given special attention. The literary-political establishment viewed the stories as trifles, bound to be thrown out with the newspaper in which they appeared. The original readers of these stories saw in them much more than entertaining trifles. In fact, while ironically musing on the absurdities of reality, these stories provided an escape from that reality. They were both an attribute and an expressive medium for intellectuals in Soviet society of the 1970s. The stories are also revealing in terms of ironic outlook; unlike the examples given previously, they present the ironic worldview in its pure form. This approach to ironic themes accounts for the restrictions of the subgenre that eventually led to its decline, yet it yields an almost "chemically pure" specimen of the ironic mode in a literary work.

Part 2 is an anthology of stories in the genre of ironic prose, the first of its kind either in Russian or in English translation. The anthology is preceded by a select bibliography of ironic prose, based on the stories discussed in Chapter 3, Part 1.

Irony as term and concept is so elusive and broad that, "like beauty, [irony] is in the eye of the beholder and is not a quality inherent in any remark, event, or situation."[15] This can also be illustrated by the definition of irony offered by Booth: "For both its devotees and for those who fear it, irony is usually seen as something that undermines clarities, opens up vistas of chaos, and either liberates by destroying all dogma or destroys by relieving the inescapable canker of negation at the heart of every affirmation."[16] An analysis of the ironic mode in the literary-cultural atmosphere of the 1970s must be preceded by a working definition of irony as it appears in the writing under study. Establishing such a definition is impossible without classifying the different kinds of irony.

I call *stylistic* the kind of irony in which the nature of the phenomenon is revealed at the level of speech. Stylistic irony in its etymology as well as in its meaning goes back to ancient Greek comedy and is connected with the *eiron*, a buffoon who pokes fun at his antagonist, the *alazon*. The eiron is small and frail but smart and resourceful and is a master of understatement. The seemingly simple eiron encourages other characters to laugh at him by assuming a heavy accent or funny gestures. The alazon (imposter) represents the principle of overstatement. His distinguishing features are pride and boastfulness carried to caricature. The comedy always ends with the defeat of the alazon, as the triumphant eiron spitefully watches the downfall of his so-called friend. Such ungracious behavior does not bring the eiron much sympathy from the audience, and thus *eironeia* in ancient Greek had a pejorative connotation. This use of irony is now universally referred to as verbal irony.

Socrates makes use of certain elements of verbal irony by presenting himself as a subtle eiron, ignorant and willing to learn from the wiser ones. He accepts his opponent's argument and humbly helps him, trying to prove the argument on the simplest levels of common sense and logic, thus driving the argument to the extreme and destroying it. This use of irony, called Socratic irony, irony of character, or irony of manner, differs from verbal irony. Here the intentional deception found at the basis of the relationship of the eiron-alazon pair disappears. The irony is no longer presented in the form itself, but in the manner of conveying the truth. A vivid example of Socratic irony is found in the writings of Alexander Zinovev. The conscious viewpoint of his narrators is full acceptance of reality as it appears in the communist state. Everything finds an explanation in the words of the narrator, who proceeds from the sophistic assumption that the existence of the state is good enough proof for its purpose, hence the bitter and satirical connotation that surrounds the picture of the "perfect society." This satirical element in stylistic irony is well described by Connop Thirlwall: "The writer effects the purpose by placing the opinion of his adversary in the foreground, and saluting it with every demonstration of respect, while he is busied in withdrawing one by one all the supports on which it rests: and he never ceases to approach it with an air of deference, until he has completely undermined it, when he leaves it to sink by the weight of its own absurdity."[17]

I call *structural* the kind of irony that is an element of the structure of the work. An example of this kind of irony is so-called Sophoclean irony, as found in ancient Greek tragedy. It occurs when the hero's situation bears for the audience an ominous sense. This sense is hidden from the hero and others on the stage. Hence Oedipus, in trying to avoid his destiny, unintentionally approaches it. Such irony, although widely used in Greek tragedy, was not perceived as irony until Bishop Thirlwall introduced the idea in 1833: "Without departing from the analogy that pervades the various kinds of verbal irony, we may speak of a *practical irony*, which is independent of all forms of speech, and needs not the aid of words."[18] The type of irony Thirlwall termed practical is also found under other names: irony of fate, dramatic irony, or tragic irony. Hutchens calls it a "dramatization of irony" and draws a line between this type of irony and irony as a rhetorical (verbal irony) or dialectical (Socratic irony) device.[19]

In dramatic irony the role of the audience takes on prime importance. Ancient Greek tragedies were almost always based on mythology, so the plots of the plays were known to the spectators before they came to the theater. The role of the audience was not to follow the plot impatiently, trying to guess what would happen next, as in detective or adventure stories, but rather to watch ironically how the characters unwittingly approach their destiny by frantically trying to avoid it. The pleasure that the Greek audience derived from performances was to some extent comparable to that which the Romans felt at gladiators' contests, where the defeated gladiator lived or died according to the whim of the audience. In the play it is the author who takes the role of fate (and even he is limited by the fabula of the myth) and decides the destiny of the characters. Nevertheless the audience becomes a silent coexecutor of the author's will. Knowledge of the plot gives the spectators the feeling of coauthorship. The possession of such secret knowledge and the detachment of the audience are the main distinguishing features of dramatic irony or irony of fate. In Shakespeare's plays chance is often substituted for fate, and we have irony of events. Both irony of fate and irony of events can fall into the more general category of tragic irony. But since they can also be found in comic situations, dramatic irony would be the more appropriate heading.

Weltanschauung is the kind of irony in which the world is perceived and evaluated from the point of view of irony. Whereas the previous kinds of irony were rhetorical or dialectic, this kind is metaphysical. David Worcester writes, "This shift of meaning, from the objective appearance of irony to the internal attitude of mind of its author, opened the door to the subjective, mystical, and ego-worshiping properties of the German romanticists."[20] The type of irony described by the critic is called Romantic irony, which, while making use of existing types of irony, was a qualitatively new phenomenon connected with the German Romantic movement. It resulted from Romantic writers' realization of the inadequacy of the written word for the expression of ideas. Novalis defined irony as "genuine consciousness, true presence of mind."[21] To some extent Romantic irony is an illustration of the Nietzschean idea that life is a spectacle, a performance, staged by a superior force. The realization of this idea and its presentation in literature illustrate the writer's wisdom and, to some degree, his controlling position. The term Romantic irony does not represent a particular concept, universally accepted by German Romantics (in fact, there are two distinct perceptions of Romantic irony, that of Friedrich Schlegel and that of Karl Solger), but rather a more general approach to life and literature.

Romantic irony is close to general irony, which sees the whole of humankind as victim of the irony inherent in the human condition. According to Søren Kierkegaard, "Irony in the eminent sense directs itself not against this or that particular existence [*Tilværende*] but against the whole given actuality of a certain time and situation."[22] This view of irony, developed almost two hundred years ago, is connected with the skepticism and frustration that people have experienced since the time of the industrial revolution. The questions that general irony deals with are fundamental issues of existence: the mystery of death; the unpredictability of events; the conflicts among reason, instinct, and emotion, the individual and society, the humane and the scientific; tedium (which includes both the boredom of life and the vacuum in the human heart); the revolt against God; and, finally, the vision of the earth as a speck of dust. It could not have appeared in Europe had Christianity not lost its power. After the foundation of Christianity was undermined, the universal balance that its teaching provided was lost. The world suddenly became vast and incomprehensible and humans weak and alienated in the cold cosmos. General irony is also sometimes called cosmic irony (or rarely world irony or philosophical irony). Distinguishing between these terms is difficult, and critics often use them as synonyms.

Weltanschauung irony (worldview), became a dominant ideological current in the modern world.[23] Haakon M. Chevalier sees irony and pity as the ruling sentiments of the contemporary world. In its social function, the critic sees it as a "mode of escape from the fundamental problems and responsibilities of life."[24] Irony is not just a device. "Irony characterizes the attitude of one who, when confronted with a choice of two things that are mutually exclusive, chooses both. Which is but another way of saying that he chooses neither. He cannot bring himself to give up one for the other, and he gives up both. But he reserves the right to derive from each the greatest possible passive enjoyment. And this enjoyment is Irony."[25] Alan Thompson defines irony as an "incongruity that rouses both pain and amusement."[26] The critic captures the character of irony in the modern world, as well as the character of the ironist. "The ironist is generally a passive person who looks on as the world goes by. He is not indifferent to it, but whenever he has an impulse to act he reflects that reform is hopeless and rebellion perhaps worse ultimately than submission. Futility and vanity are his final terms for human effort."[27] The writer-ironist is a detached narrator who understands the paradoxes and absurdities of existence and humanity but can only muse ironically on them, for he himself is human and knowledge is the only power he has. Such writers would like to do something but can do nothing; their hands hang useless while they, like an old, kindly, and experienced doctor, smile sympathetically at the patients—their characters.

Chekhov is a good example of a Weltanschauung ironist, whose heroes let the stream of life carry them without trying to swim against the current. The writer does not believe in action, activity. It either leads to nothing or ruins people's lives when it becomes the only thing important to them (e.g., "House with a Mezzanine" [«Дом с мезонином»]). Chekhov's heroes are given dreams that constitute the essence of their existence. These dreams never come true, nor can they. Petya Trofimov dreams out loud of the beautiful future life people will see. He speaks of the world as one huge orchard, but at the same moment he stumbles and clumsily falls down (Cherry Orchard [*Вишневый сад*]). A young and energetic doctor grows into a fat and stingy old man, indifferent to anyone's life and happiness, including his own ("Ionych" [«Ионыч»]). A man with a dream becomes a slave of his fixed idea and buries his life in the ground together with several gooseberry bushes ("Gooseberries" [«Крыжовник»]). An old bishop is tied in this world to the lives of thousands of people. He is indispensable, yet when he dies everyone forgets him ("Bishop" [«Архиерей»]). A boy writes a letter to his grandfather in the village. He dreams of going back; he asks the old man to take him away from the city. Ironically, the letter the boy drops into the box is addressed only "To grandfather; the village." Again, the dream does not come true. It would not, even if the old man took the boy home. Behind the idealized picture of village life drawn in the letter the reader sees the same dull, eventless, and hard existence ("Vanka" [«Ванька»]).

Chekhov's hero is always alone: alone in happiness and alone in grief. Chebutykin gathers recipes from a newspaper to cure hair loss while Irina pours out her heart to him on her name day (Three Sisters [*Три сестры*]). The horse becomes the only creature with whom the old coachman Iona Potapov can share his grief ("Heartache" [«Тоска»]). Doctor Kirilov and the landowner Abogin from the story "Enemies" («Враги») are both struck by destiny—the first loses his son, the second his wife. And it does not matter that the boy dies tragically, whereas the wife of Abogin elopes in an "operetta" way with her lover. Each of the two men loses the thing most dear in his life. But the only feeling their grief brings is hatred. They do not want to understand each other's sufferings; they are wrapped up in themselves.

Chekhov rarely takes sides. He is as sympathetic to the doctor as to the landowner. But it is not just the fact that there are no heroes or villains in Chekhov's works that makes them ironic. We can hardly find a strict differentiation between hero and villain in the works of Tolstoy or Dostoevsky, but the characters in their novels can be unsympathetic or even repugnant. There are few in Chekhov's stories or plays toward whom we do not feel sympathy or at least pity. Charles I. Glicksberg writes, "If he is frequently ironic in his reading of life, his irony is invariably kindly and compassionate in tone rather than bitter or cruel; he has no desire to hurt or deride."[28]

The Weltanschauung irony of Chekhov and his heroes is combined in his works with different stylistic and structural kinds of irony. The general themes of boredom, failure, futility, and impossible desires, for example, dominate the play *Three Sisters*. In the play they find their echo in ironic remarks, dialogues, and situations. For instance, the fact that Irina starts working at the post office brings to mind the irony of fate that now she is sending other people's letters to Moscow. She, who wanted so passionately to work, is now burdened by work to the point of fatigue and irritability—and certainly is not ennobled by this labor.

Three Sisters was produced by Yury Lyubimov at his Taganka Theater in 1981. Ironically, this was the last work by Lyubimov to reach the Moscow audience before the director was forced to leave the country. This production marked the end of Lyubimov's Taganka Theater; it also dropped the curtain on the epoch of which it was a powerful symbol. The connection between Chekhov and the audience of Lyubimov's *Three Sisters* was made by means of a visual metaphor: a side wall of the theater would slide open, exposing a view of the Moscow evening. In Lyubimov's production Chekhov's play did not have the nostalgic sentimental overtones traditionally ascribed to it in the Russian theater. The play, with its final words directed into the future ("If one could only know, if one could only know!"), was dominated by an "ironic undercurrent" that brought it closer to its modern-day audience. "Chekhov lived in this production as our contemporary. He spoke to us, and we spoke to him as equals, without holding anything back."[29]

The Weltanschauung irony that dominated Lyubimov's performance was indicative of the whole cultural atmosphere of the Soviet Union in the 1970s. It was expressed through different media: literature (the printed word), *magnitizdat* (tapes of the bards: the recorded word), stand-up comedy (the oral word), and film (the word presented in images), all of which are connected by a common denominator, the vision of a lonely person in a hostile and alienating environment, a vision that dominated the country's cultural atmosphere for more than a decade.

1. Irony In Siberian Literature

Works of Siberian writers have been chosen in this book to demonstrate the prominent role of irony in Soviet literature of the 1970s.[1] Although irony is neither restricted to nor dominant in Siberian literature (it can be seen in the works of different writers as well as different genres), for the sake of convenience I have tried to give a homogeneous picture, and the short works of Siberian writers provide a good example. While it is also true that irony does not exhaust the scope of these works, it is irony that made them (especially the stories of Shukshin and the plays of Vampilov) so popular with the intellectual audience. Ironic tendencies in Siberian literature are rooted in the peculiarities of this literature's development, and the 1970s happened to be an appropriate time for the expression and perception of these tendencies.

The frequency of ironic themes in Siberian prose comes as no surprise. The Siberians (сибиряки)[2] are a relatively young group, having developed mainly in the eighteenth and nineteenth centuries, in a constant struggle with nature. The vastness of the rich Siberian *taiga* dictated a special relationship between humans and nature, a special psychology. That is why the themes of nature and humans in nature[3] are so prominent in the works of the Siberian writers (V. Rasputin, V. Astafev, G. Markov). A special hero was also created: a strong individual, a natural man confronted with society's rules.[4] This character of Siberian writers is close to a romantic hero, and the irony found in their works, to Romantic irony.

In his analysis of Vasily Shukshin's works, Bocharov isolates "mischief" (*ozorstvo* [озорство]) as the basic feature of the author's characters. The critic explains ozorstvo as a reaction to the character's realization of the futility of life and the hostility of society. "This is . . . the bitter irony of an individual confronted with insurmountable circumstances; an individual realizing his inability or reluctance to adapt to these circumstances, whether it's the monotony of everyday routine, the unaccustomed structure of life or the spiritual emptiness of a consumer society."[5] Bocharov characterizes the kind of irony present in the works of Shukshin as Romantic irony. At the same time the critic distinguishes the traditional romantic hero from Shukshin's hero.[6] Whereas the former detaches from society, the latter acts in a mischievous way (озорничает). Ozorstvo is a safety valve that helps Shukshin's characters survive. Their recklessness indicates their helplessness and, consequently, becomes a source of irony. "Both in Shukshin's and Vampilov's works irony arises from the fact that neither the characters nor the authors themselves can find self-confidence."[7]

The chudaki (чудаки) and ozorniki (озорники) of Siberian authors are also close to the fool-in-Christ (*iurodivyi* [юродивый]). The eccentricity of iurodivyi was based on the gap between the better world of Christianity that comes after death and the actual sinful world of the living. The iurodivyi escapes into a world that is as real to the iurodivyi and the audience as the real world. In the world of medieval Russia the iurodivye had their own venerable place: they were believed to be the only ones to "know the truth";[8] they acted in a prophetic way, their actions were always taken seriously, as they were meant to be by the iurodivye themselves. In this religious context the iurodivyi took on the aspect of a saint. Chudaki and ozorniki of the Siberian writers, on the other hand, do not have this dimension; in their world they are perceived as square pegs in round holes. Their actions are nothing more than a protest against a hostile reality and a futile attempt to escape it, since for them there is nowhere to escape to.

Shukshin's chudaki are people from the village. Because of his characters' rustic origins most critics label Shukshin a "village prose writer" (*derevenshchik* [деревенщик]). Nevetheless, Shukshin's irony distinguishes him from other derevenshchiki. Whereas in some works of the village prose writers (e.g., V. Belov, F. Abramov) irony is present as a satirical device, Shukshin is an ironist whose ironic view is directed toward people at large—rural and city dwellers alike. His chudaki also differ. Sergey Ivanovich Kudryashov, for example, from the story "Psychopath" («Психопат»), has an obsession rather than a dream. "Psychopath"—as he is called in the village—is a librarian who spends all his free time in search of old books. He visits distant villages, digs through dusty piles in attics. He has hardly any education and he is not much of a reader. Finding old books and sending them (sometimes for money, sometimes free) to libraries and archives is his *idée fixe*. He is both unfriendly and denounces people to the police.

Hooligans (ozorniki) and eccentrics (chudaki) are characteristic not only of Shukshin's works but become an essential element of Siberian prose. One finds them in the works of E. Gushchin, E. Popov, V. Rasputin, A. Vampilov, and others. Ozorniki and chudaki are a modernized version of the old romantic hero, yet in the twentieth century this hero appears pitiful. Romantic irony is replaced by Weltanschauung irony, and admiration of the hero's action is replaced by pity and understanding.

One of the major ways of escaping reality as well as one of the major ironic themes in the stories of Siberian writers is escape into a dreamland. This dreamland can be a real place; when a hero is idealizing a place he had left—usually home—the theme of escape is expressed in a real flight from a prison or a front line. But usually it is an escape into a world of dreams, the world that does not exist. Naive, well-meaning, and funny dreamers—the heroes of Siberian writers—invent for themselves unattainable yet lofty tasks: to build a helicopter, to rid humankind of illnesses, to invent a perpetual motion machine. Deep down the heroes understand the futility of their efforts: the main thing for them is not to solve the problem but to tackle it, not to solve the secrets of the world of microbes but to peep into this world—to "touch" a dream.

In their imaginary world the heroes could live and be happy, but any attempt to affirm themselves in the real world is bound to fail. These heroes are idealists; they look for beauty and goodness in life, for the ideal love of a woman, and for an ideal relationship between people. But even their most modest and at times petty dreams remain unfulfilled and unattainable. In the real world these heroes who crave to be heard, recognized, and acknowledged are constantly confronted with lack of understanding and compassion, indifference, suspicion, and doubt of the goodness of human nature. All this causes them, as well as the reader, to sense the futility of life and dullness of everyday reality. The writer-ironist sympathizes with the characters, for the writer-ironist, too, lacks faith in people and is skeptical about the heroes' achieving their goals, ideals, and dreams. There is no possibility of escaping reality, which unfailingly shatters the dreams of the alienated hero.

For example, Andrey Erin, a carpenter in Shukshin's story "Microscope" («Микроскоп»), one day brings home a microscope that he claims he received as a prize for his shock labor (ударный труд). The microscope changes Andrey's life drastically. He stops drinking and spends all his evenings at home, watching a fascinating new world on the other side of the lens. The hero's "discoveries" in the microworld and his naive interpretation of the phenomena are funny and touching, yet the reader respects Andrey's devotion and thirst for knowledge. The hero's goals are also honorable. He is dreaming to free mankind from microbes and bacteria, and thus to prolong human life up to one hundred fifty years. The microscope is not a toy or a hobby for Andrey Erin, but rather his chance to prove that his life is not in vain. The reader knows, though, that this attempt to escape reality is doomed, and the dream is going to be shattered. Even if a drunken friend had not accidentally revealed Andrey's secret (the microscope was bought with the money that the hero claimed to have lost) to the hero's wife, the ending would be the same. Andrey himself accepts this stroke of destiny with surprising passivity, as if he expected it. Life assumes its normal path; Andrey goes back to drinking. He does not even try to stop his wife from returning the microscope, not because he is submissive, but because he understands that the money is needed to buy coats for the children. "Real life" was always in the back of Andrey's mind. From the beginning his protest was a momentary escape, rather than a breakout, as is the case with the romantic hero.

Chudaki always mean well, but they are naive and unable to adapt to the conventions of society. In Shukshin's story "A Strange One" («Чудик»), the protagonist comes to visit his brother who lives in the city. To gain the favor of his brother's wife, he paints a baby carriage when everyone is away. At the sight of cranes, green grass, flowers, roosters, and hens on the sides of the carriage, the woman gets angry and orders her husband to throw his brother out. Chudik (a nickname for the protagonist, and also the title of the story) overhears her outburst. "Chudik hurried away from the porch. . . . Then he did not know what to do. It became very painful again. When people hated him, it always got very painful and scary. It seemed like: well, that's it now, what's there to live for? And he wanted to go away somewhere far from people who hated him and laughed at him."[9]

Another dreamer is the chudak Mitka from Shukshin's story "The Strong Ones Go On" («Сильные идут дальше»). His life is a succession of dreams. As a boy Mitka dreamed of sailing to the North Pole. Then he dreamed of finding gold in the Altay mountains. Shukshin states finally: "Mitka turned into the most absurd and hopeless kind of

Vasily Shukshin.
Courtesy of Ardis
Publishers.

dreamer—an overgrown one. Life chewed his dreams lazily, people laughed at Mitka, but he continued to dream with indestructible persistence."[10] Mitka dreams of an herb that can cure cancer in three days and imagines himself in a big house, the whole second floor of which is a bedroom where he lives openly with young and beautiful women whom he cures of cancer. Drinking helps Mitka to withdraw into his dreams. When the hero tries to affirm himself in the real world, he fails. In an attempt to prove his courage and physical fitness to some "city fellows with eyeglasses" (очкарики) and especially to a certain young woman, he swims in cold Lake Baikal and almost drowns when his swimming trunks slip down and tie up his legs. Mitka drifts into a new dream; he will invent a printing press for making counterfeit money and will help the poor and women. Shukshin concludes ironically: "Mitka is a kind man but very naive: the poor and women will definitely get caught with the counterfeit money! And it will be they who will suffer after all. It's better to cure cancer—less dangerous."[11]

Monya Kvasov from Shukshin's story "A Stubborn One" («Упорный») is obsessed with an idea of inventing a perpetual motion machine. It is not the problem itself that stirs the character's mind so much as the predetermined attitude of the educated people of his village—the teacher and the engineer—who say the scheme cannot work. Monya, nevertheless, tries and fails. The dream does not come true, and he ends up drinking brandy with the engineer.[12] Monya Kvasov's return to reality, though, is less painful than that of the others. He watches the sun rise and thinks that at least here everything is clear. The sun completes its cycle every day—unreachable, inexhaustible, eternal—while people are doing their routine work: shouting, hurrying, watering the cabbage, counting their joys and successes. The story ends on an optimistic note: "Hey! . . people, dear people . . . Good morning!"[13] For Shukshin's heroes the main objective is not to achieve a dream—they know it is impossible—but to give it a try.

The same is true for Vasily Atyasov from Evgeny Gushchin's "Shadow of a Dragonfly" («Тень стрекозы»). The young carpenter's dream is no less incredible than those of Shukshin's heroes; he decides to build and fly his own helicopter. The dream comes suddenly, like a disease, and the only way to get rid of it is to fulfill it. Neither the probable break-up of his marriage nor the scowling of his fellow villagers detracts Vasily from his task. His wife, Varya, worries about him and seeks advice from the village palm-reader, who tells her: "Every man has some kind of a safety-valve. He either drinks or tells wild stories, or sometimes, like yours, builds some kind of trash, wasting himself" (У каждого мужика есть какая-то отдушина. Либо он пьет, либо треплется, а то как твой—строит какую-нибудь холеру, зря изводится).[14]

"Shadow of a Dragonfly" is the name the palm-reader gives to Vasily's disease. The helicopter built by the young carpenter becomes the manifestation of this name. Made of plywood, the small, light, and fragile machine is the symbol of a dream in the story. In contrast, a log house built by Vasily for his family stands as an assertion of material values. This huge, shining, new, laquered home with carvings of kissing doves on the shutters is bound to win out over a fragile dream helicopter made from odds and ends from a junkyard. The machine takes off but cannot fly high enough, and it crashes into the trees. The description of the scene with the pine trees glowing in the sun and the "wall of the forest" (стена леса) brings back the image of the lacquered log house.[15]

Vasily's dream is shattered under the ruins of his plywood helicopter, and he returns to his usual routine. The story ends with a picture of the delayed arrival of winter. The author writes: "Something had shifted in the customary flowing of the seasons."[16] The character's actions are shown as part of the natural pattern, in which an occasional loss of rhythm is as essential as the regularity of nature's cycles.

Escape into a dream world sometimes takes the form of an actual escape, as in Valentin Rasputin's *Live and Remember* (*Живи и помни*) or in Shukshin's "Styopka" («Степка»). Andrey from Rasputin's novel cannot stand the reality of war any longer and leaves the front a few months before the war ends. Styopka, the character in Shukshin's short story, escapes from prison only a short time before the end of his term. Both are drawn to their homes, which in the cruel and depressing environment of the characters assume for them the qualities of a dream. In both cases escape into the dream is as short-lived as in the other stories, but the consequences are more serious. Both Andrey and Styopka realize that they cannot escape punishment, although they do not regret their deeds.

Another kind of "dreamer" is shown in Shukshin's "Desire to Live" («Охота жить»). He is a convict who escapes from a camp in the taiga and comes to the hut of an old hunter. The young man tells the hunter his dream—to live free in a big city, drink champagne, and feel that the whole world is his. "But you do not know how bright the lights of a big city are. They lure you. Kind and sweet people live there; it is warm and soft in their apartments, and music is playing. They are polite and very afraid of death. And I am walking through the city, and it is all mine."[17] At the end of the story the convict kills the old man, just to be on the safe side. In this story Shukshin is no longer an ironic detached narrator. The writer is embittered by human cruelty. This theme is present in a number of Shukshin's stories and becomes especially significant in "The Smear" («Кляуза»), an account of events that ultimately brought about Shukshin's death. But even in these stories we can find, if not sympathy for the characters, then at least understanding for their bitterness and cruelty. L. Annensky suggests that in "The Smear" we should not see the ward supervisor in the hospital as just a "stupid fool" or her demands for a bribe as just a demonstration of power. The bribe has symbolic value for her—it is a token of respect («знак уважения»).[18] Her rudeness is a defense against reality, where she occupies the lowest position, and her demands are for the attention she lacks.

A woman often becomes a symbol of the ideal, and love for an ideal woman, a way to escape reality. For example, in Shukshin's story "Illegitimate" («Сураз») the jailbird Spirka commits suicide because he cannot win the love of the music teacher—a slender and delicate city girl. Vaska Metus, the hero of Evgeny Popov's story "I Wait for a Non-Treacherous Love" («Жду любви не вероломной»), lives an unhappy life because he cannot find the one and only, the ultimate woman. The new wife he brings home, literally to replace the old one, does not fulfill his ideal. The ideal is not beauty, intelligence, or moral qualities. In fact, Vaska himself does not know what he wants from his wife. He constantly searches in himself for love "non-treacherous, but big and limitless" (не вероломной, а такой большой огромной), as in the words of a popular song, but cannot find it and moves on to a new object.[19] The hero takes the notion of an ideal love literally, and he actually tries to find it. Once he "escapes" to the city and is picked up by a prostitute. A fight with a policeman sends the hero to jail. Yet the author believes that the first thing Vaska will do when he comes back from jail is to marry, to continue his search.

For a burned-out and disillusioned hero, the search for ideal love can turn in the end into an incessant succession of love affairs. Shukshin's story "Step Bigger, Maestro!" («Шире шаг, маэстро!») is a modern variation of Chekhov's "Ionych." But unlike Chekhov's hero, Solodovnikov, who is a womanizer and a young country doctor, does not develop as a character. It does not take him a lifetime to turn from a young and naive dreamer into a burned-out cynic. He appears as a cynic at the beginning of the story. A sunny spot on the wall reminds him that spring is approaching and changes the young doctor's mood. He dreams, but his dreams are far from idealistic. Solodovnikov dreams of doing complex operations and writing a book—both to make him famous. But even these dreams are shattered by the routine. Spring does not seem to affect the drowsiness of the village people. The cycle of their lives is unaffected by the cycle of nature. The chief doctor of the village hospital is busy getting sheet metal from the sovkhoz (state farm) director. A young farmer is busy guarding his hay from the neighbors. The sovkhoz warehouse manager is busy making money from government property. To Solodovnikov's questions, "Don't you notice anything? What is going on in the world?" the chief doctor answers: "War in Vietnam."[20] The author is equally ironic toward the petty dreams of Doctor Solodovnikov and the dull life of the country people. At the end of the story the young man abandons his ambitious dreams; he is not even going to do the simple operation that he scheduled for the morning. His thoughts return to the familiar subject—women.

In Popov's stories love is as far from romantic as Popov's heroes are from being ideal dreamers. They are people with human vices and imperfections. Their dreams are often petty but are still unattainable. In "A Front Garden" («Палисадничек») a young man dreams about his sister's girlfriend. The story is an account of several short episodes, none of which is crucial to the protagonist's fate. An obscene incident in the front garden is also more humorous than tragic. Yet the author's point is that the character's fate *is* tragic («Трагична судьба отдельных молодых людей»).[21] The tragedy, though, is not in the fact that Vitalenka grew a beard and changed jobs eighty-one times in just a few years. The tragedy is in life itself, mundane reality, filled with dull and uneventful days and petty desires; it is in the clash between the hero's obsession with love and his inability to love. Love in the story becomes a device for exploring the futility of human aspirations.

Dreams of love and women in Popov's stories must be viewed through the central element of the writer's poetics—"parodic *skaz*"—in which the narrator's voice is different from the author's. Such "parodic word," as Mikhail Bakhtin calls it, usually coincides in contemporary instances of skaz with the ironic use of the "other's word."[22] Popov's skaz has its peculiarities, the first being that the author breaks the cause-effect relationship and substitutes associative links. Second, even though Popov's skaz reflects the free flow of speech of a semi-literate narrator—a conventional feature—it is also unconventionally rich in literary, philosophical, and other allusions. One of the characteristics of Popov's skaz is a constant digression from the line of narra-

Evgeny Popov.

tion into wordy and seemingly unnecessary reflections. These passages are usually pseudorevelations and are heavily charged with irony. "See how interesting it turns out to be! He studied, his sister studied and his love—his sister's friend—also studied! All three of them studied. And that's not all! Look around you—practically everyone is studying. I studied too. I graduated from the Sergo Ordzhonikidze Moscow Geological Institute. Everyone is studying. And what difference does it make that one person is studying to become a high level diplomat, and another to be a meat-cutter. We are all building and will, undoubtedly, finish building [communism]."[23]

Popov parodies fairy-tale dreams in the short story "Heavenly Life and Eternal Bliss" («Райская жизнь и вечное блаженство»). It opens with a pastoral description of a quiet summer street where a heavenly voice is heard. Details of a nightingale singing, a girl, a sticky maple leaf, and a ladybug crawling up the narrator's hand contribute to the serenity of the picture. At the same time the bucolic feeling is interrupted by stylistically contrasting sentences. For instance, after the description of the song that promises heavenly life and eternal bliss, the narrator continues: "But my head got scorched, so I sat me down in the shade to get some rest."[24] From this point the story becomes openly ironic. The singer appears in the window: a young saleswoman from a grocery store with heavy make-up—"a doll" (куколка). The girl is waiting for her prince, in this case a producer, to take her to the "fairy-tale world" of show business. The illiterate idiom of the characters mixed with pathetic pronouncements adds stylistic irony to the Weltanschauung irony of the story. The reader perceives the events in a different light from the one presented by the narrator. Here the belief in a dream is being questioned, the dream itself turns out to be a longing for prestige and material wealth, and the nightingale appears to be a common sparrow.

A similar parodic rendering of a fairy tale can be found in Popov's story "A Jam" («Раззор»). It tells the story of a poor village orphan girl who comes to the city to study. She meets a boy from a rich family and gets pregnant. He is a playboy rather than a prince and has no intention of marrying the girl. But the boy's father, afraid for his good name, intervenes, and the story ends in a wedding. The story carries stylistic analogies to a fairy tale, such as: «жила-была тихая девочка» (there once lived a quiet girl); «девочка погоревала, распростилась . . .» (the girl grieved for a while, said "good-bye" . . .); «на столах было всего видимо-невидимо» (there was plenty of everything on the tables). At the same time, constant divergence from the fairy-tale style and structure create irony. Often this is achieved by illiterate idiom, slang, and the breaking of the logical sequence of the narration: «Имелась даже красная икра. Со стороны невесты родственников не имелось. Зато со стороны жениха многие говорили речи и желали молодым различных благ» (There was even red caviar. But there were no relatives from the bride's side. On the other hand from the groom's side a number of speeches were pronounced wishing the young people good fortune).[25]

The story is a grotesque stylization of Nikolay Karamzin's "Poor Liza" («Бедная Лиза»). The tragedy remains, but in Popov's story it is shifted into everyday life—its futility, boredom, and inevitability. This is why what seem to be traditional tears of joy at the wedding that concludes the story actually mean something quite different. "The groom smiled graciously, but many others also cried. The mother cried, wiping her eyes with a lace handkerchief. The father cried, grimly biting his well-trimmed moustache. A lot of them cried! And they cried, naturally, out of joy. What other reason could there be?"[26]

A similar device, where what appears to be straightforward proves deceptive, is found in Shukshin's novella *Point of View* (*Точка зрения*). Matchmaking (сватовство) is a recurring motif. The story is rendered several times, each time from a different point of view. In the version told by the pessimist the people are vain, greedy, and vicious. In the optimist's rendering the characters are so insipidly positive that they become caricatures. The magician tries to derive objective truth by combining the two contrasting views and presents a grotesque picture, devoid of any common sense. The conventionally realistic rendering of the episode, given at the end, is ironic, for the reader tests its seeming truthfulness against the previous renderings. As a result, the last episode seems as false and meaningless as the others.

The heroes have a need to be heard, and they will do anything to attract people's attention. Gleb Kapustin from Shukshin's "Cut-Down" («Срезал») lives only for his "starry moments"—when the whole village listens to him, waiting for him to bring about the downfall of another distinguished visitor to the village. Gleb Kapustin is a village authority on all matters. Like Kudryashov from the story "Psychopath," Gleb is uneducated, and the knowledge he has is superficial, drawn from popular magazines, radio and TV shows, and common superstitions. He is famous in his village for "cutting down" distinguished visitors (знатные гости). Inability to answer even one of Gleb's questions immediately diminishes the authority of the visitor and leads to his complete downfall. Gleb enters into verbal combat with two scholars—a husband and wife, both Ph.D.s—who do not really understand what is going on. Gleb discusses problems of medicine men in the north districts of the country, something that he might have read in a popular science magazine. Then he switches to philosophy and uses a number of specialized bookish idioms that are meaningless out of context. Finally, Gleb challenges the scholars with the question of whether the moon is artificial and propounds a "scientific hypothesis" that it is hollow and inhabited by intelligent creatures, a notion obviously picked up from a science fiction story. The guests' astonishment and inability to refute Gleb's ridiculous statements are viewed by the villagers as the scholars' lack of knowledge and Gleb's complete victory.

The desire for attention drives Bronka Pupkov, in Shukshin's "A Thousand Pardons, Madame" («Миль пардон, мадам»), to invent a ridiculous story of how he made an attempt on Hitler's life and how it failed. The story makes him the laughingstock of the village and causes him trouble with the village authorities and with his wife. Bronka's story is so outrageous that he has to drink before and after telling it to stifle his embarrassment, yet he does not stop telling it.

Attempts to communicate usually run into indifference. Sashka Ermolaev, in Shukshin's story "Offense" («Обида»), goes to a store where a saleswoman mistakes him for someone else and offends him in the presence of the public and his little daughter. Sashka tries to explain the misunderstanding, but neither the salespeople in the store nor the people in line will listen. Further attempts cause a fight. Even his wife does not understand; at the end of the story Sashka is on the verge of a nervous breakdown.

A plea for compassion and understanding is also at the center of Shukshin's story "'A Story'" («Раскас»). The wife of Ivan Petin has run off with an army officer, and the abandoned husband writes "a story," which is the confession of the victim of the insult. The language is full of jargon and the spelling is poor, but that only emphasizes the pain that Ivan suffers. The "story" ends with the words, "Yours, Ivan Petin. Driver First Class."[27] This line serves two functions. For the reader it reveals the real purpose of the "story." It is a letter that is addressed and signed and presupposes a reply. It is addressed to people who will read it and understand Ivan's grief and to his wife, whom it will cause to repent and come back. With a firm belief in the power of the printed word, Ivan Petin takes the "story" to the local newspaper.

The editor sympathizes with Ivan, but sees that the "story" cannot be published in the present form; it also cannot reach its addressee—the woman has already gone far out of the newspaper's circulation area. The editor offers Ivan help in writing a letter to his wife, but Ivan is offended and leaves. The conflict lies in lack of understanding: the editor approaches Ivan's situation from a commonsense perspective. For him this vaudeville situation with an eloped wife and an illiterate husband is not without humor, but for Ivan the grief is personal. His world has collapsed.[28]

The mother from Shukshin's story "Mother's Heart" («Материнское сердце») is also looking for understanding. Her son, Vitka Borzenkov, who has been swindled out of his money, starts a fight and injures a policeman. The hero's mother tries to save him from jail by appealing to the feelings of the policemen and then of a prosecutor. Their behavior, though, is dictated by law, which blocks understanding between the authorities on the one hand and the mother on the other. In the conflict between natural and social law, Shukshin does not take sides; the mother's emotional plea and the lawmakers' reasonable arguments sound equally strong.

Lack of understanding is often connected with hostility. It is the reason that Sashka Ermolaev cannot find even one sympathetic ear among the people in the line. The law that governs them is "Guilty until proven innocent." People do not trust one another, they do not believe in one another's good intentions. Suspicion and doubt of the goodness of human nature are the theme of Alexander Vampilov's one-act play *Twenty Minutes with an Angel* (*Двадцать минут с ангелом*). Ugarov and Anchugin, who are in a provincial town on a business trip, need money for a drink. As a joke, one of them sticks his head out the window and cries out, "Good people! Help! Hard predicament! A no-exit situation! . . . Citizens! Who will lend a hundred rubles?"[29] A man appears and offers them money. The heroes cannot understand such generosity and start guessing about why the man made the offer. They suggest that the man might be a policeman or a KGB agent trying to provoke them into something illegal, or that he is from the underworld—a counterfeiter or a thief trying to get rid of illegal money. They think he might be a recruiter for some distant *kolkhoz* (communal farm) or gold mine, or a journalist getting material for a satirical article. Ugarov and Anchugin tie the man to the head of the bed and invite other hotel guests to help in their investigation. None of the characters wants to accept the man's offer as altruistic; they all look for a hidden reason. They finally decide that the man is crazy, that he thinks of himself as Christ. The thought of seeing someone good and virtuous, someone better than they are—even if it is because of mental illness—enrages the characters and makes them ready to lynch the man. The man finally confesses that the money was intended for his mother, whom he had not seen for a long time. She died before he found time to visit her, and now, as a gesture of repentance, the man wants to give the money away. This confession of the man's sin suddenly makes him understandable; the other characters can genuinely sympathize with someone else's vice, but cannot accept someone else's virtue.

Lack of belief in humanity and pessimism about its future are also at the center of Sergey Zalygin's "Festival" («Фестиваль»). The story is told by a deceased film director and opens, "All of us are mortal and everyone will die, and I also died last fall on a nice morning."[30] The story is an evaluation of the character's life by an objective observer (the hero states that anxieties and desires of the living do not bother him anymore). The hero reminisces about his last moments, when his life passed before his eyes. The title of the story is symbolic; besides a film festival that the hero remembers, the story itself is a kind of festival, with winners and losers. In the hero's personal festival he sees a succession of people and characters that are in some way connected with his life or art. Characters from his movies and books are indistinguishable from real people; art and life become interwoven in his last moments.

The hero is confronted with figures, each of which is symbolic. The actress who approaches him first stands for the hero's subordinates as well as his victims in the world of art; the Basso stands for colleagues or fellow artists. Next comes a fellow countryman, an old man whom the hero depicted in his works. Then two young people who look and think alike confront him representing the new generation, which has substituted the knowledge of do's and don'ts for moral values. A man and a woman, symbolic of militant banality (пошлость) in which emotions are reduced to a single one—hatred—pass before him followed by a little boy who stands for the future generation, already corrupted by pragmatism and cynicism. And finally, a woman, the hero's love, appears as a fairy from a dream and this is the "Beginning"—the origination of the feeling. The hero reluctantly gives the "Continuation" where the same woman is shown old, worn out, and mundane. She is constantly carrying something on her shoulders. "I did not understand what it was—either a basket or a bag or a box or a trunk or a shopping bag or a coffin or a mixture of all of the above. 'What's this?' I exclaimed. 'Nothing important. It's weight of time. A horrible weight of time.'"[31]

According to the hero, mankind is buried under the weight of time's running out («дикий цейтнот»); natural feelings are dead; people are too busy playing their roles. The earth is presented as a theater where a performance is going on constantly, and the hero himself is an actor in this huge spectacle. The only way out is solitude. "Maybe the greatest role intended for the greatest actor who has never yet lived on earth is the role of a hermit."[32] The hero has no faith in humankind. Its future is nonexistent; instead an apocalypse is approaching. "I want to learn what is heard there, in the cosmic stillness, what is heard about the immediate future, about war and peace? . . . How is human tragedy felt there and how much longer will it last?"[33] At this point the title of the story assumes an ironic meaning: the festival becomes «пир во время чумы», a celebration in the midst of death and destruction. The only two positive figures in this festival of human futility are the narrator's friend and the nineteenth century. Yet the friend in the story is the second self of the hero, his own better half, his conscience. Admiration for the nineteenth century—the century of realism in literature—is a nostalgic feeling, a kind of escape in the past.[34]

Another form of escape, probably the most frequent in Russian literature (and daily life), is drinking. Vodka accompanies almost all of the characters of Shukshin, Vampilov, Gushchin, Popov, and other writers. The action in Vampilov's play *Twenty Minutes with an Angel* centers on the problem of getting money for a morning drink. Knyazev in Shukshin's story "A Strange One" and Mitka in his "Strong Ones Go On" drink constantly. Monya Kvasov in "A Stubborn One" drinks with an engineer, and even Gushchin's Vasily in "Shadow of a Dragonfly," who never drinks (a fact stressed in the story), will probably start after his dream fails. Although drinking commonly appears in the works of Siberian writers, its presentation is restricted by publishing regulations and censorship. The picture drawn in works published outside the Soviet Union is much more expressive and gloomy.[35]

Popov's story "Why Was There Shashko?" («Зачем был Шашко?») begins with a statement of the protagonist, who has been cured of alcoholism. "I am cold. I am sober and self-controlled. I bought myself a Finnish corduroy sport coat."[36] Then follows the story, which is a detailed account of the slaughter of a little devil Shashko that the character finds one day in his apartment. At the end the reader learns that it was all a fit of delirium tremens and that the opening statement of the story ("I am sober and self-controlled") refers to the character's present state, not to his condition at the time of the account. The opening statement of the story is repeated at the end. Coldness, soberness, and the corduroy sport coat become the symbols of the real world, but the nightmarish quality remains even when the character is cured. In the closing lines the author suggests that the two worlds co-exist. "Answer me, why *did* I see Shashko, when as a matter of fact he never was and never could have been? Tell me, why is the real world more unreal than the unreal one and why are the faces of people in the street seized with meaningful horror and meaningless joy? Explain it to me, why do Gogol, Hitler, Breugel, Hoffmann, Swift, and Stalin exist?[37] This mixture of names comes from the narrator himself rather than from the agitated mind of an alcoholic character. In a world where the wildest dreams of medieval and romantic fantasies are brought to reality by people like Stalin or Hitler, there is no longer a clear distinction between life and art. Hence the escape into the world of dreams is impossible.

Siberian writers are ironists, for they do not blame their characters for failures, they do not take a judgmental stance. They exhibit, if not pity, then understanding, and attribute their heroes' inadequacies to the human predicament. Vampilov and Gushchin muse ironically at their heroes, Shukshin tries to understand and explain even the most vicious of human actions, and Popov pities his characters. In the story "A Plane for Köln" («Самолет на Кельн») an insignificant incident triggers a stir in the hierarchy of a provincial town. At the bottom of this hierarchical ladder is an ageless cleaning woman named Glafira, whose failure to shovel the snow has caused the accident that kept a city official from reaching the airport to greet the leader of a friendly African nation. Crying, Glafira tells her superior the reason she was late for work; she was making love with her husband, an occasion so rare in Glafira's life that in her rendering it acquires festive elements. Even the woman's superior—a petty Stalinist bureaucrat—is touched by her story: "Something shuddered—I swear—something shuddered, in Ivan Ivanych's heart or in his body."[38]

The dull and monotonous life of the characters in the works of Siberian writers is reduced to a mechanical existence. The mechanization of life as depicted by Popov reminds the reader of Evgeny Zamyatin's We (*Мы*), with the difference that the society Popov depicts is very much real. Society not only turns people into mechanical particles, but also kills them. A failure to reach the airport to greet the

African guest causes the high official Kozorezov heart trouble. Glafira is turned into a sexless creature, Ivan Ivanych's mental activity is limited to speculation on the advantages and disadvantages of ballpoint pens (the character is a modernized version of Gogol's Akaky Akakievich Bashmachkin). In this context the thoughts of Mandevil Makhur, the leader of a backward African nation, about the "barbarism" of these "funny Russians" sound ironic and true.

The heroes in the works of Siberian writers appear displaced in the hostile world around them, hence their escapist philosophy, which most often takes the form of drinking. The heroes do everything to escape reality; the writers face it, but do not have the answer and regretfully abandon their characters in this cold world.

2. Irony in Soviet Culture

_____

_____

_____

_____

Georgian Film

In cinematography, irony is a prominent feature of the Georgian films of the 1970s. Its roots can be traced to the pioneering directors of the 1920s: D. Rondeli, N. Shengelaya, M. Kalatozov, and especially M. Chiaureli, about whom it has been said, "These experiments are surprisingly daring, for only a resilient and courageous people can be so ironic toward itself, while showing such great love toward humanity."[1] The major themes in the 1920s were the breakdown of the patriarchal Georgian community, the penetration of corruptive modern industrial relationships into the centuries-old natural society, and the loss of traditional values. While the cinematography of the 1920s was characterized by its monumentalism, its epic and tragic character (with humor as part of an epic picture), the cinema of the 1970s directs its attention to the individual, usually an alienated individual in a hostile world. The destruction of the natural human qualities that started in the late nineteenth and early twentieth centuries has been completed, and the tragic figures of the films of the 1920s have become the fumbling and ridiculous eccentrics (чудаки) of the 1960s.[2]

The incongruity between dream and reality, between the desires of the natural man and the structure of a society founded on mechanics and regulations becomes a major theme of Georgian films of the 1970s. They have been termed _philosophical comedies_, which is just a euphemism that the Soviet critics have used for what is in fact irony.[3]

An example of such a comedy can be Mikhail Kobakhidze's short film[4] from 1965, _Marriage_ (_Свадьба_). The whole plot is built on the discrepancy between dream and reality. The hero of the film, "a funny man with sad eyes," reminds the viewer of a clown or of a Charlie Chaplin silent film hero.[5] In fact the film does not have any words—a characteristic of a number of Kobakhidze's short films (*Umbrella* [*Зонтик*], *Men's Choir* [*Мужской хор*], *Serenade* [*Серенада*], *Musician* [*Музыкант*]). Music takes the role of narrator. Familiar song melodies comment on the events of the film by the associations that their words, not sung but well known by the audience, create. These comments are ironic as is the film itself. The film can be described as a parable of a loser. A young man, a pharmacist, meets a young woman, a violinist, and immediately falls in love. He then dreams about making a proposal and also imagines their marriage. In reality, though, when the hero arrives, with flowers in hand, at the young woman's house, she is getting married. The ironic tone is reenforced by the parallels of the dream and reality sequences, the fact that in details they coincide yet in the outcome are opposite.[6]

One of the major features of Georgian philosophical comedy is its lyricism. But it is perceived as something more than just a sentimental mood: "It is a whole philosophy of life, the means of reacting to life and the last chance not to notice it."[7] In other words, it is an attempt to escape reality. Such an attempt becomes the main theme of *Eccentrics* (*Чудаки*), the 1974 film directed by Eldar Shengelaya (script by R. Gabriadze). Its heroes try to escape from prison, but the underground passage they have been digging for months just brings them back to it. Then another way is found, a dream machine the heroes call a skyflier (неболет)—a hybrid of a carriage and a zeppelin. They float in their skyflier and see the earth from above. It is beautiful, but the extreme brightness of the colors and prop-like appearance of the world below suggest that the characters are not just seeing the real world, but the projection of their most beautiful hopes and illusions. There is no escape from reality; humanity is an eternal prisoner, and whatever road they take out will inevitably bring them back to their cell. Soaring over reality in a dream-machine is an ironic victory, for what is seen as victory in the fairy-tale reality of the film becomes bitter defeat when applied to the reality of life. Yury Bogomolov admits: "The more absolute the hero's victory within the plot, the more conventional the plot becomes, and, therefore, the more doubtful the victory is."[8] Originally the film is called *The Tetched* (*Чокнутые*). The natural, ideal world has changed, and the heroes who cannot adapt to reality but remain "ideal" are bound to become "abnormal" in the new world.

Nostalgia for the old natural world is another theme of Georgian films such as G. Danelia's *Don't Despair!* (*Не горюй!*), a 1969 film in which the script is based on a French novel, by G. Danelia and R. Gabriadze; G. Shengelaya's *Melodies of the Veriisk Block* (*Мелодии Верийского квартала*), a 1973 film with a script by G. Shengelaya and A. Salukvadze; and Revaz Gabriadze's 1977 short film *The Caucasus Romance* (*Кавказский романс*). The last is a hilarious account of how a young and beautiful girl is kept locked away from the temptations of the world by her militant and savage-looking grandmother. The boyfriend manages to abduct the girl (with her consent, of course); the old woman and her two old friends, who have been the girl's guards, come home, sit at the fireplace, and turn into three tombstones. A tragic folk melody that sounds in the background and the sight of the three obelisks make the audience reevaluate the characters. Sympathy toward the abandoned old folks grows into nostalgia for the abandoned old natural way of life.

The rupture of centuries-old ties between man and nature is the main theme of Georgy Shengelaya's short film *Alaverdoba* (part of the 1963 film *Two Stories* [*Два рассказа*]), which is based on a script by the director's friend, G. Rcheulishvili and dedicated to Rcheulishvili's memory. The film concentrates on a fall holiday at the end of the field-work season. This Georgian holiday was traditionally celebrated with a feast accompanied by singing, dancing, and athletic competition. Yet the modern holiday, as it is seen in the film, is quite different; it becomes an orgy of excessive eating and drinking, an ugly spectacle of the worst in human nature. At the same time the people are viewed, ironically rather than satirically, as victims of circumstance: "And it looked as if not a happy event was celebrated here, but rather something heavy and gloomy was being buried in wine, as if all these people gathered here with the sole reason of escaping into some kind of mad trance (погрузиться в безумное забытье)."[9] The degenerated ancient tradition becomes a negative symbol and is contrasted with a beautiful white cathedral[10] and the valley of the Alazon River that the hero sees from its height—symbols of natural life and work, and also of the human potential that can be realized only when people are in harmony with the world around them. The cathedral can also be read as a symbol of faith and a reminder of the danger that lies in losing it.

The break with tradition is also the theme of Merab Kokochashvili's 1968 film *Big Green Valley* (*Большая зеленая долина*), with a script by M. Kokochashvili and M. Eliozishvili. In this film the traditional world of the shepherd Sosana is shattered by advancing technological civili-

Director Georgy Shengelaya (top) and stills from *Alaverdoba* (middle) and *Pirosmani* (bottom). Reprinted from R. Tikanadze, *Gruzinskoe kino*.

zation: his wife leaves him, bored with her lonely life in the mountains; his friend goes down into the valley; his best cow dies and the herd is lost. But Sosana still does not succumb. He stays in the mountains. The hero is a part of the ancient tradition, the bearer of the old moral laws; he cannot adjust to the new world and passes into legend together with the old world to which he belongs.

The natural way of life is the world we see in G. Shengelaya's *Pirosmani* (script by E. Akhvlediani), a 1970 film about the great Georgian artist Niko Pirosmanishvili. The people in the film are never predictable. Niko's greedy sister, who took all he had at the beginning, becomes kind and caring at the end. Dmitry, an energetic and business-oriented young man, by the end of the film turns into a poor old sufferer, whose appearance arouses only pity. In the film are Good and Evil, but they come from the same source. Understanding their balance is the key to an understanding of *Pirosmani*. The film presents an ironic view of a world where the artist has to make a choice: to live for the present or to work for the future. The artist in *Pirosmani* chooses the future, or rather, the future chooses him. All his life Pirosmani has made signs for local stores and painted walls in the city's taverns. His bears, giraffes, and janitors—humans and animals alike—have sad eyes that are turned toward people with a reproachful smile. In the words of a critic, "The tragic and the comic in his paintings are not in contradiction, but are unified."[11] The artist is seen as a natural man, unspoiled by civilization, and he lives in the only way he knows how: "Pirosmani's nature is in his identity with nature" (Природа Пиросмани в том, что он равен природе).[12]

Given the same choice between the present and the future, the hero of *An Extraordinary Exhibition* (*Необыкновенная выставка*), E. Shengelaya's 1969 film with a script by R. Gabriadze, chooses the present. He is also an artist who has a dream—to create a masterpiece, his *magnum opus*, out of a piece of Italian marble that he is saving. The hero comes back from a war and his dream begins to take form; he decides to create a sculpture entitled "Spring," inspired by a local girl. The girl soon becomes the artist's wife; mundane troubles with home and children delay the realization of the artist's dream.

This clash of dream and reality comes through in one of the key scenes of the film, the scene of the class reunion. Aging "boys and girls" are getting together in a mountain retreat. They have not kept in touch over the years and can hardly recognize one another, yet the atmosphere at the beginning of the party is joyful. Soon, though, everything

Director Eldar
Shengelaya (top left)
and stills from *An
Extraordinary
Exhibition*. Reprinted
from R. Tikanadze,
Gruzinskoe kino.

changes. Meeting their old teachers and peers brings more than memories to the aging participants. It brings a peculiar feeling of shifted time,
throwing everyone back to the school days and bringing back memories
of youthful plans, hopes, dreams, and ideals. Yet the projected future of
these plans is present, and the party continuously grows grimmer as its
members feel, almost as a physical weight, the implications of the
ironic law of the incongruity between dream and reality. The party
finally breaks up, and everybody dashes off, abandoning its organizer—
whether unconsciously or consciously—for having brought them to
this bitter realization. This clash between dream and reality is also
evident in the main character of Aguli Eristavi, whom critics see as an

amalgam of Charlie Chaplin's "little man" and Miguel Cervantes' Don Quixote.[13]

Yet the conflict in this case is more complicated, the irony is hidden deeper. The artist who hopes one day to create "Spring," a sculpture celebrating life, spends his life making monstrous busts for people's tombstones—without any spark of talent or resemblance to the deceased. Inability to create his ultimate masterpiece is not an indication of the hero's lost talent; the talent was never there in the first place. Even the initial idea of the sculpture—"Spring" was to be shown as a beautiful young girl—strikes one as trite and mediocre. This creates a double irony and changes the focus from the contrast between dream and reality to that between the debased, unromantic dream and lack of potential on the part of the artist to achieve even this unimpressive goal.[14]

At the end of the film the hero, who spent his entire life making tombstones, bequeaths his Italian marble to a young pupil. The film ends with both hope and the ironic realization that the story of the old "cemetery sculptor" may be repeated in the fate of his pupil. Neither G. Shengelaya nor E. Shengelaya makes value judgments, and they do not make a hero of Niko Pirosmanishvili or a villain of the old sculptor. They sympathize with their characters, who have to make the choice between "historical destiny and private fate, God's gift and a filling omelette."[15]

The natural world of old Georgia is gone, and the natural man cannot survive in the new world. The hero must accept the new social laws or disappear. This choice becomes the main theme of the films of Otar Ioseliani. In the 1968 film The Falling Leaves (Листопад), with a script by A. Chichinadze, the natural hero is confronted with a mechanistic factory staff. The individual's sensitivity clashes with the collective consciousness. Nothing in the modern world supports the hero, only nostalgic old photographs on the walls. The hero of The Falling Leaves is another eccentric who lives in an ideal world. People surrounding the hero perceive him as strange, for he never hides his feelings and does not accept compromise. This brings about a conflict at work, where he refuses to take part in selling spoiled wine to the public (the hero works at a wine factory), and makes him an object of ridicule on the part of the young woman he loves. Unlike other films with a similar hero, the protagonist of The Falling Leaves develops throughout the film. He manages to retain his values while turning into a cold and

Director Otar Ioseliani (top);
still from *The Falling Leaves*
(middle); still from *Once There
Lived a Singing Thrush*
(bottom). Reprinted from
R. Tikanadze, *Gruzinskoe kino*.

calculating player in a game into which he has been drawn against his will.

The hero of the 1971 film *Once There Lived a Singing Thrush* (*Жил певчий дрозд*) is a young kettledrum player who drifts through life trying to manage everything, yet fails to achieve anything. He deals with the world on his own terms. He always does what he wants to do at any particular moment, not what he is supposed to. Everyone likes him, but he does not have either a real friend or a real love. His problem seems to be the lack of time; he even dies at the end of the film in what appears to be an accident, in a hurry to get to the other side of the street. But his problem is much more serious than running out of time, and his death is not accidental. At the end of the film the audience sees a close-up of the inside of the hero's watch, which an acquaintance is fixing for him. It is a symbol of modern life, mechanistic and inhuman: "Mechanized time has pushed the living man off the screen."[16] Some critics made value judgments about the lack of heroic qualities in the protagonist. But the author's position is clear; he pities his hero, whose nature does not allow him to adjust to the world.[17] The accident is a natural end for this natural man who tries to fit in, to become a "part of that mechanism, something like a minute hand, relentless in its circular movement."[18]

In the 1980s irony ceased to dominate the Georgian film industry. It was replaced by satire or humor. E. Shengelaya's 1984 film *Blue Mountains or an Unbelievable Story* (*Голубые горы или неправдоподобная история*) is a parable in which the old world of bureaucrats and laggards literally collapses. The world is presented as a publishing house where outdated forms of doing business are employed. In the course of the film cracks start to appear in the walls of the building, and it finally falls down. The reason for the collapse turns out to be the new subway line—a sign of change—being constructed under the building. The publishing house is moved to a new building, and everything seems to be the same, although now changes start to take place even in the psychology of the old-timers. A similar point can be made about R. Chkheidze's 1981 film *Your Son, Earth* (*Твой сын, земля*), which has a script by R. Chkheidze and S. Zhgenti. In *Your Son, Earth* nostalgia for the old natural ways of life, the ironic worldview of changes brought about by the new ways and the destruction of centuries-old traditions—themes of the 1970s—are counteracted by a new dominant view. The film's hero, party secretary of the local district, decides to plant grapes in a valley where the vines had long ago been destroyed. Such turning back to the tradition in a new and constructive way can be seen as a response to the ironic view of the previous years. The hero himself is different, too. He is far from a naive and disillusioned dreamer or a natural man who is fading away with his disappearing world.[19]

The Bards

To the end of the 1940s, the only songs permitted in the Soviet Union were the so-called *mass songs*. They were written by professional composers and poets employed by the state. These songs, which appeared in large quantities, were approved and often commissioned by the party and reflected party policy. The songs were always optimistic, proclaiming the happiness of the people of the Soviet Union and the advantages of the socialist system. They were openly ideological and portrayed a positive hero—the builder of communism. It would be unfair to say that all these songs were inferior—a number of talented people wrote them and many had catchy tunes and easily memorizable verse (e.g., the wartime "Katyusha" [«Катюша»]). The mass songs were in the tradition of prewar times of the 1930s; they were not only created for the masses, but also meant to be sung by choirs. These upbeat songs followed people everywhere: to music (choir) lessons from elementary school to high school, to regular Saturday labor outings (трудовые субботники), to parades and meetings, and, through the radio, to people's apartments. The youth of the new times yearned for different songs containing different messages.

The *author's songs*, or songs of the bards, emerged after World War II and are connected with the more liberal political atmosphere in the mid 1950s. In some respects the songs that appeared at the time were in the same vein as the Young prose: romantic, hopeful, youthful, and directed toward a better future. The two songs that became beacons for the authors at that time were "The Brigantine" («Бригантина») and "The Globe" («Глобус»). "The Brigantine" cannot be called an author's song; it was written in 1937 by the poet Pavel Kogan in collaboration with the composer Georgy Lepsky—both then young men. Kogan perished during the war, and the song was never sung by either of its authors before an audience. "The Brigantine" tells about a pirate's ship ready to embark on its next pursuit of adventure and gold. A catchy tune, romantic lyrics, and a theme far removed from socialist reality made this song practically folklore among the young generation. The second song, "The Globe," was also written by two people: the lyrics by M. Lvov and the music by the famous Russian poet M. Svetlov. Like "The Brigantine," "The Globe," a 1947 song about friendship and great distances that challenge it, was written on the spur of the moment. The authors viewed it as a minor piece and could not have predicted its enormous popularity—the song became the students' anthem. When later sung on the radio, "The Globe" was introduced as a *students' song*. It was also extended—students in the geography department at Moscow University added several verses to the original two. It is said that with the addition of verses from students all around the country, eventually the song reached ninety-three verses.[20]

The 1950s and 1960s were the years of development of the "virgin lands" (целина). Thousands of young people went to farm these vast territories in the southern Soviet Union which had not been used for agriculture. The romantic tone of "The Brigantine" and "The Globe" fitted the romanticism of the road and of the distant lands. At the same time, industrial development created a sharp rise in the popularity of science and technology among young people. There emerged a new kind of technical intelligentsia—young, intellectual, well educated in various areas, and creative. Science and technology became a field of battle for young people, who, nevertheless, were not satisfied by science alone. They were interested in poetry—and wrote it. They were interested in theater—and organized amateur companies at their institutes where they wrote and performed sketches as well as entire humorous shows.

The young people were also interested in songs, but they wanted a new kind of song, which had intimacy as a main characteristic. It was a conversation between friends, and it dwelt on the common interests, desires, and hopes of youth. These new songs became a tradition on student outings, at the students' summer construction sites, on geological expeditions, at biological stations, on hiking trips, and at parties in apartments. The songs told romantic stories of danger and heroics. They talked of travel to distant lands, of wild and rough nature, of conquering high mountain peaks, of hard work in the coal mines and on the trawlers in far seas, of the dangerous work of drivers on serpentine mountain roads, and of innovative experiments in science labs. The recent war continued to be a theme of songs, but the new songs portrayed the war primarily as a tragedy; the emphasis was not on the patriotic message (even though it remained), but on the death and hardship brought by the war.

A number of songs were devoted to nature and that became the new generation's idol. These songs were named *tourist*. Students' (студенческая песня) and tourist (туристская песня) songs were not necessarily author's songs (авторская песня), since some of them were written by two people (a poet and a composer) and were not sung by their authors. They can be called *amateur songs* (самодеятельная песня). Yet these songs were connected with the author's song in their main characteristics, intimacy and sincerity of expression. One of the bards (the name used for the authors of the author's songs) said that this criterion of sincerity is in the "degree of frankness that the song projects." The songwriter argues that if the song "does not work," the fault is not necessarily in the writer's work, but in his person: "Lack of precision in expression is caused by lack of precision of feeling."[21] The advantage of the amateur songs was that they were not accountable to the institution of censorship. As such they were not approved for publication, recording, or performance at official concerts, but they were never intended to be official. These songs were sung with the accompaniment of the seven-stringed acoustic guitar—an inexpensive, portable instrument also known for its romantic connotations (e.g., Spanish serenades, Gypsy songs).

Since the songs were never recorded by the official state company, *Melodiia*, they were distributed on tape. The tape players in the early 1960s were crude, and the open-reel tape often tore, but this turned out to be the way to promote the songs. The tape players were expensive. People would save for months to buy them and immediately fill the complimentary free cassette with the songs. This form of distribution was called *magnitizdat* (магнитиздат). It worked like the *samizdat* (самиздат), the system of retyping a work using about eight carbon copies; and the *tamizdat* (тамиздат), the system of distributing works published in the West. All of these works were either unavailable or forbidden in the Soviet Union.[22]

The amateur songs represent a wide range of works, from semiofficial songs by professionals that made their way into the young intellectual crowd, to songs written by students and young scientists, to the author's songs. The emergence of the genre of author's songs was influenced by the works of Berthold Brecht and of the French chansonniers Yves Montand and Georges Brassens, who were admired in the Soviet Union. In the Russian tradition, the bards are close to Aleksander Vertinsky, the author of the *mood songs* and a famous prerevolutionary cabaret author and singer who returned at the end of the 1940s to the

Soviet Union from his emigration to the West, and to Yury Morfessi, a salon Gypsy singer.

The author's songs are not homogeneous; being intimate expressions of individual feelings, they differ as much as the personalities of their authors. Yury Visbor, for example, brought the romanticism of the heroism of soldiers, workers, truck drivers, pilots, submarine sailors, fishermen, and northern explorers into his songs. The message of his songs was not much different from that of the propaganda media, but the fact of the author's participation in the events he depicted (Visbor was a journalist and always volunteered for the most challenging assignments), as well as the tone of the songs that evoked trust, gained him wide popularity. Alexander Gorodnitsky sang about the hardships of Antarctica, which he visited a number of times as a geologist, yet his general tone differs from Visbor's. Gorodnitsky is interested in such themes as betrayal ("Betrayal" [«Предательство»]), memory, and the unimportance of an individual in the universal scheme ("The Flood" [«Наводнение»], "Atlantis" [«Атлантида»], "There Are Few of Us Left" [«Нас осталось мало»]).[23] Gorodnitsky asserts the importance of dreams and fairy tales for adults as a way of escape. He is pessimistic about efforts to change the world with his songs.

Yuly Kim (pseudonym Mikhailov) started as a teacher and then became a writer for theater. In Kim's songs the author's two callings merge; the recurrent themes of his songs are truth, kindness, war and peace, dignity, and knighthood. Kim's songs are often theatricalized monologues or dialogues in which the author, like Socrates, poses questions that make his listener think and draw his own conclusions. He himself questions his ability and right, to use the words of his hero teacher from the song "A Duet for a Teacher and a Student" («Дуэт учителя и ученика»), to "show people the way" (указывать людям дорогу).[24] The songs of other bards (such as Yu. Kukin, M. Nozhkin, N. Matveeva) also have their peculiarities; what unites them all is the fact that the bards come to their audiences and sing their songs. These songs, most of all, are conversations about life, intense yet intimate talks among friends. "The singer was needed as an interlocutor, as a friend, with whom communication is meaningful, excitingly interesting."[25]

This is especially true in respect to the three major Russian bards: Bulat Okudzhava, the acknowledged founder of the genre; Vladimir Vysotsky; and Alexander Galich. Their uniqueness was reflected not only in the content of their songs, but also in the music and the way it was performed. A widespread fallacy is that text occupies the central place in the bards' songs, that the tune is unimportant and merely functional. This fallacy might have been started by the bards themselves, who often stressed that they were not musicians. It is true that the bards' music itself is often unprofessional and uninteresting, but the product of the genre *is* a song—the text and the tune are blended together to achieve a specific result. The performance of the author becomes crucial; it is he who knows how the tune must be handled to project and enhance the text. Sinyavsky's term *one-actor-theater* (театр одного актера), which he uses to describe Galich's performances of his own songs, to some extent applies as well to the performances of Okudzhava, Vysotsky, Kim, and Nozhkin.[26] The bards' special intonation is achieved by merging all three elements: text, music, and the author's performance. The amateur tune is juxtaposed with the well-harmonized professional mass song as another way of rejecting the official art. Vladimir Frumkin notes that it was precisely the "intonation" of Okudzhava's songs that attracted a wide audience. People then started thinking about the lyrics. In this intonational novelty, the critic sees one of the bards' major accomplishments: "In some two to three years Okudzhava, Galich and Vysotsky implemented an 'intonational' revolution in the country; a fatal blow was struck to the well-rounded and dead state intonation that nested in our songs, cantatas and operas, in the speeches of officials, on the radio, in the theater and in the movies."[27]

Notwithstanding obvious similarities, the three major bards differ in several ways. Okudzhava developed over the years from an optimistic dreamer into a semiskeptic who found his only escape in personal and historical memories and in friends.[28] Vysotsky and Galich, who started to write songs later, came to the genre as authors with fully developed world views: Vysotsky as a rebel who understands the futility of his efforts to change life and people but cannot live in any other way, and Galich as a pessimist whose bitter satire of the Soviet system of values grows into an ironic musing on the inadequacies of life and humanity in general. It is irony that, although not exhausting the scope of analysis of these writers, gives the three bards (and other prominent figures of the genre) a common denominator; ironic themes form parallels between the bards and allow discussion of their works in the boundaries of one narrative mode.[29]

Life is a recurring theme in the songs of the bards. For Okudzhava it is mysterious. Using imagery the poet presents life as a cycle that does

Bulat Okudzhava.
Courtesy of
V. Frumkin.

not end with death. In "Song of the Blue Balloon" («Песенка о голубом шарике») a little girl's tears for her lost balloon develop into the tears of a young woman waiting for Mr. Right, then the tears of a mature woman who is left by her husband, and finally the tears of an old woman who does not want to die. The end of the song, "and the balloon has returned / and it is light blue" (а шарик вернулся / а он голубой) brings us back to the beginning of the cycle of life.[30] In the song "The Miraculous Waltz" («Чудесный вальс») the author transforms a picnic scene into a symbolic picture of life: "The music plays for an age. Our picnic drags on and on. / That picnic where they drink and weep, love and leave" (Целый век играет музыка. Затянулся наш пикник. / Тот пикник, где пьют и плачут, любят и бросают).[31] The love triangle presented in the song acquires universal qualities. The musician who grows into the earth, becoming a birch tree, is another symbol of ongoing life, the unity of all living nature. Okudzhava's view of life is that of an ironist: the cycle of life is ongoing, but its elements are too short; the beginning of each element of the cycle already contains its end. In "The First Nail" («Первый гвоздь») the refrain discloses the symbolic meaning of the housewarming party, that of the ephemeral character of human life and material values: "we drink and it gets rusty, we drink and it gets rusty" (мы пьем, он ржавеет, мы пьем, он ржавеет).[32]

In the songs of Galich the truth of life is bitter. In his "A Song of the Islands" («Песня про острова») the fairy-tale wonders of the distant islands are listed along with truth, conscience, and freedom. At the end of the song the author ironically states that the islands are the fruit of his imagination, thus undermining the moral values mentioned along with the islands. The world is corrupted and life is worthless. In "A Merry Conversation" («Веселый разговор») Galich compares the passing of the life of an elderly cashier to coins passing through her hands: "And the cash register clicks and clicks / counting life, not coins" (А касса щелкает, касса щелкает, / Не копеечкам—жизни счет).[33] In another song, "With the Cat-Like Paws of a Willow"[34] («Кошачьими лапами вербы»), the author characterizes life as devoid of sense («ни лада, ни смысла, ни склада»). Everything ends with a person's death:

А только и есть, что ограда
Да склепа сырое жилье . . .
Ты смертен, и это награда
Тебе—за бессмертье твое . . .

(And the only things that exist are the gate / and the damp burial vault / you are mortal, and this is your reward / for your immortality.)[35]

Galich's irony is often aimed at the Soviet system; his generalizations are based on life in the Soviet Union. In the poet's works, art and life are tightly connected, and the theme of futility of life is present alongside the theme of the death of art under the Soviet regime. In "This Is How Poets Lived" («Так жили поэты») the symbolic Pegasus is replaced by a wooden horse from a merry-go-round, "a wooden dummy:"[36]

Ни печали не зная, ни гнева,
По-собачьи виляя хвостом,
Он кружит все налево, налево,
И направо, направо потом.

(Devoid of sorrow and anger / wagging his tail like a dog / he goes in circles to the left and to the left / and then to the right and to the right.)[37]

The rotation of the merry-go-round becomes the rotation of the earth. The futility of the ongoing cycle of life is present in "About the Painters, the Stoker and the Theory of Relativity" («Про маляров, истопника и теорию относительности»). The song, written in the manner of skaz, is a story told by one of the painters.[38] It tells how three friends decided not to work anymore because some physicists have changed the direction of the earth's rotation on a bet («раскрутили шарик наоборот») and thus exposed all people to deadly radiation and other hazards. The heroes of the song quit working and start treating themselves for radiation with Stolichnaya vodka. The song is an example of structural irony, but the last two lines, which convey the point of view of the author, bring us back to Weltanschauung irony: "And the sphere is rotating and rotating / and all the time in the wrong direction!" (А шарик вертится и вертится, / И все время не туда!)[39]

Vysotsky sees life as a rut in which everyone is doomed to follow in the tracks of others. Loss of freedom in the rut is compensated by comfort: "There is no lack of food and drink in this cosy rut / and I convinced myself that I am not alone here, not alone" (Отказу нет в еде-питье в уютной этой колее, / И я живо себя убедил—не один я такой, не один). The ability to move forward along with others on a marked path is only an illusion of individual progress, and that is why the words "you want to move forward—please, do" (желаешь двигаться вперед—пожалуйста) sound so ironic. One man's attempt to free himself from the rut, in the song "A Strange Rut" («Чужая колея»), ends in his death—it is impossible to fight the rut: "In the confrontation the resources of his soul were wasted, / And the valves were gone" (Он в споре сжег запас до дна тепла души, / И полетели клапана и вкладыши).[40] The rut is a lucid allusion to the Soviet regime; the narrator's successful escape from the rut is not a sign of general hope, but rather a reflection of the poet-state relationship in the author's personal experience.

The plight of the individual in the world is another major theme found in the songs of the bards. It is connected with the theme of life. The world is hostile, enigmatic, and incomprehensible, and the individual feels weak and alone. Weakness and loneliness are recurring motifs in the songs devoted to humanity. In his songs "I Need Someone to Adore" («Мне надо на кого-нибудь молиться») and "A Moscow Ant" («Московский муравей») Okudzhava compares humankind to an ant, sympathetically yet ironically stating humanity's weakness in the huge world represented by the city of Moscow. The author's irony is rooted in the incongruity between the individuals' high expectations and dreams and their inability to achieve them. In "A Paper Soldier" («Бумажный солдат») the plot of Hans Christian Andersen's tale about a tin soldier becomes the basis of Okudzhava's parable: a paper soldier is ready to go into the "fire and smoke" for his love and does so forgetting that he is made of paper: "And there he perished all for naught, / he was just a paper soldier" (И там погиб он ни за грош— / ведь был солдат бумажный).[41] The author feels pity for human beings but cannot help them, since the author is also human and weak. The only thing he can do is pray to God in his song "François Villon's Prayer" («Молитва Франсуа Вийона»): "Grant Thou a little something to everyone . . . / and don't forget about me" (Дай же ты всем понемногу . . . / и не забудь про меня).[42]

Galich's hero is more susceptible to evil than to good. In "Once More about the Devil" («Еще раз о черте») he pictures the seduction of a man by the devil. A proposition to get additional time to sin on earth receives prompt consent from the hero. The price of the soul is low and the agreement is signed in the modern way, in ink instead of blood: "In our nuclear age, in our stone age, / Decency costs a penny!" (В наш атомный век, в наш каменный век, / На совесть цена пятак!).[43] Vysotsky's view of man is more complex. In "Mangustos" («Мангусты») he writes that people cannot survive without venom and snakes, they do not want to get rid of evil. This leads to imagery in the song "Case History" («История болезни») in which the snake is the biblical serpent and its venom is of forbidden knowledge. The author sees the history of mankind as the medical record of an incurably ill person:

У человечества всего
То колики, то рези
И вся история его
История болезни.

(All humankind / Has cholic or the gripes / And its whole history / Is a case history.)⁴⁴

Humans are weak, and to survive in the hostile world they must wear masks: "Everyone has learned to wear a mask, / So as not to smash the face against the stones" (Все научились маски надевать, / Чтоб не разбить свое лицо о камни). But the masks have been on for so long that the author fears that there are no more faces behind them: "What if the masks are removed—and there—/ The same half-masks—half-faces?" (Что если маски сброшены—а там— / Все те же полумаски-полулица?).⁴⁵

The hostility of the world makes people isolated and lonely. In Vysotsky's song "I Have a Fit of Drinking Out of Loneliness" («У меня запой от одиночества»), the character drinks in the company of a devil. The realization of the metaphor «напиться до чертиков» (to drink until you see devils) bears a strong irony in the song—there is nobody who can keep the man company. The song "We've Never Talked" («Не поговорили») by Yu. Levitansky and L. Kritskaya as performed by Elena Kamburova dramatizes lack of communication.⁴⁶ Each stanza begins against the background of a monotonous noise—the result of at least a dozen people talking at the same time. Each stanza ends in a similar line. At the end of the first stanza it is: "The day passed without a trace—and we never got to talk" (День прошел, как не было—не

Vladimir Vysotsky.
Courtesy of
V. Frumkin.

поговорили). In the second stanza the word "year" (год) replaces the word "day," and in the third line, is in turn replaced by the word "life" (жизнь).[47] The lack of communication thus becomes connected with the futility of human life.

Escape from reality is the way the hero of the bards tries to evade the "atomic age—stone age." The symbolic character of Okudzhava's "Last Pirate" («Последний пират») finds shelter in a small provincial bar (в районной пивной). In the song's closing statement the author suggests that life would be worthless without the "smiles of the bar crows," "singing of factory sirens," and the motion of the platform as if it were the pier of fate.[48] All of these are obviously products of intoxication, and their consolation is as ephemeral as the image of the last pirate. The blue trolley[49] from "The Last Trolley" («Последний трол-лейбус») acquires the same fairy-tale and dreamlike features. It is the last resort for the hero and similar "unlucky ones," who were "shipwrecked in the night" (потерпевших в ночи крушенье).[50]

Another remedy is suggested in "A Song about the Danish King's Drops" («Песенка о каплях датского короля»), where all the troubles of humanity can "be dissolved easily in the dripping sound of these drops" (растворяются легко в звоне этих капель).[51] The drops, though, cannot be found, and escape is not possible. A similar theme is found in Vysotsky's series "Moscow—Odessa" («Москва—Одесса») and "After Ten Years It's All the Same" («Через десять лет всё так же»). The hero waits in the airport for his flight to Odessa. The flight is delayed, and the waiting room of the airport becomes the hero's prison; weeks and months pass, and he still cannot get to his destination. The words of the drunkard "So how is it that the whole country does not fly anywhere?" (Как же так,—говорит,—вся страна, / Никогда, никуда не летит?) can be taken as an ironic comment on the contemporary poet's life.[52] Galich's songs lack even an attempt to escape reality. The only way to survive is to accept it. The poet calls it "nonresistance of one's conscience" («непротивление совести»).[53] Even the world of dreams becomes inaccessible to modern man. In "Song about Major Chistyakov" («Песня про майора Чистякова») the hero dreams that he is Atlas and carries the earth on his shoulders. He eventually gets tired and drops it. The hero wakes up in horror, but by ten o'clock he has forgotten his nightmare. At twelve Major Chistyakov comes to work, where he is in charge of the letter "G" (first letter of the poet's name) and puts an entry into the poet's file: "He wrote I dreamed / that I am Atlas" (Написал он, что мне во сне / Нынче снилось, что я атлант).[54]

Escape from Soviet reality into a dream world becomes as impossible in Galich's songs as escape from the Soviet state into some other country; both borders are closely guarded and controlled by Major Chistyakovs.

Reality is often contrasted with the past, which assumes nostalgic and dreamlike qualities. In Okudzhava's "Song of a Lady Fair" («Песня о прекрасной даме») the image of the poet's past love turns into the image of the ideal woman and also the yardstick against which the present is judged: "What are we ourselves, gentlemen, compared to that fair lady? / And what are our lives, what are our ladies, gentlemen!" (Ведь что мы сами, господа, в сравненье с дамой той прекрасной, / и наша жизнь, и наши дамы, господа!).[55] The past is often presented in the songs of the bards through images of concepts and objects long gone, such as the hand organ from Yu. Levitansky's "Remembering a Hand Organ" («Воспоминание о шарманке») and horse cabs in Okudzhava's "You Cannot Turn Back Time" («Былое нельзя воротить»). Nostalgic feelings toward the past are usually accompanied by the bitter realization that it is irretrievable. In Okudzhava's "Old House" («Старый дом») the sight of an abandoned and delapidated house triggers the poet's memories of the people and things that inhabited it long ago. But the illusion is momentary: "The doors are wide open. And there is no soul inside" (Двери распахнуты. И ни души).[56] Memories from the past are a kind of escape from reality, but they can neither substitute for nor alter it. In the song "The Old Jacket" («Старый пиджак») the alteration of the old jacket becomes an attempt to change the character's fate. The poet ironically concludes:

Он представляет это так:
едва лишь я пиджак примерю—
опять в твою любовь поверю . . .
Как бы не так. Такой чудак.

(He pictures it this way: / As soon as I try on my jacket—/ I'll believe in your love again . . . / And that just couldn't be. What a character.)[57]

In Galich's songs, longing for the past is connected with the country he left. It is a complex feeling, in which nostalgic tones are frequently replaced by bitter, realistic memories of personal hardships as, for example, in "Exercise in Nostalgia" («Опыт ностальгии»).[58] Vysotsky has neither nostalgia for the past nor illusions about the future. The change in time for him is merely quantitative, not qualitative:

Слышно в море мелодии
Повторение нот.
Все былое уходит, уходит, уходит, уходит,
Пусть придёт что придет.

(In the tempest of melody one can hear / a repetition of notes. / All past passes, passes, passes, passes, / and let whatever comes come.)[59]

Lack of hope is yet another major theme in the songs of the bards. In the "atomic age—stone age" nothing is left for human beings but to sell their souls or to put on masks that hide their identity and human nature. They have become like ants, incapable of controlling their destiny. Even their dreams and fairy tales are ruined by the age. Vysotsky's song "There Is No More Lukomor'e" («Лукоморья больше нет») is a bitterly ironic account of the fate of Pushkin's fairy-tale land in modern times. Bureaucracy, moral failure, corruption, and greed ruin the fairy-tale land, transforming it into a part of the modern world: the oak trees are cut down and turned into coffins, the house on chicken legs is burned, thirty-three fairy-tale heroes (*bogatyrs* [богатыри]) are raising chickens, the learned cat has turned his golden chain into money and dictates his memoirs, the sorcerer Chernomor finally abducts Lyudmila, etc. Evil prevails in the fairy-tale world, and this is just the beginning:

Ты уймись, уймись, тоска
У меня в груди!
Это только присказка,
Сказка впереди.

(Oh, please, subside, you wistfulness / In my heart! / This is just the introduction, / The tale is yet to come.)[60]

A similar device is found in Galich's "A Salon Romance" («Салонный романс»), which transforms the romantic world of the songs of Alexander Vertinsky. Two lovers' farewell candlelight dinner is turned into a drunken party («сто пятьдесят под боржом»), the traditional love triangle is destroyed by a banal "ménage à trois," masters and servants change places:

Все предано праху и тлену,
Ни дат не осталось, ни вех,

Alexander Galich.
Photo by Lev
Nisnevitch.

И нашу Елену—Елену
Не греки украли, а век!

(Everything is given over to dust and rot, / there are no dates, no memorable markers left, / and our Helen—Helen / is stolen by the age, not by the Greeks.)[61]

In the song "A Business Trip Pastoral" («Командировочная пастораль») illusions of ideal love are shattered by mundane reality. The world of pastorals («страна пасторалия») is replaced by the gray and monotonous life of the real world («страна постоялия») where nothing changes, no dreams come true, and people have grown tired of waiting for miracles:

Но, видно, здорово мы усталые,
От анкет у нас в кляксах пальцы!

Мы живём в стране Постоялии—
Называемся—постояльцы . . .

(But it seems we are too tired, / and our fingers are in ink with filling in forms! / We live in the country Habitualia— / we are called— inhabitants. . . .)[62]

The songs of Okudzhava contain an affirmation of hope. It is the force that helps his heroes persevere. In "Castle of Hope" («Замок надежды») the character's life passes while he attempts to achieve a dream—to fulfill a hope. Okudzhava believes in eternal values, which for the poet himself are art and friendship. This theme is prominent in many songs, especially "Song of Mozart" («Песенка о Моцарте»), "The Brotherhood of Friends" («Союз друзей»), "Georgian Song" («Грузинская песня»), and "A Word of Advice to My Friends" («Пожелание друзьям»). But the hope that sounds in these songs is not hope for the future. Friends and art are the last stand where the poet escapes reality, a defensive line. For Vysotsky, though, even his art is unable to help the poet overcome reality: "Oh, how bored I am of singing and playing. / I would rather lie on the bottom like a submarine, / and quit transmitting signals" (Ох, надоело петь и играть. / Лечь бы на дно, как подводная лодка, / И позывных не передавать).[63]

In Okudzhava's words, the genre of the author's song is now dead: "It seems to me that the author's song as we know it and as it existed before, has successfully passed away. It passed away, and left several names behind. What exists now is not an author's song. It is an amateur song, a mass culture phenomenon, which has nothing in common with what we had started some time ago."[64] The death of the genre is demonstrated by the number of festivals of the author's song that were organized by the VLKSM, the national young communist league, in the 1980s. The rebel song, the song that had always been the bane of officialdom, was embraced by its former enemy. This fact is especially ironic since the VLKSM itself was on its way out.

There are people who continue to write and perform their songs, some of them talented, but the message they carry is becoming outdated. N. Senkova, for example, sings about escaping from oneself, and S. Matveenko and B. Gordon sing about solitude, disillusionment, and inability to attain dreams. Others, like M. Shcherbakov, express confusion in the state of the world; his hero's world is devoid of order and his hero's life of meaning. These themes are prominent in the cultural and literary world of today's Russia, yet the prevailing forms of expression are different; the time for the intimate low-key conversations with friends is gone. After all, in the words of a modern bard: "I don't see the world in the daylight, / I don't believe in my best friend" (Я при свете света не вижу, / я не верю в лучшего друга).[65]

The culture of the bards and magnitizdat are part of the past. Vysotsky and Galich died; Okudzhava hardly writes songs anymore. The old songs of the bards are available on Melodiia records. The meaning of the songs for their audience has changed, too. Now they are nostalgic reminders.

Stand-up Comedy

The performance of humorous short stories, sketches, and monologues on stage has been a tradition in Russia since the 1840s. One of the most famous Russian actors, M. Shchepkin, took part in the emergence of this form of theater art. Several prominent names are connected with the genre: P. Sadovsky, a contemporary of Shchepkin; I. Gorbunov and V. Davydov in the 1870s; and V. Andreev-Burlak in the 1880s and 1890s. The actors took part in gala performances, or performed during the intermissions of full-length plays. The years immediately preceding the October Revolution of 1917 in Russia brought a new turn to the genre; the master of ceremonies (конферансье) was introduced. The master of ceremonies assumed great importance at the Crooked Mirror (Кривое зеркало) and the Bat (Летучая мышь), two cabarets in Petrograd before the revolution. The Crooked Mirror had O. Ozarovskaya and V. Khenkin, who both came to the cabaret as beginning actors, and K. Gibshman, who played the part of an awkward and inexperienced performer. The owner of the Bat—the rival of the Crooked Mirror—N. Baliev, was a master of ceremonies himself. The master of ceremonies in the cabaret introduced the individual numbers and performed monologues on issues of the day—not unlike stand-up comedians today. One of the most popular prerevolutionary masters of ceremonies in Moscow was N. Smirnov-Sokolsky. He started as a writer of humorous sketches and monologues, but then came onto the stage. His performances in the Moscow movie and variety theaters were marked by the "intonation of the public speaker and an interlocutor."[66]

In the Soviet times, the master of ceremonies became a permanent figure at variety shows (концерты) that included choirs, folk dances, solo singers and ballet dancers, magicians, and poetry readings. The purpose of the master of ceremonies was to tie all these numbers together with a theme, introducing the patriotic and pompous as well as the satirical interludes. The figure of the master of ceremonies deteriorated into an ideological messenger whose jokes were rude and humorless. Because of the low artistic quality of the shows and the kind of audience they attracted, the figure of the master of ceremonies and his jokes soon became symbols of bad taste. Some masters of ceremonies tried to use humorous literature on the stage, but literary humor did not appeal to the audience. Only the stories of Mikhail Zoshchenko succeeded. The shortage of scripts for these shows in the 1950s and 1960s brought to life writers for stand-up comedy (писатели-эстрадники) and the new genres—stand-up monologue (эстрадный монолог) and sketch (эстрадная сценка). The higher quality of the variety shows, which at this time started to be broadcast over radio and TV, appealed to a more sophisticated public, and this in turn promoted a higher quality in the master of ceremonies texts.

Better performers also appeared in stand-up comedy. The most popular of them, Arkady Raikin, was a favorite for more than thirty years. Richard Stites accurately describes the main characteristics of the Soviet stand-up comedian: "The Soviet comedian must not only amuse and entertain, but also display empathy and an understanding of everyday problems: work, in-laws, dating, corruption, bureaucracy, and especially neighbors (who in the Soviet context are often across the wall, not the hall). Satirical comedy is partly created by its audience and its environment. The laughter connecting the standup comics with their listeners about the shortcomings of Soviet life may be more socially significant than the muted exclamations and breathless silences of the Taganka theater that Western visitors have so often noted."[67] Raikin organized his own theater that toured the Soviet Union. He also mobilized the best writers to work for him: S. Altov, A. Kanevsky, M. Mishin, M. Zhvanetsky, and others. The most talented of them all was Mikhail Zhvanetsky. For many years Zhvanetsky, like the rest of Raikin's writers, was in the shadow of the actor, but in the late 1960s Zhvanetsky started his own theater with the young performers V. Ilchenko and I. Kartsev. The author himself came out onto the stage, and his name soon became as well known in the Soviet Union as those of the bards.

The figure of Zhvanetsky stands out for several reasons. First, he combined writing skill with performing artistry, making the genre the

Mikhail Zhvanetsky.

author's (авторский жанр). Second, he concentrated on the monologue, developing it into a completely new genre. Zhvanetsky's monologues represent a departure from their literary counterparts and at the same time show great similarities with the ballads of the bards. (As writer Felix Krivin once noted in a conversation with the author, Zhvanetsky's monologues are almost impossible to read—they have to be heard.) Third, he created a new style (эстрадный стиль), with its own vocabulary and syntax. And finally, in the works of Mikhail Zhvanetsky we find a particular orientation that we call ironic.

Zhvanetsky's view of the world is similar to that of Galich, who saw the "socialist camp" (социалистический лагерь) as a concentration camp. In Zhvanetsky's monologues the dullness of life and the decline of morals are restricted to the country he lives in. Nevertheless, on a larger scale these seemingly satirical texts become ironic. Foreign countries are presented in the aura of a dream. This device, through which a real territory is given dreamlike qualities because of political restrictions and closed borders, makes Zhvanetsky's irony up-to-date. The source of irony here is suppressed satire that could not be openly stated because of censorship.

If foreign countries in the works of Zhvanetsky represent the unattainable dream, television is the means of dreaming. Several monologues present television as a safety valve, a way to escape reality. It is ironic that Zhvanetsky was often allowed to read his monologues on TV for the same reason—they were viewed by the authorities as safety valves and accepted as an unavoidable compromise. In the monologue "A Monologue Something Like This" («Вот такой монолог»), exotic places are represented as huge stores, dealing in dreams: "Fiji, Tahiti, Las Palmas—such are the names; and the islands were opened[68] a very long time ago, they say, by someone, and now [the inhabitants] live off tourists of some kind. An exhibition of flowers on Tahiti: and Tahiti was opened a long time ago and is open twenty-four hours a day."[69]

At the end of the monologue Zhvanetsky tells of the new device invented for TV that allows viewers to experience the physical effects of the picture: feel the breeze, the splashes of the ocean waves, and the insect bites. "One can lose oneself in dreams!" (Ох, можно забыться!), concludes the author. Foreign countries in Zhvanetsky's monologues are presented like the earth as seen by E. Shengelaya's chudaki from their skyflier. And not only foreign countries, but domestic reality is also altered, "touched up" by television.

In the monologue "How TV Programs Are Made" («Как делается телевидение»), a woman tells the story of making a show about her family—an ideal family. This story, like most of Zhvanetsky's monologues, does not have a plot and is based on a number of complex cultural allusions. Suffice it to say that the program, which supposedly depicts an average Soviet family, says little about the family itself. The "friends" of the family are filmed in a zoo (people laughing) or at a Richter concert (people applauding the wife's story of her shock-labor at the factory). The family members are played by actors, the apartment is a stage set ("The door is mine—the rest is painted scenery" [Дверь моя—а остальное дорисовано]), and the store was filmed abroad ("The editor said that even in the supermarket in the picture the selection was poor and there were too many people"). Even the silver wedding anniversary is filmed in Japan: "The restaurant was filmed in Japan, that is why the faces at the tables are slanting. We were filmed here, and then superimposed on the Japanese by a matte technique."

The image of the iron curtain is constantly present in Zhvanetsky's works. In his monologue "Let's Argue" («Давайте спорить»), the author ironically criticizes Hollywood without seeing its productions; mentions philosophers—Western, no doubt—without reading their works; argues about the taste of oysters and coconut, usually known in the Soviet Union only by their names; and exhorts his audience to aspire to international standards of which he is actually ignorant. He predicts that the ability to intuit a proper opinion will develop to such a level that it will replace information. The closed and excluded nature of Zhvanetsky's world dictates new morals and a new code of behavior. The monologue "Friendship Isn't What It Used to Be" («Дружба видоизменилась») is used by the author to draw a picture of morals in the new society: friendship has been changed to such an extent that it allows betrayal, does not need communication and survives with only one member; kindness has incorporated in itself ruthlessness and cruelty; mutual aid and support can be distinctly observed through a microscope; feelings of deep trust and complete control have merged, forming a "perfect combination." The closing of the monologue is an ironic generalization in which all this is seen as intrinsic in human nature, rather than the result of territorial or political conditions. This transformation of meaning is achieved by the double meaning of the phrase «белый свет» (literally meaning "[white] light," metaphorically—"our world"): "Feelings and concepts have lost the repugnant clearness they used to have in the past, they easily blend into one another, as do the different colors of the spectrum that form our contemporary light [modern world]."

Zhvanetsky does not have much faith in people; he sees their major concern not as how to change the world, but rather as how to adapt to it. The heroes of his monologues are very similar to those of Zoshchenko's stories. The device of skaz is widely used by Zhvanetsky. The hero of the monologue "Yes, Yes, That's Right" («Да, да, именно») is a frightened individual whose only concern is survival. Every second word of the text is "thanks": "Thanks, that I live, that I exist. Hurray, that I woke up; viva, that I had breakfast. . . . For buttermilk a separate thanks to everyone!" The character from the monologue "In Excellent Spirits" («А настроение—отменное!») simply turns away from problems and convinces himself that his life is the best. The lack of objective reasons for being satisfied with life is replaced by absurd arguments, such as the high quality of the honor guard («Зато почетный караул—во!»). The narrator of the monologue "People Are Better Off Now" («Лучше стал жить народ») argues that the people are better off, while he is fishing things out of the rubbish chute. These are all forms of escaping from reality by turning away from it, as an ostrich hides its head in the sand. Drinking is another form of escape, as seen in the monologue "My Friend and I" («Мы с приятелем»), where the narrator presents vodka as the only remedy against bad moods, depression, and the hardships of life.

The author sympathizes with his characters and is in fact one of them. In the monologue "What's Good?" («Что такое хорошо?») the author says: "My gloves pinch and the world is too tight" (Давят, давят перчатки; тесен, тесен мне так плотно облегающий меня мир). In the struggle for life in the hostile world where Zhvanetsky's characters live, there are no winners. A man flees and locks himself in his apartment, his own microcosm. His only refuge is his family, especially his wife. It is she who gives him strength to fight his way through every day: "Give me some more strength, and I'll rush there again."

The attitude toward a wife, a woman, in Zhvanetsky's works is illustrated by the title of one of the Okudzhava songs: "Your Majesty, Woman" («Ваше величество, женщина»). Women in Zhvanetsky's monologues are stronger and more enduring than men. This incurs both the author's admiration and his bitter irony. He is worried that the woman is turning into a working machine, her functions being reduced to those of the family breadwinner and mainstay. In the monologue "Everyone Makes a Big Deal Over French Women" («Все говорят: француженка!»), praise of the woman's ability to keep her place in numerous shopping queues, carry "five hundred kilogram" bags of groceries, raise children, cook, and still manage to help her husband sounds ironic and sad. According to Zhvanetsky, such a life has deprived woman of her femininity, turned her into a bag (баба). The narrator dreams of the time when "the corns on the best feet in Europe will disappear together with the shoes [of poor quality that cause these corns]" and only the woman-gymnast will have muscles, and the man will watch her and be happy that she is not his wife. But the natural woman—tender and free—is forced out into the realm of dream. The young heroine of the monologue "I Can't Stand in Lines" («Я не могу в очереди стоять») is Georgian and very similar to the "natural man" of Georgian films. She cannot live in a big city, cannot adapt to the modern way of life: "I cannot live with pedestrian crossings, rings, whistles, barriers. . . . We protect birds, so that they fly where they want, so why do we tell people: live here, walk there, don't walk here, don't sing here?!" The heroine leaves the big city and returns home to Georgia: "Come to Batumi, take the road to Mikhindzhauri, go into the woods and call: 'Diana!'—and I will come out." The heroine's name and dwelling place allude to the Greek goddess. Thus the hope for the natural woman is transferred from the realm of dreams into the realm of myth.[70]

The hero's attempts to overcome the modern life-style are ironic. Thus, in the monologue "Do You Want to Grow Younger?" («Хотите помолодеть?»), the narrator proposes to eliminate watches and clocks and to live by the natural cycle of human life: "The birds start to sing—it means it's morning; it gets dark—it's evening."[71] To live by the sun, to rejoice when one is happy—not just on the designated holidays—would be ideal. But reality is different, and time flies faster and faster: "and I subscribe to newspapers more and more often—and it is only once a year!" (и газеты выписываю все чаще и чаще—а ведь это раз в год!). The same idea is expressed in the monologue "I Did Not Lose a Second!" («Ни секунды не потерял!»), where the Weltanschauung irony is emphasized by the structural irony.[72] The narrator is proud of his little victories. Whereas the lucky are born with a silver spoon in their mouths, he was clever enough to be born with a watch on his wrist. His whole life, told on the space of a typewritten page, is a chase from one queue to another. The process itself soon replaces the reason for standing in lines, and the character buys swimming trunks in February (his number in line has come up) and simultaneously gets in two lines for tickets, one to a resort and the other to get back home. Lines to eat, to drink, to ride, to buy, to get undressed at the beach, to take a shower, to swim, to get dressed, fill all his time. The character considers himself lucky—he manages to get a place in all the lines. When his turn comes in the cemetery line, he happily grabs what is offered: "I am on time!" (Успел!) is the last word of the monologue.

The pressure of time (цейтнот) does not allow Zhvanetsky's characters to stop and think about their lives. When they do, they realize that they have lived in vain. The hero of "Portrait" («Портрет») leaves his will for his son. The monologue is structured around the word "not": the hero did not become (and never will become) tall, handsome, or lucky. He will never fall in love with a famous movie star, conduct a symphony orchestra, command a battleship, or become a great sportsman: "There is no time. There is no more time." The end of the monologue is ironic. In form it contrasts with the rest of the story, in fact it stresses the shortness and futility of human life, the features that the character's son is bound to inherit from his father: "But on the other hand. . . . On the other hand now I will tell my son: 'Boy, I've gone through everything, I did not become this, and I did not become that, and I will pass my knowledge of the world on to you.'"[73]

Ironic worldview brought an additional attraction to the monologues of Mikhail Zhvanetsky, an additional bond and common ground between him and his intellectual audience. This bond was based on some common understanding, a knowledge shared by the author and the viewer but unknown to the uninitiated. This knowledge can be explained as a sort of passive opposition to the system, an emotional outlet for the system's critics. It was based on certain taboos that were not even broken but just skillfully alluded to by the author, which brought him his audience's gratitude and laughter. Such practice, though, is impossible without restrictions and prohibitions imposed by censorship. Zhvanetsky himself once noted that as an author he thrives on "closed doors." These closed doors created his special relationship with the intellectual audience, and Weltanschauung irony was the vehicle for expressing this relationship. With the opening of doors in the middle of the 1980s, with the lifting of a number of taboos—although Zhvanetsky is still performing—his special relationship with his audience ceased to exist.

Growth of Humor Forms in the Soviet Media

There were two roles that the media played in the Soviet Union. The establishment tried to educate people in the spirit of communism, delivering propaganda both in its pure form and camouflaged as entertainment. People, on the other hand, tried to get from the media as little propaganda and as much entertainment as possible. The media was used as an escape, not only for the broad base of the population, but also for the intellectuals. In television, for example, the college education of a viewer translated into specific programs that he watched, but his reason for watching television in general was not entirely different from that of a less-educated member of the audience. One of the main forms of relaxation in the media in general was humor, and for the well-educated audience in the 1970s it was humor with ironic undertones. The process of relaxation itself—passively spending time in front of television—can be viewed as an ironic activity of an individual who does not believe in his potential to change his life actively. The popularity of humor in the Soviet media of the 1970s could partially be explained by the demand for such escapist material. In a sociological experiment, when asked to write an essay "A Letter to My Favorite TV Personality," a number of high school students addressed their letters to Pani Monika from the TV humor show "A Tavern of 13 Chairs."[74]

The popularity of humor brought the demand for more humor programs in the national media in the 1960s. Several programs of satire and humor appeared on the radio, the most famous of which—"Good morning!" («С добрым утром!»)—was heard on Sundays by millions of people. It consisted of popular songs, celebrity interviews, and humorous stories. One of the most popular and widely watched TV programs was the "KVN"—Club of the Joyful and the Resourceful («Клуб веселых и находчивых»). The "KVN" was a game in which teams of students competed for the title of most witty. The "KVN" games drew as many people to the TV screens as did the most popular soccer matches. The program was curtailed at the end of the 1960s, but the enthusiasm it generated did not disappear. At the end of the 1960s television introduced a new humor program, "A Tavern of 13 Chairs" («Кабачок 13 стульев»). It was originally to be based on Polish humorous stories and songs. The program was the first TV show with a permanent cast of characters. Polish humor was chosen for two reasons: first, because of censorship it was easier to present some questionable situations as set in liberal Poland, and second, Polish humor at the time was rich and innovative (especially popular in the Soviet Union were the stories and sketches by S. Mrozek, A. Potemkowski, J. Osenka, S. J. Lec, and H. Bardijewski). Nevertheless, the program soon began to be infiltrated by Russian humorists who wrote sketches especially for the show's characters: Pan Professor, Pani Monika, Pan Wladek, Pani Zosia, Pan Direktor, Pan Gimalaiski, and others.

At the beginning of the 1970s the city authorities of Odessa agreed to sponsor a Festival of Humor, which was to take place on April 1. The festival was organized by enthusiastic former "KVN" players and humor writers. It consisted of a huge parade, which started at the street named after Ilya Ilf and Evgeny Petrov. The street was renamed after the two great humorists by the festival organizers, and two city cafes, the Golden Calf (Золотой теленок) and Twelve Chairs (Двенадцать стульев), were named for the writers' most famous novels. On the first and second of April all theaters and movies showed comedies exclusively, amateur theater groups staged Gogol's stories in the city's courtyards, and concert halls were given to comedians and humorous writers who read their stories. The culmination of the festival was a show and race of antique cars to win the "Antilope Gnu" (на приз

«Антилопы ‹гну›»). The festival, called "Iumorina" («Юморина»), was repeated for several years but then was banned in 1976 after severe criticism by the party press.

One of the most significant events at the end of the 1960s was the opening of the "department of humor" on the sixteenth page of the *Literary Gazette*, the publication's last page. Until that time the only national humorous periodical in the Soviet Union was the journal *Krokodil*, the mouthpiece of the party's central committee. *Krokodil* had a distinct satirical direction and published mostly feuilletons and political cartoons. Humorous stories were variations of satirical articles. The "administration"—as the organizers called themselves—of the humor page of *Literary Gazette* set forth their program in the opening issue of 1967.[75] They distinguished their goals from those of *Krokodil*: "We want to be the apostles of angry satire and subtle humor (naturally, with a lyrical undercurrent)." In reality, the department was carrying out only the latter.

A number of gifted young authors contributed to the sixteenth page of *Literary Gazette*, including S. Altov, A. Arkanov, G. Gorin, L. Izmailov, F. Kamov, A. Khait, A. Kuchaev, A. Kurlyandsky, M. Mishin, M. Rozovsky, V. Slavkin, V. Tokareva, E. Uspensky, E. Shatko, and A. Zhitinsky. Most of them were not professional writers, at least not at the beginning. Some well-known and popular writers (such as V. Aksyonov, A. Bitov, A. Gladilin, and F. Krivin) also published their works in the department of humor.

The department was given the name "Twelve Chairs" («Двенадцать стульев»). It was organized and run by I. Suslov and V. Veselovsky. The materials on the page were arranged under various headings: "Second-Hand Bookshop" («Лавка букиниста»), which published stories of old humorists, such as S. Cherny, A. Averchenko, D. Kharms, P. Romanov, I. Ilf and V. Petrov, M. Bulgakov, F. Sologub, and Teffi; "Phrases" («Фразы») for short witty pronouncements; "Eccentrics" («Чудаки») for cartoons; "Mockingbird" («Пересмешник») for parodies; "Boomerang" («Бумеранг») for answering alleged letters to the editor; "Horns and Hoofs" («Рога и копыта»), an absurd news column; and "Translations" («Переводы») for foreign humor. In the last, stories by Kurt Vonnegut and James Thurber along with those of Yugoslav, Bulgarian, and Polish humorists often appeared. Parody was a dominant genre in both prose and poetry. A number of parodic poems, interviews, and the "novel of the century" *Turbulent Stream* (*Бурный поток*), which was serialized, appeared in the department under the name EvGENII

The opening of the "department of humor" on the sixteenth page of *Literary Gazette* (January 1, 1967).

SAZONOV («гений» in Russian means "genius"). The works of Ev-GENII SAZONOV were written collectively by the administration and authors of the humor department.

The success and popularity of the sixteenth page of *Literary Gazette* was so great that soon other periodicals established humor sections. In 1968 *Literaturnaia Rossiia* added "The Eccentric" («Чудак»), which had the same format as "Twelve Chairs" but with different headings. In 1970 a humor section in *Iunost'* with the threatening name "Vacuum-Cleaner" («Пылесос») was renamed "Green Briefcase" («Зеленый портфель»). A new student magazine, *Studencheskii meridian*, came out in 1974 with a humor section called "Parallel" («Параллель»). In Leningrad a humor department was started at the magazine *Avrora*. It was given the name "Elephant" («Слон») and was modeled after "Twelve Chairs." In the 1970s humor sections also appeared in the magazines *Teatr* and *Sovetskii ekran*.

The section "Ironic Prose" («Ироническая проза») was introduced by Ilya Suslov in the seventh issue of *Literary Gazette* for 1967. One should distinguish between the heading "Ironic Prose" in *Literary Gazette* and ironic prose as a subgenre of the humorous short story. Although they often coincided, satirical or humorous items were also published under the heading "Ironic Prose." Also, quite a few stories of this subgenre appeared under different headings in the magazine: "Intellectuals of the Club TC" («Интеллигенты Клуба ДС»), "Summer of the Club TC" («Лето Клуба ДС»), etc. The same authors who contributed works of ironic prose to *Literary Gazette* were also publishing their stories in other periodicals. In addition to ironic prose the journals published ironic poetry, which I will not deal with here. It would, however, be fair to say that the poetry also enjoyed immense popularity and attracted as contributors a number of famous poets, such as Andrey Voznesensky, David Samoilov, Yunna Morits, Alexander Bezymensky, Eduardas Mezhelaitis, Vladimir Lifshits, Konstantin Vanshenkin, and Yulia Drunina.

The decline of the ironic narrative mode in the late 1970s and early 1980s coincided with the tightening of censorship and the disappearance of a number of humor sections. In 1978 "Elephant" and "Parallel" ceased to appear; the humor sections in *Teatr* and *Sovetskiiekran* also disappeared; "The Eccentric" was purposely renamed" The Inspector General" («Ревизор»). "Green Briefcase" converted to harmless humor, and "Twelve Chairs" became satire, a variation of the hard party line of *Krokodil*. The original headings in "Twelve Chairs" were re-

"Departments of humor" in Soviet periodicals of the 1970s.

placed with straightforward satirical clichés dealing with lazy workers, drunkards, bribe-takers, and bribe-givers («Не прикладая рук», «Не лезь в бутылку», «Вы—нам, мы—вам», «Под колпаком Клуба ДС», «Рвачи прилетели», «Дисциплинарий Клуба ДС»). The number of stories was greatly diminished, and the greatest importance was given to satirical articles and feuilletons. Although censorship was partly to blame, the main reason for the decline of the ironic prose was that the genre had reached its limits. The number of ironic themes was restricted; innovations were finally exhausted. The stories started to resemble one another to a startling degree. Ironic prose suffered from a disease that it had formerly studied—loss of identity. Gradually the best authors moved on to other genres and fields. Those who remained produced mediocre satirical and humorous stories. As a result, *Literary Gazette* lost its intellectual reader.[76]

3. Ironic Prose as a Subgenre of the Humorous Short Story

Ironic prose came as an alternative at a time when more and more themes became forbidden for satirical approach. In the late 1960s and early 1970s on the humorous pages of the Soviet periodicals, attempts were still made to tackle problems people encountered in daily life. Since restrictions on the themes were getting more rigid, authors resorted to Aesopian language. Exotic foreign countries became veiled expressions of real problems; forbidden issues were raised in the form of an innocent children's rhyme or a mock news chronicle or letter to the editor. Here are two rhymes, the first by Vladimir Lisichkin and the second by Emma Moshkovskaya, that were published under the rubric of "The Children's Room" («Детская комната») that appeared in *Literary Gazette* at the end of the 1960s:[1]

Апельсин

Если нужен
Апельсин—
Вы зайдите
В магазин,
И купите
Пластилин
И слепите
Апельсин.

("An Orange." If you need / An orange / Go to / A store / And buy yourself / Some play dough / And make yourself / An orange out of it.)

Суп

Если в миске мало супа,
вам нужна большая лупа.
Поглядите в эту лупу,
будет много-много супу!

("Soup." If there is little soup in the bowl, / you need a big magnifying glass. / Look into this magnifying glass, / and there will be a lot of soup!)

Both rhymes are satirical commentaries on the food shortages and low standard of living in the Soviet Union. If recognized as such by the censors, they would undoubtedly be taken out. The rhymes were saved by the unassuming place they occupied in the newspaper—on its last page—as well as by their presumed audience—children.

The battle between censor and author was fought constantly. Their relationship was not simple; the official censor was responsible only for making sure that no state secrets were revealed. The censorship of the ideas, though, was done on the level of the editor, senior editor, and managing director of the newspaper, who read the material before its publication and made sure that it corresponded to the party line and did not mention forbidden topics. Such a list of topics and names of nonpersons was always at hand at every media office, and these lists were updated regularly. But the censorship started even earlier. The author, who was aware of the forbidden topics, was his own first censor.[2] Daring editors, such as Suslov and Veselovsky of the humor page of *Literary Gazette*, were playing the game of trying to pass hidden messages in the stories they published. This game was played openly. The senior officials of the newspaper knew they should look for hidden messages in stories in the humor section; the editors knew how to present the material so that the questionable item would not stand out among conventional stories and jokes. The editors also knew which of the managing directors was more receptive to certain material, which was more rigid in his ideological views, and which would be more likely simply to overlook a risky subject.

In *Literary Gazette* some leniency was shown to minor diversions from the party line. This leniency was the result of the special mission the newspaper acquired when its format was changed in 1967. The newspaper was the party's publication for the intelligentsia. As such, it was allowed to publish material that would have been unthinkable for

The first page of a special issue of *Literary Gazette* (January 1, 1991) completely devoted to the "department of humor."

the state's and party's main organs, *Pravda* and *Izvestiia*. The articles in *Literary Gazette* never crossed the line, but the material was presented in a subtle and sophisticated way. Things presented as orders and decrees in other periodicals were explained, and the rationale given, in *Literary Gazette*. The same bitter medicine was prescribed, but reasoned out for the patient and sweetened by occasional little bribes—humorous stories with allusions to forbidden subjects. Usually these allusions were quite innocent and provided a safety valve, channeling people's discontent into the safe avenue of laughter and ridicule of the authorities. This was "part of the deal," and was tacitly agreed to by editors and party bosses. The senior editors of the newspaper, its managing directors, and the editor-in-chief, Alexander Chakovsky, had a difficult task: to allow some evidence of freedom, or even hints of mild opposition to the leading view on certain issues of minor importance, but to preserve the appearance of a party line periodical to the hardliners, who also were reading the paper.

The censorship games between the authors and humor page editors on the one side and the newspaper's officials on the other sometimes turned into exercises in wit. The story may not have carried any message, but a mere allusion to a serious ideological matter or a political leader in a joke became a challenge for authors. Suslov tells of a story[3] about a drunkard who on his way home at night sees a figure with a raised hand in the street evidently trying to stop a taxi. It is a cold winter day, and the pedestrian seems to be frozen stiff. The hero takes him home to thaw, only to discover in the morning that he had carried home a statue. The publication of the story brought hundreds of angry letters to the editorial office and the Party Central Committee; good communists were infuriated with what they perceived as an allusion to Lenin—the only monument with a hand stretched out in the manner described in the story. The incident almost cost Suslov and Veselovsky their jobs.

At the end of the 1960s and the beginning of the 1970s, *Literary Gazette* managed to preserve this equilibrium between the intelligentsia and the authorities, but with the advancement of the conservatism in the country's political and cultural atmosphere, even these meager and semisanctioned attempts at subversion became impossible. Suslov writes about it, using some of the current jokes: "They demanded from us only positive satire. Do you know what this is? It is when it is considered that the goal of satire is to project Hurray in the scream Disaster! It is when at Genghis Khan's funeral someone says that he was a sympathetic and sensitive person. It is when in reality the things are different from what they really are."[4]

Ironic prose came as a temporary compromise between the intelligentsia and the authorities. It never raised any forbidden topics or alluded to famous political figures, and it concentrated on the predicament of an individual living in a society of conventions, on a personal striving of an individual for recognition of his personal achievement in the society where everything is communal and collective. The readers of *Literary Gazette* found their double in the hero of ironic prose and, in the life of the hero, an accurate account of their own life. The readers' skepticism about the values of society reached toward universal values, which also came under suspicion. In the series of fables by Felix Krivin, children's heroes of fairy tales and world literature switch places with villains or ordinary characters, and vice versa. Even though the author summons the heroes (readers) not to accept the roles thoughtlessly and to try to perform the role given to one by life to the best of one's ability, the fact of role-playing and role-switching brings in an ironic perspective of a person as a speck of dust manipulated by impersonal powers ("If Such a Thing Should Happen . . ." [«Если бы такое случилось . . .»]).

The stories of ironic prose, found in the 1970s on the humor pages at the end of various periodicals, are unique in the sense that they developed a special bond between the author and the intellectual reader. This bond is common to these stories and to some other cultural phenomena of the time (such as Zhvanetsky's monologues) and is based on a specific kind of relationship. To become a part of this relationship one has to follow in the footsteps of a Soviet intellectual: read the same books, listen to the same records, and laugh at the same jokes. Such a relationship is based on a cultural text that is found behind the literary text and that is known to all the participants in the relationship. This cultural text is not just a "cultural glossary" of the time, but an entity that has its own integral structure as a genre. This cultural text could be shown in detail, yet here we will only state that at its base lies certain conventions describing human life, specifically, the life of an intellectual reader of these stories. This description of life looks like a computerized image, a picture of a person evolving. It is like a statistical presentation of a mathematically average individual. Yet all the elements of this skeletal structure are so characteristic of all those who are part of the cultural structure that any individual can substitute this presentation for his life, with all its intricate and inimitable details, and suddenly realize that his life, even in its most unique details, completely coincides with the programmed general image. To some extent this scheme can be illustrated by a rhyme of O. Molotkov published in *Literary Gazette*:

Человеческая комедия. Инженерный вариант.

Мама, сказка, каша, кошка,
книжка, яркая обложка,
Буратино, Карабас,
ранец, школа, первый класс,
грязь в тетради, тройка, двойка,
папа, крик, головомойка,
лето, труд, река, солома,
осень, сбор металлолома,
Пушкин, Дарвин, Кромвель, Ом,
Гоголь и Наполеон,
Менделеев, Герострат,
бал прощальный, аттестат,
институт, экзамен, нервы,
конкурс, лекция, курс первый,
тренировки, семинары,
песни, танцы, тары-бары,
прочность знаний, чет-нечет,
радость, сессия, зачет,
стройотряд, жара, работа,
культпоход, газета, фото,
общежитье, взятка-мизер,
кинотеатр, телевизор,
карандаш, лопата, лом,
пятый курс, проект, диплом,
отпуск, море, пароход,
по Кавказу турпоход,
кульман, шеф, конец квартала,
цех, участок, план по валу,
ЖСК, гараж, квартира,
теща, юмор и сатира,
детский сад, велосипед,
карты, шахматы, сосед,
сердце, печень, лишний вес,
возраст, пенсия, собес,

юбилей, часы-награда,
речи, памятник, ограда.

("The Human Comedy. Version for Engineers." Mama, fairy tale, kasha, kitty, / book, bright cover, / Pinocchio, bad Karabas, / nap-sack, school, first grade, / dirt in notebook, C, F, / dad, yelling, scolding, / summer, labor, river, straw, / fall, collecting scrap-metal, / Pushkin, Darwin, Cromwell, Ohm, / Gogol and Napoleon, / senior prom, diploma, / college, exam, nerves, / college entrance exams, lecture, freshman year, / working out, seminars, / singing, dancing, chatting, / depth of knowledge, flip a coin, / joy, finals, exams over, / work force, heat, work, / cultural field trip, newspaper, photo, / dorm, trump—miser, / movies, TV, / pencil, shovel, crowbar, / senior year, senior project, B.S., / vacation, sea, ship, / Caucasus, pleasure trip, / drafting-table, boss, end of the quarter, / shop, workplace, production plan, / apartment building cooperative, garage, apartment, / mother-in-law, humor and satire, / kindergarten, bicycle, / cards, chess, neighbour, / heart, liver, extra weight, / age, retirement, social security office, / jubilee, gold watch, / eulogies, tombstone, fence.)

In this rhyme, human life is taken in its entirety by simply naming its particular points. To understand the connotations (and sometimes even denotations) of the objects and activities described in the rhyme, one has to know the cultural text—then each of the noun-points becomes a center of a rich associative field. In the structure of the stories, these points, including birth and death, have equal importance, and each of them taken separately can be extended into an independent story. Such a story, though, will still allude to the whole cultural text, as well as to all other points constituting it. In some sense Molotkov's rhyme reveals the basis for the covert relationship between the author and the reader by making an entire cultural text the topic of the literary text. The cultural text is unmasked by the simple enumeration of noun-codes well known to the reader. The act of reading itself becomes a game, since the readers not only are perceiving the account of personal past and future life, but also see themselves involved in this process (mother-in-law, humor and satire). The stories of ironic prose are based on the same principle: each story deals with one of several points from the cultural text. These points are developed in a separate structure, but the cultural text "human life" can be seen behind each story. It is up to the reader to apply the known cultural text to the story and to find the connection that constitutes the reader's special relationship with the author and other readers.[5]

Thematic, structural, and stylistic elements in ironic prose are tightly interwoven, forming a peculiar unity that contributes to the uniqueness of the subgenre. The stories of ironic prose are short, from two to ten typewritten pages. The writer's attempt to approach global ironic themes within this restricted format dictates the skeletal character of the stories. Characters are symbols and types, rather than individuals. The narrowness of themes and devices in ironic prose often leads to close similarities between stories. This process also helps to explain the way the subgenre developed. The schematic nature of the stories forces the writers to put great emphasis on formal features. Experiments in style are common, and the stories abound in such elements as ruptured casual relationships, mixing of first- and third-person narration in the same story, tautology, and, most often, actualization of metaphor as a plot device. There are stories written exclusively in nouns, adjectives, verbs, or proper names. At the structural level, the use of convention is common: elements of science fiction, fantasy, fairy tale and myth, the absurd, and the supernatural are often intertwined. Writers experiment with the form of the stories, introducing various plot devices.

Human beings and their place in the world stand as the central theme of the subgenre. Humans are weak and vain, their desires are petty, their dreams are bound to be shattered by reality. Loneliness, lack of communication, loss of identity, and fear of breaking a dull and routine yet orderly existence characterize the hero of ironic prose. Happiness is unattainable, reality is cruel, and escape is impossible. Life is too short, and no individual achievements are significant on the scale of eternity. Life is governed by unpredictable forces, and any human efforts to change life are destined to fail. The writer is usually present in the story as an all-knowing, all-understanding ironic narrator. The writer feels pity for the story's heroes, but also an element of self-pity, for common human life makes them one. That is why a large number of the stories are narrated as monologues.

Life (in the sense of one's fate, destiny, or one's lot) is a major theme of the stories. But the approaches and ways of dealing with this theme are numerous and varied.

In stories of ironic prose one often finds the motif of the dull and routine character of human life. This could be called the "absence of life," for real life is buried in everyday reality. Uneventful and monotonous Chekhovian reality turns human life into mere existence, the only goal of which lies in physical self-preservation. In Vladimir Todorov's story "Wings" («Крылья») this theme is treated by means of comparisons. The story begins with a miracle—two newlyweds grow wings and fly happily and carelessly above the world, oblivious to worry. But the gravitational pull of reality overcomes their capacity for flight and they soon find themselves on the ground. The husband's wings disappear, and the wife's are cut off and used to make a pillow. The irony is that only when the spouses "come down to earth," suppressing their desire to dream and soar, do their lives become orderly and normal. "The Bibikovs had a good marriage, fought within reasonable limits, watched television till late, visited friends and even gained weight. . . . Their friends held them up as an example and envied them."

The invisible hat in Viktoria Tokareva's "Ruble Sixty Isn't Much" («Рубль шестьдесят—не деньги») is a catalyst that forces the protagonist to reevaluate his life. The fairy-tale convention—a hat that makes the wearer invisible—puts reality in perspective and reveals its routine and mundane nature. People do not notice the protagonist whether he wears the magic hat or not. He suddenly realizes that other people, including his wife and friends, never notice him. They never look directly at him, but rather at the place where he was supposed to be. Living is replaced by mechanical movements, which become automatic. Communication is dead, words have no meaning and become trite components of mechanical existence. "I understand that she's more or less indifferent to my presence. I don't know myself whether I live here or not. I eat, sleep, play with my daughter and talk with my wife. We say all the necessary words to each other—hello, how are you, change the channel, don't spoil her she'll take advantage of it. But in point of fact I'm not here. She's gotten used to that and stopped noticing me."

The futility of human life is expressed in the key words of the hero: "If I suddenly vanished, no one would notice." He tries to escape, but the attempt is doomed, for his hopes are directed toward the past. Yet the past is gone, and he cannot return to the woman he once loved.

An attempt to escape mundane reality is the subject of Alexander Kurlyandsky's story "Cheating" («Измена»). The husband's decision to commit adultery comes from the mere desire to break the monotony of his life. It is characteristic that he makes this decision after watching a foreign film that depicted a "rotten bourgeois society." Being inexperienced in such matters, the hero approaches adultery in the way he knows best; passion is discussed with a possible love object in the manner of a business meeting. The businesslike atmosphere is sustained in the hero's apartment, where the adultery is to take place. The climax of the story comes when the protagonist's wife suddenly arrives at home and discovers Nina Borisovna on the sofa. A clichéd humorous story situation ends unexpectedly: the wife rushes back to work, and Nina Borisovna goes home to do the laundry. Nothing can stir the stagnant life of the protagonists. The hero's meek attempt to bring excitement into his life has failed.

In the stories of ironic prose, life is seen as a vicious circle of dullness and monotony from which no one can escape. Boris Gureev's "Monday Is a Hard Day" («Понедельник—день тяжелый») portrays the circle through a formal device. A day in the protagonist's life is expressed by a series of verbs, most of which are repeated several times. This technique is used to show the vanity of life as well as its cyclical nature. The story begins with the words "I stretched. I yawned" and ends with "I yawned. I stretched." The hero's mechanical "functioning," expressed by verbs, is clarified by several nouns, which are given in parentheses as an explanation of the verbs. Whenever the verbs denoting communication are used (побеседовал, потрепался, послушал, поговорили), the nouns in the parenthesis—the topics of the conversation—are always the same, only their order is changed: TV, wife, hockey, events of the previous day. Arkady Arkanov's "Ravioli on the Floor" («Пельмени на полу») likewise employs the ring device, an identical beginning and conclusion—the first and last words describe a meaningless and dull conversation between a wife and husband. The story proper, framed by these two conversations, consists of a dream—a kind of escape for the hero. The hero reveals his frustration with the boredom of life in the imaginary scene of selling his wife in the market. This grotesque detail serves as a counterpoint to the mundane reality of life and intensifies the bitter irony at the end of the story, when the hero returns to his familiar real world.

The same constant flow of invariable events is seen in Nikolay Shakhbazov's "My Circle of Friends" («Мои знакомые»). It is obvious that the "friends" who meet regularly for conversation do not have anything to talk about. Long pauses are interrupted by meaningless remarks, which, by association rather than interest, stretch out the thread of the conversation. The characters are not named, they are presented by descriptive details: a young man, the hostess, the wife of an army officer, the hostess's husband. Often impersonal pronouns are used to emphasize their lack of identity. "Someone said that someone had died of cancer. Nobody present had known the deceased; still, they all nodded their heads and each of them mentioned somebody else that had died, and of cancer, too. The conversation turned to the dead and someone recalled that cremation had been practiced even among the ancient Hindus." The conversation jumps from Leonardo da Vinci to the price of milk at the collective farm market. The purposelessness of such communication is expressed by a tautology—the same thought is constantly reiterated by different characters. The irony of the boredom and lack of purpose in life is underscored by the stylistic irony in the last sentence where the end of one meaningless cycle becomes the beginning of another. "The conversation in the hallway concerned minutiae which there is no need to mention here, and as they were leaving, everyone felt himself particularly happy, having come to the conclusion that, whatever the others might have said to the contrary, life was in fact pretty curious." The final phrase, in Russian «что жизнь, что бы там ни говорили, довольно любопытна», alludes to two famous closing statements from Gogol's stories "The Nose" («Нос»): «Кто что ни говори, а подобные происшествия бывают на свете,—редко, но бывают» (Whatever anyone may say, such things do happen—rarely, but they do happen) and "Ivan Ivanovich and Ivan Nikiforovich" («Повесть о том, как поссорились Иван Иванович с Иваном Никифоровичем»): «Скучно на этом свете, господа!» (It is a dreary world, gentlemen).

Life is also seen as a meaningless cycle, and human striving for knowledge as a futile effort. In A. Inin and L. Osadchuk's story without a title, this idea acquires universal dimensions. The life of an ordinary scientist is viewed in the light of brilliant moments in the history of science. A conventional device—the breaking of time restrictions—lets the reader approach the hero of the story as Everyman. Testing his life against those of geniuses, the narrator shows the futility of ordinary efforts, which only lead to one end—a tombstone with the ironic inscription: "Live and learn" (Век живи, век учись). (This proverb also serves as a title for Alexander Kulich's story "Live and . . ." [«Век живи . . .»], which conveys a similar idea, although presented satirically rather than ironically.)

In the stories of ironic prose, death is usually viewed as just another in the meaningless succession of many ordinary events. In Alexander Zhitinsky's absurd parable "The Airplane Crash" («Катастрофа»), the description of a plane crash reminds the reader of the breaking of a pea pod: "An airplane was flying high up in the sky, and for some reason it cracked open. And all of the passengers spilled out of it."[6] People who only seconds later will die cannot find anything more important to talk about on their way down than the advantages and disadvantages of various Crimean resorts. When this topic is exhausted, nothing is left to talk about. "They had run out of things to talk about. They sighed and flew on in silence, approaching the earth at the speed of an express train."[7] In Arkanov's "Before You Go" («Перед уходом . . .»), grim and absurd conventional detail is developed into a humorous situation from everyday life. Suddenly and for no reason, feeling that death is approaching, the hero finds no better way to spend the last days of his life than in arguing with his wife about the funeral preparations and the length of the guest list. At the end the character is persuaded to move the "event" of his death up a day, so that it won't conflict with his wife's appointment at the dressmaker. The significance of death is reduced to nothing more than a nuisance for the dying man's acquaintances.

Life's events are insignificant. In Alexander Kabakov's "New Happiness" («Новое счастье»), the hero chooses New Year's Eve to evaluate the past year. He remembers each individual month, but they all seem to resemble one another. Work, illness, and purchases are three major occasions around which the hero's life has revolved. Sometimes a whole month is remembered for an insignificant event: "In November we paid a visit to friends" (В ноябре были в гостях). At the end of the story the reader feels pity for the character, whose life is passing in vain, devoid of interesting experience. But the character himself concludes his monotonous account of petty achievements and minor mischief-making with an unexpected statement: "I hope next year is no worse than last." "No news is good news" becomes the motto of his life, and the monotony of everyday existence is justified by the fact that life could always be worse.

Another justification of *tedium vitae* is found in Herman Drobiz's "Lamppost and the Tower" («Столб и башня»), which centers on the idea that there are no petty events and insignificant people—everyone is important in his own place. This idea derives from a popular Soviet cliché: that a minister and a cleaning lady are equally valuable and should be treated equally. The role of the cleaning lady is given to an ordinary lamppost, whereas the minister is represented by the Ostankino Tower—the famous Moscow TV tower. The correspondence between the two is a parody of letters to the editor, a tradition started in Russian literature by Fonvizin and Novikov in their humorous journals in the late eighteenth century. In this story, however, not only are the letters of the simple lamppost parodied, but also the answers of the famous tower. In its letters, the young lamppost expresses despair at the uneventful and boring life at the Razuvaevka station on the eastern railroad where it "works." It is depressed by its inability to leave, to explore new places: "From me to the station it's only twenty yards, but I will never see what's there, behind it, on the other side."[8] The tragedy of the lamppost's life parallels that of the electrician Semyonov. The life of the man is revealed in occasional references made by the lamppost in its letters. Semyonov is not subjected to the same torments as the lamppost. Drinking and going out with women seem to take all of his time. He finally marries and soon thereafter visits the lamppost at night and repeatedly strikes his head against it in despair. The electrician gets a divorce, and the lamppost becomes old and is replaced by a new, concrete one. The realization that comes to the lamppost at the end of its short life is ironic; the conclusion it makes is comforting—the thoughts of the vanity and boredom of life are replaced by a conviction that dreams are vain. "Now I'm older and I understand that nothing good can come of it if all lampposts suddenly decided to become Ostankino Towers. Who needs that many towers? But lampposts are needed, and lots of them.[9] It has taken me years to reach this realization, and now I am truly happy."[10] The story ends with a telegram—the last reply of the famous tower. It is not addressed to the lamppost, for it has already been used as firewood by the electrician Semyonov. The telegram is a parody of a formal obituary, and its clichés serve as an ironic commentary on the lamppost's optimistic conclusions: "station razuvaevka eastern railroad / in connection beginning heating season express deep grief regard to deceased my old friend modest worker wooden lamppost wish workers of station success in work stop / ostankino tower."[11]

The ephemeral nature of human life is the central theme of a number of stories. People make mistakes, they waste their days and weeks on insignificant and futile pursuits, and when they realize that they have not lived properly, it is too late for them to correct their mistakes. The character of A. and B. Nastroev's[12] "Turkish Sabers" («Турецкие сабли») spends all his time away from home. He has cheated on his wife, but the explanation that he concocted could serve as an ironic commentary: "He studied some cosmic object, whose life span was ridiculously short—only some eight million years."[13] At the end of the story the hero is left alone. He realizes that a human life span is much shorter than that of even the most short-lived star, and that happiness is not equated with high position or material wealth. Turkish sabers stand as a metaphor for happiness. The hero seeks them at the beginning and does not have them at the end. A character in Alla Bossart's "Rose-Colored Music" («Розовая музыка») is also an astronomer. The story is a condensed account of the heroes' lives: it starts with them in high school. The boy and the girl meet every day in the courtyard where they take out the trash. They pass their lives trying to prove to each other that they have independence and outstanding abilities. The boy becomes a renowned scientist, and the girl writes a book on the English family novel. At the end of their lives they are still alone and still talk to each other only in a courtyard where they come to take out the trash. The people who were meant to be together spend their lives proving something to each other, and when they finally decide to live together, they have nothing to talk about. Their lives resemble those of the heroes of the English family novel discussed in the woman's book: "And they lived, really, kind of dully" (А жили они, правда, скучновато). In Mikhail Mishin's "What Didn't Happen to Nenashev" («Что не случилось с Ненашевым») the same theme is expressed through the formal device of negation (even the name of the character starts with the negative particle ne). Without the negative particles the story reads as an ironic realization of the vanity and shortness of life. The character understands that despite an interesting job and a happy family something is missing from his life. Repeated use of the negation ne shifts the center of gravity in the story from the character to the author. Alexander Kanevsky, in "Save Your Years" («Храните свои годы»), also employs a conventional device: the character actually saves his years by taking them to the bank. He economizes minutes and seconds at the expense of visiting his parents, spending time with friends, and building a family with the woman he loves. His aim is to establish himself, to save enough time so that he will feel secure later in life. But when the goal is achieved and the time comes to spend the savings, the character cannot break his habit. He becomes a victim of his own obsession.

The theme of the ephemerality of life is often combined with the theme of wasting life on accumulating material wealth. The attainment of money and luxuries has always been a target for satirical writers. When the theme is presented ironically, the characters are not ridiculed but pitied; their obsession is seen as their cross, rather than as a social vice. They are victims who pay a high price for their wealth. In Alexander Khort's "Something for a Rainy Day" («Заначка»), the character's life passes in the accumulation of money and no time is left to spend it. The character's secret passion turns out also to be the secret passion of his whole household: his wife hides money in a gramophone, his grandson piles up coins under an aquarium, and even the cat, catching a goldfish from the water, hides it away for a rainy day. In Zhitinsky's "Tree" («Дерево»), the theme is presented as a parable. The tree of life is blooming with money and man devotes his life to picking the harvest: "Judging by the amount of money, he probably had enough work there for a lifetime."[14]

Mikhail Kazovsky, in "A Miracle on My Nose" («Чудо на переносице»), uses a conventional device; the character's view of life is changed by a fancy pair of blue sunglasses. They make his life easier, for everything around him seems pleasant and important. The hero marries a woman he does not love and buys furniture that he does not like and a car that he does not need. He surrounds himself with objects of material value and loses his moral values. For a moment, when the glasses break, he realizes the futility of his life. "I became lonely and sad. I suddenly had a desire to buy a train ticket and go somewhere." But his wife buys him a new pair of glasses and the anguish is soon forgotten. The character of Vladimir Klimovich's "In the Nick of Time" («Кстати») never has any doubts. When the office manager who was gravely ill suddenly recuperates, the question arises of what to do with the expensive funeral wreath, the plot in a nice cemetery, the prepared eulogy, the marble tombstone, and the paid musicians; the protagonist seizes the opportunity—and dies. A failed hope to achieve a respectable and profitable position in life naturally grows into a desire to get at least a nice spot after death. "And here I lie beneath all my wreaths in the cemetery for dignitaries. My neighbour to the left is a famous actor, and there is a general to my left. What bliss!"

The hero of Mark Zakharov's "One Life to Live . . . or a Tavern Story" («Жизнь прожить . . . или шашлычная история») does not have any desires or needs except for the ordinary. His life, or rather existence, is shown as a continual feast in a cheap tavern. The character enters upon it as a young man, and while there, between exotic Georgian dishes, he meets his future wife, marries, and watches his children grow and leave. He, however, never leaves the table. While meeting his future wife, the hero says: "Those were wonderful moments" (Это были чудесные мгновения).[15] His words are ironic, for it is difficult to determine whether they refer to the woman or just to another dish. The end of life is also described in restaurant terms: " 'Time to settle up. . . . Bring me the check, please,' I asked and sat back in my chair once and for all."

Sometimes the character's obsession with material goods and money passes, as in Andrey Kuchaev's "Your Money or Your Life" («Кошелек или жизнь»). The green purse that the heroine finds in the street obliges her to acquire other green objects: a coat, a bag, boots, a car, a country house (дача). The character grows greenery and sells it at the market. She collects green paper money in the bank and sees the world through green sunglasses. Her obsession stops as suddenly as it starts. The author, in the manner of a *deus ex machina*, arranges a happy ending. This turns the story into a kind of a game—another conventional device that bears an ironic connotation. The narrator in Semyon Altov's micromonologue "Car on a Stick" («‹Жигули› на палочке») tries to find an answer to the problem of a constant lack of money. In childhood it is a nickel for an ice cream, later three thousand rubles for a car. The narrator proposes to change the measure of values: let the person who tries to get the car spend all his money on ice cream. Then he could really feel rich. The monologue is just a joke with a sad ironic smile, but its solution to the problem is not much more incredible than a seemingly plausible ending.

Sometimes the characters try to change their lives but fail. This can be illustrated by two stories; Arkady Inin's "And the Years Fly . . ." («А годы летят . . .») and Vladlen Bakhnov's "Seasons" («Времена года»). In both the authors accelerate time; the entire life story of their characters fits on two typewritten pages. The frame that Inin uses in his story is a recurring New Year's greeting. With each "Happy New Year" the progressively aging character makes a new resolution. While each crucial year should bring new meaning and new achievements into the life of the hero, at the end of the story his life has passed and nothing has been done. Bakhnov's story takes place in a bar, where young heroes who are full of good intentions try to plan their lives more fruitfully. The story reads as though it takes place in the course of an evening party, but its span is twenty-five years. Violet December twilight yields to February snowstorms, which in turn give way to the scorching August sun, autumn slush, October winds, hot July breezes, and snow again. The heroes grow bald, the drinks become stronger, and the plans for the future are still the same.

A major problem facing the heroes of ironic prose is that they occupy the wrong place in life. The hero of Tatyana Slutskaya's "Mediocrity" («Бездарь») fails in his duties as an accountant and is fired. At the same time he makes an important discovery, solves a chess problem at the request of a desperate grand master, and analyzes a play, the review of which in the next day's newspaper is written exactly as he had thought of it. But the character is known as a mediocre person (бездарь), for he has the wrong job and occupies the wrong place in life. In other stories, characters are also doing the wrong job, spending time in the company of the wrong friends, or living with the wrong wives. It is as if someone had shuffled a deck of cards and the people had become mixed. Precisely this analogy comes to mind when one reads D. Ivanov and V. Trifonov's "Sugar, Sugar" («Сахар, сахар! . . .»). Sitting across the table from his wife, the character sees her reflection in the kitchen table and compares her to a queen of diamonds. Himself he fancies as a jack of clubs. The hero is convinced that both of them are in the wrong place. Remembering what happened six years before when he met his wife, he suddenly realizes that he went on a blind date in place of his friend. He also remembers that the date was supposed to be a brunette, yet his wife is blond. The hero wonders whether one can possibly be in the right place in life. "I wonder, could anything worthwhile have happened if two other people had met? I already know the answer, never in a lifetime." In E. Abramov's "Sun Was Shining" («Сияло солнце»), this idea is expressed in circular form. The gardener envies the driver, who envies the scientist, who envies the writer, who envies the gardener. The circle closes, confirming the thought of the impossibility of finding one's proper place in life.

Attempts to change life are uncommon in ironic prose. The monotony of life also means the predictability of events and a comfortable assurance in the future, which is nothing but a repetition of the past. Life has its own norms and rules, which are never broken. It is governed by stereotypes, which are based on the customs, norms, and traditions of society. They are the routine, the ordinary, and the assurance of their unshakeable existence. Anything unusual is either overlooked as unimportant or is changed to meet the norm. Pyotr Semyonovich Blinov from A. Kurlyandsky and A. Khait's "Sixth Sense" («Шестое чувство») suddenly acquires a sense of "abscyllochordia"—an elusive feeling for things around him that he cannot explain. The appearance of the new sense leads to conflicts with his wife and friends. People get angry with him; as long as they do not understand what he means, they conclude that this sense does not exist. The hero is alone in the world until he meets another man with the sense of abscyllochordia. It turns out, though, that the man has also another feeling, for "lipotapia," which is unknown to Pyotr Semyonovich. At the end the hero turns away from the man, rejecting the existence of the unknown feeling.

Often, when something extraordinary happens, people do not notice it. Ivan Ivanovich, in Vladimir Gonik's "Ikarus" («Икар»), finds one morning that he can fly, yet nobody notices. He comes to work through the window, and the only reaction he gets from his colleagues is: "Close the window, it's drafty!" People do not see him fly because it cannot happen. A doctor prescribes medicine for his nerves, his wife treats him as if nothing has happened, and the audience in the circus perceives it as a trick. Ivan Ivanovich's boss tries to reason with the hero. "Why do you need it, my dear? Just think! Today you are flying along the hall and tomorrow you will flee from your family, and then find yourself on the dock. I beg you . . . so that I won't have to take measures." The boss treats the extraordinary event as misconduct on the part of the character. He is not surprised, because he does not think of the fact itself. The word "fly" (летите) refers to Ivan Ivanovich's ability to fly, whereas the second "flee" (улетите—the word has the same root in Russian) is already used in the metaphorical meaning. Such stylistic transition from the supernatural into the familiar world of verbal stereotypes is the way for the boss to escape facing the extraordinary. A similar device is employed by Gonik in "A Malady" («Хворь»), where the supernatural and stereotypes are mixed on a structural level. A doctor who is afraid of infection sterilizes his clothes and washes his hands with alcohol. It is a standard procedure, but the illness of his patient is not usual: the man does not have a face. The character in Boris Lobkov's "Wrong Creek" («Неправильный ручей») sees a lamp take off and fly into the sky. Another man who witnesses this unusual event concludes: "It should not fly, . . . because it cannot fly." The man refuses to believe his eyes, for he is afraid to shake the familiar. In Zhitinsky's "Pedestrian" («Пешеход») a man walks along streetcar wires. He is finally taken off by firemen because he interferes with public transportation. The character in Otto Novozhilov's "Tra-la-la-isms" («Тралялямс») tries to get noticed. He walks along the street with a glass lampshade on his head. The character is stopped by a policeman for crossing the street outside the pedestrian crossing.

The rules and stereotypes apply to both concrete objects and abstract concepts. In Boris Rakhmanin's "Non-Standard Bulbs" («Нестандартные лампочки»), the director of a factory of electrical appliances conducts a meeting concerning defective goods. Defects of the bulbs are strange: one of them has a live fly inside it; another transmits music. One bulb is unbreakable, and one shines without any source of electricity. But everything is perceived as a defect that has to be eliminated to achieve the standard. In Herbert Kemoklidze's "Truth" («Истина»), the truth itself is perfected so that it will acquire a stereotypical form. Blue and rose colors, as well as sugar, are added; it is sprinkled with cologne, adorned with bells, and beaten to make it harder. Only in this "standardized" form is the banal truth (избитая истина) accepted by the committee.

Along with stereotypes of general human nature in ironic prose, a number of stereotypes are specific to Soviet society of the 1970s. In Rafael Sokolovsky's "Echo" («Эхо»), the hero loses his echo. His colleagues are surprised, not by the fact itself, but that his echo could leave such a good citizen and worker. The hero files the necessary papers in the appropriate office and the echo is forced to return to him. In Inin and Osadchuk's "Good Whistling!" («Счастливо свистеть!»), a man running through the country with a whistle in his mouth is a central absurd proposition. Yet the circumstances are familiar— meetings of workers to greet the enthusiast, interviews, and media clichés in the coverage of the event. In Lev Lainer's "Responsibility" («Ответственность»), the character responds seriously to a ridiculous street joke just because it is put in recognizable stereotyped form. A stranger tells him: "You are appointed the one responsible for spring," and the hero starts thinking of spring as a job he has to do. The character in Anatoly Chudinov's "Puddle" («Лужа») gets stuck carrying people from one side of a puddle to the other because nobody believes that this is not his official job. To escape he uses the stereotypical behavior of a salesman and rudely "closes for lunch." Evgeny Arkadevich in Grigory Pruslin's "Purple-Colored Camel" («Фиолетовый верблюд») sees a violet camel in his dream. He is as much perplexed by the fact that the camel speaks and smokes as by the animal's strange color. "More than anything in the world, Evgeny Arkadevich valued clarity, always and in all things. He felt at ease on the job and at home only when everything could be readily understood." Evgeny Arkadevich begs the camel to tell him the reason for the inexplicable phenomenon, to which the camel replies: "That's the way it has to be. Do you read me? The way it has to be!" (Так на-до. Ясно? На-а-до!). This meaningless phrase calms the hero down. It is a cliché often used in Soviet society when logical explanations and reasoning are inapplicable. Yet for Evgeny Arkadevich "the world once again became clear and rational."

The individual's place in life, his relationship to the world around him and to other people, is a major theme of ironic prose. The subject is approached from different angles in a quest for answers to such universal questions as: Who are we? Where are we going? What is the purpose of our existence?

In Zhitinsky's parable "The Microbe" («Микроб»), a simple question asked by a cholera microbe from the other side of the microscope barrel confronts a man with an unsolvable problem. "Which one are you?" (Ты какой?), asks the microbe, and when no satisfactory answer is given, concludes: "There, you see? . . . And here you come nosing into my life with your microscope. Figure yourself out first."[16] An unexpected view of humanity is given in Bakhnov's story "The Sleep Walker" («Сомнамбул»). It is set on another planet where a science fiction writer creates a story about an imaginary planet Earth. Using the device of "making strange" (остранение), the author forces us to look at ourselves from a distance. An editor on a distant planet makes the writer change his story and the physical appearance of "peoples" (человеки) because in his view they are too weak and unadaptable to survive in the world. Their natural means of communication is as imperfect as their bodies.[17] The editor convinces the writer that human civilization cannot exist and is too bold even for a fantasy, since people cannot possibly understand each other. The irony of the author is combined with a double dramatic irony; the reader of the story is human, yet the editor's argument for the improbability of communication on Earth is understood as the author's ironic comment on lack of communication among human beings. As weak and imperfect as men and women are, they are needed in the universe. They serve some unknown purpose. In Zhitinsky's "Loafer" («Лентяй»), this idea is expressed in the form of a parable: a man is always seen in the hall, where he never does anything—he just smokes cigarettes, leaning against the wall. The man is fired for doing nothing, and the next day the wall falls.

An ironic view of humanity includes the realization of the duality of human nature. Good and evil are as inseparable in a human being as they are in life. In Zhitinsky's "Glasses" («Очки»), strange glasses show both natures, good and evil. The same smile is seen as a friendly grin and as a treacherous sneer. A friendly slap on the shoulder is combined with a blow, and laughter is seen as snickering. A similar device is used in Vagrich Bakhchanyan's "Man" («Человек»). This microstory consists of one paragraph written entirely in adjectives modifying the opening words: "Man was . . . ." The adjectives used in the story are divided between those with negative and positive meanings:

Человек был молодой, здоровый, сильный, крепкий, жизнерадост-
ный, бодрый, энергичный, деятельный, увлекающийся, трудолю-
бивый, дельный, образованный, умный, смышленный, прекрасный,
хороший, добрый, честный, искренний, открытый, скромный, оду-
хотворенный, солидный, музыкальный, экономный, бескорыстный,
самоотверженный, неутомимый, общительный, гостеприимный, га-
лантный, щедрый, свободомыслящий, благовоспитанный, порядоч-
ный, наивный, неряшливый, незначительный, ограниченный, глу-
поватый, неотесанный, льстивый, ничтожный, уродливый, злой,
подлый, трусливый, жестокий, коварный, хитрый, мстительный,
старый.

(Man was young, healthy, strong, sturdy, life-affirming, robust, energetic, active, committed, industrious, well qualified, educated, intelligent, bright, wonderful, nice, kind, honest, sincere, open, modest,
inspired, established, musical, frugal, unselfish, selfless, untiring, sociable, hospitable, gallant, generous, open-minded, well bred, decent,
naive, unkempt, insignificant, limited, silly, unrefined, ingratiating,
petty, ugly, mean, base, cowardly, cruel, deceptive, cunning, vengeful,
old.)

As seen by the authors of ironic prose, one of people's problems is
their dependence on material things. It is not the craving for wealth,
already mentioned, but rather the inability to soar above reality that ties
people to earth. In a complex story by Kuchaev, "What Happened to
Sergeev" («Случай с инженером Сергеевым»), this idea is expressed
through a surrealistic scene in a washroom. The reflection of the setting
sun on the tile floor of the room distorts the engineer's perception of
reality. For a second he finds himself suspended between life and
death, earth and heaven. This symbolic picture is reinforced by the
things that start to fall out of the engineer's pockets: first a passport,
notebook, pen, comb, cigarettes; then a diploma, university class notes,
grade school watercolors; and finally a pacifier. These are all objects
that tie him to the world. Having lost them, the engineer becomes "as
light as the poplar fluff" (легким, как тополиный пух).[18]

In ironic prose, dependence on material things is often exaggerated.
In a grotesque story by Inin and Osadchuk, "The Fall of G. Dugin"
(«Падение Г. Дугина»), the character tries to celebrate the New Year in
the "Italian way." He knows that in Italy on New Year's Eve people

throw old and unnecessary things out into the street. Dugin's house is filled with furniture and accessories, but he cannot find a thing that he could dispose of. Finally the hero finds something—he throws himself out the window. Yet his wife pulls him out of a snowdrift and puts him back into his armchair under a print called "Spring," between the "Ruby" TV set and "Symphony" stereo. The story ends with the ironic remark: "Now all the objects in the house were again in their proper place." In Felix Kamov's "Souvenir" («Сувенир»), the grotesque is taken to the extreme. The narrator of the story tries to convince the character that the character is a souvenir, a thing to be used by others in decorating their rooms. An absurd dialogue ends in a no less absurd consequence. The character is finally convinced and finds his place on the wall of the narrator's apartment. The dubiousness of man's value as a species is expressed in the story by means of a parody of the famous line from Act 4 of Gorky's play *The Lower Depths* (*На дне*): "Man! . . . It sounds . . . proud!" The word "man" is replaced by "souvenir," and "proud" is replaced by "nice."

In Tokareva's "Japanese Umbrella" («Японский зонтик»), the narration, which starts as realistic, suddenly turns absurd. People and objects change places. "Things stretched out into a long line and selected people for themselves. And people sat in carton boxes, the kind used for packing TV sets. Their heads stick out and they breathe the fresh air." The device demonstrated here can be called depersonification, people merging with nonorganic nature. The same idea of the relative value of man or woman can also be expressed by a contrasting device—personification, in which human qualities and characteristics are attributed to material objects, natural phenomena, and animals. Another world is being created—sometimes hostile to the human world, sometimes indifferent, but always distinctly different from it. In Nina Katerli's "Autumn" («Осень»), the world surrounding humans lives its own life, and no more attention is paid or importance assigned to people than to cars, which look the same on the gray and rainy day: "identical people in identical drenched overcoats go scurrying about in the rain."[19] In Katerli's "Victory" («Победа») the two worlds are in a state of war. The idea of war is emphasized by an allusion to a famous painting by Vereshchagin—"The Apotheosis of War." A cabbage display in a store window reminds a woman of the pyramid of skulls in the painting. Her strategy is to "give in," to play along with the hostile objects until they give up. She does not try to cook a meal because she is sure that the water will boil over and extinguish the fire. She does not buy mandarin oranges, which are to be had on the street without standing in line, because the opportunity is too good to be true. She pricks her finger and falls down in the street on purpose—so that objects cannot take credit for the accidents. The war ends in the woman's victory; perplexed by her unconventional tactics, the objects give up. In Drobiz's "It's Raining" («Дождь идет»), the world of nature and the world of humanity are contrasted. A man's shallow and monotonous life is tested against the vital world outside his apartment. The natural world is compared to poetry, social reality to prose. The man's attitude toward the outer world is nostalgic and pitiful. The world of nature is alive and is compared to the world of art in Katerli's "Thunderstorm" («Гроза»). A thunderstorm is music; it brings to life the paved courtyards, buildings, monuments, palaces, trees, and a stone statue of a musician, who plays in harmony with the music of nature. Only humanity is not touched by this feast of life; its life is governed by other laws. "The wind on tiptoes came out of the hallway, raised its collar and started up the street. This time it did not push anyone, only in the garden it suddenly lost its control: as hard as it could it pulled a young full-cheeked linden by the ear so that the raindrops rushed in all directions, and wetted a new sport-coat of a gloomy man with a big brown briefcase."[20] Animals constitute a part of the natural world and are contrasted with people. In Andrey Bitov's "Someone Else's Dog" («Чужая собака»), the condescending and scornful silence of a fat boxer is compared with the banal remarks of pedestrians. Rakhmanin, in "The City's Wild Animals" («Городское зверье»), draws a picture of a different world, where humans are not permitted. In his "poems in prose," city animals acquire almost diabolic features. They watch people, they understand everything, but they never disclose their intelligence to the inferior humans.

In Ivanov and Trifonov's "My Second Self" («Второе ‹я›»), the theme of the predominance of the material in the lives of people merges with another key theme found in ironic prose, the loss of identity. Fashions in art objects, books, topics of conversation, women's hair color, and music homogenize people so much that it is impossible to tell one apartment from another, one couple from their neighbors, one man or woman from hundreds of their twins. The character of the story mistakes his neighbor's door for his own, and it is not until several hours later that he realizes the mistake. The convention used in the story is a device that intensifies the author's idea. When a woman realizes that she had mistaken a strange man for her husband, she begins to cry. "She broke into tears, just the way my wife would. Just the way hundreds of blondes would, faced with any of hundreds of brunets, if they were in our place." The hero of Arkady Khait's "When I Look in the Mirror" («Когда я смотрюсь в зеркало») has a face that is "reminiscent of all the faces in the world" (напоминает все лица сразу). He is constantly mistaken for someone else and does not have a life of his own; everything that happens to the character is meant for his doubles.[21] A woman mistakes him for her lover and brings him home; the woman's husband sees in him a colleague who borrowed money; the hero gets hit without knowing why and ends up taking home a strange baby. Loss of identity to a large extent is a social problem; the individual is "averaged." In Mark Rozovsky's "Slick Kid" («Глянцевый мальчик»), the character meets a man who is "working" as a picture on a page of an illustrated magazine. He is a "new hero," materialistic and rational, who plans the time to fall in love and treats romantic sentiments as a commodity. His speech is filled with official statistics, and he estimates his achievements in percentages.

In the world of the averaged faceless people, individuality is a sin and even a slight deviation from a physical or moral norm is a drawback. In Kuchaev's "Nothing Special" («Ничего особенного»), an engineer named Malkin cannot find a hat that will fit. His wife complains to the salesman: "You see, . . . my husband's not quite like other people. He's different. It's really a shame." The problem, though, is soon resolved. The salesman squeezes Malkin's head and presses it into the "normal" shape. The hat fits and the engineer is no longer different from everyone else. In Grigory Gorin's "Kurentsov Unclad" («Обнаженный Куренцов»), the character's sudden realization of his loss of identity drives him insane. The semiliterate Kurentsov accidentally finds himself at an art exhibition. There he sees himself in one of the paintings and tries to persuade the exhibition authorities to take the picture down. They refuse, and the character breaks into the building at night and steals the "caricature." On the way out he sees that other paintings also depict members of his family. "No longer surprised, no longer shaking, he wandered through the darkish halls of the gallery and with a kind of dull indifference inspected the paintings. Kurentsovs were looking down at him from all sides. . . . Naked, or dressed in the most outlandish costumes, with red, blue or green faces, the Kurentsovs watched Vasily Mikhailovich from all sides."

Whereas in Gorin's story loss of identity makes the character ill, in Gonik's "Malady" loss of identity is a disease. The character literally loses his face—a realization of a metaphor that intensifies the idea of the story. The character of Ruslan Kireev's "To Be Oneself" («Быть самим собой») tries to preserve his identity, but whatever he does is just a repetition of someone else's actions. Tired of being unoriginal, the character flies from his chair only to discover that he acts exactly like a fly. In fact, he himself becomes a fly (a turn of plot reminiscent of Kafka's "Metamorphosis").

The theme of loss of identity is connected with the theme of lack of communication. In a society where life is monotonous and people lack individuality, communication is often impossible. Questions are predictable and so are the answers. In Ivanov and Trifonov's "Sugar, Sugar," the white kitchen table that separates the husband and the wife becomes an insurmountable obstacle in their efforts to communicate. Alienation between people grows into a boring habit. Conversation is used not as a means of communication and understanding, but as a way to kill time, as in Shakhbazov's "My Circle of Friends." People do not know anything about one another, and they do not want to know. "Nobody knows anything about anyone" (Никто ни про кого ничего не знает),[22] says the narrator of Katerli's "Autumn." A character from Zhitinsky's "Earring" («Серьга») wears an earring that allows him to switch off his hearing whenever anything unpleasant or bothersome comes up. In B. Briker and A. Vishevsky's story "Made in Heaven" («Небесная история») the heroes, who sit next to each other on the plane, strike up a conversation, fall in love, and make a commitment to each other, all in their thoughts, yet when the flight ends they go their separate ways without ever actually saying a word to each other. The hero of Tokareva's "One, Two, Three . . ." («Раз, два, три . . .») tries to find someone with whom he can share his thoughts, but he fails. "The earth is covered with telephone cables, like nerves. You can dial any combination of digits and call any apartment you want. That is, you can call, but you can't get through to anybody. Is there a number you can call to actually reach another human being?"

The individual is alone in the world. Loneliness is a frequent feeling among the heroes of ironic prose. It drives a provincial lamppost to write letters to the famous Ostankino Tower in Drobiz's "Lamppost and the Tower"; it makes another character in the story—the electrician Semyonov—strike his head against the lamppost in a fit of despair. The protagonists of the Nastroevs' "Turkish Sabers" are alone and unhappy. "After all it is quite dull—to be alone. Even though everything is going well. Even in a three-room apartment. And even though he is sitting across the room from a female TV announcer. And even though it's a color TV."[23] For the character of Tokareva's "Ruble Sixty Isn't Much," this feeling becomes especially acute when he buys a hat that makes him invisible. The hero suddenly realizes that with the hat or without it, people do not notice him. By the end of the day he feels extremely tired and discovers why: "I suddenly felt how exhausted I'd gotten in the course of the day, most likely from loneliness." In Viktor Gastello's "Stulchikov's Illness" («Болезнь Стульчикова»), a realization of the character's loneliness comes at the crucial moment in his life. Convinced that he is dying, Stulchikov turns to his friends and colleagues for compassion, but nobody listens to him. People are wrapped up in their own affairs, and when the hero finds out that the hospital has made a mistake and there is nothing wrong with him, he again becomes as indifferent to the needs of others as they were to his. On each birthday cashier Kozin, from Inin's "Cake, Delivered Home" («Торт с доставкой на дом»), sends himself a bottle of champagne and a cake with the inscription: "Happy birthday, Boris Borisovich!" He usually ends up celebrating with the delivery man, who happens to be as lonely as Kozin. Neither money nor a successful career can substitute for the need for attention and interest from other people. The feared boss in Slutskaya's "I Also Want to Go to Shumerov's . . ." («Я тоже хочу к Шумерову . . .»), envies his worst worker because the worker gets telephone calls from friends all day, whereas the director had only two calls: the first was the wrong number, the second from his son asking for money.

The theme of loneliness is often presented through conventional or fantastic elements. The hero of Katerli's "Firfarov the Man and the Tractor" («Человек Фирфаров и трактор») is an old abandoned tractor, which occupies the empty garage of Firfarov's old car. The tractor's longing for love and affection is both funny and touching; and even though Firfarov grows used to having a tractor around, he is ashamed of the old machine and drives it away. The hero of Bakhnov's "Loneliness" («Одиночество») is an old man who lives in the future. The old man looks for company, but finds a toll robot that talks to him about the "old days" and stops in the middle of a word when its meter runs out. He tries a bar, but the special drinks that bring an illusion of communication do not satisfy him. Finally, he is approached by another old man, as lonely as himself, but the hero flees for he is afraid that this is just another illusion that will end in another disappointment.

People try to get the attention of others, they want to be noticed at any cost, even if it means putting a glass lampshade on their head, hanging chains on their trousers, or inventing some elusive "tra-la-la-isms," as does the character in Novozhilov's story. Characters in Rakhmanin's "Invention" («Изобретение») try to attract people's attention by flying. But, ironically, together with the flying pills they took vanishing pills, and nobody notices them. In Arkanov's "With the Chin on One Side" («Подбородок набекрень»), the hero's desire to stand out and be noticed drives him from one grotesque situation to the next. He walks barefoot in winter, and everyone starts walking barefoot, even the cars drive without tires. He runs and everybody runs, he flies up and sits on the roof and finds hundreds of people sitting there. The hero concludes: "Nothing came of it after all. I did not achieve anything. Nobody noticed me. . . . So I started to shout out of despair. And everyone started to shout, as if 'Spartacus' [a soccer team] had lost a game."[24]

Almost as pervasive in ironic prose as the desire to be different is its counterpart, the desire to conform. People do not accept deviations from the norm, but try to align everything with known patterns and standards. A character from Nikolay Bulgakov's "No Use Denying" («Что греха таить») tries to talk a neighbor into surgery because his ears are uneven. The hero of Sokolovsky's "Echo" insists that the echo that abandoned him be returned, so that he will be the same as everyone else. In Lobkov's "Wrong Creek," someone alters the course of a spring so it will not flow under a stone, thus acting against the laws of physics and common sense. The common sense here is represented by a popular proverb: "Water does not flow under a lying stone" (Под лежачий камень вода не течет). (The proverb is usually used in the metaphorical meaning, so this is another case of realization of a metaphor.) The light bulbs in Rakhmanin's "Non-Standard Bulbs" are labeled defective because they do not correspond to the standard, and nobody notices that each defect constitutes an invention of its own. Even truth itself has to be recognizable, has to be "standard," and should not be a surprise or be innovative (Kemoklidze's "Truth").

The other way of fighting the unconventional in life is not to notice it, not to believe that it exists. Thus nobody believes that Blinov, from Kurlyandsky and Khait's "Sixth Sense," has the feeling of abscyllochordia, and Blinov, in his turn, does not believe the stranger who claims he can feel lipotapia. Nobody notices that Ivan Ivanovich from Gonik's "Ikarus" flies.

People are afraid to confront the unknown, they are comfortable in their boring and predictable world. A character from Zhitinsky's

"Temptation" («Искушение») turns down the offer to fly with a man outside his window. Fear of the unknown is combined here with unwillingness to break society's conventions, in this case, rules of decorum. "It was indeed too cold to go flying in my shirtsleeves, and it seemed downright indecent to go flying in a coat. Who ever goes flying in a coat?"[25] In Arkanov's "Old Man in the Fur Hat" («Старик в меховой шапке»), the character meets a strange old man at a local railway station cafeteria. It becomes clear from the conversation that the immortal old man met with Pushkin and gave the poet the idea for one of his fairy tales. He also motivated scientists to invent penicillin and suggested the theory of relativity to Einstein. And when the old man is about to share his new thought about some "horrible regularity" (ужасная закономерность), the terror-stricken character flees. Terror is the usual reaction to the unnatural and unexplainable. Ivan Ivanovich Marchenko, from Vitaly Korotich's "Something about Astronomy" («Кое-что об астрономии»), worries because he hears on TV that whether life exists on other planets is unknown. Uncertainty even in a remote matter that should not concern the character causes him to become ill. A comforting thought comes in the hero's dream: "The one who should know apparently already did, and would reveal it to him, Marchenko, at the appropriate time." (A similar situation is found in Pruslin's "Purple-Colored Camel.") Ivan Petrovich Sidorov from Lev Novozhenov's "One Fifty Four" («Шестьдесят четыре») shields his life from anything unexpected. He does not speak to people on the street, refuses to recognize the wallet that he lost, and turns down a business trip to France. His main concern is that his life continue exactly as it has been. The hero comes home and finds out that his wife weighs one hundred fifty-four pounds—the same as before. "'Thank God,' Sidorov sighed in relief." The bureaucrat Modest Ionovich Rykalin from S. Viktorov's "Trochee" («Хорей») suddenly begins to speak in verse. His inability to speak in the usual clichés drives him to a hospital bed and eventually brings about his death. Relief comes immediately before Rykalin's end, when, to the satisfaction of all the friends gathered at his deathbed, he utters a meaningless bureaucratic cliché. "The sick man was breathing with difficulty, all the time licking his dry lips, then leaning on his elbow and making a stately gesture with the other hand, he said in a low but firm voice: 'Comrades, I draw your attention to the fact that according to the results of the past financial quarter . . .'—and stopped. Relaxed, he leaned back on the pillow and died. Maria Ignatevna froze in a stupor of grief, and old Tomilina made a sign of the cross: 'Thank God, at least he died like a human being.'"

Time is another major theme in the works of ironic prose. Two main approaches to the theme can be identified: sociological and metaphysical. The sociological approach can be viewed as a part of the broader theme of life. In this approach time presents a dilemma. Human life is too short, its rhythm too intense. There is no time for individual achievement. In V. Sinakevich and V. Skvirsky's "Idea" («Идея»), a man needs "one week, just one" to formulate his idea, an important discovery that will make his life worth living. Yet constant disruptions prevent the hero from fulfilling his goal. The trifles of life fill all his time, and the daily routine buries the idea together with its inventor. At the end of the story the hero, now an old man, is still optimistic about the future, yet the structure of the story undercuts his optimism. The last words are charged with irony: "I am not dead yet, and I still have a head on my shoulders. Back in school I was considered talented, and in college they said I showed great promise. I'll get it all unravelled, personally I have no doubts about it. I'm looking confidently into the future, as the saying goes."[26] In Elena Baranovskaya's "If I Get Up at Seven A.M. . . . ." («Если я встану в семь утра . . .»), running out of time is present as a regular feature of an ordinary day. Here it is concrete and is connected with the reality of Soviet life.

In Altov's "There Is No Time!" («Некогда!») running out of time assumes universal qualities. From a fact of life it becomes life's substitute. The micromonologue starts with an enumeration of things and people. The character rushes by, missing these things and people in a hurry to get somewhere. The author then switches from the specific to generalized notions. If at the beginning the hero hurriedly passes familiar faces in the crowd, scents in the marketplace, museums, and parks, at the end he is rushing past such notions as happiness, family and children, and compassion. Humanity's striving is shown as an effort that does not bear any result and does not lead to any goal. Striving for the sake of striving has become a human obsession, a substitute for life, an escape from its problems. The meaninglessness and irony of human striving are revealed through the stylistic ambiguities in the last words of the monologue, "on Mondays, on Thursdays, on puddles, on thin ice, running across the street, through red lights, forward!"

When writers approach time as a metaphysical category, they try to understand its meaning, as well as its significance in human life. The stories of ironic prose often relate to human life. In Novozhenov's "Call" («Звонок»), the hero's trip to another room to answer a telephone turns into a lifelong ascent of the hierarchical ladder. The unnatural acceleration of time in the story is an artistic device through which the futility of human life and ambitions is revealed. Years that pass in a succession of eventless days and weeks can easily be condensed to seconds and minutes. In Evgeny Shatko's "Date" («Свидание»), waiting for a girlfriend turns into a situation from the theater of the absurd. Years pass, but the hero does not leave the square where they agreed to meet. The conventional time element changes the general view of the story and the heroine. From a young woman, "delicate and slim, as if from a painting by Giotto," she turns into a dream, a symbol. And now everyone in the square is waiting for her. "Gladioli withered, it began raining, it started snowing. I am not leaving the square, I made friends with the policeman, with the wise shoe-shiner, with the ever high-spirited ice cream vendors. And now all of us are waiting for her together, we are waiting patiently and have been for a long time, because she is just late."

In Arkanov's "And the Soup Has Always Been Hot" («А суп был всегда горячим»), a conventional time element turns a banal story of two people falling in love into a dramatic tale with a universal scope. Fairy-tale elements also contribute to the story's effect on the reader. The character has been waiting for seven years for his wife to come home. In all this time nothing changes. "The mushroom soup still remained hot, as if it was just taken off the stove. The bread did not go stale. The sour cream did not go bad."[27] In fact, time has stopped for the character. When he realizes that his wife does not love him anymore, he jumps on the wall and turns into a picture, thus perpetuating the present moment.

Ironic prose is interested mainly in the present. The future enters only in dreams or projections, the meaning of which is analyzed later in the text. References to the past are rare, and when found, they represent an attempt to escape from reality. In Tokareva's "Ruble Sixty Isn't Much" a man suddenly realizes that he is not needed by his wife or friends. He takes a taxi into his past («я сел на заднее сиденье и поехал в свое прошлое») and visits a woman he once loved and whom he still loves. The woman loves him too, yet the four years that they have spent apart stand between them. The past is gone and there is no return to it, as there is no escape from the present.

An attempt to escape is a recurring theme in ironic prose. The character in Novozhenov's "Platform Number Nine" («Девятая платформа») comes to a railway station in order to leave Moscow. He does not care where he goes, as long as it is far away from the snowy city streets, his cold and unhospitable apartment, and his wife to whom he has become a stranger. The character's story is paralleled by that of a little boy who is going to Africa with his toy rifle. He is promptly found and taken home; and the hero's escape seems now as ephemeral as the boy's attempt to reach Africa. The man in Kazovsky's "Miracle on My Nose" wears sunglasses with blue lenses, which change his view of life. When the glasses break, the character sobers up. "I became lonely and sad. I suddenly had a desire to buy a train ticket and go somewhere." Yet his wife buys him another pair of wonderful glasses, and the problem is solved. The heroes cannot escape reality, so they adapt to it. In Inin and Osadchuk's "On the Same Day Every Month" («Каждый месяц, в один и тот же день»), a lonely middle-aged man invents his own way of fighting the dullness of everyday life. Every month on payday, he packs and goes to the airport, chatting on the way with the taxi driver about where he is going on a business trip. After having a cup of coffee with brandy in the airport bar, the hero returns home, inquiring on the way in the taxi about the city news. This monthly trip is a form of escape, which helps the hero live through another month of his eventless life. "He arranges a little holiday for himself, he creates his own *haut monde*, where someone is overjoyed and anxious to pick him up and see him off."

Escape, no matter how insignificant and temporary, is impossible. The heroes of Mikhail Zadornov's "Still Young" («Молодые») decide to add a taste of adventure to the dull routine of their lives. All they can think of is to stay on the metro and get off one station past their usual stop. The young couple discuss the idea as a bold and reckless act. "Think about it, life is trickling away and we never get to see anything. At this rate we won't have anything to reminisce about in our old age." Yet even this pitiful attempt to escape turns out to be in vain: the train does not go beyond the heroes' station. "It wasn't meant to be!" (Не судьба!), concludes the husband. In Kamov's "Bald Angel" («Лысый ангел») the theme of escape is presented in a story of black humor. The hero convinces people that they are angels. His present victim is an accountant, a sick old man. As crazy as the idea sounds, the accountant easily believes in it—reality is too dull and eventless, and therefore, any opportunity to escape it is welcome. The old man kills himself, as did others before him, and the character goes on looking for angels.

The theme of escape from reality is often presented through a convention or an absurd situation. The character of Arkanov's "Early in the Morning after a Good Mood" («Рано утром после хорошего настроения») voluntarily turns into a sheep to escape reality. The story seems to be a joke, and the hero's transformation just a symbolic reaction to the absurd ideas of his boss. But the symbolism lies deeper. The boss's stupidity and demagogy are grotesque, yet recognizable as characteristic of reality. The character is escaping from human life and everyday problems rather than the stupidity of his superior. In Nikolay Konyaev's "Nastenka the Tree" («Настенька-дерево»), the story is written in the form of a modern fairy tale. In an ending similar to that of the traditional Russian fairy tale "A Tale about Alyonushka and Her Brother Ivanushka" («Сказка об Аленушке и ее братце Иванушке»), the girl turns into a tree. Yet the similarity stops here. In the traditional fairy tale the girl turns into a willow, trying to save her brother from a wicked witch. In the modern fairy tale the girl voluntarily becomes a tree as an escape from a strange and hostile world.

Fate is important in ironic prose. Human life is predetermined, nothing can change the order of things. In Shatko's "Wheel of Fortune" («Колесо Фортуны») the character accidentally gains access to the tape of his life. The attempt to change the future almost brings irreversible damage to the character's life and the lives of people around him. The predetermined nature of life does not let the characters of ironic prose escape. The hero of Tokareva's "One, Two, Three . . ." explains: "When a man doesn't know what will be, he fantasizes. Fantasy is creation, and creation is a flight from mundane reality. . . . I know everything that will happen an hour, a day, ten years from now." Such predetermination suggests that people are puppets in the performance of life. Writers of irony see the world as a stage or a movie set. In Gorin's "Cut! Let's Call It a Day" («Стоп! На сегодня хватит!»), the reality of life is replaced by a surreal sequence of movie-making scenes. Each episode brings more and more people into an artistically created reality. The bank robbery is fake, the weapons are loaded with blanks, nature is a backdrop, and conversations are merely an exchange of lines from a cheap melodrama. The movie-making stops only at night. In Briker and Vishevsky's "My Life in Art" («Жизнь в искусстве») and Khait's "One-Man Show" («Театр одного актера»), life and theater merge. The character does not live, he acts. He is not an individual, a person, but rather a conglomerate of parts that he plays at different times of day: loving husband, talented engineer, museum visitor, bus passenger, and so on. His vocabulary is full of theatrical expressions; people around him are mere costars; morning, evening, sun, and stars are just stage props.

Dreams are a frequent motif in ironic prose. They are usually connected with the theme of escape from reality. Heroes try to escape into the world of dreams, but even there reality catches up with them. The character from Arkanov's "Ravioli on the Floor" complains of the undreamlike nature of his dream. "Instead of the sky being blue from early in the morning and the snow in the street—white, so white that it would make you squint and sneeze, instead of all this there is grayness, and not just grayness but the grayness of the asphalt which makes your head ache slowly. For me it's the most boring time: the fall seems to be over, and so is the rain; the temperature is below zero yet there is no trace of snow. There is just asphalt everywhere. And the sky is like asphalt. And the wind is gray. And this has been going on for two weeks now. . . . And it's not our first year together." Gray and dull weather in his dream causes the character to think about life with his wife. Later in the dream he takes her to the pet market and gives her away to a passerby. Yet the dream ends with an awakening and the story ends in the way it started—with the eternal morning conversation of the hero with his wife. The hero of Gorin's "Dream" («Сон») even in his dream does not attempt to escape. In fact, he dreams of his wife telling him about her dream. She dreams that he abandoned her and left for the mountains in a car with another woman. Both the car and the other woman are the fruit of the hero's (heroine's?) imagination, yet the husband and wife get into a fight, and he accidentally kills her. The character wakes up horrified to find that reality exactly repeats his dream, but without the grim ending.

Reality and dream often coexist in ironic prose. The hero of Arkanov's "A Bed, Put Up on Its Side" («Кровать, стоящая вертикально»), the poor student Sanya, imagines that he is a musketeer, a cowboy, and an alien, while riding in the back of a freight truck with a beautiful woman, the client whose furniture he is going to unload. The dream here is another attempt to escape reality in which the hero is poor, lonely, and insignificant.[28] A similar situation is found in Mark Vilensky's "Star Dust" («Звездная пыль»), where a common clerk suddenly gets a day off. Walking along the street, he fantasizes a whole new life, glamorous and full of adventure, yet the sight of a grocery store brings him down to earth—he remembers his wife's request to buy potatoes.

In ironic prose the dream is always contrasted with reality and is always unattainable. In Altov's "Tube of Ultramarine" («Тюбик с ультрамарином») irony is combined with structural irony; the reader cannot believe in the fairy-tale happy ending to the story. The tavern artist will never go to the shore to treat his lungs. He will never use his tube of ultramarine, which he saves for his seascapes; and the only foam he is going to see is that in the beer glasses in a dirty bar, where he draws portraits for a draught of beer. The irony of this situation is juxtaposed with the one created by the artist. His idealized portraits of drunkards give them hope for the future, which is unfeasible under the circumstances. Human dreams are always unattainable, and humanity cannot reach happiness. That is why characters from Abramov's "Sun Was Shining . . ." long for something that the others have, never realizing that those others, in their turn, long for something else. In a similar circle, Arkanov in "And They Started to Cry . . ." («И они заплакали . . .») puts forward the idea that nothing is new in the world; everything has already occurred in the past. Humans cannot discover or create anything; their dreams, hopes, and efforts are futile. The story ends on a grotesque note; after watching people from inside her cage the ape reconsiders her decision to turn into a human being.[29]

In ironic prose the characters understand that their dreams are unattainable, yet they dream. It is a dream for the sake of dreaming, for they must have something in this life to which they can escape. For Ralf Pontyagin, the hero of Vassily Aksyonov's "Cabdriver's Dream" («Мечта таксиста»), the fantasy is Vanya the gold miner (Ваня Золотишник). Someday this ideal person will come, he will get into Pontyagin's car, he will become the taxi driver's friend. "And off they race through the night toward the lights of the city. Vanya sits in the back seat eating salmon caviar and gurgling his brandy, while Pontyagin sings rapturously, glancing down at an immense gold nugget the size of a radio, with an inscription: 'To Ralf from Vanya, from Siberia with love.'" Vanya comes indeed, but without the nugget. Pontyagin treats him like royalty and gives him money when he leaves. Pontyagin does not want gold; it is the "beautiful and human dream" (красивая человеческая мечта) that he needs: "The main thing for me is to know that my gold miner's there, that he exists in nature."

Alongside the "high" dreams that fail, in ironic prose we find petty dreams—the result of human insignificance in the world of the ironist (for example, the characters from the story "Still Young" dream of riding on to one more metro station to see what is there). People's dreams are also bound to the conventions of the society in which they live. The values come from newspapers and TV programs, and the dreams often look like media clichés. When the hero of Tokareva's "Ruble Sixty Isn't Much" dreams of how he will greet his former girlfriend, he thinks of a scene from a popular spoof of a horror movie: "I'll wait until she leaves the room, then I'll close the door and appear before her like the ghost of Spessart Castle." The naive hero of Arkanov's "Nightingales in September" («Соловьи в сентябре») dreams entirely in media clichés and words from popular songs. "And so a new, young family is formed, cutting a path for itself, unnoticed, through the thicket of false pleasantries, animal sensuality, and outward well-being. One cell will form, and then strengthen. 'I don't need any other fate,' Lyosha thought, 'for in you I've found my lifelong mate.' He had etched this thought in his memory forever when he heard it on the radio from the well-known singer Eduard Khil, and when he had memorized it, he entered it in his notebook" (Вот так и возникает новая молодая семья, незаметно пробивая себе дорогу в зарослях показной красивости, животной чувственности и внешнего благополучия. Возникает ячейка, а потом крепнет. «Мне не надо судьбы иной,—думал Леша,—лишь бы день начинался и кончался тобой». Эту мысль, услышанную по радио от Эдуарда Хиля, он запомнил навсегда, а когда запомнил—переписал в записную книжку).[30] On a nice spring day the hero of Kazovsky's "My Fair Lady" («Моя прекрасная леди») dreams of a "tender song" (о ласковой песне) and "of course, 'good and great love'" (и, разумеется, хорошей, большой любви). His dream, based on popular songs, unexpectedly comes true. A dream girl appears and is ready to bring him happiness, yet at the last moment he decides that it is more secure to stay in his old and predictable life.

The theme of happiness also enters ironic prose frequently. It is connected with the theme of dreaming. Characters are constantly dreaming of and longing for happiness, yet they can never attain it. Kuchaev in his story "Happiness" («Счастье») shows that a feeling of complete happiness is impossible. Happiness is a natural feeling and can be experienced only instinctively. Rationalizing always puts an end to the feeling, for it brings in the reality of social life, which is incompatible with happiness. Morozov experiences happiness waking up in the morning («Морозов проснулся от счастья»). But when he begins thinking of the reason for the feeling, the hero remembers only the ugly reality of the previous night's drunken orgy, and the feeling vanishes. In the story "What Happened to Sergeev," Kuchaev returns to the theme of happiness. The hero of the story reaches a state of absolute happiness only when in a surrealistic situation he is relieved of all his worldly possessions and memories of his past life. Happiness is timeless, and Sergeev, who experiences it, is described as suspended in air between heaven and earth. The story of engineer Sergeev is framed by short conversations in which different people present their understanding of the notion of happiness. For one it is money, for another it is nuts and coffee. These are all ironic examples of how happiness has been degraded in society. Similarly ironic are the words of the narrator in the story "Turkish Sabers," which are, in fact, almost a direct quote from the opening paragraph of Tolstoy's *Anna Karenina* (*Анна Каренина*): "All happy families resemble each other" (Все счастливые семьи похожи одна на другую). In the context of the story, these famous words of Tolstoy express nothing but despair for the dullness and boredom in the life of "happy" families.

The stories of ironic prose usually convey only one message. Yet many of the ironic themes are closely connected, and this brings an opportunity for incorporating several themes in a short story. Two stories are prime examples of multiple themes in ironic prose of the 1970s. They are Gorin's "Stop Potapov!" («Остановите Потапова!») and Arkanov's "Peaches" («Персики»). Potapov, from Gorin's story, has adapted to life perfectly. Nothing bothers him, nothing can disturb his equilibrium. The price that Potapov pays for his adaptation is high—he loses his human qualities. He is devoid of love, compassion, and sense of duty. He turns into a well-oiled machine that functions with frightening precision and accuracy. The mechanization of Potapov's existence is emphasized by the significance of mechanical objects in the character's life. Every new cycle of Potapov's functioning ("life" is not an appropriate word here) starts and finishes with an alarm clock. The character does not wake up in the morning; he is "wrenched out of his sleep" (ровно в семь утра звонок будильника вырвал Потапова из сна). He does not fall asleep, but rather "begins to sleep" (ровно в двенадцать часов ночи Потапов начал сон). The story covers one day in the character's life; and in the same way that Potapov winds up his clock every night, someone or something winds up Potapov for every new day, indistinguishable in the succession of identical Potapov days. Confronted with an unpleasant conversation with his wife, the character blocks it out with his electric razor. Nothing touches Potapov, nothing can penetrate the protective covering. In fact, his feelings are gone, replaced by the drive to satisfy his natural instincts. It is characteristic that Potapov remembers the woman who loves him while eating lunch. It is also characteristic that while he is making love to this woman later, the taxi meter is ticking outside, measuring Potapov's life, running it. The character becomes a victim of his own device.

In the story we find the usual ironic themes: lack of communication, loneliness, and desire to be unoriginal (как все). The hero understands that his life is passing in vain, but he never makes an effort to change it. He finds his temporary escape in dreams. "Potapov had had a pleasant, technicolor dream about the sea and a little cafe atop a cliff, where he sat beneath a striped beach umbrella, waiting for somebody. This waiting had been both excruciating and exquisite." In reality Potapov does not wait; he is always on the run, in a time crunch. The hero is constantly lying; his whole life is a performance, in which he plays different parts every day. In fact, the artificial world of theater is closer and more understandable to him than the lives of actual people. Potapov is more touched by the death of Polonius in the Taganka Theater performance of *Hamlet* than by the death of a friend from his student years.

When the story appeared in *Literary Gazette*, it attracted wide attention. In the words of Vail and Genis: "In its time, the story had the effect of a bomb exploding. Probably for the first time since psychological realism, in this short newspaper story one could hear: 'Good lord, look how we are living?!'"[31]

Special attention must be given to the title "Stop Potapov!" which was proposed to Gorin by the editor Ilya Suslov. On the one hand it looks like a recognizable Soviet cliché, something like «Пьянству— бой!» (A Fight against Drunkenness!) or «Остановить гонку вооружений!» (Stop the Arms Race!). As such it served as a camouflage that helped to get the story through the censors. On the other hand, it has an ironic meaning, for the alleged Potapov is inside the reader and to stop him is impossible; Potapov's way is the only way to survive.

The hero of Arkanov's "Peaches," Nikolay, is another Potapov. His romantic interlude (курортный роман) with Raya (Rayukha) is a tribute to the clichés of society rather than to natural desires, much less to love and affection. The heroes are bored alone, but they are bored together, too. The story is a kind of ironic rendering of Chekhov's "The Lady with the Lap Dog" («Дама с собачкой»), yet the love and pity that the author and the reader feel toward the heroes of Chekhov's story are replaced by pity and understanding toward the characters of "Peaches." If in Chekhov's story Anna Sergeevna and Gurov turn to love as an escape from boredom, Arkanov's characters fully accept boredom's reality. In fact, their relationship is just another convention of the mundane world, where love is replaced by an affair; tender love letters, by a banal *poste restante* correspondence. Arkanov sees this as a weakness of human nature rather than of Nikolay's character. Nikolay does not differ much from the rest of humankind, which is revealed at the end in his dream: "That night in a dream he saw himself as a peach among identical Nikolays in a plywood box with holes. He was cramped and hot. Then the lid was removed and someone's hand took him out of the box and started to touch and squeeze him, examining him carefully. 'Eh-h, they are all second grade!' he heard the voice above him say, and suddenly felt the arm drawing back and pitching him somewhere."

Ironic prose has a limited thematic scope. Restrictions that the ironic subjects impose on a writer cause him to search for new formal elements to make the stories original. Thus structural and stylistic innovations are an intrinsic feature of ironic prose. Common forms are stories within stories; stories with circular form, in which the beginning and the end are identical; and stories written by means of negations. There are stories with a twist at the end and those in which the absence of any kind of an ending becomes a formal device in itself. Time is often used as a formal device; a number of stories are written to represent a day, a year, or a life span. Such forms underline the circular nature of life, as well as the fact that no day in a person's life is different from any other day, and a close look at one link will reveal the whole chain of eventless and dull days in a human life.

Conventionalities are common in ironic prose. People in the stories become objects, are hung on the walls as souvenirs, acquire additional senses, speak in verses, turn into animals, save seconds and minutes of their lives in the bank, or take responsibility for the change of the seasons. In a number of stories people acquire the ability to fly—a formal element that opens a number of possibilities for exploring ironic themes. Other elements found in the stories—fantasy, science fiction, fairy tale, myth, the supernatural—perform a similar function as the conventional elements of ironic prose. Absurd elements are common too.

Schematization is another structural element pertinent to ironic prose. The peculiarities of ironic vision and the brevity of the stories create a special world where people are replaced by their caricatures, life by theatrical performance, and feelings by their parodies. Everything becomes building material for the plot-puzzle. Even death loses its metaphysical eminence. In Zhitinsky's "Airplane Crash," for example, the insignificance of human life, the pettiness of humanity, the lack of communication are revealed through an absurd form. The plane crash is depicted as a routine incident. Where life has no meaning, death becomes merely an artistic device.

In ironic prose, realization of a metaphor is an important element both in structure and in style. It is an element of structure whereby the whole story can be read as a stylistic device. Short parables by Zhitinsky ("The Drops" [«Капли»], "Cabbage" [«Капуста»], "Fishing Pole" [«Удочка»]) and several other stories serve as examples. In one of them, Kemoklidze's "Truth," the whole story centers on a revival of a trite metaphoric expression. There are also numerous examples of the stylistic application of the metaphor—when the realization of a metaphor is incorporated in the text of a story as a stylistic device and does not affect its structure.

Other stylistic features of ironic prose that should be noted are the intellectuality of the texts (the stories abound in both direct and subtle allusions to literary works, works of art, philosophical concepts, etc., which require a certain level of sophistication on the part of the reader), the mingling of first- and third-person narration (e.g., in Arkanov's "Peaches"), and the linking of parts of the story by association rather than logic, as in Kireev's "My Strength of Character" («Твердость моего духа») and in Arkanov's "Peaches."[32]

The special relationship between the author and audience based on a cultural text of human life (particularly that of the reader—an urban intellectual), creates favorable conditions for the realization of the elements of irony. The averaged and schematized hero of the stories is a perfect subject for an ironic outlook. In many instances such ironic formulas as "to be a puppet in the hand of fate" or "to be devoid of identity" materialize literally in the stories. Irony as the worldview, on the other hand, fills the lifeless form of a human being with existential meaning, making it not just recognizable for its readers but also emotionally and intellectually stimulating and identifiable. The special relationship between the writer and the reader and their common ironic worldview brings to life ironic prose that is based on a specific cultural text. This text, though, was limited in its application and identical stories and characters that were created as a result eventually brought the subgenre to its natural end.

Conclusion

————————
————————
————————
————————

Irony is a mirror of the epoch and generation of the 1970s, and it passed together with the epoch and its generation. Irony projected the present into the future and showed that there was no hope for improvement. It became a final word of the epoch and also its dead end. By 1986 the works of Soviet writers and artists had begun to manifest a mood of gloom, pessimism, and skepticism. This mood was evident in the preceding decade in Russian literature published outside the USSR, but it was suppressed in the country during the Brezhnev-Andropov-Chernenko era. Lifting the ban on such topics as violence, prostitution, drugs, alcohol, and corruption brought a flood of works dealing with these social vices. The "rehabilitated" works of the writers of the 1920s (Platonov, Bulgakov, Zamyatin, Kharms, Vvedensky, and others) fell right into place in this environment. But although glasnost let the gloom and skepticism out into the open, the seeds of these sentiments were already evident in the ironic mode present in a number of works and genres of the 1970s. This ironic worldview characterized the literature and culture of the so-called period of stagnation; it also was the most visible evidence of a complex subterranean creative ferment. Suppressed by censorship, ironic tendencies found an outlet in regional literature (Siberian prose), in smaller genres (chansons, stand-up comedy, humorous short stories), in a national art form (Georgian film).

The changes currently taking place in the former Soviet Union help to put in perspective the decade of the 1970s. In his essay "On Tyranny," Joseph Brodsky, while concentrating on the generalized image of a "contemporary Russian tyrant" of the Brezhnev-Andropov-Chernenko era, gives a picture of the world and the values created by such a social order: "The droning dullness of a party program and the drab, unspectacular appearance of its leaders appeal to the masses as their own reflection. In the era of overpopulation, evil (as well as good) becomes as mediocre as its subjects. . . . There is something haunting about these bland, grey, undistinguished faces: they look like everyone else."[1] Irony came as a reaction to this dullness and grayness in both the political and cultural atmosphere, where any change in the country's political leadership means nothing but the fact that "it's simply going to be more of the same."[2] The dullness and monotony of everyday life are reflected in the ironic themes of loss of identity, lack of communication, boredom, the unattainability of dreams, the petty nature of human beings and their desires, the limitation of human potential. Expressing and acknowledging this, irony tried to find an escape, yet the attempt failed: the road of irony leads nowhere—it is an end in itself.

The dead end revealed by irony in the 1970s brought into the open a generalized feeling of frustration and pessimism. A sense of doom, of an approaching apocalypse descended on the country. What started at the end of the 1960s as an intellectual's skeptical view of the human predicament, in just fifteen years, at the beginning of the 1980s, had grown into a perspective common to the whole country; continuing to lead the same life was impossible. This feeling now permeated all layers of society and even reached its top. It brought down the Communist party and its system of government, and ultimately led to the disintegration of the Soviet Union. The dramatic events of the 1980s, as well as those now taking place in the territories of the former Soviet Union, overshadow the short and seemingly uneventful period of the 1970s. Yet the full scope of contemporary events cannot be assessed accurately without taking into account all the contributing factors. The pervasive irony, the disillusioned laughter of the preceding decades that we have studied here is one of those factors. It may not have been so dramatic as growing nationalism and economic deterioration, but it certainly made an impact in its own unassuming way—like a sad smile on the lips of an all-knowing and all-understanding ironist.

NOTES

Introduction

1. Friedberg, *Russian Culture in the 1980s*, 25.
2. Irony was often associated in critical literature with the "Young prose." One should not confuse the ironic mood of the 1970s with the ironic tone of narration of the Young prose.
3. Slobin, "Aksenov beyond 'Youth prose': Subversion through Popular Culture," 51.
4. Chudakova and Chudakov, "'Sovremennaia povest' i iumor," 232.
5. Terts, "Chto takoe sotsialisticheskii realizm?" 433.
6. Bocharov, *Beskonechnost' poiska*, 347.
7. Jauss, "Literary History as a Challenge to Literary Theory," 10, 13.
8. "No matter who or what he may be, the real reader is always offered a particular role to play, and it is this role that constitutes the concept of the implied reader": Iser, *The Act of Reading*, 34–35.
9. Suleiman, "Varieties of Audience-Oriented Criticism," 32–33.
10. Jauss, "Literary History as a Challenge to Literary Theory," 15.
11. Ibid.
12. Booth, *The Rhetoric of Irony*, 222.
13. Bitov, "Vybor natury (Tri gruzina)," 583.
14. For the last, see Vishevsky, "Unconventional Literature in a Society of Conventions."
15. Muecke, *The Compass of Irony*, 14.
16. Booth, *The Rhetoric of Irony*, ix.
17. As cited in Wright, "Irony and Fiction," 111.
18. As cited in Hutchens, *Irony in Tom Jones*, 17.
19. Ibid., 20.
20. Worcester, *The Art of Satire*, 124.
21. As cited in Wellek, *A History of Modern Criticism*, 86.
22. Kierkegaard, *The Concept of Irony*, 271.
23. In the subsequent chapters, by *irony* we will mean Weltanschauung irony. The term *Weltanschauung irony* will be used only when different types of irony are contrasted.
24. Chevalier, *The Ironic Temper*, 12.
25. Ibid., 79.
26. Thompson, *The Dry Mock*, 247.
27. Ibid., 255.
28. Glicksberg, *The Ironic Vision in Modern Literature*, 134.
29. Gershkovich, *Teatr na Taganke*, 135, 141.

1. Irony In Siberian Literature

1. Here I mean Russian writers who originally come from or live in Siberia and who write about the land and its people.

2. Here I consider Siberians (сибиряки) to be the Slavs who colonized the country beyond the Ural Mountains. It is not my intention to discuss the folkloric and literary tradition of the native peoples of the region, even though the native Siberian cultural and folkloric tradition had considerable influence on the colonists.

3. The personification of nature is common in contemporary Siberian literature. Among numerous examples I could mention here are Rasputin's *Farewell to Matyora* (*Прощание с Матерой*), with its fairy-tale nature spirit, or Astafev's *Tsar-Fish* (*Царь-рыба*), in which the fish that embodies the power of nature becomes personified.

4. "Natural man" is used here loosely. The hero does not live among nature, but his perception of life, spontaneity of reactions bring him closer to his romantic counterpart and, at the same time, cause his alienation in the modern world.

5. Bocharov, *Beskonechnost' poiska*, 354.

6. Galina Belaya traces the roots of Shukshin's *chudaki* to the fools (*duraki* [дураки]) of the Russian popular theater (балаган) and fairy tales. Yet chudaki, whose dreams are dashed against a hostile reality, have little in common with duraki, especially Ivanushka-durachok (Иванушка-дурачок)—the embodiment of the common folk's dream of happiness. Ivanushka-durachok from Shukshin's *Before the Sun Goes Up* (*До третьих петухов*) is a parody of his fairy-tale counterpart rather than its derivative, as Belaya claims; Belaia, *Khudozhestvennyi mir sovremennoi prozy*, 102.

7. Bocharov, *Beskonechnost' poiska*, 353.

8. Bakhtin, *Problemy poetiki Dostoevskogo*, 175.

9. Shukshin, *Rasskazy i povesti*, 287.

10. Ibid., 288.

11. Ibid., 293.

12. In Vassily Aksyonov's story "A Wild One" («Дикой») a similar situation results in the achievement of the "dream machine"—a convention that only emphasizes the irony of the situation.

13. Shukshin, *Rasskazy i povesti*, 323.

14. Gushchin, "Ten' strekozy," 97.

15. A parallel is found in Yury Olesha's *Envy* (*Зависть*), where the dream-machine Ofelia is made for the destruction of "Chetvertak," a symbol of the material world. However, in Gushchin's story the machine is a means of escape, not an instrument of destruction.

16. Gushchin, "Ten' strekozy," 97.

17. Shukshin, *Rasskazy i povesti*, 204.

18. Annenskii, "Put' Vasiliia Shukshina," 664.

19. Popov, "Rasskazy," 165.

20. Shukshin, *Rasskazy i povesti*, 157.

21. Popov, *Veselie Rusi*, 14.
22. Bakhtin, *Problemy poetiki Dostoevskogo*, 225.
23. Popov, *Veselie Rusi*, 14.
24. Ibid., 61.
25. Ibid., 10.
26. Ibid.
27. Shukshin, *Rasskazy i povesti*, 252.
28. The story is strongly influenced by Chekhov, particularly his stories "Enemies" and "Vanka."
29. Vampilov, *Dvadtsat' minut s angelom*, in *Proshchanie v iiune*, 97.
30. Zalygin, *Rasskazy ot pervogo litsa*, 334.
31. Ibid., 379.
32. Ibid., 369.
33. Ibid., 358.
34. Andrey Sinyavsky calls "dreams of good old honest 'realism'" the "secret heresy" widespread in contemporary Russian literature. See Siniavskii, "Chto takoe sotsialisticheskii realizm," 446.
35. Drinking is common in Siberian folklore as well. Heroes of Siberian fairy tales drink often and a lot. There is even a fairy tale that is named after its central character—"A Drunkard" («Пьяница»)—a real fairy-tale hero who rescues the princess and marries her at the end; see *Russkie geroicheskie skazki Sibiri*.
36. Popov, *Veselie Rusi*, 112.
37. Ibid., 114.
38. Ibid., 80.

2. Irony in Soviet Culture

1. Tikanadze, *Gruzinskoe kino . . . Problemy, iskaniia*, 12–13.
2. The process is very similar to that seen in Siberian literature; see Levin, "Uvidet' vovremia," 109.
3. Runin, "Amplituda kolebanii," 102.
4. Short takes, or "short stories for cinema" (киноновеллы) as they are called, are a distinctive feature of Georgian cinematography. These constitute, as has already been stated, a fruitful form for irony.
5. Tikanadze, *Gruzinskoe kino . . . Problemy, iskaniia*, 344–45.
6. This device is common for ironic works of different art forms and genres (for example, see Shukshin's *Point of View*, in *Rasskazy i povesti*).
7. Bogomolov, "Gruzinskoe kino: otnoshenie k deistvitel'nosti," 48.
8. Ibid., 46. Conventions are very common in Georgian films. The plot of I. Kvirikadze's 1977 film *Little Town Anara* (*Городок Анара*) is based on a conventional situation—in the whole region there is no barrel big enough to hold the wine that comes from the ten-liter horn owned by the hero. The hero of Kvirikadze's 1970 short film *A Jug* (*Кувшин*) (the script is based on a Pirandello short story, by R. Gabriadze) accidentally walls himself up in a huge wine jug. Fairy-tale elements are also common in Georgian movies: in G. Danelia's *Don't*

Despair! (*Не горюй!*); T. Abuladze's *Tree of Desire* (*Древо желания*), in which the script is based on a G. Leonidze short story; G. Shengelaya's *Melodies of the Veriisk Block* (*Мелодии Верийского квартала*).

9. Tikanadze, *Gruzinskoe kino . . . Problemy, iskaniia*, 172.

10. The same image-symbol appears later in O. Ioseliani's film *The Falling Leaves* (*Листопад*) when, after showing a table at which wine factory workers gather for celebration, the camera turns upward to show a church on top of a hill.

11. Tsereteli, "Ot smeshnogo do vozvyshennogo," 61.

12. Bitov, "Vybor natury (Tri gruzina)," 585.

13. Tikanadze, *Gruzinskoe kino . . . Problemy, iskaniia*, 247–48.

14. In T. Abuladze's 1968 film *Prayer* (*Мольба*) as well as in his 1986 film *Repentance* (*Покаяние*) the poet-hero enters into an active struggle of good versus evil; yet, as critics mention, Abuladze's themes, even though closely linked to Georgian cultural tradition, are not dominant characteristics of Georgian cinematography of the 1970s; Tikanadze, *Gruzinskoe kino . . . Problemy, iskaniia*, 325.

15. Bogomolov, "Gruzinskoe kino: otnoshenie k deistvitel'nosti," 43.

16. Ibid., 53.

17. On unherioc heros in Georgian film, see Mamatova, "Gruzinskoe kino: k probleme traditsii," 86.

18. Bogomolov, "Gruzinskoe kino: otnoshenie k deistvitel'nosti," 53.

19. Mamatova, *Vetvi moguchei krony*, 238.

20. Belen'kii, ed., "*Voz'memsia za ruki, druz'ia!*" 22.

21. Kliachkin, interview in *Literaturnaia Rossiia*, January 23, 1987.

22. For a discussion of magnitizdat, see Sosin, "Magnitizdat: Uncensored Songs of Dissent."

23. The theme of historical memory and tradition that are dead is also present in E. Klyachkin's "Valaam" («Валаам»), named for an island not far from St. Petersburg known for its ancient architecture.

24. Belen'kii, ed., "*Voz'memsia za ruki, druz'ia!*" 101.

25. Rudnitskii, "Pesni Okudzhavy i Vysotskogo," 397.

26. Siniavskii, "Teatr Galicha," 143.

27. Frumkin, "Ne tol'ko slova: vslushivaias' v Galicha," 16.

28. Zholkovsky calls this motif in the bard's songs "a glance into the past: nostalgia"; Zholkovskii, "'Rai, zamaskirovannyi pod dvor'," 293.

29. Irony in the works of the bards was noticed before. Sinyavsky writes about irony as that "always trembling string in Galich's songs"; Siniavskii, "Teatr Galicha," 147. Vysotsky is described by his critics as an ironic author; see Rudnitskii, "Pesni Okudzhavy i Vysotskogo," 408, and Krymova, "O poezii Vladimira Vysotskogo," 494. Smith talks about Okudzhava's ironic view of life as "unknowable, leaving humans baffled in their attempt to encompass it"; Smith, *Songs to Seven Strings*, 231.

30. Okudzhava, *65 pesen*, 32. «Голубой шарик»—a "blue balloon" or a "blue sphere" in Russian—also means the earth, which brings an additional symbolic meaning into the song. The device found here is a kind of hyperbole in which a balloon grows to the size of the earth. This device is very popular in

the songs of the bards. Another song by Okudzhava tells of janitors who walk around the planet and "rustle with their brooms against it" (о планету метлами шуршат); Okudzhava, *Proza i poeziia*, 180. In the song "Clouds" («Облака») Galich states that he is cold "for ages" (на века); Galich, *Kogda ia vernus'*, 79. In Vysotsky's song "Glare Ice" («Гололед») the poet pictures the earth in the grip of ice. This concrete and hyperbolic image conveys the lack of understanding and brotherly love on the planet. "If not one then the other would fall, / The earth is covered with ice / And he would be trampled down to death" (Не один, так другой упадет,— / Гололед на Земле, гололед— / И затопчут его сапогами); Vysotskii, *Pesni i stikhi*, vol. 1, 65.

31. Okudzhava, *65 pesen*, 97.

32. Okudzhava, *Proza i poeziia*, 180.

33. Galich, *Kogda ia vernus'*, 179.

34. The poem is also a reference to Chekhov: "*Ich sterbe*," words from this song, were also Chekhov's last words.

35. Galich, *Kogda ia vernus'*, 159.

36. The title of the poem—«Так жили поэты»—is a line from Blok's poem "The Poets" («Поэты»).

37. Galich, *Kogda ia vernus'*, 179.

38. Skaz is a widespread device among the bards. It is particularly popular with Vysotsky. It can be explained by the peculiarities of the genre—the bards' songs are usually ballads or stories which traditionally have a narrator. Skaz as a device is also suitable for irony (for example in Zoshchenko's stories).

39. Galich, *Kogda ia vernus'*, 195.

40. Vysotskii, *Pesni i stikhi*, vol. 1, 314.

41. Okudzhava, *65 pesen*, 53.

42. Ibid., 121.

43. Galich, *Kogda ia vernus'*, 108.

44. Vysotskii, *Pesni i stikhi*, vol. 2, 70.

45. Ibid., vol. 1, 331.

46. This is one of the songs that cannot be called an author's, but in its ideas and in the manner in which it is sung by Elena Kamburova it stands close to the bards' songs.

47. Kamburova, *Poet Elena Kamburova*.

48. Okudzhava, *Proza i poeziia*, 207.

49. For Okudzhava the color blue is a symbol of hope. Blue stars shine in the sky for the hero's love in "You Are Running Around All Day Long" («Все ты мечешься день деньской»); Okudzhava, *Proza i poeziia*, 172. In "Conversation at Night" («Ночной разговор») the goal of a dreamlike journey is the Blue Mountain; Okudzhava, *65 pesen*, 119. The painters in "Painters" («Живописцы») are asked to dip their brushes in blue paint, the color that has for the poet a nostalgic meaning of Moscow courtyards (дворы); Okudzhava, *65 pesen*, 100. Zholkovsky calls Okudzhava's hope "conscientiously unfounded faith/hope" (осозноваемо необоснованная вера/надежда) and ties it to the low estimate that the author places on subjective human potentials of an ordinary individual; Zholkovskii, "'Rai, zamaskirovannyi pod dvor,'" 291. For Galich's hero there is no more hope and blue is the color of shattered expectations. In

"Song of the Blue Bird" («Песня о синей птице») the hero bitterly summarizes his quest for the blue bird: "And when I found its blue trail—/ I got fifteen years in jail" (А нашел ее синий след—/Заработал пятнадцать лет); Galich, *Kogda ia vernus'*, 81.

50. Okudzhava, *65 pesen*, 39.

51. Okudzhava, *Proza i poeziia*, 213.

52. Vysotskii, *Pesni i stikhi*, vol. 2, 10.

53. Galich, *Kogda ia vernus'*, 61.

54. Ibid., 104.

55. Okudzhava, *65 pesen*, 169.

56. Okudzhava, *Proza i poeziia*, 217.

57. Okudzhava, *65 pesen*, 77.

58. Galich, *Kogda ia vernus'*, 340.

59. Vysotskii, *Pesni i stikhi*, vol. 1, 82.

60. Ibid., 122.

61. Galich, *Kogda ia vernus'*, 144.

62. Ibid., 188.

63. Vysotskii, *Pesni i stikhi*, vol. 1, 66.

64. As cited in Belen'kii, ed., "Voz'memsia za ruki, druz'ia!" 5.

65. Sergey Matveenko, as cited in Belen'kii, ed., "Voz'memsia za ruki, druz'ia!" 313.

66. Kuznetsov, *Iz proshlogo russkoi estrady*, 336.

67. Stites, "Soviet Popular Culture in the Gorbachev Era," 3.

68. In Russian, the word for "opened" also means "discovered."

69. Unless otherwise stated, the monologues of Zhvanetsky are quoted from Zhvanetskii, *Riskovannye shutki*.

70. In Zhvanetsky's monologues, when the natural man is found in reality, he is seen as an abnormality and arouses nothing but pity. This character type, however, is rare, and when at some office a man appears who believes everything he is told, does not understand double talk, and trusts in people's honesty and good will, crowds come to see the queer fish; "He Is Our Pride" («Он—наша гордость»), Zhvanetskii, *Roman Kartsev, Viktor Il'chenko, Mikhail Zhvanetskii*.

71. Zhvanetskii, *Roman Kartsev, Viktor Il'chenko, Mikhail Zhvanetskii*.

72. Zhvanetskii, "Ni sekundy ne poterial!" 79.

73. Zhvanetskii, *Riskovannye shutki*.

74. Vil'chek, "Kinematografiia i televidenie," 167–68.

75. *Literaturnaia gazeta*, January 1, 1967.

76. "In 1967 the well educated accounted for some 73 percent of the readership of this paper. A resurvey in 1977 found that the college educated had dropped to 64 percent of the readership. . . . The proportion of young readers *Literary Gazette* has also diminished from 46 percent in 1967 to 23 percent in 1977. As is usually the case, the younger age groups tend to be better educated than the older ones, and as the readership structure shifts to the older groups, it shifts automatically to the less well educated. This drop in young readers brings *Literary Gazette* closer to the average" (Mickiewicz, *Media and the Russian Public*, 55).

3. Ironic Prose as a Subgenre of the Humorous Short Story

1. For bibliographical information on the works mentioned here, see the Bibliography of Ironic Prose.

2. For an exhaustive treatment of censorship in Soviet literature and media, see Loseff, *On the Beneficence of Censorship.*

3. Suslov here means V. Klimovich's "A Story" («История»). See Suslov, "I bitvy, gde vmeste . . . ," 179–181.

4. Suslov, "I bitvy, gde vmeste . . . ," 181.

5. For more detailed theoretical treatment of the ironic prose, see Briker and Vishevskii, "Iumor v populiarnoi kul'ture sovetskogo intelligenta 60-x–70-x godov."

6. Zhitinskii, "Fantasticheskie miniatiury," 264.

7. Ibid.

8. Drobiz, "Stolb i bashnia," 109.

9. The irony here could be reinforced by the slang meaning of the word "post" (столб) in Russian: a dumb, stupid person. This would bring an additional *Aesopian* meaning to the phrase.

10. Drobiz, "Stolb i bashnia," 109.

11. Ibid., 110.

12. Nastroevy (Настроевы) is a pseudonym of three students from the Moscow aviation institute which literally means "there are three of us" (нас трое). The same pseudonym was used even when only one or two members of the group were involved, as is the case here.

13. Nastroevy, "Turetskie sabli," 110.

14. Zhitinskii, "Fantasticheskie miniatiury," 264.

15. The phrase has an additional ironic meaning, for it is an allusion to Pushkin's famous poem "I Remember a Wonderful Moment" («Я помню чудное мгновенье»).

16. Zhitinskii, "Novogodnie fantazii," 115.

17. Creatures of the imaginary planet communicate by thoughts. Telepathy is a popular theme in ironic prose. In Anatoly Eiramdzhan's "Telepathy" («Телепатия»), the character suddenly discovers the ability to read other people's thoughts. Luckily for him he soon loses this ability, for the hostility he feels in other people makes it impossible for him to lead a normal life.

18. Kuchaev, "Sluchai s inzhenerom Sergeevym," 111.

19. Katerli, "Osen'," 263.

20. Katerli, "Groza," 262.

21. The theme of doubles is popular in ironic prose. Besides an ironic theme of loss of identity, where all people look alike, in the stories one often encounters real doubles—a feature of the Romantic and Symbolist traditions. Such are the characters from Anatoly Gladilin's "The Double" («Двойник»). The most famous example of this theme is found in Dostoevsky's *The Double.*

22. Katerli, "Osen'," 263.

23. Nastroevy, "Turetskie sabli," 110.

24. Arkanov, "Podborodok nabekren'," 22–23.

25. Zhitinskii, "Fantasticheskie miniatiury," 262.

26. Sinakevich and Skvirskii, "Ideia," 57.

27. Arkanov, "A sup byl vsegda goriachim," 112.

28. This story by Arkanov may have been influenced by James Thurber's "The Secret Life of Walter Mitty," which could have reached the Russian writer as a story, a film, or a retelling of one or the other.

29. The story could also be an allusion to Zoshchenko's famous "Adventures of a Monkey" («Приключения обезъяны»).

30. Arkanov, "Solov'i v sentiabre," 108.

31. Vail' and Genis, *Sovremennaia russkaia proza*, 51.

32. Alexander Slonimsky points to this device as one of the variations of "comic alogism" (комический алогизм) in his study on the comic in Gogol; Slonimskii, *Tekhnika komicheskogo u Gogolia*, 11.

Conclusion

1. Brodsky, "On Tyranny," 116, 120.

2. Ibid., 119.

General Bibliography

Annenskii, L. "Put' Vasiliia Shukshina" (The path of Vasily Shukshin). In *Do tret'ikh petukhov*, by Vasilii Shukshin, 638–66. Moscow: Izvestiia, 1976.

Bakhtin, M. *Problemy poetiki Dostoevskogo* (The problems of Dostoevsky's poetics). Moscow: Sovetskaia Rossiia, 1979.

Belaia, G. *Khudozhestvennyi mir sovremennoi prozy* (The artistic world of contemporary prose). Moscow: Nauka, 1983.

Belen'kii, L. P., ed. *"Voz'memsia za ruki, druz'ia!" Rasskazy ob avtorskoi pesne* (Let's take each other by the hands, friends! Stories of the author's song.). Moscow: Molodaia gvardiia, 1990.

Bitov, Andrei. "Vybor natury (Tri gruzina)" [Choosing a model (three Georgians)]. In *Sem' puteshestvii*, 523–91. Leningrad: Sovetskii pisatel', 1976.

Bocharov, A. *Beskonechnost' poiska* (The infinitude of the search). Moscow: Sovetskii pisatel', 1982.

Bogomolov, Yu. "Gruzinskoe kino: otnoshenie k deistvitel'nosti" (Georgian film: relating to the contemporary). *Iskusstvo kino* 11 (November 1978): 39–56.

Booth, Wayne C. *The Rhetoric of Irony*. Chicago: Univ. of Chicago Press, 1974.

Briker, B., and A. Vishevsky. "Iumor v populiarnoi kul'ture sovetskogo intelligenta 60-x–70-x godov" (Humor in the popular culture of the Soviet intellectual of the 1960s–1970s). *Wiener Slawistischer Almanach* 24 (Winter 1989): 147–70.

Brodsky, Joseph. "On Tyranny." In *Less than One*. New York: Farrar, Straus, Giroux, 1986.

Chevalier, Haakon M. *The Ironic Temper*. New York: Oxford Univ. Press, 1932.

Chudakova, M., and A. Chudakov. "Sovremennaia povest' i iumor" (The contemporary novella and humor). *Novyi mir* 7 (July 1967): 222–32.

Friedberg, Maurice. *Russian Culture in the 1980s*. Significant Issues Series 7, no. 6. Washington: Center for Strategic and International Studies, 1985.

Frumkin, Vladimir. "Ne tol'ko slova: vslushivaias' v Galicha" (Not just words: a close reading of Galich). *Obozrenie* 9 (April 1984): 15–22.

Galich, A. *Kogda ia vernus'* (When I return). Frankfurt: Possev-Verlag, 1981.

Gershkovich, Aleksandr. *Teatr na Taganke: 1964–1984* (The Taganka Theater). Benson, Vt.: Chalidze Publications, 1986.

Glicksberg, Charles I. *The Ironic Vision in Modern Literature*. The Hague: Martinus Nijhoff, 1969.

Gushchin, E. "Ten' strekozy" (Shadow of a dragonfly). *Nash sovremennik* 3 (March 1974): 84–101.

Hutchens, E. N. *Irony in Tom Jones*. University, Ala.: Univ. of Alabama Press: 1967.

Iser, Wolfgang. *The Act of Reading: A Theory of Aesthetic Response*. Baltimore: Johns Hopkins Univ. Press, 1978.
Jauss, Hans Robert. "Literary History as a Challenge to Literary Theory." *New Literary History* 2 (Autumn 1970): 7–37.
Kamburova, Elena. *Poet Elena Kamburova* (Elena Kamburova sings). Phonographic recording. Melodiia, n.d.
Kierkegaard, Søren. *The Concept of Irony, with Constant Reference to Socrates*. London: Collins, 1966.
Kliachkin, E. Interview in *Literaturnaia Rossiia*, January 23, 1987.
Krymova, N. "O poezii Vladimira Vysotskogo" (On the poetry of Vladimir Vysotsky). In *Izbrannoe*, by Vladimir Vysotsky, 481–502. Moscow: Sovetskii pisatel', 1988.
Kuznetsov, Evg. *Iz proshlogo russkoi estrady. Istoricheskie ocherki* (From the past of Russian variety shows. Historical sketches). Moscow: Iskusstvo, 1958.
Levin, E. "Uvidet' vovremia" (To catch in time). *Iskusstvo kino* 12 (December 1979): 101–10.
Loseff, Lev. *On the Beneficence of Censorship: Aesopean Language in Modern Russian Literature*. Arbeiten und Texte zur Slavistik Series, no. 31. München: Verlag Otto Sagner in Kommission, 1984.
Lvov, A. "Predislovie" (Introduction). In *Pesni i stikhi* (Songs and poems), by Vladimir Vysotskii. New York: Literaturnoe zarubezh'e, 1981.
Mamatova, L. "Gruzinskoe kino: k probleme traditsii" (Georgian film: the problem of tradition). *Iskusstvo kino* 12 (December 1979): 76–89.
Mamatova, Liliia. *Vetvi moguchei krony* (Branches of the mighty tree). Moscow: Iskusstvo, 1986.
Mickiewicz, Ellen Propper. *Media and the Russian Public*. New York: Praeger, 1981.
Muecke, D. C. *The Compass of Irony*. London: Methuen and Co., 1969.
Okudzhava, B. *Proza i poeziia* (Prose and poetry). Frankfurt: Possev-Verlag, 1968.
———. *65 pesen* (65 songs). Ann Arbor, Mich.: Ardis, 1982.
Popov, Evgenii. "Rasskazy" (Stories). *Novyi mir* 4 (April 1976): 164–72.
———. *Veselie Rusi* (The merrymaking of Russia). Ann Arbor, Mich.: Ardis, 1981.
Rudnitskii, K. "Pesni Okudzhavy i Vysotskogo" (The Songs of Okudzhava and Vysotsky). In *Teatral'nye siuzhety*, 394–411. Moscow: Iskusstvo, 1990.
Runin, B. "Amplituda kolebanii" (The pendulum's arc). *Iskusstvo kino* 11 (November 1979): 98–104.
Russkie geroicheskie skazki Sibiri (Russian heroic fairy tales of Siberia), ed. R. P. Matveeva. Novosibirsk: Nauka, 1980.
Shukshin, V. *Rasskazy i povesti* (Stories and novellas). Kishinev: Literature artistike, 1978.
Siniavskii, A. [Abram Terts, pseud.]. "Teatr Galicha" (The theater of Galich). *Vremia i my* 14 (1977): 143–50.
———. "Chto takoe sotsialisticheskii realizm" (What is socialist realism). In

Khudozhestvennyi mir Abrama Tertsa (The artistic world of Abram Terts), 399–446. New York: Inter-Language Literary Associates, 1967.

Slobin, Greta N. "Aksenov beyond 'Youth Prose': Subversion through Popular Culture." *The Slavic and East European Journal* 31 (Spring 1987): 50–64.

Slonimskii, A. *Tekhnika komicheskogo u Gogolia* (The comic technique in Gogol). Brown University Slavic Reprint Series, no. 2. Providence, R.I.: Brown Univ. Press, 1963.

Smith, Gerald Stanton. *Songs to Seven Strings: Russian Guitar Poetry and Soviet "Mass Songs."* Bloomington: Indiana Univ. Press, 1984.

Sosin, Gene. "Magnitizdat: Uncensored Songs of Dissent." In *Dissent in the USSR: Politics, Ideology and People*, ed. Rudolf L. Tökés, 276–309.

Stites, Richard. "Soviet Popular Culture in the Gorbachev Era." *The Harriman Institute Forum* 2 (March 1989): 1–8.

Suleiman, Susan R. "Introduction: Varieties of Audience-Oriented Criticism." In *The Reader in the Text: Essays on Audience and Interpretation*, ed. Susan Suleiman, 3–45. Princeton, N.J.: Princeton Univ. Press, 1980.

Suslov, Il'ia. "I bitvy, gde vmeste. . . ." In *Moi avtografy* (My autographs), 165–83. Tenafly, N.J.: Hermitage, 1986.

Tikanadze, Rusudan. *Gruzinskoe kino . . . Problemy, iskaniia* (Georgian film: problems and explorations). Tbilisi: Khelovneba, 1978.

Thompson, Alan Reynolds. *The Dry Mock*. Berkeley: Univ. of California Press, 1948.

Tsereteli, K. "Ot smeshnogo do vozvyshennogo" (From the ridiculous to the elevated). *Kino i vremiia* 2 (1979): 61–77.

Vail', Petr, and Aleksandr Genis. *Sovremennaia russkaia proza* (Contemporary Russian prose). Ann Arbor, Mich.: Hermitage, 1982.

Vampilov, A. *Proshchanie v iiune* (Farewell in June). Moscow: Sovetskii pisatel', 1977.

Vil'chek, V. "Kinematografiia i televidenie" (Cinematography and television). *Kino i vremiia* 2 (1979): 156–72.

Vishevsky, Anatoly. "Unconventional Literature in a Society of Conventions." *Slavic Review* 47 (Winter 1988): 709–15.

Vysotskii, Vladimir. *Pesni i stikhi* (Songs and poems). New York: Literaturnoe zarubezh'e, 1981.

Wellek, René. *A History of Modern Criticism: 1750–1950*. Vol. 2: *The Romantic Age*. New Haven and London: Yale University Press, 1965.

Worcester, David. *The Art of Satire*. Cambridge, Mass.: Harvard Univ. Press, 1940.

Wright, Andrew H. "Irony and Fiction." *The Journal of Aesthetics and Art Criticism* 12, no. 1 (1953): 111–18.

Zalygin, S. *Rasskazy ot pervogo litsa* (Stories in the first person). Moscow: Molodaia gvardiia, 1983.

Zholkovskii, A. K. "'Rai, zamaskirovannyi pod dvor': zametki o poeticheskom mire Okudzhavy" ('Heaven disguised as a courtyard': remarks of Okudzhava's poetic world). In *Mir avtora i struktura teksta: stat'i o russkoi literature* (The world of the author and the structure of a text), ed. A. K.

Zholkovskii and Yu. K. Shcheglov, 279–308. Tenafly, N.J.: Hermitage, 1986.
Zhvanetskii, M. "Ni sekundy ne poterial!" (I have not wasted a second!). *Avrora* 1 (January 1972): 79.

———. "Portrait" (The portrait), *Moskva* 9 (September 1972): 220.

———. *Riskovannye shutki* (Risque jokes). Phonographic recording. Russian and International Songs Record Co., 1982.

———. *Roman Kartsev, Viktor Il'chenko, Mikhail Zhvanetskii*. Phonographic recording. Melodiia, 1973.

Bibliography of Ironic Prose

Abramov, E. "Siialo solntse" (The sun was shining). *Literaturnaia gazeta*, November 22, 1972.

Aksenov, V. "Mechta taksista" (A cabdriver's dream). *Literaturnaia gazeta*, August 26, 1970.

Al'tov, S. "Nekogda!" (There is no time!). *Literaturnaia gazeta*, November 12, 1976.

———. "Tiubik s ul'tramarinom" (A tube of ultramarine). *Literaturnaia gazeta*, November 11, 1975.

———. "'Zhiguli' na palochke" (Car on a stick). *Literaturnaia gazeta*, June 16, 1976.

Arkanov, A. "A sup byl vsegda goriachim" (And the soup has always been hot). *Iunost'* 6 (1982): 111–112.

———. "I oni zaplakali" (And they started to cry). *Literaturnaia gazeta*, May 22, 1968.

———. "Krovat', stoiashchaia vertikal'no" (A bed, put up on its side). *Literaturnaia gazeta*, December 10, 1969.

———. "Pel'meni na polu" (Ravioli on the floor). *Literaturnaia gazeta*, October 20, 1971.

———. "Pered ukhodom" (Before you go). *Literaturnaia gazeta*, September 10, 1969.

———. "Persiki" (Peaches). *Literaturnaia gazeta*, October 10, 1973.

———. "Podborodok nabekren'" (With the chin on one side). In *Solo dlia dueta*, 20–23. Moscow: Iskusstvo, 1975.

———. "Solov'i v sentiabre" (Nightingales in September). *Iunost'* 2 (1972): 108–10.

———. "Starik v mekhovoi shapke" (The old man in the fur hat). In *Solo dlia dueta*, 28–34. Moscow: Iskusstvo, 1975.

———. "Rano utrom posle khoroshego nastroeniia" (Early in the morning after a good mood). *Literaturnaia gazeta*, March 8, 1967.

Arkanov, A., and G. Gorin. *Solo dlia dueta*. Moscow: Iskusstvo, 1975.

Baranovskaia, E. "Esli ia vstanu v sem' utra . . . " (If I get up at seven A.M.). *Avrora* 3 (1972): 79.

Bakhchanian, V. "Chelovek" (Man). *Literaturnaia gazeta*, January 20, 1971.

Bakhnov, V. "Odinochestvo" (Loneliness). *Literaturnaia gazeta*, November 29, 1978.

———. "Somnambul" (The sleep walker). *Literaturnaia gazeta*, July 3, 1968.

———. "Vremena goda" (Seasons). *Literaturnaia gazeta*, February 12, 1975.

Bitov, A. "Chuzhaia sobaka" (Someone else's dog). *Literaturnaia gazeta*, July 31, 1968.

Bossart, A. "Rozovaia muzyka" (Rose-colored music). *Literaturnaia gazeta*, July 31, 1974.

Briker, B., and A. Vishevskii. "Nebesnaia istoriia" (Made in heaven). *Iunost'* 12 (1976): 106.

———. "Zhizn' v iskusstve" (My life in art). *Teatr* 1 (1977): 189.

Bulgakov, N. "Chto grekha tait'?" (No use denying). *Literaturnaia gazeta*, December 4, 1968.

Chudinov, A. "Luzha" (The Puddle). *Avrora* 4 (1978): 80.

Drobiz, G. "Dozhd' idet" (It's raining). *R. T.* 11 (1966): 13.

———. "Stolb i bashnia" (A lamppost and the tower). *Iunost'* 10 (1975): 108–10.

Eiramdzhan, A. "Telepatiia" (Telepathy). *Literaturnaia gazeta*, July 24, 1974.

Gastello, V. "Bolezn' Stul'chikova" (Stulchikov's illness). *Literaturnaia gazeta*, August 15, 1979.

Gladilin, A. "Dvoinik" (The double). *Literaturnaia gazeta*, March 22, 1967.

Gonik, V. "Ikar" (Ikarus). *Literaturnaia gazeta*, June 13, 1969.

———. "Khvor'" (A malady). *Literaturnaia gazeta*, January 14, 1970.

Gorin, G. "Obnazhennyi Kurentsov" (Kurentsov unclad). *Literaturnaia gazeta*, February 12, 1969.

———. "Ostanovite Potapova!" (Stop Potapov!). *Literaturnaia gazeta*, February 16, 1972.

———. "Son" (The dream). *Literaturnaia gazeta*, May 29, 1968.

———. "Stop! Na segodnia khvatit! . . ." (Cut! Let's call it a day). *Iunost'* 12 (1967): 104–106.

Gureev, B. "Ponedel'nik—den' tiazhelyi" (Monday is a hard day). *Literaturnaia gazeta*, February 1, 1978.

Inin, A. "A gody letiat . . ." (And the years fly). *Literaturnaia gazeta*, January 16, 1980.

———. "Tort s dostavkoi na dom" (Cake, delivered home). *Literaturnaia gazeta*, October 21, 1981.

Inin, A., and L. Osadchuk. "Kazhdyi mesiats, v odin i tot zhe den'" (On the same day every month). *Literaturnaia gazeta*, March 22, 1978.

———. "Padenie G. Dugina" (The fall of G. Dugin). *Literaturnaia gazeta*, December 29, 1976.

———. "Schastlivo svistet'" (Good whistling). *Literaturnaia gazeta*, January 24, 1968.

———. "***." *Studencheskii meridian* 2 (1974): 46–47.

Ivanov, D., and V. Trifonov. "Sakhar, sakhar . . ." (Sugar, sugar). *Literaturnaia gazeta*, October 4, 1972.

———. "Vtoroe 'ia'" (My second self). *Literaturnaia gazeta*, March 17, 1971.

Kabakov, A. "Novoe schast'e" (New happiness). *Literaturnaia gazeta*, January 5, 1977.

Kamov, F. "Lysyi angel" (The bald angel). *Literaturnaia gazeta*, August 11, 1971.

———. "Suvenir" (Souvenir). *Literaturnaia gazeta*, January 7, 1970.

Kanevskii, A. "Khranite svoi gody" (Save your years). *Literaturnaia gazeta*, August 7, 1974.

Katerli, N. "Chelovek Firfarov i traktor" (Firfarov the man and the tractor). *Avrora* 1 (1978): 77–79.

———. "Groza" (Thunderstorm). In *Molodoi Leningrad* 75, 261–62. Leningrad: Sovetskii pisatel', 1975.

———. "Osen'" (Autumn). In *Molodoi Leningrad* 75, 262–63. Leningrad: Sovetskii pisatel', 1975.

———. "Pobeda" (Victory). *Avrora* 9 (1977): 79.

Kazovskii, M. "Chudo na perenositse" (A miracle on my nose). *Literaturnaia gazeta*, January 17, 1979.

———. "Moia prekrasnaia ledi" (My fair lady). *Literaturnaia gazeta*, May 17, 1978.

Kemoklidze, G. "Istina" (The truth). *Literaturnaia gazeta*, December 13, 1967.

Khait, A. "Kogda ia smotrius' v zerkalo" (When I look in the mirror). *Literaturnaia gazeta*, November 17, 1976.

———. "Teatr odnogo aktera" (One-man show). *Literaturnaia gazeta*, June 15, 1977.

Khort, A. "Zanachka" (Something for a rainy day). *Literaturnaia gazeta*, March 31, 1971.

Kireev, R. "Byt' samim soboi" (To be oneself). *Literaturnaia gazeta*, April 18, 1973.

———. "Tverdost' moego dukha" (My strength of character). *Literaturnaia gazeta*, July 26, 1972.

Klimovich, V. "Istoriia" (A story). *Literaturnaia gazeta*, January 13, 1971.

———. "Kstati" (In the nick of time). *Literaturnaia gazeta*, November 11, 1970.

Koniaev, N. "Nasten'ka-derevo" (Nastenka the tree). *Studencheskii meridian* 12 (1976): 46.

Korotich, V. "Koe-chto ob astronomii" (Something about astronomy). *Literaturnaia gazeta*, June 27, 1973.

Krivin, F. "Esli by takoe sluchilos' . . ." (If such a thing should happen). *Iunost'* 12 (1969): 105–107.

Kuchaev, A. "Koshelek ili zhizn'" (Your money or your life). *Literaturnaia gazeta*, February 27, 1980.

———. "Nichego osobennogo" (Nothing special). *Literaturnaia gazeta*, November 11, 1970.

———. "Schast'e" (Happiness). *Literaturnaia gazeta*, December 11, 1974.

———. "Sluchai s inzhenerom Sergeevym" (What happened to Sergeev). *Iunost'* 9 (1975): 110–11.

Kulich, A. "Vek zhivi . . ." (Live and . . .). *Literaturnaia gazeta*, August 30, 1973.

Kurliandskii, A. "Izmena" (Cheating). *Literaturnaia gazeta*, November 16, 1977.

Kurliandskii, A., and A. Khait. "Shestoe chuvstvo" (The sixth sense). *Literaturnaia gazeta*, March 13, 1968.

Lainer, L. "Otvetstvennost'" (Responsibility). *Literaturnaia gazeta*, October 29, 1980.

Lisichkin, V. "Apel'sin" (An orange). *Literaturnaia gazeta*, April 21, 1971.

Lobkov, B. "Nepravil'nyi ruchei" (The wrong creek). *Literaturnaia gazeta*, April 5, 1967.

Mishin, M. "Chto ne sluchilos' s Nenashevym" (What didn't happen to Nenashev). *Avrora* 3 (1975): 78.

Molotkov, O. "Chelovecheskaia komediia" (The human comedy). *Literaturnaia gazeta*, December 3, 1975.

Moshkovskaia, E. "Sup" (Soup). *Literaturnaia gazeta*, February 19, 1969.

Nastroevy, A., and B. "Turetskie sabli" (Turkish sabers). *Iunost'* 2 (1976): 110.

Novozhenov, L. "Deviataia platforma" (Platform number nine). *Literaturnaia gazeta*, January 28, 1976.

_____. "Shest'desiat chetyre" (One fifty four). *Literaturnaia gazeta*, January 23, 1974.

_____. "Zvonok" (A call). *Literaturnaia gazeta*, May 8, 1974.

Novozhilov, O. "Tralialiams" (Tra-la-la-isms). *Avrora* 12 (1977): 75.

Pruslin, G. "Fioletovyi verbliud" (Purple-colored camel). *Literaturnaia gazeta*, November 12, 1971.

Rakhmanin, B. "Nestandartnye lampochki" (Nonstandard bulbs). *Literaturnaia Rossiia*, June 25, 1969.

_____. "Stikhotvoreniia v proze" (Poems in prose). ["Gorodskoe zver'e" (The city's wild animals), "Strannyi chelovek" (A strange man), "Izobretenie" (Invention)]. *Literaturnaia gazeta*, December 25, 1968.

Rozovskii, M. "Gliantsevyi mal'chik" (A slick kid). *Iunost'* 1 (1968): 106–108.

Shat'ko, E. "Koleso Fortuny" (The wheel of fortune). *Literaturnaia gazeta*, April 16, 1969.

_____. "Svidanie" (A date). *Literaturnaia gazeta*, October 11, 1967.

Shakhbazov, N. "Moi znakomye" (My circle of friends). *Literaturnaia gazeta*, April 24, 1968.

Sinakevich, V., and V. Skvirskii. "Ideia" (An idea). *Korotkometrazhki (Short subjects)*, 56–58. Leningrad: Iskusstvo, 1975.

Slutskaia, T. "Bezdar'" (A mediocrity). *Literaturnaia gazeta*, December 10, 1975.

_____. "Ia tozhe khochu k Shumerovu . . ." (I also want to go to Shumerov's). *Literaturnaia gazeta*, December 25, 1974.

Sokolovskii, R. "Ekho" (Echo). *Avrora* 2 (1975): 78.

Todorov, V. "Kryl'ia" (Wings). *Literaturnaia gazeta*, June 1, 1983.

Tokareva, V. "Iaponskii zontik" (Japanese umbrella). *Literaturnaia gazeta*, March 20, 1974.

_____. "Raz, dva, tri . . ." (One, two, three). *Literaturnaia gazeta*, June 18, 1969.

_____. "Rubl' shest'desiat—ne den'gi" (A ruble sixty isn't much). *Literaturnaia gazeta*, July 10, 1968.

Viktorov, S. "Khorei" (Trochee). *Literaturnaia gazeta*, May 8, 1968.

Vilenskii, M. "Zvezdnaia pyl'" (Star dust). *Literaturnaia gazeta*, December 27, 1978.

Zadornov, M. "Molodye" (Still young). *Literaturnaia gazeta*, November 7, 1979.

Zakharov, M. "Zhizn' prozhit' . . . ili shashlychnaia istoriia" (One life to live . . . or a tavern story). *Literaturnaia gazeta*, February 15, 1967.

Zhitinskii, A. "Fantasticheskie miniatiury" (Fantastic miniatures). ["Iskushenie" (Temptation), "Dom" (The house), "Kapli" (Drops), "Derevo" (The tree), "Katastrofa" (The airplane crash), "Taksist" (The taxi driver), "Sobaka" (The dog), "Devochka" (Little girl), "Peshekhod" (The pedestrian), "Lentiai" (The loafer), "Ochki" (Glasses), "Ser'ga" (The earring).] In *Molodoi Leningrad* 73, 261–68. Leningrad: Sovetskii pisatel', 1973.

———. "Novogodnie fantazii" (New Year's fantasies). ["Mikrob" (The microbe), "Kapusta" (Cabbage), "Udochka" (The fishing pole).] *Studencheskii meridian* 12 (1974): 46–47.

PART 2

Anthology of Ironic Prose

Emil Abramov

—————————

—————————

—————————

—————————

Emil Abramov (real name Emil Abramovich Draitser, b. 1937 in Odessa, Ukraine) was a student first at Odessa Polytechnical Institute (1960) and at two journalism institutes in Moscow. After working as an engineer in Kiev, he moved to Moscow to work in various publishing and newspaper jobs. His stories appeared in the leading Soviet periodicals. Draitser left the Soviet Union in 1974, earned a Ph.D. in Russian literature from UCLA in 1983, and is currently an associate professor of Russian at Hunter College in New York. In the United States he has published both original prose and critical studies of Russian satire and folklore. "The Sun Was Shining . . ." was published in 1972 in *Literary Gazette*.

The Sun Was Shining . . .

The sun was shining and all was right with the world. A gardener was watering his flower bed. A car drove past. A scientist was sitting next to the driver. He was reading a book by his favorite author.

"Daisies and violets," the gardener thought as he guided the stream of water from side to side. "Shrubs and bushes. Leaves and stalks. What a blooming bore. He has it good," he thought, glancing after the driver in the limousine as it passed. "Something new and different every day. He gets to see the world, show himself. Maybe I should study to be a driver. While there's still time. . . ."

The car was already driving down the next street. "Got to change the left rear tire. It's veering left," the driver thought. "On second thought, to hell with it. This crate can fall apart for all I care. I'm just a high-falutin flunky. But him," he looked at the scientist, "he's really got a purpose in life—conducting experiments, constantly looking for something. It's for sure better than hugging a steering wheel all day long. Maybe I could be a technician, work in a laboratory. Then take some more courses, find myself a field."

"So what if I discovered the formula for that wax," the scientist thought as he sat with the book in his lap. "So what if I've published twenty-three articles. So what if I'm about to finish a postdoctorate. If only I could write a single story like his, then I could feel that it's all been worth something."

At that moment the writer was looking down at the street from his study window. "Still and all, what he does is the most wonderful kind of work in the world. Creating beauty that doesn't need any reviews, artists' committees, or critique sessions." He was gazing enviously at the gardener watering his flowers. The sun was shining and all was right with the world.

Vassily Aksyonov

Vassily Pavlovich Aksyonov (b. 1932 in Kazan, Russia) is a major contemporary Russian writer. He has written numerous novels, plays, and short stories, many of which have been translated into English and other languages. He completed his medical studies in Leningrad and began practicing as a physician in 1956. *Colleagues*, Aksyonov's first novel, published in 1960, takes his medical experience as its point of departure and marks the author's transition to a full-time writing career. In 1981, while on an author's tour of the West which the Soviet authorities had "strongly advised" him to undertake, he was deprived of his Soviet citizenship. He lives in Washington, D.C., and is a distinguished professor of Russian at George Mason University in Virginia. Recent English translations of his work include *The Island of Crimea* (1984), *The Burn* (1984), *In Search of Melancholy Baby* (1987), *Say Cheese!* (1989), and *The Destruction of Pompeii and Other Stories* (1991). Both "A Cabdriver's Dream" and "A Vulnerable Ego" were published in 1970 in *Literary Gazette*.

A Cabdriver's Dream

It was about the time when Alex Dimsky started to work out of the one of the taxi parks in Moscow. His supervisor and partner was Ralph Pontyagin, an old hand among Moscow cabdrivers.

Everyone knows the old song with the magical and truthful lyrics: "It's the dream of every flyer, / Take me higher, higher. . . . "

While pilots dream of greater heights and submarine captains of greater depths, Ralph Pontyagin dreamt of Vanya the gold miner. Pontyagin had nurtured this dream from the very beginning of the 1950s and had never parted with it. It kept him going. Here is what his dream looked like: Pontyagin would be walking past the line of "guests of our beautiful capital" at Kazan Station, whistling and clacking his teeth. He would indifferently call out, "Anybody for Savelov Station? Anyone for Fili?" And suddenly, bang! Here he comes, his hero Vanya, wearing a sleeveless Harris tweed vest and a silver fox caftan, carrying two wooden trunks with locks. Here he comes, big, pink-cheeked, a little tanked already, cheerful and good-natured. Vanya obligingly slides right into Pontyagin's taxi. He gets in and starts draping wreaths of hundred ruble notes over all of the car fixtures . . . It's as though we were driving to a wedding.

"Where you from?" Pontyagin asks in trepidation.

"From there," Vanya answers in his bass.

"Know what you mean," Pontyagin replies glibly. "Still digging?"

"Sure am," Vanya says, "let's you and me take a spin on down to the Black Sea, partner. Feel like taking a swim. . . ."

That's Vanya's life philosophy, you see: live and enjoy.

"That's a fairy tale, it's all made up," Alex Dimsky condescendingly smiled at his dream. "There aren't any more gold miners like that. Quite a yarn you spin, Pontyagin."

But it's hard to deprive grown men of their dreams. Pontyagin brushed off what Dimsky had said and saw before him, just like in real life. . . .

Here he is, approaching Domodedovo Airport, the western terminus for trans-Siberian airliners. Pontyagin parks off to the side, he waits patiently, refuses all fares. First, he turns down some newlyweds; second, he turns down Bozo the clown; third, he turns down a blonde in an evening dress. And there it is, the reward for his patience, here, straight toward him comes his hero, Vanya the gold miner.

And off they race through the night toward the lights of the city. Vanya sits in the back seat eating salmon caviar and gurgling his brandy, while Pontyagin sings rapturously, glancing down at an immense gold nugget the size of a radio, with an inscription: "To Ralph from Vanya, from Siberia with love."

"Wow, that bit about the gold nugget is really good," Alex Dimsky gaped. "Really powerful, but the business with the caviar is too much."

And once, right downtown, on Plyushchikha, no less, out of the most ordinary crowd you can imagine, Vanya the gold miner got into

Pontyagin's cab, hungry and in tatters, and without a penny to spare. Can that be? I ask you, can it be? Of course it can, and no one is exempt.

So Pontyagin took Vanya the gold miner home, he introduced him to his wife, to his brothers; together they partook of borsht, emptied a bottle, and poured out their souls.

Pontyagin prepared the most comfortable bed in the house for Vanya the gold miner; he got up at night and tucked in his blankets.

The next day Pontyagin bought Vanya some shoes, a scarf, a ticket home, and gave him three rubles. Goodbye, Vanya the gold miner, till next year, Vanya, dear friend.

"You see, I don't need any of his incredible money," Pontyagin suddenly admitted to Dimsky one day. "The main thing for me is to know that my gold miner's there, that he exists in nature. . . ."

"Now that I can understand," Alex said gravely. "I understand you and I respect you, Ralph Pontyagin, for such a beautiful and human dream."

A Vulnerable Ego

I've been thinking back to my younger days. There were always plenty of first-rate guys in the crowd I went with, aspiring architects, writers, and fashion designers. I remember we used to get together and sing till daybreak.

Stas Rassolov wasn't particularly different from any of us. Sure, he was talented, sure, he was physically strong, sure, he was good-looking, but then nature hadn't stinted the rest of us in any of these qualities, either. There was just one thing that was uniquely, personally his—an incredible, acute vulnerability. The guy had no skin, figuratively speaking, of course; in point of fact his skin was flawless, smooth as a new shoe sole.

I remember one of our picnics. It was out by the sky blue waters of Kratov reservoir. Lena Ryzhikova, our budding ballerina, was all aflutter and aglow from her debut the night before in one of the country's biggest theaters. Really, she could scarcely contain herself. We all showered her with questions and adulation and fluttered in harmony with her. Only Stas Rassolov, blushing in embarrassment, stood off by himself and vigorously had to with the processed cheese slices, beef jerky, smoked fish, olives, smoked ham, brisket, and bacon, washing it all down with healthy doses of beer, Georgian white, Bulgarian brandy, and some well-spiced punch. They say that kind of thing happens to some people, sort of a nervous tic.

Finally Rassolov, seizing a pause in all the exuberant chatter, fixed his gaze on Lena and bellowed as best he could, "Oh, come on now, really. I was at this theater of yours last night, and I saw you there, cavorting about with all the grace of a she-elephant. Sorry, sweetheart, better not push the ballet stuff with your qualifications. You're better off sticking to the three S's: scouring, schooling and . . . I forget, what's the last one?"

Lena gasped and clutched at her heart. As fate would have it, a soaked newspaper with the review of her performance floated past us just then. Everyone could make out the headline: "Young Elena Ryzhikova delights spectators with enormous charisma." The review was signed by Gleb Kokorev, who was sitting with us now and looking at Lena.

The poor girl broke out in sobs and slipped away into the wild roses, Kokorev at her heels. The rest of us followed suit.

"Lena, don't let Stas upset you. He doesn't mean it, he's just uncomfortable. You don't know how vulnerable he is."

We glanced back. Stas was sitting beside our devastated picnic smoking a cigarette, and flicking the ashes into the reservoir. At that moment his massive figure looked so lonely that all of us felt a twinge of guilt.

"Let's go join him," Lena whispered.

Another time we got together on the twenty-eighth floor. We were celebrating Gleb Kokorev's first published book. From the doorway Stas belted out, "Hello, hello, you miserable little hack. Admit it now, aren't you ashamed to look people in the eye? Don't worry, you'll get used to it, you hopeless mediocrity."

Kokorev's parents were horrified, and his aunt pitched over in a faint. His uncle was furious.

"Please don't be upset with Stas," we tried to explain to his relatives. "He doesn't mean that; it's like his camouflage, his armor. He's so vulnerable, delicately constituted, incredibly thin-skinned, you can see for yourselves."

Gleb's parents and relatives nodded understandingly and were filled with compassion for the young man.

All evening Rassolov defended himself as best he could. With one hand spearing slices of roast pork and the other pouring out homemade gin, he proposed toasts to the lady of the house, calling her Mr. Kokorev, as well as to the father, whom he addressed alternately as Mrs. Kokorev and ma'am. When he left, it was with bulging pockets stuffed with leftovers, unfinished bottles, and the family's most prized possession—a "Three Horsemen" desk set. "Mrs. Kokorev" had given it to him as a gift right after Stas slapped him on the stomach and said with a wry grin, "Well, Mrs. Cockroach, don't you think it's about time to relinquish some of this excess baggage?"

All of us watched from the twenty-eighth floor as Rassolov's big, lonely figure cut across the parking lot.

"He reminds me of a Hemingway character," Zyablova, a biologist, said softly, and in her blue eyes you could see the pity from which, as we all know, it's but a small step to love. "There's definitely something Hemingwavian about him, or better yet Fitzgeraldian, with those steel blue eyes."

"He may even have something of the young Mayakovsky about him, with his yellow cardigan sweater," offered Pkhakadze, a chemist.

The rest of us agreed with the women. What a defenseless, vulnerable ego.

And so our happy company, including Rassolov, carried on. With the years his vulnerability increased. He began blowing his nose into his dinner napkin, telling himself racy stories at the table, copping books from household libraries—and ties, sweaters, and socks from the closets—making messes on floors, breaking light fixtures and hi-fi equipment, and laughing at the community and literary work of his peers. He called us no less than retards, senile, nouveaux riches, intellectual snoots, horses' asses, and soap bubbles—but this last only on holidays. We never took offense, because we knew the cause of it all— he didn't really mean it, he was just uncomfortable. A defense mechanism, if you like, naive, pathetic attempts to disguise his own deep-seated vulnerability.

Years passed, and we grew older. On one occasion we met in Timiryazev forest preserve and sat in a circle, bloated and variously afflicted. We sang some old rock hit in chorus (though Stas insisted on droning out "Katyusha" the whole time), and then we became silent, pensive.

"Tell us, Stas," I said, "here you've been insulting us all our lives, mocking us, robbing us. You haven't really meant to do all that, have you? It's been because of your own deep-seated insecurity, hasn't it?"

"You know, I think you may be right," Rassolov said in a subdued, atypical voice. "I may do those things because I am insecure." And then he thought for a minute. "Then on the other hand, I'm pretty sure you're all wrong. Maybe it's just because that's the kind of jerk I am."

Semyon Altov

Semyon Teodorovich Altov (b. 1945 in Sverdlovsk, Russia) completed his studies at Leningrad Technological Institute in 1968. He held a spectrum of jobs from chemical engineer to night watchman. He has been a free-lance writer since 1978, authoring collections of satire and a number of comedy shows. Altov also performs his stories from the stage. "A Tube of Ultramarine" appeared in 1975 in *Literary Gazette*.

A Tube of Ultramarine

Vitya Burchikhin drank the first glass of beer in four gulps, as was his habit. He poured himself a second glass, watched the foam seethe, then lifted it to his lips. It was then that he felt someone looking at him. How irritating, these precious moments when it's just you and the beer, and suddenly some interloper spoils it all. People are hanged for lesser things than that.

Vitya tossed off his beer in a few jerky gulps, banged his glass down on the table and turned around. Sitting two tables away was a haggard man in a sweater, with a long scarf wound around his nonexistent neck. He was holding a pen. The guy kept casting penetrating glances at Burchikhin, as though he were making some comparisons, which he then set out on paper.

"Taking inventory, are you?" Burchikhin spat and made for the man, who smiled and continued marking up his paper. Burchikhin approached ponderously to take a look. On the paper he saw his native Kuzmin Street, and on the sidewalk—Burchikhin. The houses were green and Vitya was yellow. But the most horrible thing was that Burchikhin wasn't really Burchikhin at all.

Burchikhin on paper differed from the original in his smooth-shaven chin, his lively eyes, and his kind smile. His posture was unnaturally good, even proud—irritatingly so. Vitya was dressed in a magnificently tailored suit. The graduation pin of some college or other was attached to his lapel. He was wearing yellow shoes and a yellow scarf. In a word, dressed to kill.

Burchikhin couldn't recall a worse insult, even though he had many to remember. "So," Vitya said hoarsely, fixing the collar on his crumpled shirt, "finger painting, are we? Who gave you the right to make a mockery of people? If you don't know how to paint, why don't you go sing or something? Just who is this supposed to be, huh? Who? Who? Is that supposed to be me? And in a tie at that? Bah!"

"That's you," the artist smiled. "Of course it's you. Only I took the liberty of imagining how you could have been. Artists do have the right to invent things, you know."

Burchikhin stared fixedly at the sheet of paper. "What's that sticking out of my pocket?"

"That's a handkerchief, of course."

"You've got to be kidding. Me with a handkerchief?" Vitya blew his nose. "And why'd you think up eyes like that? And that foreign haircut. Now the chin actually came out well, that I can recognize. Say, maybe you're right after all. I haven't done you any harm. What reason should you have for making all this up? Why, give me a shave, a shower, and some nice clothes and I'd be just like in the picture. Why not?"

Burchikhin looked at his clear eyes, tried to smile the smile in the painting, and felt a pain in his cheek from an aggravated cut. "You smoke?" Vitya held out his pack of Belomors which had been torn down the middle. The artist took a cigarette. They both lit up. "And what's that?" Burchikhin asked, tentatively reaching toward a hair-thin line drawn on the face in the picture.

"It's a scar," the artist answered. "You've got a cut there now. It will heal, but there will always be a trace of it."

Vitya drew in deeply on his cigarette. "You say it won't go away? That's a shame. Could have been a handsome cheek. What's the pin?"

The artist bent over the paper. "See, it says here Institute of Technology."

"You think I'll graduate from college?" Burchikhin asked quietly.

The artist nodded toward the drawing. "See for yourself. You'll be accepted and you'll graduate."

"What can I expect in the way of family life?" Vitya nervously flicked the cigarette away.

The artist picked up his pen and sketched a woman's silhouette on the balcony of one of the buildings. Then he paused, and dashed on a child, too.

"Is it a girl?" Vitya asked, his voice breaking.

"A boy."

"Who is the woman? Judging by the hair color it's Lyusa."

"Galya," the artist corrected him.

"Galya? So that's why she doesn't seem to want to have anything to do with me. She's flirting. That's a woman for you." Vitya laughed and no longer felt the pain from his cut. "You're a good guy, you know that?" He slapped the artist on his narrow shoulders. "Want a beer?"

The artist swallowed and whispered, "Sure. I'd like one a lot."

Burchikhin called to the waiter. "Bring us two beers." Vitya poured the beers and they began to drink in silence. Catching his breath halfway through, the artist asked, "What's your name?"

"Burchikhin."

"You see, Burchikhin, I've actually got this thing for seascapes."

"I understand," Vitya said, "they can cure that now."

"There you go," the artist said, obviously pleased. "I have to paint the sea. My lungs are weak. I ought to be in the south, by the sea. Using lots of ultramarine. The color's useless here. I have a passion for pure, unadulterated ultramarine. Like the sea. Can you imagine it, Burchikhin, the sea. Itself, in the flesh. Waves, cliffs, and foam."

They tossed the foam from the top of their glasses under the table and lit cigarettes.

"Don't worry," Burchikhin said. "Everything's going to work out. You'll for sure be sitting in your shorts at the seaside with that ultramarine in your hands. You've got everything ahead of you"

"Really?" The artist's eyes lit up and suddenly looked as though they were painted. "Do you think I'll ever get there?"

"Oh, sure," Vitya replied. "You'll live at the seaside, you'll forget about those lungs of yours, you'll become a famous artist, you'll buy a house, land, a yacht."

"Oh, come on now, a yacht?" the artist said, shaking his head deliberately. "Maybe a boat, do you think?"

"Of course, and better yet, both a boy *and* a girl," Burchikhin said and hugged the artist around the shoulders, which required half his arm, from the elbow to the fingers. "Listen, pal, sell me this picture."

The artist shuddered. "How dare you? I could never sell it to you. If you like it, take it as a gift."

"Thanks a lot," Vitya said. "Could you get rid of the necktie, though? I can't stand seeing me in one. Can't breathe."

With one pen stroke the artist changed the tie into the shadow of a lapel. Burchikhin cautiously picked up the sheet of paper and, holding it out in front of him, walked off between the tables. He was smiling the smile in the drawing, and his stride became more confident and sure.

The artist got out a fresh sheet of paper and set it down on the wet table. Smiling, he affectionately patted his coat pocket, which held an unused tube of ultramarine. Then he sighed, picked up his pen, and started to scrutinize the next table over.

Arkady Arkanov

_____
_____
_____
_____

Arkady Mikhailovich Arkanov (b. 1933 in Kiev) completed his medical studies in Moscow in 1957, worked as a doctor for three years, and has been a professional writer since 1960. He is the acclaimed author of many short story collections, plays, and screenplays. "Humor and irony are the way I see the world, not a literary method," he states. "Nightingales in September" was published in 1972 in *Iunost'*; "Peaches" in 1973, "Cross Country" in 1970, and "Before You Go" in 1969, all three in *Literary Gazette*.

Nightingales in September

On a warm September evening a certain young man by the name of Lyosha was headed for the house of a certain young lady by the name of Lida. In one hand the young man was carrying a bottle of dry red wine (one ruble sixty-five kopecks). In the other he carried a bouquet of carnations (one ruble twenty-five kopecks). Of course, Lyosha would have gladly carried a cake, and a book, too—"the best kind of present"—but he only had two hands.

The young man had waited for this evening perhaps all his life, but then again perhaps not quite so long, because he harbored the loftiest hopes for it.

For he loved the aforementioned young lady, Lida, in a pure kind of Komsomol way, unburdened by any coarse overtones of the let's-go-stand-in-the-entryway or the why-don't-we-go-sit-on-the-bench variety. He loved her in the only true way—he didn't stroke her blonde hair; he didn't put his hand on her knee and say "Hey, Lida baby"; he didn't gaze mysteriously into her eyes and flare his nostrils as he did so. And because of all this, he rightly hoped that his love would be requited, a hope which would be realized precisely on this warm September evening. This was Lida's birthday, which Lyosha had been mindful of daily, and although no invitation had come, he knew he would be welcomed, because true friends come without an invitation. Yes . . . and so a new, young family is formed, cutting a path for itself, unnoticed, through the thicket of false pleasantries, animal sensuality, and outward well-being. One cell will form, and then strengthen. "I don't need any other fate," Lyosha thought, "for in you I've found my lifelong mate." He had etched this thought in his memory forever when he heard it on the radio from the well-known singer Edward Hill, and when he had memorized it, he entered it in his notebook.

Lida will really be surprised when she opens the door. And he'll hand her the bouquet of carnations and say, "Lida, this is for you in honor of your birthday. . . ." And she'll understand at once that he is her true friend, for true friends don't have to be invited, they come of their own accord. And then Klavdia Martynovna, covered with flour, will come out of the kitchen, clap her hands, and sob. And he'll hand her the bottle of dry red wine and say simply, "Klavdia Martynovna, this is for you in honor of our Lida's birthday."

Lida and he will go into her room. He'll help her with her solid geometry, and her blonde curls will brush against the sheet of poster board. And it will become obvious that in just four and one-half years they will observe their entrance into lawful matrimony with an effulgent, Komsomol wedding. Why should it be any sooner? Certainly there was no need to test the waters; Lyosha could vouch for his and Lida's feelings. It's just a matter of them getting their degree, of getting set up with a job and an income. And two years or so after that, Mitka will come along. Why should it be any sooner? Certainly it's not because they're egocentric. It's just a matter of giving the family time to solidify, to go to the theater, the exhibits, the skating rink. There'll be no harm in that: When Mitka's born they'll both be twenty-seven. When Mitka's ten, they'll be thirty-seven. When Mitka's twenty, they'll be forty-seven. When Mitka's thirty, they'll be fifty-seven. When Mitka's forty, they'll be sixty-seven. When Mitka's fifty, they'll be seventy-seven. When Mitka's sixty, they'll be eighty-seven . . . . When he reached eighty-seven, the future father of the sixty-year-old Mitka rang the doorbell of the apartment of Mitka's future mother, who had just turned twenty today.

"For God's sake, who is it now?" he heard the voice of Klavdia Martynovna from the other side of the door. "Who's there?"

"Robbers," Lyosha good-naturedly joked, then coughed and said seriously, "It's me, Klavdia Martynovna."

"Who's 'me'?"

"Me, Lyosha."

"Lyosha who?"

"Lyosha nobody. Just Lyosha."

The lock clicked and the door opened slowly.

"This is for you, Klavdia Martynovna, in honor of your daughter's birthday," Lyosha declared simply and handed his future mother-in-law the bottle of dry red wine.

"Oh, you came to see Lida?" the future mother-in-law asked, peering down her nose suspiciously at the bottle.

"Yes, Lida!" the future son-in-law said in a sad and solemn way.

"Well, she's just not home now. You want me to give her a message?"

"I'll do it myself," Lyosha smiled, sniffing the carnations. "She'll be really surprised when she sees me."

"Do you want to come in or something?" Klavdia Martynovna said without any particular enthusiasm.

"Well yes, of course, on a day like this one ought to wait."

"And just who are you?" Klavdia Martynovna took a step backwards.

"Do you mean to say you don't remember me? I was here in March. Lida and I were studying together."

"Maybe," Klavdia Martynovna said, shrugging her shoulders. "Lots of people come to see Lida."

From the living room came the typical sounds of people at table: knives scraping on plates, glasses clinking together in toasts.

"Are you celebrating?" Lyosha wondered out loud.

"Some relatives have come over," Klavdia Martynovna said. "The kids have gone out to a restaurant. Armaz and Levan came up from Sukhumi. Lidochka spent her summer vacation at their place. Well, so in return they've invited her and all her friends out for dinner."

"Personally, I like Georgians," Lyosha said. "Moldavians are a nice bunch, and Estonians. . . . "

"Lida didn't say anything to you about it?" Klavdia Martynovna asked.

"She probably just forgot. You know how she gets carried away with things," Lyosha said.

"Sure. She won't be back very soon, probably not until morning, I figure."

"Don't trouble yourself, Klavdia Martynovna. You go drink the wine, share it with your company, and put the carnations in water. I'll just wait here for Lida. I'll stand in the hallway. And anyway, I don't think that Lida will be able to stay away much longer. She'll rush home to celebrate with kith and kin. After all, it's that kind of day."

"Klava, who are you out there gabbing with?" came somebody's stale voice from the living room.

"Coming!" Klavdia Martynovna called back. "Some guy just came to see Lida."

"Well, so what are you standing there for?" the stale voice continued. "If he's one of us, then he should be drinking with us, and if he's not, then why did he bother to come in the first place?"

"No, please," Lyosha said hastily. "Give my regards to everybody, and I'll manage fine right here. I've already eaten today, thank you."

"Suit yourself," Klavdia Martynovna said. "But why stand around like a butler in the hallway? It can't be very comfortable. Wipe off your shoes and go sit in Lida's room. Believe me, though, she's not checking in again till tomorrow morning. Why not just write her a note if it's anything important."

"Klavdia Martynovna," Lyosha said soulfully. "Dearest Klavdia Martynovna, I am her friend!"

And he tightly clasped Klavdia Martynovna's hand.

When he was alone in Lida's cozy little room, Lyosha thought: "Perhaps I should go ahead and tell everyone about my decision. No, I'll wait for Lida and then hand in hand we'll go in together and make the announcement. Lida is a real human being. She understands what friendship is all about. She's proud, that's why she doesn't notice me. She'll come home, see me, and then lower her gaze and rest her head on my shoulder." And everything would be clear without having to say a single word—why she didn't say hello to him, why she didn't go up to him, why she had her own circle of friends, and why Lyosha didn't even seem to exist. Because one has to know how to hide one's real, pure feelings, once they've shown themselves. And they had shown themselves as far back as last March, when he had helped her make conical sections. It was then that she said, "Thank you." Now, half a year later, he had made the decision. He had weighed his feelings, he was not mistaken. And on the day of her twentieth anniversary he had come to tell her that he remembered her simple, sincere, and maidenly "thank you," and that he was prepared to extend to her his youthful and comradely "you're welcome."

Outside, despite its being September, the nightingales were bursting forth in song. Lyosha picked up a photo album from the table. Here was Lida at one year—just like their Mitka would be, only a boy. And here were some summer landscapes: Lida in a bathing suit; one leg on the running board of a new Volga, the other on a mustachioed young man lying on the sand; a wine glass in her hand; the sea to the right; citrus trees to the left. And here was Lida, naked to the waist, her blonde curls strewn over a pillow, and a cigarette in her mouth. Probably on the beach of some health resort, doctor's orders. Next a color portrait of the same young man with the mustache who had previously been lying beside the car; glossy hair, neat part on the side; and an autograph: "To unforgettable Lidushka from Levan! Remember, Lidushka, how we partied, and then how much we loved. . . . " Loved what? He hadn't been able to write that, because he'd run out of space. Probably, loved to take walks. "After all, the weather is magnificent down there, and there's all that subtropical vegetation," Lyosha thought.

For a long time he continued to leaf through the photo album, then he put it back in its place and began to inspect the room. If the labor union committee refuses to supply them with a special dorm room for married couples, then they'll have to live here and apply to the local residential authority for an apartment. And just about then Mitka will be born, and the residential authority will have to give in. They'll be a little crowded, of course, but it won't be too close for comfort, as the saying goes. The main thing is to respect one another and help each other both at work and at home. Klavdia Martynovna will surely be understanding, and they'll finally hit it off. If need be, he could paint the walls and hang wallpaper and make trips to the market. And they'll all come to live together happily and harmoniously, and Mitka will call Klavdia Martynovna "Gramma." They'll call a cab, and he'll bring Mitka home from the maternity ward himself. And Lida, sitting in the car, will rest her head against his shoulder and quietly say, "You know, he looks just like you."

Klavdia Martynovna checked in on Lyosha. "You don't happen to have some smokes on you? My smokers in there have just run out."

"I've only got this low-tar and nicotine brand," Lyosha said apologetically and pulled a pack out of his pocket.

"Tar or no tar, just as long as they can be inhaled," said a man standing behind Klavdia Martynovna, who then squeezed by her into the room and held out his hand to Lyosha. "I'm Pavel Stepanovich, Lidochka's uncle."

"Nice to meet you. I'm Lyosha," Lyosha said, firmly shaking the hand of his relative-to-be.

"Now there's a good Russian name!" Pavel Stepanovich enthused. "So what does that give us now? Armaz, Levan, David . . . Lyosha! Short and sweet for a change! What do you say, Lyosha, let's go drink to Lidka's happiness."

"Lida will be happy," Lyosha said. "But first of all, I don't go in for that sort of thing, and secondly, the name is insignificant. As long as the person is decent."

The remaining relatives and guests poured out into the hallway and began to sing and dance riotously. Then they seized up Lyosha and dragged him into the living room. He picked up a guitar and began singing cheery songs by Pakhmutova with lyrics by Grebennikov and Dobronravov. They poured vodka down him, and he started to get gloomy. Before long he became totally depressed and went out to the kitchen. He sat down on a kitchen stool and became lost in thought. Outside the nightingales were singing as before.

The guests began to disperse, and before long they had all left but one, a middle-aged man by the name of Sergey. Klavdia Martynovna, in a totally intoxicated state, was clinging to him and saying, "Where are you going? Tell me! You don't have to go to work tomorrow. Lidka probably won't be home till morning, if at all. Well, how about it?"

"I don't know, Klava," Sergey answered and gazed longingly at the door. "I don't feel right about it. And then there's that guy in the kitchen. No, I'd better go."

Lyosha fidgeted on his stool. Klavdia Martynovna appeared in the kitchen.

"Well?" she said with malice in her voice. "Why are you sitting there like a lump? I told you in perfectly clear Russian—they've gone out to a restaurant. She's not coming back soon! If she wanted, she would have invited you along."

"Lida is proud," Lyosha said quietly and not as confidently anymore, and stayed seated.

The outside door slammed.

"She's back," Lyosha gave a sigh of relief.

Klavdia Martynovna poked her head out into the entryway and said dejectedly, "He's gone. And now you go. She's not going to come. I'm telling you."

"Even so, Klavdia Martynovna," Lyosha said as though getting his second wind, "mother or no, you don't really know Lida. She's a person of integrity. She can't help having certain feelings for me. She'll be back soon, and you'll see."

"What, I don't know her? I don't know Lida? She has feelings for you? She doesn't even give you a thought! Now go home, or else you'll miss the last train."

Lyosha slowly got up off the stool. There was a lump in his throat. His entire life philosophy had cracked. They hadn't prepared him for this in school. Edward Hill hadn't sung about this. Was it possible that he, a simple, forthright fellow, like thousands of others, was not worthy of a girl's intimate feelings?

"And the nightingales started whistling, to spite me," he said for some reason as he buttoned all three buttons of his sportcoat.

"Those aren't nightingales, Lyosha, those are the neighborhood punks," Klavdia Martynovna said, and Lyosha finally understood that she was not fated to become his mother-in-law.

I ran into him that night on the embankment of the Moscow River. And he related his plight to me just the way I've set it forth here. I suggested that he jump, but he firmly rejected my suggestion and marched away, singing an enthusiastic explorer's song, "Stand fast, old fellow, hold on, old boy."

As for me, I believe in guys like him. He'll get his degree, he'll become an engineer, and he'll spend all his vacations on hiking trips. With his guitar. Around the campfire. Singing songs.

After all, there are quite a few songs that help one live and build the future.

Peaches

"How much are your peaches?"

"Three fifty a kilo."

"I'll give you three."

"For that much I could eat them myself."

"How about if you sell them to me for three and eat them yourself for two fifty."

The man selling the peaches stared off to one side, as though he had no interest in continuing the conversation.

"Nice-looking peaches," a young woman said. "The lady over there is selling them for three, but hers are damaged, with bruises."

"You think so?" Nikolay said. "All right, rob me. I'll give you ten rubles for three kilos. Fifty kopecks shouldn't make that much difference."

"So give me eleven," the peach vendor rumbled. But by then it was clear that the deal was done, and he began to set immense, obnoxiously sun-ripened peaches onto the aluminum tray of his scales.

"If these don't keep all the way to Moscow, you'd better watch out," Nikolay said ebulliently and handed the man a ten-ruble note.

"They'll keep all the way to Siberia if you want," the man said and buried the note deep down in an inside pocket of his jacket.

"How about these prices," Nikolay thought out loud, glancing now and then at the peaches in his shopping net. "Three fifty, that's practically a full day's work."

The young woman walking next to him, Raya, was silent. She only stopped for a second, took off one sandal, and shook a pebble out of it. From that moment on Nikolay thought only about how to get the peaches home in good condition, and a few other things.

The peach vendor covered his scales with a towel, asked the woman next to him to keep an eye on things, and headed for a nearby Georgian restaurant, because he had worked up an appetite.

After waiting at his table in the restaurant for a good half hour and losing his temper, he ordered tossed salad with egg and sour cream, a bowl of spicy tomato soup with rice, two shish kabobs Georgian style, a soda, two different kinds of bread, and a bottle of Psow wine, since they had run out of beer.

When he had eaten and drunk everything with long breaks between the courses, and when he had waited another thirty minutes for the check, he handed the waiter the ten-ruble note, complained to him about the slow service, and headed back toward the market stalls to sell his peaches. On the way he thought how good it would be to have that strapping waiter working in the orchards growing peaches.

The waiter stuffed the ten-ruble bill into the pocket of his tuxedo and thought how much he'd like to get that pig farmer into a restaurant, running around all day with his tongue out, and then see what he said.

But just a moment later his attention was drawn to the table by the window, where a mixed black and white party had sat down, emitting baritone jokes in a foreign accent and feminine giggles.

"What's with you, Raya?" Nikolay asked as he arranged the peaches in a plywood box with holes, which he had just bought for two and one-half rubles. "Why so sad all of a sudden?"

"It's hot," answered the young woman, who really was hot, because she had arrived at this seaside resort in the southern Crimea in July rather than September, as she had been expecting. (At the last minute she had been offered early vacation leave, which she couldn't pass up.)

"Chin up, Raya," Nikolay said. In four hours his vacation would end with a jet flight from Simferopol airport back to Moscow. His stay in the trade union resort on the south shore of the Crimea was ending. It was here, on the fourth day of his vacation, that he met Raya on the beach and suggested that they both swim out to a buoy, and then take a ride on a sight-seeing boat with an accordion player and Czech beer in the bar. It had seemed so unusual to her, the way this unique southern cameraderie had developed so quickly between them, and with it an exchange of the most diverse information and fresh impressions. That's how she had learned that he was from Moscow. "And where are you from? I'm from Tyumen." That's how he learned that she had read a book about dolphins. "And I recently saw Memoirs of the Future. Have you seen it yet?" "No, Lyudmila Zykina, the singer, was on tour in our town, and by the way there's supposed to be a Georgian restaurant somewhere around here. And they recently discovered so much oil in Tyumen province that you wouldn't believe it." And so 88 degrees in the shade and 75 in the water were producing the usual effect. And moreover it turned out that his supervisor was a real blockhead, and that dancing had been forbidden in the workers' dorm where she lived, and that there was nothing better than dry wine after a good swim, and tonight they're showing the miniseries "Seventeen Moments of Spring" on television. And they watched their seventeen moments of spring night after night, moment by moment, saving a place for each other in the lobby. And when Stierlitz, the Soviet spy, fell asleep exhausted in his car, that thing happened between them that caused him to go diving all the next day like a madman, that compelled him to beat a vacationing professor at a game of go fish, that moved him to sing the songs of his favorite singer—Edward Hill—from morning to evening, and that made her cast furtive glances to all sides under the naive assumption that everyone was looking at her and conspiratorially whispering. They spent the rest of their holiday looking at each other with bedroom eyes, although for meals in the cafeteria they replaced them with the dull, vacant ones of typical vacationers. Anyway, he rather liked this place, although she was perpetually hot, and she began to count the days nervously.

Then the last installment was over and the rains came. And for days on end he played go fish or chess with the professor, quietly humming "Water, Water Everywhere" and looking out the window in expectation of a change in the weather, because he shared a room with three other men and Raya shared hers with three other women. She felt hot as ever and continued counting the days.

When his leave time had expired, Nikolay felt rested and revitalized. That same day the sun came out and they went to the market to buy peaches. Being the man, Nikolay felt sorry for her, having to part with him. "Chin up, Raya," he repeated just before the bus arrived. "You can't change anything." The time of his departure had come. They had scarcely been acquainted when the snow began to fall. "We can write each other. General delivery, or maybe a post office box. That's how we'll do it. What's the matter with you, Raya?"

"You'll miss your bus," Raya said. She wanted his bus to leave, the sooner the better. She wanted this day to be over, because her vacation would be over tomorrow, too, and she had to send Klobukova a telegram instructing her to get everything ready for her arrival. This was the one thing she was sure of, and she was incapable of thinking about anything else.

The vacationers staying at the trade union resort on the south shore of the Crimea surrounded the bus. Nikolay carried his things into the bus and set down his box of peaches so that they wouldn't be crushed.

"Well, see you soon, as they say," he called out the window and waved as do soccer players leaving for an away game.

The bus wheezed and drove off through the gates of the resort.

The vacationers staying at the trade union resort on the south shore of the Crimea waved back and called out, "Good-bye!"

The bus turned to the left and the vacationers dispersed. The sea, which just a second earlier had been right there, disappeared and Nikolay did not see it again. He thought only about the fact that he would be back in Moscow in a few hours.

Raya's vacation ended the next day, and she flew back to Tyumen, where Klobukova was waiting for her. On the third day she went back to work.

At work people told her that she hadn't gotten much of a tan.

At the airport Nikolay heard something about a quarantine on fruit and vegetables. For a second it took his breath away. What am I supposed to do with the peaches, he thought, and within minutes he had gotten several sheets of wrapping paper from the airport news stand, wound it around the boxes of peaches, and tied it all up with a rope.

At the ticket counter, two men from the Caucasus (Nikolay could never tell an Armenian from a Georgian from an Azerbaijani) were vehemently gesticulating and expressing their outrage over the quarantine in a mixture of Russian and their own language. Two tall baskets with fruit were standing in front of them; the shift supervisor and baggage manager were standing next to the ticket agent. The supervisor kept repeating, "That's it, this conversation is over, I have no intention of going to jail for you. Next." The Caucasians' hats were set down over their eyes, and the sweat was literally streaming down their faces. But the supervisor was unbending, because he had no intention of going to jail for them.

"Can I take my dirty laundry on with me?" Nikolay asked plaintively, nodding toward the box of peaches.

"Let's have everything," the ticket agent said firmly, and Nikolay felt sick as he watched his box of peaches slam down onto the baggage cart. "Small price to pay," Nikolay thought, "at least those two guys aren't even going to be able to get past check-in." And he was thoroughly pleased with himself for having outsmarted the airline.

In the airplane Nikolay immediately fell asleep and didn't even have a chance to get his peanuts. When he woke up, the sign outside his window said Moscow instead of Simferopol.

As he was walking toward the baggage claim area, the two Caucasians overtook him, carrying heavy suitcases. Behind them a porter was carrying two tall baskets of fruit. "How do you like that," Nikolay thought.

His suitcase appeared on the conveyor belt forty minutes later, followed by the box of peaches. There was a big, wet, brownish stain on the wrapping paper. "They've smashed them, those bastards," Nikolay thought. He took his things and made for the exit, holding the box of peaches with one arm outstretched, so as not to get his clothes stained.

"Why didn't you send a telegram?" Nadezhda asked Nikolay as she kissed him.

"Fidelity check," he grinned.

"You sly devil. Mother and I had figured everything out. You had to come back today. You didn't have much of a choice."

"Daddy, what did you bring me?" Volodya clung to him.

"That's a secret," Nikolay said.

"Give me the secret, give me the secret," Volodya jumped up and down.

"After dinner," Nikolay said sternly.

After dinner Nikolay ceremoniously unwrapped the box of peaches.

"Your attention, please. One, two, three—peaches!"

He opened the box.

A good half of the peaches had been smashed by something and constituted a fairly revolting mush.

"Those bastards," he said.

"Don't throw them out," his mother-in-law interposed. "They'll do for jam."

They washed the remaining eight peaches, arranged them on a big, fancy plate, and then ate them within two minutes.

"Were they really worth all the trouble?" Nikolay said.

"It's not the gift, it's the thought that counts," his mother-in-law offered.

Nadezhda started clearing the table and Volodya ran outside.

When Nikolay was lying in bed reading *Sporting Week*, Nadezhda walked in in her nightgown.

"By the way, how much did those peaches cost down there?" she asked.

"Three fifty a kilo," Nikolay replied.

"What do you know, even here at the central market they're cheaper," Nadezhda said and turned out the light.

That night in a dream he saw himself as a peach among identical Nikolays in a plywood box with holes. He was cramped and hot. Then the lid was removed and someone's hand took him out of the box and started to touch and squeeze him, examining him carefully. "Eh-h, they're all second grade!" he heard the voice above him and suddenly felt the arm drawing back and pitching him somewhere.

"What is it? What happened?" his frightened mother-in-law asked, running into the bedroom at the sudden thud.

"I fell out of bed," Nikolay said apologetically.

"You weren't much for falling out of bed before your vacation," she droned in displeasure.

Nikolay rubbed his bruised side and went back to bed.

In the morning he caught the number 48 trolley and rode to work.

At work they told him that he had hardly gotten any tan at all.

"It's all peeled off," he said. "And then it rained a lot."

Cross Country

"Tomorrow you're going on the 10-K," my department head told me.

"Where to?" I asked.

"Not where to, but how," my department head clarified for me. "On skis, ten kilometers, cross country."

"At my age? I'm fifty-three."

"Yes, at your age, and I do remember that you're fifty-three. Have to insure the participation of broad societal segments; it's cross country after all."

Orders are orders.

"When do I get my per diem?"

"Are you serious?"

"Of course. . . . This is the 10-K you're sending me on. . . ."

"You're going at your own expense," he said. "We'll reimburse you later."

My department head pointed to the door.

My wife and I didn't sleep a wink all night, making preparations for my trip. My wife cried. We had everything. We had lived together for thirty-three years. . . . Betrayals, infatuations, exudative pleurisy, the silver wedding anniversary. . . . We still had plans to live to our heart's content. I had some specific plans regarding that.

Who could have guessed that our life would be so cruelly disrupted by the dread 10-K. . . .

By morning my suitcase was packed.

"Don't wear out your shirts," the old girl said. "Change them every day. . . ."

She packed some food in a picnic basket to last the early part of the trip.

"Here's chicken, a dozen eggs . . . meat loaf the way you like it . . . a thermos full of chicken soup, apple pie. . . . You can pick up anything else on the road. . . . ”

Then we parted. The old girl cried uncontrollably. My heart was heavy.

“Forgive me if anything was amiss,” I said with a tremor in my voice. “Whatever else, we’ve had a good life together. . . .”

“Don’t forget to write,” she said. “Don’t worry about me . . . . The main thing is to return victorious. . . .”

At ten A.M. the next day, at Reutovo railway station, I had number 184 pinned to my chest, and I shoved off from the starting line.

Regaining my composure after the initial shock, I saw some of my colleagues and a slew of coworkers that I hardly knew sliding to the right and left, behind and in front of me. Each had a number on his chest.

“Tired yet?” I asked number 12 when we reached the 8-meter mark.

“Still hanging in. . . .”

“I’m about ready to fall flat on my face.”

“Don’t give up, old guy,” came the encouragement from number 12. “They say we’re going to get our second wind soon.”

About 3 P.M., as we entered a forest, number 200 fell on the snow, mowed down mercilessly. He begged us to leave him behind and keep moving forward.

We picked him up, resuscitated him, tied him to number 95, and set out again. . . .

Once, at dawn, number 70 suddenly took the lead. “What are you doing?” we called out.

“I have to be home by Friday,” he tossed back at us. “My wife’s having a birthday.”

The poor devil must have lost his sense of time, because it was already Sunday. For a good three weeks yet his slope-shouldered back marked number 70 could occasionally be glimpsed far ahead, serving the rest of us as a trail marker. But finally even it vanished behind the trees. . . .

We kept pushing forward, heedless of all obstacles.

“When did you last get a letter from home?” number 50 asked me, fiercely working his poles.

“Too long ago,” I answered despondently, shoving on as hard as I could. “My wife writes that everything’s fine at home. She’s retired now. Our grandson has started school. . . . They’re building a new subway in our town. . . .”

"Yeah," number 121 sighed wistfully. "It's probably summer where I live. . . . Probably hot . . . birds are singing . . . ." He brushed off a tear.

Before the meet, number 92 had been a math professor and a confirmed bachelor, but still a great admirer of the female sex.

"I've heard that there's a women's meet taking place not far from here," he waggishly whispered to me at one point. "How about it? We'll catch up later. . . ."

"Where's your team spirit?" I said.

"Up to you," he rumbled and started shaving. . . . I didn't see him again.

We were about to undertake a difficult three-meter ascent, and as we approached I managed to make a few final notes in my journal, which was now in its ninth notebook since the start of the meet. . . .

Oddly enough, I got used to the skis and my new life. The image of my old girl was still in my mind, but now it looked smudgy and unreal. . . . My premeet life in general seemed like a distant dream, not quite pleasant, but not unpleasant either.

Number 2, the curator of our field library, said all the indicators were that we would reach the finish line by next spring. . . .

. . . And there's the band playing at the finish line. The March sun shines blindingly. Somebody presents us with expensive prizes and certificates. It's over. It's over. . . . A young, beautiful, fiendishly well-built girl throws herself at me. I look at her and suddenly recognize my old girl. Yes, it's her. As she was thirty-three years ago, on the eighth day of our acquaintance.

"Seryozhka," she cries. "I'm so glad that you came. I've bought two tickets to the movies. . . ."

Holding hands, the two of us rush off to the movies. I've just passed my certification exam, and we're going to get married in the summer. . . . We're young. We have a long and wonderful life ahead of us. . . .

I'm still unaware that thirty-three years from now, in my sunset years, I'll take up a sport that will bring back my youth.

Before You Go

Once, I remember, I ate a cabbage roll and suddenly felt I was about to die.

So I told the woman with whom I had somehow managed to live my whole life, "Listen, I'm most likely going to die soon."

"When?" she asked.

"I wouldn't be surprised if it happened Thursday."

"What's today?"

"Monday."

She grew gloomy and mournful. Then, when she had overcome her deep spiritual grief, she asked firmly, "Did you cash your paycheck?"

"Sure," I answered.

"Let's have it."

I put it on the table.

She counted the money and gave me a disappointed look. "Where's the other six rubles?"

"I took it," I answered timidly. "Just in case. . . . For a beer, ice cream. . . . Maybe we could go to the movies. I do have two days left."

"Selfish," she said. "Why can't you spend your last two days with your family? Let's have the rest. You think I'm going to spend it on myself? You know it'll just be spent on you anyway."

I gave her my last six rubles. "You and I need to talk about this. I'd like to be buried in decent, liveable conditions."

"Don't expect an orchestra," she said.

"Don't exaggerate. It never entered my mind to pay for a whole orchestra. I've arranged for Kolya from number 12 to play his accordion; he'll be glad to do it for five. He's taking his discretionary day on Thursday. The main thing is to decide who we want to invite."

She smiled. "You don't invite your friends. Your friends are supposed to remember these things."

"Sure, but how are they supposed to find out?"

"Pick up the phone and call."

"That's what I'm saying. For me, I'd like to see my folks, Petya and Zina, Lyusa and her husband, then we'll need to invite Nina Ivanovna from Kiev, the people at work. Then there's your mother, Veronika, the Satanovskys, Uncle Abessalom from Sukhumi."

"It would be rude not to invite the Kozovskys," she interrupted.

"I can't stand them."

"You won't have to."

"You're right, sorry. We'll move the coffin out at five, or else it will be too hot."

"Before I forget, remember to invite Kruplova and her wrestler boyfriend," she said.

"Whatever for?"

"You think I'm going to carry that coffin?"

"But they'll know that we invited them for that. . . ."

"Don't tell them what it's for, just let them come and be surprised."

She got a sheet of paper and started to draw up a guest list.

"Comes to forty-two people; we have to trim it back," she said irritably.

"Shame on you. These people are coming to pay their last respects."

She utterly lost her composure. "Last respects? Easy for you to say. I'm the one who'll have to feed all that rabble." She began to cry.

"Calm down," I said. "I'm not dying to cause you problems. It's just worked out this way. Let's work on the menu."

She stopped crying. "You don't trust me?"

"I trust you, I just don't want to have nothing but cheese sandwiches again."

"What do you mean, again?"

"Like at my birthday party. I want this to be a big, elegant spread."

"I know what I'll make," she said. "I'll make beans Georgian style."

"Beans give me heartburn," I said, grimacing.

"What do you have to do with this?"

We spent a long time negotiating the menu, and then I asked to be laid out in my blue serge suit.

"You would have to take the only nice one, wouldn't you?" she let burst. "It's up to you, of course, but I can't understand why you have to show off."

"And what would you have me wear?"

"Anything. How about your sweatsuit? What difference does it make?"

"None, to you. It's not your funeral."

I went to the closet just to be safe.

She was watching my actions closely.

"Okay. . . . I've got my tie, handkerchiefs, passport, lighter. . . . "

"You won't need the lighter. It's not a business trip," she rightly observed.

I put the lighter back.

"We'll need to surrender the passport, too."

I handed it to her.

"Please don't worry so much," I said. "Don't cry, everything will be fine. But let me warn you, if that brother of yours gets up at the funeral and calls me a bloodsucking parasite in front of everyone, I'll sit up and spit in his face."

"You're capable of anything," she said.

I gave her a hug. "Listen, honey. We've only got two days till Thursday. Let's make them enjoyable."

She looked up at me with frightened eyes. "Wait a minute. Till Thursday? I've got a fitting scheduled for Thursday. Can't you hold out till Friday?"

"Unfortunately I sense that it's going to happen on Thursday."

We started bickering again. And I suddenly felt that it was going to happen on Wednesday instead of Thursday.

She was pleased.

Children came running in. Lots of them. Ours, others', the neighbors'.

"What about the zoo?" they fidgeted. "How about the bike? How about the toy sword?"

"Kids," I shouted, "stop this ruckus. We have a whole day. We'll get it all done."

What can you do? Usually we draw broad, sweeping conclusions at the end of our lives. This happened in my case, too.

One should never leave anything to the last day.

Family squabbles can shorten your life, even if only by a day.

—Tuesday, 11:59 P.M.

Vagrich Bakhchanian

Vagrich Bakhchanian, in his autobiography written in Vienna in 1974: "I was born in Kharkov twenty-seven years after the culmination of the Great October Socialist Revolution, started school in the same year as the capitulation of fascist Germany, began my working career soon after the death of Stalin. I was drafted into the ranks of the Soviet Army twenty years after 1937. I received my discharge after the ninetieth anniversary of Vladimir Ilich Lenin's birth. I moved to Moscow six years prior to the demise of Marshal of the Soviet Union Semyon Mikhailovich Budyonny. In the decisive year of the ninth five-year plan I left the USSR." "Man" appeared in 1971 in *Literary Gazette*.

Man

Man was young, healthy, strong, sturdy, life-affirming, robust, energetic, active, committed, industrious, well qualified, educated, intelligent, bright, wonderful, nice, kind, honest, sincere, open, modest, inspired, established, musical, frugal, unselfish, selfless, untiring, sociable, hospitable, gallant, generous, open-minded, well bred, decent, naive, unkempt, insignificant, limited, silly, unrefined, ingratiating, petty, ugly, mean, base, cowardly, cruel, deceptive, cunning, vengeful, old. . . .

Vladlen Bakhnov

———————

———————

———————

———————

Vladlen Efimovich Bakhnov (b. 1924 in Kharkov, Ukraine) graduated
from the Gorky Literary Institute in Moscow in 1949. He is a free-lance
writer living in Moscow, the author of a number of screenplays and
books of poetry and prose. Much of his work is markedly satirical and
fantastic, but as Bakhnov himself observes, "Reality far outstrips my
fantastic creations and ideas." "The Sleep Walker" appeared in 1968 in
Literary Gazette.

The Sleep Walker

The elderly but still quite purple der Esss, publisher of the daily science fiction magazine "The Sleep Walker," was hurriedly sleeping out
the last episode of a new story line.

He had just opened his eyes when he thought to contact the author,
the well-known fantasy writer der Elll.

"I'm afraid it's not going to be quite so simple, der Esss," his quite
blue secretary der Errr thought to him in reply. "You see, he advised us
that he was planning to take a vacation on the moon, but he didn't
specify which one."

"Good grief, aren't you familiar with the theory of probability?"

"Of course I am."

"Then use it in this case," the publisher thought angrily and signed
out.

"Der Elll is on the wave-length," he picked up a few minutes later
from his secretary.

"Fine. Connect us, would you?"

"Hello, der Esss," the writer linked up.

"Oh, der Elll, glad to be bringing you in. How's your vacation going?"

"Fine, thanks. There's excellent weather here on the eleventh moon. I'm sensing that you already slept through my story line."

"Most certainly did, der Elll. You know I always like to sleep through your works before all the others. But I have to admit that this new one had me a bit puzzled."

"Why is that?" the writer thought, surprised.

"Der Elll, let me be perfectly frank with you." The publisher knew that the writer had one major idiosyncracy—he couldn't stand it when people were overly familiar with him and he allowed no one, except for his mothers and wives, to call him simply Ell, let alone just El. This is why the old publisher called him by his full name—Elll. "I'd like to share some of my doubts with you, der Elll."

"I am sensing."

"We've been working together for quite some time now, and I trust that you won't accuse me of impatience, deviousness, or conservatism."

"Absolutely not!"

"Fine. It seems to me that logic should figure in any work of science fiction."

"Are you implying that my story line . . ." the writer started to think, but Esss immediately cut him short in his thoughts.

"That's just it. I realize that the events you describe take place outside of our solar system, perhaps even in a different galaxy. I realize that the sentient creatures you have invented may be totally unlike us. But these, these . . . What do you call them? Plippos?"

"Peoples . . ."

"That's right, peoples. Unusual name, I rather like it. Well, then, if these peoples of yours really looked the way you've described them, they would have had to perish in the course of the evolutionary process. And perish not long after they appeared, I dare think."

"Why is that?"

"Because the fittest survive. And it's as though you made your peoples helpless and defenseless on purpose. Judge for yourself. Each people has only two sight organs, both of which are located in the same plane for some reason, on the front side of what you call the head. That just can't be. How do these peoples of yours know what's happening behind them? Their rear is totally undefended, and that in itself is reason enough for them to have become extinct. Let's go on. Your peoples fashion their own work implements. They make them with the help of their upper extremities, is that right?"

"Yes."

"But you'll recall that when we have to plane, drill, or hammer nails, we do that using a minimum of two upper extremities, and we hold the object we are working on in the others. And here your peoples only have two upper extremities. That's too few for performing any kind of useful labor. Furthermore, as we all know, in order for a three-dimensional body to be firmly positioned it must have at least three resting points. These creatures of yours only have two, so that the slightest blow can knock them off their lower extremities. So what do we have? Only one pair of light perceptors, one pair of upper extremities, and one pair of the lowers. This is ingeniously creative, but extremely improbable. But, my dear der Elll, this is not really what's bothering me."

"Then what is?" the writer thought impatiently.

"It's this: This planet you've invented has a rather developed civilization. But you'll have to admit that in order for a civilization to exist, its members have to be able to communicate with each other, exchange information, and so on."

"Indisputably."

"But don't you see there has to be some kind of constant communication between them? Your peoples are separated from each other, and consequently any communication is impossible."

"Oh, no, they do communicate."

"I beg your pardon. How can they communicate if they don't have any telepathic link?"

"But you must admit that in other worlds a different, non-telepathic kind of link could exist."

"What, precisely?"

"Der Esss, I thought you'd slept through my story line. It's all there. Peoples converse. Conversation is a variety of communication by means of an acoustic link."

"Oh, come on, der Elll, you can't be serious. What kind of communication is that—conversation? And to be honest with you, I couldn't quite see how this acoustic link of yours could work."

"Let me explain. Imagine that each of us had a speech organ and an acoustic organ. In order to relay information to you, I would have to transform my thoughts into words and then, by means of the speech organ, cause disturbances in the air with these words. This would form sound waves which would spread and eventually reach your acoustic organ. From there the waves would be reanalyzed as words and the information I was conveying to you would be sent to your brain. Your brain would process the words and you would respond by causing air disturbances with sound waves which would be transformed. . . ."

"My God, all these transformations! Do you see how entangled this entire hypothetical acoustic link of yours has gotten?" Tiring from the strain, der Esss took out a cigar and felt his pockets for a match.

"Here you are," the writer offered, and a flat, silver lighter appeared in the publisher's hand.

"Thank you," der Esss thought as he lit the cigar, and he tele-transported the lighter back to the writer. "Yes, I'm sure it must be very complicated, this thing you call conversation. And totally unreliable. You and I can exchange thoughts directly, and even at that, you some-times don't quite get my drift, or vice versa. Or our thoughts reach their destination distorted due to some atmospheric disturbance or other. Just imagine how distorted a thought can get if it goes through this acoustic link! Why, it could be distorted to the point of unrecog-nizability on account of all these transformations alone. And that, I should think, is sufficient to rule out the possibility of any kind of exchange of thoughts by means of conversation."

"I agree that telepathic links are simpler and more reliable," der Elll thought. "But you must allow that the peoples are incapable of using a telepathic link."

"I don't quite follow what there is to be capable of. But if these peoples are incapable of that, then that means they can't exist."

"What are you implying?"

"I'm implying nothing. I'm thinking it. I have already sufficiently proved to you that normal communication is impossible with this so-called acoustic link. And where there is no communication, there is no society. And where there is no society, there cannot be a civilization. And without a civilization, these civilized beings that you call peoples cannot exist, either. Are we in agreement?"

"But I'm not a science writer, I'm a science fiction writer."

"Absolutely. Tell me, why is it your fans like you so much? Pre-cisely because your story lines have always been marked by a convincing verisimilitude, an uncanny authenticity, and at the same time you've always had a proclivity for these daring flights of irrepressible fancy. Your last story line doesn't have that."

"What do you suggest I do?"

"Oh, I'm not the one to be giving you advice, der Elll. But I'm confident that if you keep working on it, this story will shape up, too."

A few days later the story was finished and released. The strange reasoning creatures that the writer called peoples had four pairs of organs of sight (one in front, one behind, one on top, and one on the bottom). They also had three pairs of upper and two pairs of lower extremities. The peoples communicated by means of a telephonopathic link that differed from the usual kind only in that it relied on wires. Science fiction lovers everywhere slept through this new story in raptures and thought to each other in delight:

"My God, that Elll makes his stories so believable! You could really think that der Elll himself had actually been on that planet with those, those . . . what are they called—peoples?"

Andrey Bitov

Andrey Georgievich Bitov (b. 1937 in Leningrad) is a prominent contemporary Russian prose writer. He graduated from the Leningrad Mining Institute in 1962 and has been a free-lance writer since the early 1960s. His most acclaimed novel, *Pushkin House*, was published in English translation in 1987. Two collections of his stories have appeared in English translation: *Life in Windy Weather* (1986) and *A Captive of the Caucasus* (1992). "Someone Else's Dog" was published in 1968 in *Literary Gazette*.

Someone Else's Dog

At work I received a reprimand. My neighbors declared a boycott. My wife ran off with my best friend. Of course, I can go to my aunt's and take her dog for a walk. . . . It's you-know-who's birthday today—I mean the dog's. My aunt will bake a cake.

The dog is a young, heavy boxer. Still, I don't have anything against him. A powerful beast. When he walks, he wags the stub of his tail and yanks on the leash. I have to hold him back the whole time, and it's like running downhill. From a middle-class point of view his face leaves something to be desired. I think he's a fine animal.

So I put on dark glasses and I take old yellow for a walk down Nevsky.

And they say about him, "Ooohhh, Churchill, you devil! What a misanthrope. . . ."

And they say about me, "Look at the owner. . . . He's even got dark glasses."

And one of them says, "Poor boy. . . . So young and already blind."

And a kid shouts, "I want a doggie, pleeease buy me a doggie."

And someone says, "Why don't you put a muzzle on your dog?"

And I think, "Why don't I put one on you?"

So I walk down the street in my dark glasses with the boxer. And I feel attached to him. The dog probably wouldn't even have noticed that guy. He doesn't pay attention to anyone. Apparently he lives in his own dog's world, and I'm not allowed there. I respect him for that. He and I could get along. But he's not interested in my world, smart beast! With a thinker's forehead. And what eyes. Everyone should have eyes like that.

People glance at him—at me, at me—at him. But he's not fazed, just keeps dragging me on. Focused and intent in all things. It looks like he has someplace to go. He's probably ashamed to show that he's just out for a walk. . . .

And here I am, walking the dog. . . .

It's the dog's birthday today. . . . My aunt will bake a cake. . . .

Then again, I don't have to go to my aunt's.

Boris Briker and Anatoly Vishevsky

Boris Lvovich Briker and Anatoly Mikhailovich Vishevsky (both b. 1954 in Chernovtsy, Ukraine) attended high school and college (Chernovtsy University) together, majoring in Russian and English literature, respectively. Both writers emigrated from the USSR, Vishevsky in 1979 to the United States and Briker in 1980 to Canada. They received doctorates in Russian literature, and both teach, Briker at Rutgers University and Vishevsky at Washington University in St. Louis. In North America they have published both fiction and critical studies of Russian literature and humor. "Made in Heaven" was published in 1976 in *Iunost'*.

Made in Heaven

"I can't understand why people feel they have to elbow their way onto planes. Do they think they're going to take off without them?" a young man thought as he waited calmly, aloof from the nervous crowd.

When he climbed up the empty walkway to the airplane, there was only one seat still free. His seat. There was a young woman in the seat next to it.

"How the hell do these belts go on?" she thought as she bemusedly examined the strange contraption.

"No trick to it," he thought and casually inserted the belt into the buckle.

"Got himself comfy, and now I suppose he's going to start flirting," she thought, having finally figured out her seat belt.

"Everyone assumes that a guy and a girl flying together in an airplane have got to get acquainted. Just what I need. Though she does have nice legs . . . ," he thought as he opened his newspaper.

"Fresh!" she thought, tugging down the hem of her skirt and turning to look out the window. The plane was slowly ascending. Raindrops shivered across the glass. Looking down she could see squares of fields, triangles of gardens, ellipses of lakes, and two small towns. A truck was driving out of one of the towns, while almost simultaneously a person on foot was walking out of the opposite one in the direction of the truck.

"I wonder," she thought. "If the truck is going 35 miles per hour, and the pedestrian is going three, where will they meet?"

Absorbed in thought, the girl leaned back in her seat.

Then he looked out the window. The plane had risen over the clouds. Breaking out from behind a fluffy cloud, the sun suddenly splashed its rays in his face, and he shielded himself with the paper.

"I don't get it. Why fresh? Just because you like the way a girl looks, does that mean you're fresh?" he thought while reading the sports section.

"Do you really?" she thought and smiled at a child who was running up and down the aisle.

"Sure, why not? Everything's where it should be, and she likes kids, too," he thought, lowering the seat back.

"He's not such a bad fellow. Kind of cute . . . even reads newspapers. I just don't like these casual relationships," she thought as she scrutinized the No Smoking sign that had just lit up over the doorway.

"Nothing casual about it. Do you think you and I are sitting next to each other like this by chance?" he thought, and yawned.

"You'd think I'd never sat next to a stranger before in my life. But why am I so nervous?" she thought and sqeezed a fly against the window with one long fingernail. But she didn't kill it.

The airplane lurched, and his hand brushed against hers.

"What soft, warm hands she has. I wonder what she felt just now," he thought and took a salami sandwich out of his briefcase.

"He's nice," she thought and glanced at her compact mirror to see how her cheap Polish mascara was holding up.

"Now I'm going to kiss her," he thought.

"No, not here. There are people," she thought as she took a piece of candy from the stewardess's tray.

"Hmmm, the stewardess isn't bad, either," he thought as he smiled at the flight attendant and scooped up a handful of candy.

"Skirt-chaser!" she thought, and took a couple of dramamine in anticipation of landing. "Good thing I found that out in time."

"Where's this skirt-chaser business come from?" he thought as he unfastened his seatbelt. "Aren't I even allowed to smile in gratitude at the service personnel?"

"I'll forgive him. But he'll have to swear never to cheat on me again," she thought as she went down the stairway with two heavy suitcases.

"I swear," he thought, running down the stairs carrying his attaché case.

Then they walked down the street side by side, entered an underground passageway, turned a corner, and crossed under a square, emerging at a trolley stop.

"I love you. You're the one I've waited for all my life," she thought, shoving her two heavy suitcases into a number 12 trolley.

"I don't see how I could live without you," he thought as he hopped up onto the platform of a number 7 streetcar.

"I suspect we can end the story here," one author thought as he finished reading.

"Agreed," the other thought sadly.

Herman Drobiz

Herman Fyodorovich Drobiz (b. 1938 in Sverdlovsk, Russia) graduated from Ural Polytechnical Institute in 1960 and the Graduate Program of Directors and Screenwriters in Moscow in 1969. After working first as an engineer, then as a journalist, he became a free-lance writer in the mid-1960s. He is the author of collections of satirical stories and of numerous scenarios for animated and feature films. He considers that "besides the five senses that either nature or God has bestowed on man, any integral personality has to possess a sixth—the sense of humor. In humor, irony, and derision I see a manifestation of common sense, so lacking in our embittered society." "The Lamppost and the Tower" appeared in 1975 in *Iunost'*.

A Lamppost and the Tower

Dear Ostankino Tower,

Permit me to introduce myself. I am a lamppost at the Razuvaevka Station of the Eastern railroad and I would like to greet you most heartily. You probably receive many letters from such as I. If so, please excuse me. But I am not writing as a curiosity seeker to a celebrity, but rather for the purpose of asking you a serious question.

But first something about myself. I am a simple wooden lamppost employed by the power and light system. I illuminate the station platform. It's not difficult work. A 500-watt lamp under a tin shade is all my equipment. The station is a small one: a one-story building, a platform, and a garden with poplars. Life here runs strictly on schedule. At 2:00

A.M. the express train to Moscow passes through, and at 8:00 A.M. the express from Moscow. Neither one stops here. At 7:15 the local stops here for five minutes. It stops again at 2:50 P.M. on the way back. At 6:30 A.M. the commuter train pulls in. At 6:40 P.M. it stops here again on the way back. There's our entire schedule for you. However, please don't think that I am complaining about our life here, as uneventful as it may be. Folks here are nice, down-to-earth, and sincere—both the people and our kind, the lampposts. The people own televisions and thanks to you, dear Ostankino Tower, they watch all kinds of things on them. Sometimes they like to pace up and down the platform and discuss, so that even I keep more or less abreast of things.

But sometimes one can get really down, because here in Razuvaevka nothing ever happens.

It can be especially depressing when my lamp burns out, and Semyonov, the electrician, doesn't get around to replacing it for several days. Instead he stands next to me, in complete and utter darkness, kissing girls. He presses them up against me and kisses them. He also likes to sit with his friends in the garden at night and guzzle beer. I am just amazed, looking at him. I am young and he is young, but he doesn't dream about anything and still he's happy. I practically feel like I'm being split apart on those dark, quiet nights, it's so sad and lonely. I'd just like to break loose from here and take off into the blue. This leads me to the question that I've decided to ask you: Can I, a simple wooden lamppost, ever hope to become as famous and popular as you? Or is this just impossible? Please write me frankly and don't laugh at my letter. I am, after all, still young, fresh, only recently debarked. The older lampposts laugh at my dreams. I find their attitude repugnant and despicable.

As darkness awaits the light, I wait for you to write.

Most sincerely yours,

A lamppost.

Dear little lamppost,

Please excuse me for not writing sooner. Indeed, I receive a great many letters like yours.

What can I tell you? Of course the older lampposts are wrong. One has to dream. But as you dream, don't forget that even now you are engaged in interesting and somewhat creative work. You are bringing light to people, and consequently happiness, and in a sense even truth. Just consider how many people have walked down your platform without stumbling, thanks to you. Try to understand that one can be happy even on the platform of a modest, provincial train station, and not just in the capital. Yet one must dream, and there you are right.

Forgive me for being so brief. I am extremely busy. I have been broadcasting programs, I am being featured in a movie, I have been posing for photojournalists. Just now I am hosting a Belgian delegation on the observation deck, and any minute I expect to have a group of Japanese and Mexicans in my Seventh Heaven restaurant.

Warm regards,

Your Tower.

Dear Ostankino Tower,

I received your letter a long time ago, but hesitated to reply due to your heavy schedule. Still, I would like to continue our correspondence, provided it hasn't bored you.

You write how eventful your life is—all those Belgians, Japanese, and Mexicans. We don't have anything like that here. But you are of course right when you say that my work is beneficial to people. Recently a girl who was hurrying to catch a train dropped her change, but thanks to my light she was able to recover all of it, to the last coin. True, she missed her train.

But I must tell you frankly that my dreams seem less and less attainable, and I feel oppressed as ever by this immobility. It's only twenty yards from me to the station, but I will never see what's there, behind it, on the other side. Maybe it's nothing special, but when you can't see it, you imagine all kinds of wonderful things, and you get even more depressed.

Semyonov the electrician got married. One night recently he came onto the platform and started banging his head against me. Please, I beg you, answer me. For me your letters are like a voice from a world that I still dream about, though I'm not sure why I bother anymore. I'm not so young anymore. I've dried out, gotten discolored, and hardened.

I remain sincerely yours,

Your lamppost.

My dear lamppost,

Forgive me once again for the delay in answering you. I've had quite a bit of work to do and my correspondence is immense. But your letters touch me, and I want you to understand that I really do take your situation to heart. Don't lose heart, and do not hesitate to write me. If I don't answer this year, then definitely I will some year soon. Sorry, must go now. I just got a call and will have to link up with Paris.

Chin up.

Best wishes,

Your Tower.

Dear Tower,

It's been such a long time since I wrote, and really, what is there left to write about? I have to laugh when I think of the nonsense that I used to profess when I was young and that you encouraged in me when you advised me to hold firm and have faith. There was a time when I laughed at the old lampposts' fear of leaving their accustomed places. Now I'm older and I understand that nothing good can come of it if all lampposts suddenly decided to become Ostankino Towers. Who needs that many towers? But lampposts are needed, and lots of them. It has taken me years to reach this realization, and now I am truly happy.

We're experiencing changes here, both good and bad. The primary change for the good is that they've torn down the old station and built a beautiful glass one.

There's other news, too. Some new guys have started working in our power and light system. These are a completely different kind of post, if you can imagine it, not wooden but concrete. They're doing a fine job, I can't deny it. But if only you could hear how they drone at night. We never ever droned like that.

I suspect that at long last you will be satisfied with one of my letters, since, as you can see, my worries are over.

Respectfully,

Your lamppost.

P.S. Semyonov the electrician has left his wife. He beat his head against a post again, but not against me. He used one of the new, concrete ones.

My dear, old friend,

It seems as though I'm late with every answer to your letters. There's more and more work, and I'm not getting any younger, either.

Let me say frankly, your last letter disappointed me greatly. You are mocking the dreams of your own youth. What good is that? Everyone has dreams that never came true, even I do. There is a drama unfolding in each of us, but we must not allow it to turn into a tragedy. These thoughts are not exactly new with me; I'm writing under the influence of a discussion by a certain established playwright who recently appeared on one of my programs. Just this morning. I think he's right. Think about it, and don't be offended.

Yours,

The Tower

Dear sweet, old Tower,

Pardon my familiarity, but I'm writing you now for the last time. You're a fine one to pontificate about not all dreams coming true. There's an important difference here; just some of your dreams didn't come true, none of mine did. If, God forbid, anything should ever happen to you, the whole world would know about it. But no one except the inhabitants of Razuvaevka know what happened to me, and even they don't much care about it.

You may ask why I'm using this tone and why this should be my last letter. Well, it's because I no longer exist in my previous form, although I am still alive. There's a new concrete post standing in my place. You may ask where I am now. I'll tell you; in Semyonov's backyard. What am I doing there? How to explain it? . . . I've been chopped into kindling. The heating season here begins early, at the end of September, so if you answer before then, add this to the address— Semyonov's yard, second cord (from the fence).

Life is over. If there were any bright moments in it, then they were my correspondence with you.

Farewell. Forever yours, I don't even know how to sign this, "Forever yours, Firewood?" Funny, isn't it?

STATION RAZUVAEVKA EASTERN RAILROAD

IN CONNECTION BEGINNING HEATING SEASON EXPRESS DEEP GRIEF REGARDS TO DECEASED MY OLD FRIEND MODEST WORKER WOODEN LAMPPOST WISH WORKERS OF STATION SUCCESS IN WORK STOP

OSTANKINO TOWER

Nikolay Elin and Vladimir Kashaev

Nikolay Lvovich Elin (b. 1921 in Dnepropetrovsk, Ukraine) moved at age two with his family to Moscow, where he still lives. He received his engineering degree in Moscow in 1939 and served in the Soviet Army during World War II. A free-lance writer since 1958, he has authored numerous books, including some for children.

Vladimir Grigorevich Kashaev (b. 1940 in Moscow) graduated from Moscow Pedagogical Institute in 1964, the year that he left his career as a physics and mathematics teacher to become a free-lance writer. He has published several books of stories, most of them in collaboration with Elin. "In the Woods" appeared in 1977 in *Literary Gazette*.

In the Woods

Gleb Nikolaevich Shlykov got lost in the woods. He was hunting for mushrooms and he got lost. It could happen to anybody. And so he panicked and set out blindly, anything to keep moving. He walked for a long time; a very long time; and constantly in the wrong direction. Finally he came straight to the edge of a swamp and sat down beside it to catch his breath. And he saw a bush with some kind of berries growing on it. They might have been boysenberries, or they might have been black cherries—Gleb Nikolaevich didn't have time to figure that out, he was too hungry. He pulled off the biggest, ripest berry and swallowed it so fast that he didn't even taste it. Suddenly, in that same instant his head felt heavy, as though it were New Year's. He was also suddenly thirsty. As Shlykov slid down toward the swamp, he caught a glimpse of his reflection in the water and gasped. His reflection had antlers, big, branchy antlers like a genealogical tree. And one of the antlers was even broken at its tip, as though Gleb Nikolaevich had caught it on the edge of a cabinet or maybe butted an enemy with it.

Shlykov rubbed his eyes, but the antlers were still there. He shook his head back and forth, hoping they would drop off, but it didn't work. Probably the season for antlers to drop off hadn't yet started.

"Well," Gleb Nikolaevich thought, "shoot! I'm stuck, and for what? The berries weren't even that good. Damnation! Now how am I going to get home with these antlers? No way I can fit in the train with these things. And if I could, they'd probably make me pay an extra fare. Now I'll have to buy a new bed, and widen the neck on my sweater. What a nuisance."

As he thus pondered, he kept looking around for the broadest passage through the trees. Suddenly he saw yet another bush, with a different kind of berries. The others had been orange, but these were brick red.

"Maybe I should try these, too," Shlykov hesitated. "All or nothing. Either I lose the antlers or grow hooves. Maybe I'll even start mooing. What if I start with just half a berry. That's not taking too much of a risk."

He went up to the bush and bit off half of one berry. Immediately one of Gleb Nikolaevich's antlers vanished. His head even tipped to one side. Shlykov was overjoyed, and he unhesitatingly sped the other half into his mouth. In an instant he reverted to his former, antlerless self. There weren't even any bumps left on his head.

Shlykov was amazed at this state of things. He carefully felt all over his head; he looked at himself in the swamp; and when he had calmed down, he tried to think of what to do next and of what kind of use he could make of these wonder-working berries. Of course, they were not a flying carpet, or even seven-league boots, but even so, it might be possible to harness them for some use or other. He thought about them this way and that, but try as he would, he could think of no tangible way he could use them for himself.

"All right," Gleb Nikolaevich said to himself. "I don't need them anyway. What I'll do is feed them to my enemies. That'll give them something to remember me by."

He poured all the mushrooms out of his basket and filled it to the top with berries from the first tree, without even glancing at the second.

"They're no lords of the manor," he thought. "These will suit them fine; they've probably got just as many vitamins as the others."

He heaved the basket onto his shoulder, turned, and marched off in the direction he had come. He walked and thought about who he would treat to his berries.

"First thing," he decided, "I'll slip some to Yardov. The year before last he called me a buffoon. Let's see him dance now. Oboznikov is a good candidate, too. He's been trying so hard to get a promotion. Before you know it he'll get one, but who would promote him if he had antlers? With antlers he couldn't make it higher than senior draftsman. Let's not forget to acknowledge Shaparov, too. Always coming over to borrow my tape player when he has guests. They like to dance, don't you know. Though they couldn't care less that they could practically wreck the machine each time. Fine, Shaparov, you won't feel like dancing now."

And in this way Shlykov so completely lost himself in reveries that he didn't even notice that he had come out of the woods and up to the train station. He boarded the commuter train and within twenty minutes was back in town. By then he had already made a list of seventy-two candidates. As he was riding in the streetcar he ticked off another forty-three. He got off at his stop elated and excited. While he walked down the street he kept worrying that he had overlooked someone. And suddenly he saw a consignment store, and in the window—what do you know—there was a set of antlers! Exactly like the pair that Gleb Nikolaevich had tried on in the forest. Well, maybe just a little smaller and not quite as branchy, but still very similar. Underneath them there was a price tag, "40 rubles."

No sooner had Shlykov seen the price tag than he lost his breath. Forty rubles? Forty rubles!?! Suddenly he felt weak, his head started spinning, and all the candidates went flying out of it. And a very good thing they did! What kind of blunder had he been on the verge of making? Give away forty rubles to a bunch of good-for-nothings? Apiece?! Just think! A mighty fine thing that he caught himself in time. Sorry, pals, you're gonna see this money the same day you see your . . .

Gleb Nikolaevich chortled sadistically, grabbed two big fistfuls of berries out of the basket and without losing a minute propelled them into his mouth.

Anatoly Gladilin

Anatoly Tikhonovich Gladilin (b. 1935 in Moscow) is an alumnus of Gorky Literary Institute. He was one of the founders of the Young prose movement of the 1960s. He published a number of novels and collections of stories before emigrating from the Soviet Union to France in 1976. He continues to write in emigration. His novel *Moscow Racetrack* came out in English translation in 1990. "The Double" was published in 1967 in *Literary Gazette*.

The Double
(from the Brazilian Stories)

My friend looked a little embarrassed. "You know," he said, leading me into the living room, "that can happen to anyone, but I must admit that I didn't expect it from you. Sure, the fact that you got as shitfaced as you did—I'd never seen that in you before—but it was bound to happen sometime. And nobody could understand why you had to throw a bottle at poor old Gaspar. And then you smashed up our family china. . . . Maybe some people find that amusing, but you know that I've got money problems. But when you started putting the moves on my daughter in front of my guests, that's where you went too far, amigo."

You can imagine how floored I was.

"You're out of your mind, friend," I exclaimed. "Just when am I supposed to have done all this?"

"What do you mean when?" he was puzzled. "You were here all last evening."

I was incensed.

"If you want to play a trick on me, you had better try again. I was home all yesterday evening. My wife and mother-in-law can vouch for me."

My friend blushed a bright red.

"You mean, that wasn't you? I thought I noticed something strange. That jerk behaved so totally different from you that for a moment there I thought . . . But damned if he isn't a dead ringer for you. Dressed just like you, used all the same words."

My God, I had a double!

From then on my life became a living hell.

This person began to visit my friends, go to my cafes. He even spent a night with senhorita Silvia, and he left his dirty tracks everywhere. At the cafes he never paid his checks, and he borrowed money from the waiters. He caused scenes at my friends' houses, and he offended senhorita Silvia's most refined sensibilities. Somehow he managed to sneak through to my boss and spill an entire bottle of ink in his lap.

Then, after a multitude of humiliating scenes and attempts on my part to set things straight, the waiters, my friends, and my co-workers finally seemed convinced that it wasn't me. They usually apologized, said it was all right, said it really was a shame, said it would be unpleasant if I had changed so suddenly for the worse.

But my double continued to get himself in trouble. Whenever my friends met him, they still kept taking him for me.

This is when I started to hunt down my double. I set out all kinds of traps. Once I almost caught up with him when he provoked an ugly fight on our street with a retired general, dom Miguel. That time I showed up literally one second after my double had struck his last blow against dom Miguel. All my neighbors saw me running after my double, but that creep managed to hail a taxi, and there were no other taxis in sight.

Lying awake late at night, I would make all kinds of plans for how I would catch this jerk. I became more and more puzzled by the behavior of my friends and acquaintances.

Everyone knows that I'm an absolute teetotaler, a good family man, and a conscientious worker. I've never in my life borrowed money from anyone, and I never raise my voice to anyone, no matter how heated the argument. Then why were all my loving friends so willing to attribute the immoral acts of my double to me?

My double did not desist from his activities, quite the contrary. He introduced more variety into them. He committed more and even fouler deeds. Again everyone was taking him for me. My tireless efforts to catch the slime in the act were in vain.

There are times when I'd like to give up the search. After all, the existence of a double could be of some benefit to me. I can borrow money and not return it, stiff waiters in cafes, get drunk, seduce women, and be disrespectful to my superiors. Then I can blame it all on him. I can embezzle large sums of the company's money, and then everyone will believe that it was my double who did it. And I need the money. I have three children, and I haven't had a raise for some time.

Unfortunately I just can't bring myself to do it. I am the same person that I've always been. Could it be my upbringing that gets in the way?

Meanwhile my double gets away with murder.

Only at times, when I am so revolted and disgusted by the baseness of it all, I give in, and I swear to myself that beginning next Monday I will try to change my behavior.

Vladimir Gonik

Vladimir Semyonovich Gonik (b. 1939 in Kiev) completed his medical studies in Riga in 1963. He has been a free-lance writer in Moscow since 1969, and in 1971 he earned a further degree in screenplay writing from the National Institute of Cinematography. He has published collections of stories and longer prose and has written several screenplays. "A Malady" appeared in 1970 in *Literary Gazette*.

A Malady

They had been expecting the doctor. The young, attractive woman of the house, her face red from crying, led him through the brightly lit apartment to her husband's bedside.

"Fine, fine . . . Have a seat, doctor," the patient said from his bed. "God, I hope you'll forgive us for inconveniencing you like this. You do understand, don't you? There wasn't much choice."

"It's all in a day's work," the doctor said encouragingly, but with restraint. "What seems to be the matter?"

"I've lost my individuality," the patient answered, wincing.

"When did this start?"

"Two days ago. So I stayed in bed, tried the usual home remedies— my wife bought vodka. It didn't help."

"There's the problem right there," the doctor said with some irritation. "You should have called me right away. You're sure it wasn't something you ate?"

The patient shrugged.

"Tell me what illnesses you've had."

"Only the usual childhood ones—measles, mumps, whooping cough. I sprained my ankle once."

"And how did you come down with this? Please think back."

"I can't for the life of me figure it out. . . ."

"Please try. I'm listening," the doctor said, and he pulled out a stethoscope and hung it around his neck.

"I guess it all started back when I got my first job. All my friends were doing the same kind of thing at their jobs as I was."

"Sorry. Open wide," the doctor interrupted. The sick man opened his mouth and stuck out his tongue.

"Not coated," the doctor thought. "Go on," he said. "What else did you notice?"

"Nothing, back then. It's only now, when I think about it. . . ."

"Go on. I'm listening."

"My apartment."

"What about it?"

"It turned out to be just like everybody else's."

"Just a second. . . ."

The doctor listened to the palpitating of the patient's heart. It proved to be normal. He inserted the earphones in his ears and placed the stethoscope against the patient's chest. "Beating clearly. No murmur," he thought. His breathing was clear, there was no congestion. "Please go on," the doctor said distractedly.

"Then I found out everyone had the same kind of furniture."

"Maybe it's the liver," the doctor thought. He tapped it, then kneaded it under the ribs on the right side. "No, it's not enlarged."

"Everyone had the same books, too," the patient said. "I'd say that's when my ailment set in. I kept writing it off to fatigue or a cold. I kept meaning to go see a doctor, but there just wasn't any time."

"Why is it people think they can ignore an illness, then just get cured?" the doctor said sternly.

The sick man gave a shamefaced smile.

"I'm amazed," the doctor continued. "Here you are, living in town, one street away from any kind of medical service you could want, all sorts of specialists. It's all free, it's all available. I assume you've been to college, but you'll forgive me, this is incredibly backward."

The patient was silent and clearly depressed. The water pipes in the kitchen could be heard whining and clanking.

"Well, then. Let's go on," the doctor said. He had the patient lie on his back, and he kneaded his stomach. It was soft, no problems there. "What happened then?" he asked.

"I had all the same stuff as everybody else—clothes, habits, conversations. Even the same kind of wife."

"And how did you feel?"

"Horrible. Couldn't have felt worse."

"I see," the doctor said thoughtfully, tugging on the rubber ends of his stethoscope.

"I feel like it's going to be all over for me soon," the sick man said woefully.

"Oh, come on, now. Things aren't all that bad," the doctor hurried to say.

"Doctor," the sick man said resolutely, "tell me just one thing, and please be honest, man to man. Is it serious?"

The doctor hesitated a minute while he collected his thoughts. There was a long silence, and some indeterminate sounds could be heard coming from the depths of the apartment.

"I . . . can't say. The fact that you put off getting treatment complicates things quite a bit. But I'd say that. . . ."

The sound of a woman pacing nervously from one corner to the other came from the next room.

"How is your wife?" the doctor asked.

"She's fine. She says she's fine. Says her individuality hasn't suffered."

"How has she taken your illness?"

"She's tried to calm me. She tells me we can get by on just her individuality."

"What do you think?"

"I can't be hanging around her neck like that."

"Have any of your friends taken ill?"

"I don't know . . . ," the patient said doubtfully.

"We need to take preventive measures," the doctor thought, then said, "Don't despair. When everybody has some kind of individuality, then its absence in one person is actually a kind of . . . individuality in itself."

The sick man was struck dumb. He tried to take these words in.

"Doctor!" he finally exclaimed. "You're terrific. You've given me hope!"

"There now," the doctor slapped him on the arm congenially, but with a sufficient degree of reserve. "You did right to call. I'm going to prescribe some medicine for you to take for a while. . . ."

The doctor raised his head and suddenly realized what had bothered him about this patient. The man had no face.

The car drove down empty streets, past unlit houses. Their residents were sleeping peacefully, unaware of everything.

"But what if, God forbid, he comes in contact with anybody?" the doctor thought. "It could start an epidemic. We have to isolate him."

The yellow eye of a traffic light was flashing above a deserted intersection.

The doctor remembered the prescriptions he had written and decided they had been appropriate. He arrived back at his office and made an entry in his journal. Then he thought, "I should disinfect myself."

He threw all his clothes off, put them in the pressurized sterilizer and washed himself with alcohol long and painstakingly.

Grigory Gorin

————————

————————

————————

————————

Grigory Izrailevich Gorin (b. 1940 in Moscow) earned his M.D. in 1963 from Moscow Medical Institute and worked for several years as a supervising physician in Moscow emergency rooms. Since 1966 he has worked as a free-lance writer. He is the acclaimed author of several plays and collections of stories. Gorin is also well known as a screenwriter. "I have worked all my life in the genre of satire, but still I hope not to lose my sense of humor completely," Gorin writes. "Cut! Let's Call It a Day" appeared in 1967 in *Iunost'*; and "Kurentsov Unclad" in 1969, "Stop Potapov!" in 1972, and "The Dream" in 1968, all three in *Literary Gazette*.

Cut! Let's Call It a Day

That morning I awoke from the bright light of the sun. It was unusual somehow—white, blinding, geometrically round.

"It's going to be nice today," I thought. "Going to be hot."

It turned out to be not only a hot day, but a happy one. I had barely gotten out of bed when little triumphs began pouring on my head, one after the other.

First of all, my wife left me.

She had been planning to do it for a long time, but kept putting it off for one reason or the other. But this morning the great event took place.

"I'm leaving you," she said and began packing her bag. I said nothing.

"I'm leaving you, and there are no hard feelings," she repeated. "Of course, breaking up is difficult, but we've become strangers. Forget about me. I didn't know that I was in your way, that you had decided to change your life so."

Then she left, the door banging behind her.

I sighed with relief and went to the bathroom.

A pleasant, grinning man was looking at me from the mirror.

"Looking good, pal!" I told myself with a measure of self-satisfaction and picked up my toothbrush.

Only last night I had had an excruciating toothache.

Today the tooth calmly withstood cold water and shone with an even, pearly white gleam, a handsome accessory in my mouth.

Over my morning coffee, I opened the newspaper and, to my delight, discovered my article there.

The editor-in-chief had obstinately and stupidly refused to print it for several months, but today either his heart had softened or he had been fired.

Humming an upbeat tune, I put on my best gray suit and went outside.

In the courtyard I ran into the head of our housing cooperative.

"You put in a request to have your ceiling painted?" he asked.

"Absolutely," I confirmed. "Turned it in about a year ago."

"The painter will be there today at three o'clock," he said. By now it had gotten to the point that I received this pleasant news as nothing out of the ordinary. I shook his hand and went out on the street.

The street appeared to be unusually well tended and festive. Squeaky clean store-front windows were glinting. Music was playing. Sumptuously dressed people were walking to work. The street sweepers whistled happy tunes as they went about their work. A seven-year-old boy in velvet shorts was accompanying them on the flute.

On the corner a redheaded salesman with a mustache, dressed in a snow white apron, was selling mandarin oranges.

"This is nice!" I thought and beamed at the geometrically round sun. "This is incredibly nice!"

As I walked, I unexpectedly came across a bank.

I went in, picked up the list of winning lottery numbers from the counter, pulled my only lottery ticket out my pocket, and won a refrigerator.

At first I couldn't believe it. This was too much even for a lucky day. I double-checked the numbers. They were exactly the same, both the number and the letter prefix. I had won. And won not just anything, not a "PS-26 ballpoint pen," and not a "combed wool scarf," and not even a "Melody brand accordion (with case)." I had won a Dnieper-4 refrigerator, suggested retail price 275 rubles!

"I won't take the refrigerator," I thought. "I'll take the money instead. I'll take a vacation to the south or the Baltic. I hear the Carpathians are supposed to be pretty nice, too."

I opened my eyes and surveyed the place victoriously.

The bank was empty. Opposite me, behind his glass window, sat the only other person there, a pleasant, elderly cashier with a smile on his face. He was looking at me. With his whole being he displayed his readiness to pay me the sum indicated in the newspaper.

Just then the door slammed and four men entered the bank: two tall, lanky men wearing caps; another, medium height, wearing a hat; and a short one with a beret.

Both of the tall guys were holding guns, the one with the hat was holding a movie camera, and the short one wasn't holding anything.

"Take it easy, everybody," the beret said loudly. "Everybody please stay just where you are and act natural! We're filming a movie here! Scene ten—bank robbery. Rolling!"

The man with the hat aimed his lens at us and began whirring.

The tall men with the guns converged on the cashier. "Hands up!" one of them said hoarsely.

"What's going on?" the cashier whispered, going white. "What do you mean you're filming a movie? Nobody told me about this!"

"Hands up!" the tall guy repeated in a frightful rattle. "Move away from the counter!"

The cashier stood up, stumbled backward and raised his shaking hands.

One of the tall men opened the counter drawer, and the other one got a folded shopping bag out of his pocket and began stuffing money into it. A violent shiver ran through me as I watched what was going on.

"Just one minute, gentlemen," I said softly. "Do you have any ID?"

"Shut up!" one of the tall men shouted at me, waving his gun and then aiming it straight at my forehead.

I lost my balance and for the first time in my life felt the perpetual rotation of the earth on its axis beneath my soles.

"Terrific!" the man in the beret shouted. "He's genuinely afraid!" And he instructed the man in the hat, "Get a close-up of this."

The camera lens approached me and drilled at me for several seconds with its penetrating gaze. "Cut!" shouted the beret. "Let's do a retake, this time with the safe."

The tall guys grabbed some keys out of the cashier's pocket, opened the safe, and stuffed bills into a second shopping bag.

"Great!" the beret approved. "That's a print." All four of them immediately left the bank, making off with the shopping bags.

Motionless with horror, we watched in silence through the window as they hopped into a black Volga.

"Police! We've been robbed!" the cashier shrieked and ran to the door.

I ran after him.

The black Volga was slowly driving away from the bank. The right rear window was down and a camera lens was jutting out of it.

We had just come even with the car, when its front door flew open and the man in the beret leaned out.

"Good job of chasing!" he shouted to us. "Could you wave your arms and shout some more?"

"Police!" the cashier shrieked and waved his arms.

"Police!" I shouted and waved my arms, too.

"Good," the beret praised us. "Now shout, 'Get them!'"

"Get them!" the cashier and I shouted.

There was quite a crowd around. As I ran I noticed some curious eyes and smiling faces. No one made any attempt to stop the car.

"Citizens!" I shouted. "This is not a movie! These are real bank robbers! Stop them!"

Two girls laughed at this. One man comprehendingly nodded his head. The policeman on duty smiled and touched two fingers to his cap. The black Volga was driving down the middle of the street. Solicitous traffic cops were waving it through all the red lights. We ran behind the car, shouting at the top of our voices and waving our arms. The man in the beret, leaning out of the door to his waist, shouted encouragement to us.

To the right I suddenly caught sight of a policeman on a motorcycle with a sidecar. Another policeman was sitting in it.

"Hey!" I shouted as I ran up to them. "Stop that black Volga. This is no movie, it's a real bank robbery! They've stolen money!"

The policemen looked at me in disbelief, then smiled, then became serious and frowned. They gunned the motorcycle, which peeled out and darted down the street.

Soon they were even with the black Volga.

I heard shouts and gunshots. Then the Volga and the motorcycle vanished around a corner.

Without stopping to catch my breath, I chased after them, and when I turned the corner, I saw an enormous crowd.

Running up to the car, I realized that it was all over. The Volga had been forced onto the sidewalk, and all four robbers were standing with their hands up, looking fearfully at the policemen's guns. The cashier was running around, picking up scattered bills and stuffing them into a bag.

"So, the jig is up, friends," I exclaimed, elated.

The man in the beret glanced hatefully in my direction.

"Let's all get into the car," one of the policemen commanded the robbers. "You're going to have to come with us, too," he addressed the cashier.

"But I have to take the money back to the bank!" the cashier said.

"The money is material evidence," the policeman said. "Bring it along."

"I'm coming, too," I said. "I was a witness to the whole thing."

"Not necessary," said the policeman. "There's enough evidence as it is. Why don't you go home."

I'm not sure why, but I didn't like the way he responded. Neither did I like the way the policemen put the robbers in the car, nor the way they shoved the perplexed cashier into it. Not until one of the policemen winked conspiratorially at one of the tall guys did I understand the truth of this horrible riddle.

"Help!" I yelled at the crowd. "These are no policemen! They're all part of the same gang! They're in disguise! Get them!"

"Shut up!" one of the policemen shouted at me and flourished his pistol in front of my nose.

I seized the policeman by the arm. With his free arm he grabbed me by the collar.

The crowd groaned and moved in on us.

"CUT!!"

This was bellowed down from somewhere high above us by a loud and commanding voice.

The big, white, geometrically round sun was extinguished.

"CUT!! LET'S CALL IT A DAY! THE EXTRAS CAN GO HOME!"

The voice from above pronounced each word with unusual clarity. The crowd obediently dispersed.

"Drop your hands!" the policeman told me. "Drop your hands, you idiot. The shooting is over."

The robbers got out of the car and lit up cigarettes. The cashier bummed a cigarette from the man in the beret, lit it, and dropped the shopping bag full of bills on the ground.

"What's going on here?" I gasped in disbelief. "What is this all about?"

"Shooting's over!" the cashier said. "Break time. Are you going to go have lunch?"

I looked around me, at a total loss.

The shop windows faded, and the music stopped playing.

The passersby were taking off their sumptuous suits and turning them in at a small window marked with a sign that said "Props." The seven-year-old stood there crying, sadly holding out his flute and the velvet shorts.

The redheaded vendor was collecting his mandarins, packing them back up in crates, and nailing the crates shut.

"Just a minute!" I said in bewilderment. "How can this be? Wait a minute!"

I ran back to the bank, grabbed the list of lottery numbers, and pulled the lottery ticket out of my pocket.

My number wasn't on the list.

I double-checked it.

It wasn't there. Not the number, and not the letter prefix.

There was no Dnieper-4 refrigerator. Not even a "combed wool scarf." Or a "Melody brand accordion (with carrying case)." Or even a "PS-26 ballpoint pen."

Nauseous, my head spinning, I went home.

The morning newspaper was posted on the bulletin board outside my building. My article wasn't in it. There was a huge crossword puzzle where it had been.

The head of our housing cooperative met me in the courtyard.

"Don't hurry," he said. "No paint job today. The painter went on a binge."

Suddenly my tooth began to throb annoyingly.

Knitting my brow from the pain, I climbed the stairs and pushed open my apartment door. My wife was home.

Her cold, narrow eyes taunted me.

I laughed nervously.

"How can you laugh when your heart is breaking?" she mimicked a hit song and set about unpacking her suitcase.

"The shooting's over," I thought. "The shooting is over!" Without looking at my wife I went into the next room, fell face down on the couch, and burst into tears.

"CUT!!"

The commanding voice had come from somewhere close by.

I wiped my eyes and sat up.

The director was sitting across from me.

"Please, no tears," he said. "That's taking it too far. You were fine doing the emotions of someone who had mistaken real life for a movie set, but the crying is just too much. That's just melodrama."

"I'm tired," I said softly. "I'm very tired."

"Fine," he said. "Let's call it a day. Go rest up."

"Thanks," I said faintly and went to wash off my makeup.

Kurentsov Unclad

His Sunday was off to a wonderful start.

Vasily Mikhailovich Kurentsov woke up early, got up, had breakfast, put on his white nylon shirt, rolled up the sleeves, and took his wife Zinaida Ivanovna Kurentsov with him into town for a stroll.

"Look, they're selling something here," Zinaida Ivanovna said, and the couple hurried toward the line.

"Pardon me, do you know what this is?" Kurentsov asked a tall young man in a suede jacket, the last person in line.

"It's an exhibit," he answered.

"How do you mean?" Kurentsov puzzled. "An exhibit of what?"

"An art exhibit," the young man said, looking both Kurentsovs over, and then he added, "modern . . . art."

"How much is admission?" Zinaida Ivanovna queried.

"Twenty kopecks," the young man said. "Five for school children and servicemen." And he smiled wryly.

If it hadn't been for that wry smile, Kurentsov would of course never have gone to that ill-omened exhibit, because he had never had any interest in art. But that fellow's wry smile, as well as their venal little conversation about the twenty and the five kopecks, had hurt his pride.

Vasily Mikhailovich turned to his wife and asked, "Well, Zina, what do you think, shall we have a look?"

"Sure," Zinaida Ivanovna agreed instantly. "What else have we got to do but wander around town?"

There were lots of people in the gallery. They crossed the room from picture to picture, whispering to each other as they went. People were intently arguing in front of some pictures. The Kurentsovs did not join in the discussions. Vasily Mikhailovich led Zinaida Ivanovna by the hand, and they dutifully traversed the entire gallery, looking both ways. By and large Vasily Mikhailovich liked all of the paintings, especially the landscapes.

"We ought to put up some kind of picture at home," Vasily Mikhailovich said quietly to his wife. "I've gotten tired of looking at wallpaper."

"You're right," Zinaida Ivanovna agreed. "They have prints at the hardware store near home."

"There you go," Kurentsov enthused. "Maybe a landscape. With trees, a little meadow. . . ."

And as his arm described an uncertain arc in an attempt to show just what kind of meadow he'd like to have in his picture, he glanced in the direction his arm was pointing and was suddenly overcome with shock.

On a huge canvas hanging in the corner, Vasily Mikhailovich Kurentsov saw himself.

The painting was titled "Night Swim." It showed the shore of a river at night. The moon was shining. Two young kids were running naked to the river. A third person, about fifty years old, was still getting ready to swim. His boxer shorts were half down, exposing his left buttock with a huge black mole on it. The man's face was turned toward the viewer, and there was positively no doubt that it was Vasily Mikhailovich Kurentsov's face.

At first Kurentsov thought he was just seeing things, but one look at his wife's blood-drained face told him he had made no mistake.

"What on earth is that?" Zinaida Ivanovna gasped almost inaudibly. "Vasya, that's you . . . naked!"

At these words a bespectacled young woman standing in front of them turned her head, looked at Vasily Mikhailovich, then at the painting, and smiled.

Kurentsov broke into a cold sweat. He clenched his fists.

"Let's go, Zina," he commanded hoarsely. "We're going to see the director."

The exhibit's head administrator listened to Kurentsov patiently, nodding and smiling in embarrassment.

"I'm sure you've made a mistake," the head administrator said. "I'm sure you were seeing things that just aren't there."

"What do you mean seeing things?" Kurentsov asked, his left eyebrow twitching nervously. "How can I be seeing things when that's me? The face, the body, even the mole is exactly on . . . that place. I can prove it to you!"

"That's quite all right," the administrator waved begrudging assent. "But even if the man in the painting does resemble you, you must agree that it's a complete coincidence. Complete, do you understand?"

"Take it down," Kurentsov said resolutely. "Take it down, period. People come here, children. . . . My coworkers could see it. It's shameful. Take it down, damn it!"

"Quite impossible," the administrator said.

"I said, take it down," Kurentsov repeated sullenly. "You don't want this to turn into a scandal."

"Don't you threaten me," the administrator said, losing his smile. "Take your complaints to the artist, though I'm sure he won't listen to them, either."

"Get him on the phone for me," Kurentsov commanded.

The administrator looked intently at Vasily Mikhailovich, shrugged his shoulders, lifted the receiver, and dialed a number.

"Hello? Kurentsov speaking," Vasily Mikhailovich said into the receiver. "Comrade artist, something has happened here, somehow I wound up in one of your paintings. You know, the one taking his pants off. I'm lodging a complaint."

"I don't follow," a voice could be heard from the receiver. "A complaint about what?"

"Distortion and misrepresentation!" Kurentsov said and peevishly realized he had said the wrong thing. "It's the spitting image of me. Comrade, apparently you saw me someplace and then made a sketch. People are looking at this, and children."

"What children?" the voice in the receiver asked, bewildered. "Comrade, I have never seen you in my life, much less painted you."

"Maybe you've never seen me, but that's still me," Kurentsov said. "Even the mole is the same."

"What mole? What does a mole have to do with this?"

"A common, ordinary mole. On the, you know. . . . Look, I'm telling you to take down the picture, or else there's going to be trouble," Kurentsov said hoarsely.

"You're drunk, comrade," the voice in the receiver said calmly. "So why don't you leave me alone."

Kurentsov listened to the dial tone for a few seconds, then he set the receiver on the table and said without looking at the administrator, "Fine. We're going, Zina."

Zinaida Ivanovna timidly held onto Kurentsov's arm, as he loudly breathed through his nose. He was crestfallen, his body convulsing periodically as though someone were poking a finger in his back from behind.

That evening Vasily Mikhailovich Kurentsov drank a lot of vodka. He drank alone, and he drank slowly, preoccupied, without anything to eat.

Zinaida Ivanovna looked at him sadly and sighed. She tried to console him.

"Forget about it, Vasya," she said. "Why do you take it so to heart? There's nothing to worry about. Nobody even knows. Who's going to go there anyway? Certainly none of our friends. You can even tell them at work not to go."

"Don't be so stupid," Kurentsov said testily. "And what if they decide to show it on TV? Or worse, make postcards of it? Five kopecks apiece."

"Then you just deny it. Say it's not you."

"Deny it!" Kurentsov interrupted her angrily. "What can there be to deny when it's undeniably my face? Trying to deny it would be really stupid."

He lapsed into silence and smoked, the skin on his forehead bunching into little accordion wrinkles, which spoke of the excruciating thoughts tormenting his brain. At last Kurentsov stood up, put on his sport coat and, avoiding his wife's eyes, said gloomily, "I'm going out, Zina."

"Where do you think you're going this late?" Zinaida Ivanovna said, upset.

"I'm going, that's it," Kurentsov repeated. "I need to get some air."

Kurentsov did not know the exact address of the exhibit, and so for a long time he cruised around central Moscow, until the taxi finally brought him past a familiar, venerable old building.

Vasily Mikhailovich walked around the building several times, and when he was sure that there were no night watchmen or policemen near, he stopped at a small window in the rear of the building. He looked around him one more time, took out a penknife, pried off the dry caulking, bent back the support tacks, and took out the double panes of glass.

When the glass was out, Kurentsov climbed up onto the ledge and squeezed his considerable weight through the narrow window frame and into a room. He was surrounded on all sides by an eerie darkness.

He walked down a seemingly endless corridor. It was very dark and very quiet, but his continuing state of intoxication removed any fear and helped him reach the door after only two falls. He shoved it open and found himself in the gallery.

In no time Kurentsov had found "Night Swim." He stood in front of it for several minutes, studying his face, which in the murk seemed to bear an even stronger resemblance. Then he fetched a chair, got up on it, and took the picture off its hook.

Suddenly Kurentsov was horrified. Not once in his life had he done anything illegal, and now his soul veritably cringed with pangs of conscience. His heart beat wildly, echoing through the empty rooms.

Yet Vasily Mikhailovich quickly managed to pull himself together. Glancing around furtively, he removed the canvas from its frame, rolled it up in a tube, and hung the frame back on its hook.

Just then a car drove past the windows, and the yellow glow of its headlights illuminated a huge painting on the wall. In the painting Vasily Mikhailovich saw his brother Viktor Mikhailovich Kurentsov, who at the time was residing in the city of Kaluga.

No longer surprised, no longer shaking, he wandered through the darkish halls of the gallery and, with a kind of dull indifference, inspected the paintings. Kurentsovs were looking down at him from all sides. Here was a portrait of his uncle Aleksey Kurentsov, and there were his cousin Sergey, his godfather Andrey Stepanovich Zhmakin, Zina's sister Olga, Bryukin his brother-in-law, his niece Spiridonova, his grandmother Anna Stepanovna, and his aunt on his mother's side Raisa Grigorevna.

Naked, or dressed in the most outlandish costumes, from all sides the red, blue, or green-faced Kurentsovs watched Vasily Mikhailovich as he stumbled around the gallery in circles, until he collided headfirst with some outsized door.

At this point, as though he were waking from a dream, Kurentsov violently yanked on the door handle, then started pounding his fists on it and shouting for help.

Within an hour Vasily Mikhailovich Kurentsov was sitting in a police van. He sat on a metal bench between two policemen and stared absently out a small window sectioned off into squares with steel rods. When the van drove past the statue of Yury Dolgoruky, Kurentsov suddenly smiled, tapped one of the officers on the sleeve and, nodding at the statue, quietly said, "Oh, ho, did you see that? That's my uncle, Mikhail Stepanovich Kurentsov. They've shown him riding a horse, the swine!"

Then he threatened no one in particular with his clenched fist and burst into tears.

Stop Potapov!

Precisely at seven o'clock in the morning the alarm clock wrenched Potapov out of his sleep. Potapov had had a pleasant, technicolor dream about the sea and a little cafe atop a cliff, where he sat beneath a striped beach umbrella, waiting for somebody. This waiting had been both excruciating and exquisite. As he crawled across his wife and put his bare feet on the floor, Potapov kept his eyes shut for a while longer, hoping to see the end of his dream; but it didn't work. His wife muttered something, the cold floor burned the soles of his feet, and Potapov opened his eyes.

The clock showed 7:05. Potapov inserted his feet in his slippers and went out into the hallway. On the way to the bathroom he grabbed the newspaper out of the mailbox, then went to the kitchen and put on water for coffee. Sitting in the bathroom, he checked through yesterday's hockey scores; having left the bathroom, he poured coffee grounds into the coffeepot, poured hot water over them, set the coffeepot on the gas burner, and began to do his exercises. While he did his exercises, Potapov kept an eye on the coffee to make sure it didn't boil over. He turned the burner off, finished his exercises, picked up a transistor radio, and went to take his shower. As he showered he listened to "News Update."

After his shower, Potapov went back into the kitchen, took cheese and sausage out of the refrigerator, then took Alyosha's school notebook off the window sill and, while he chewed a sandwich, began to go over it.

Yesterday alone, his son had gotten two F's. Potapov shook his head in disappointment, signed the notebook, and finished his coffee.

"If you don't finally go to that school today, I don't know what I'll do with you," his wife said. She had come into the kitchen and was looking at Potapov with angry, but somnolent eyes. "This is the third time the vice-principal has asked you. Are you his father or aren't you?"

"All right," Potapov said and looked at his watch. It was already 7:20. "Let's not argue, Lyubasha," Potapov said. With his right arm he embraced his wife, while his left hand took the electric razor off the shelf.

"Back off!" his wife shook herself from his one-armed embrace. "If you don't go to the school today, I'm not going to talk to you anymore."

"I promise I'll go. I swear, Lyubasha," Potapov pressed his left hand to his chest, plugging the cord into the outlet with the right.

"Andrey, this is serious, especially since. . . ." Whatever else his wife said was drowned in the buzz of the electric razor. Potapov inspected his face in the mirror and nodded to his wife. Then he yanked the cord out of the socket. ". . . or aren't you?" Lyuba finished saying.

"All right," Potapov said again. "But as far as all the rest is concerned, Lyubanya, you're absolutely right."

He pecked his wife on the cheek and quickly went out into the hallway, knotting his tie as he went. A bleary-eyed Alyosha had just come out of his room. Putting on his sport coat, Potapov gave him a quick cuff on the neck, and as he pulled on his overcoat he said, "I want to talk to you later, young man." He grabbed up his briefcase and his hat and left. . . . There was a big crowd at the bus stop, as usual. Potapov let the first two buses go by and breathed in the fresh air. The air was crisp, but there was a spice and stickiness to it reminiscent of early spring. It made him slightly dizzy, and his pulse raced.

For some reason Potapov remembered Natasha at this point. He had seen her a week ago as he was riding down Tverskoy Boulevard in a taxi. Natasha was wearing a suede overcoat with a hood. For a moment

Potapov had wanted to stop, but he reconsidered because he was in a rush. She had come to mind several times since then, but now, at the bus stop, the recollection was somehow especially sharp, even physically so.

"I'll call her today," Potapov thought. "Or better yet, I'll drop in unannounced. No, no I should probably call first."

Even so, he still hadn't decided what he should do—call first or just drop in—when a bus pulled up.

Potapov stopped thinking about Natasha, lurched forward and somehow managed to squeeze onto the bus. As he jockeyed for position he saw a familiar face—one of their neighbors at the apartment house, but then again maybe not—and greeted him with a nod of the head.

Working his way to the center of the bus, Potapov called out loudly, "I have a month pass." Then he cleverly managed to reach into his briefcase and pull out a copy of *Foreign Literature*. This issue had a sequel of a novel by Erich Maria Remarque. Potapov opened it to page 114, where it had been dog-eared, and began reading: "In the afternoon I left for Cannes. He had invited me to have dinner with him at a restaurant. . . ." The bus jolted and the magazine fell out of Potapov's hand, but he caught it in mid-air and continued to read: ". . . Mrs. Wimper had fixed a vodka Martini in anticipation of my arrival. . . ." That was page 163. Potapov tried to find the dog-ear that marked page 114, but the bus was too crowded; and besides, Potapov recalled that he was supposed to return the magazine tomorrow, anyway, so he might as well skip ahead. "She and I talked about the visit with Silvers . . . ," Potapov read, but at this point the driver announced his stop. Potapov closed the magazine, stuffed it in his briefcase, and began to work his way over to the exit. On his way he again caught sight of the same familiar face—one of their neighbors at the apartment house, but then again maybe not—nodded to him again and called out, "Why don't you stop by sometime, old buddy?"

Precisely at nine A.M. Potapov entered his department. Greeting his colleagues, Potapov sat down at his desk, pulled down a file of materials concerning standardization, and began to study the file. Everything was in its place, only the title page was missing.

"Where's the title page for this file?" Potapov asked Mikhailov, who was sitting at the next desk.

"No idea," Mikhailov said. "Maybe it's been passed on to technical application."

"That's all I needed!" Potapov said heatedly and went to the technical application department.

He needed the title page for two reasons: first, Potapov liked everything in his files to be in place, and second, on the back of this particular title page there was a chess problem that he'd copied out of *Science and Life*, and he had been planning to solve it now. In the technical application department, Potapov was told that the title page had been forwarded to the accounting department. The secretary in the accounting department told him that the title page had been sent back to the standardization department. Back at his desk, Potapov found the title page lying on his desk, but somebody had already solved the chess problem.

Heaving a sigh, Potapov put the page in the folder, put the folder in his desk, and looked at the clock.

It was noon.

"Lunch will be in an hour," Potapov thought and for some reason again thought of Natasha. "I'll give her a call," he decided, and he pulled the telephone over toward himself. But the phone rang before Potapov had a chance to lift the receiver.

"Hello?" Potapov said.

"Potapov?" a hoarse masculine voice said. "This is Kondratev."

"Hi, how you doing, guy?" Potapov said, desperately trying to remember who Kondratev was.

"I've got bad news," Kondratev said. "Alex is dead."

"That can't be!" Potapov gasped, desperately trying to remember who Alex was.

"He went fast. Took only two months," Kondratev said despondently. "So there you have it. The funeral's today at three o'clock, Vostryakov cemetery. Can you be there?"

"Can I be there? Well, sure," Potapov said, desperately trying to remember where Vostryakov cemetery was. After receiving this sad news he had absolutely no taste for work. Potapov cleared all the papers off his desk and went out into the corridor to smoke. There were lots of people smoking in the corridor. When the president's secretary saw Potapov, she cadged a cigarette from him and said, "The boss is having a general meeting of all departments at four o'clock today. Mandatory."

"Of course," Potapov said, holding a lighted match to her cigarette. "You just get better and better looking, Sonechka."

"Oh, you!" Sonya coquettishly protested and exhaled a stream of smoke. "All you're good for is making compliments, but none of you can seem to figure out how to take me to see *Hamlet.*"

"Know anyone who has tickets?"

"Yermolenko in the union office has some. But he won't give them up."

"Depends who's asking," Potapov said with a significant raise of one eyebrow and left for the union office.

"Say, Yermolenko," Potapov said as he entered the union office, "didn't you need people for the volunteer patrol?"

"Yeah?" Yermolenko said, looking at Potapov suspiciously.

"You give me two tickets for *Hamlet* and I'll volunteer."

"It won't work," Yermolenko sighed. "*Hamlet* is tonight, and so is the volunteer patrol."

"It'll work out fine," Potapov said. "*Hamlet* starts at seven and the hoods don't start till later. I'll put my time in after the show, honest."

"You're going to have to stay out till midnight," Yermolenko warned.

"You've got a deal!" Potapov promised, took the tickets, and went to have lunch.

While he was having lunch, he suddenly thought of Natasha again, and for some reason he choked up.

"I'll drop in on her without calling," Potapov decided. "I'll just go over there. Haven't seen the woman I love for half a year. What kind of . . . ?" He didn't finish the thought. The radio began to play old-time Russian love songs, and Potapov listened to them until he finished his lunch.

Once he was back in the department, Potapov glanced at the clock. It was a quarter past two. He picked up the phone and dialed the number of his friend in the ministry.

"Hello, Sergachov?" Potapov said. "This is Potapov. Say, Lyonya, could you have me summoned to the ministry for a couple of hours?"

"We can't keep doing this," Sergachov said with unmistakable displeasure. "Sooner or later they're going to get wise to us, and are we ever going to get it in the neck."

"This is the last time I'll ever ask you, Lyonya, I promise," Potapov said. "A friend of mine died. I'm going to the funeral."

Sergachov was silent for a while, then he quietly asked, "Is that the truth?"

"Would I lie to you?" Potapov sighed.

"Oh, all right," Sergachov said. "I suppose you need a car, too."

"Sure!" Potapov was rapturous. "I'll be right back. I just have to pay my last respects, and that'll be it."

Twenty minutes later the supervisor of Potapov's department entered the room.

"Potapov," he said, "the ministry called. They want you there right away."

"What is it this time?" Potapov asked angrily. "They've just got one problem after another!"

"They probably have some questions about one of your reports," his supervisor said.

"They've got nothing but questions," Potapov snapped. "I'm sick of it. I've got work up to my gills here. I'm not going, and that's that!"

"Now, stop your grousing," his supervisor said sternly. "Leave everything as it is and get going."

At the entrance to the building an official car from the ministry was waiting for Potapov. Potapov sat down in front, lit a cigarette for himself, and offered one to the driver.

"Going to the cemetery?" the driver asked.

"Yeah," Potapov sighed. "Only first would you drive me to Khimki, school number 21?"

He was in luck. He caught the vice-principal during recess. But recess was ending, and she was already hurrying back to class.

"Good afternoon," Potapov said. "I'm Potapov. I was supposed to talk with you about my son."

"Vera Mikhailovna," the vice-principal introduced herself.

"Pleased to meet you," Potapov smiled. "My mother's name was Vera Mikhailovna, too. Beautiful name."

"Thank you," the vice-principal said and blushed for some reason.

"Have I come at a bad time?" Potapov asked. "You're in a hurry, aren't you?"

"Yes, I am," Vera Mikhailovna nodded. "The kids are waiting for me. Could you come back around, say, seven?"

"Sorry, afraid I can't," Potapov sighed. "Urgent business trip to Taimyr. Couldn't you just give me the gist of it?"

"It's not something that can be talked about briefly," Vera Mikhailovna said. "Your boy isn't doing his work; he's insolent, he's lying right and left."

"I'll kill him!" Potapov said firmly.

"Oh, no, why do you say that?" the principal blushed again. "You and I just need to sit down and have a good, long talk. . . ."

"Fine," Potapov interrupted her. "I'm coming back from Taimyr in two months and we'll talk then. In the meantime, Vera Mikhailovna, I want you to take the little good-for-nothing under your personal supervision. Are we agreed? What size shoe do you wear?"

"Why do you need to know?" the vice-principal blushed again. She was very young for a vice-principal and was constantly blushing.

"I'd like to bring back some Eskimo boots for you," Potapov said. "Nice fur-lined Eskimo boots."

"But I, you . . ." the principal went totally red.

"Now, now, I insist," Potapov said with authority in his voice. "There, that's settled. I'm not going to hold you up any longer. The children are waiting for you."

Then he kissed her hand and ran out of the school.

It took them a long time to reach Vostryakov cemetery. Potapov spent a long time wandering among the snow-covered tombstones, looking for the funeral party. Finally he saw a small group of people, and when he recognized one of them to be a professor from the college he attended, he at once determined that the deceased had been a friend from his student days. Which friend exactly, he did not know, because the casket lid was closed, and the casket had been lowered into the frozen ground. Potapov recalled that there had been several Alexanders in their circle of friends, but now, as if to spite him, all of them were absent, so it was impossible for him to deduce which one of them was lying there. And he didn't feel right about asking.

Potapov removed his hat, sadly circulated among all those present, shaking their hands, and said sadly, "Ah, Alex, Alex. How could it have happened, friends?"

Then, unexpectedly, he sensed that he was crying. He started to feel terrible inside because of it; he wiped his eyes with his hands, lit a cigarette, and silently went over to the car.

When he returned to work the clock showed exactly four. The president's meeting was just beginning. On the way to the meeting Potapov stopped by his department and took his pocket chess set out of the desk drawer, and then he went inconspicuously into the conference room and took a seat in the last row. Mikhailov joined him almost immediately.

Their game was off to an interesting start. In his opening Potapov made a mistake and lost two pawns, but he recovered in mid-game and captured one of Mikhailov's knights.

"Give up, old guy," Potapov said confidently.

"No way!" Mikhailov answered. "Not while I've still got a chance."

"So, gentlemen," the president began to wrap up the meeting, "if there are no questions, shall we adjourn?"

Potapov looked at the board and found that Mikhailov had just made a daring move with his rook. Potapov countered with his queen. The end of the game promised to be exciting.

"I have a question," Potapov said, standing up. "In view of the fact that we'll be manufacturing in accordance with the new standards, how does the administration plan to dispose of our production waste?"

"That's a point well taken," the president said. "It appears to me that the problem of utilizing our waste. . . ."

"Your move," Potapov said softly as he sat down again. "We've got another half hour."

Potapov invited Sonya to supper at a cafe before the play; they each had a glass of vodka and chatted so much that they missed the beginning of it. While Potapov was making his way to their seats hunching over, stepping on various feet, and profusely excusing himself, Hamlet was already talking with Horatio about something.

Finally Sonya and Potapov got settled and looked up at the stage. A huge, woven curtain was moving slowly and horribly across the stage, crushing people beneath it.

"Neat!" Sonya whispered.

"The stage designer's a genius," Potapov said quietly.

"Who did the sets?" Sonechka asked.

Potapov had forgotten to buy a program, so he put his index finger to his lips and disapprovingly shook his head. Embarrassed, Sonechka said nothing. When Hamlet had killed Polonius and, tormented by the irreversibility of events, bent down over the corpse, Potapov shuddered and with astonishment was suddenly aware that an odd kind of shiver had run down his back. Potapov had seen the movie of *Hamlet*, but only the second part, so the death of Polonius took him completely by surprise.

Potapov watched the rest of the play entranced, deriving pleasure from his sympathy for the Danish prince and from that unwonted feeling, the shiver down his back produced by every word said on stage.

During intermission, he went up to the concession stand, had a sandwich and drank some lemonade; the tingling sensation gradually subsided. Potapov looked at the clock. It was a quarter to nine.

"They've made the play too long," Potapov thought. "They've done a good job, but it's too long."

He suddenly thought of Natasha, and his heart contracted painfully.

"I've got to go see her," Potapov told himself.

He bought some candy for Sonya, went out to smoke, and then came back with a preoccupied look on his face.

"Sonya," Potapov said, "I just called home. Alyoshka's sick. He's got a temperature of 102."

"My God!" Sonya gasped.

"It's all right," Potapov said. "Probably just the flu. I've got to go home, though. You'll excuse me, won't you?"

"Don't be ridiculous. Of course, go on home!" Sonya sympathetically squeezed his hand and kissed Potapov on the cheek.

Potapov reached his office by subway, walked into the headquarters of the volunteer patrol, picked up a red armband, and signed in. "Your beat is the square in front of the movie theater and the adjacent neighborhood," Potapov was instructed by the young man sitting at the desk. "You're on duty till midnight."

"I'll stay on patrol till one A.M.," Potapov said, "after all, I am late."

"Oh, come on, you don't need to," the young man smiled. "Midnight will do just fine."

Potapov put on the armband, left headquarters, and slowly walked toward the taxi stand. As he walked, he inhaled the fresh spring air and thought about Natasha. He waited his turn in line, and finally sat down in the front seat of a green Volga. He offered the driver a cigarette and said in a voice that broke, "Take me to Polyanka, chief."

He rang the doorbell for a long time, fearfully listening to the rustling behind the door and wondering if she was alone or not. Finally the lock clicked and he saw Natasha. Apparently she had just taken a bath—she was wearing a striped bathrobe, her hair was damp, and there were a few drops of water on her forehead.

"It's you!"

"It's me," Potapov said and removed his hat. "You can turn me away, or you can let me in."

Natasha looked at Potapov for a few seconds, then with the back of her hand she wiped the drops off her forehead and said almost inaudibly, "Come in."

In half a year Natasha's apartment had not changed at all. There were some new curtains on the windows and a television had cropped up in a corner, but that was all. The television was on.

Potapov took off his overcoat, went in, and stopped in the middle of the room. Natasha turned the television off, went over to a table, took a cigarette out of its pack, and lit it.

"Natasha," Potapov said in a hushed voice. "Please, hit me."

She smiled just noticeably.

"Hit me," Potapov begged her again. "Or if you want, you can use me to wipe your feet in the hallway."

He walked up to her and embraced her. She buried her face in his sport coat and heaved a sigh. Potapov began to stroke her damp hair gently.

"Why did you disappear like that? Why didn't you come see me even once, why didn't you call me?" Natasha said, sobbing. "Aren't you even ashamed?"

"Quiet, love," Potapov said and kissed her head. "Don't say anything just now."

Afterwards they lay in the dark, smoked, and talked about all kinds of nonsense. Finally Potapov sat up in bed, felt around for his pants, and began to get dressed.

"Leaving already?" Natasha asked him quietly.

"Yes," Potapov answered abruptly.

"Stay longer," Natasha pleaded with him.

"I can't, love," Potapov said. "I've got a taxi waiting for me, and the meter's running." As soon as it was out, he realized that he'd botched it. Natasha jumped up, and even in the dark he could see how her face had gone pale.

"You creep!" she said. "Jerk!"

"Come, come now," Potapov felt himself blushing as he tied his shoelaces. "I was just joking, silly goose. It was a joke! Don't you remember that joke?"

"Get out of here!" Natasha screamed at him.

"Go ahead, hit me," Potapov said as he put on his sport coat.

"Go to hell!" Natasha shouted and hid her face in her pillow.

"It's really a shame," Potapov sighed. "It's really a shame that we have to say good-bye like this."

He decided not to wait for the elevator and ran down the stairs instead. The green Volga was waiting for him at the entrance.

"What took you so long, buddy?" the driver grumbled at him. "I've gotta get this thing back to the park."

"No problem, chief," Potapov said, lit a cigarette, and offered one to the driver. "I'll make it worth your while. Take me to Khimki, and floor it."

He was home at a quarter past eleven. Lyuba and Alyosha were already asleep. Potapov went into the kitchen, lit a burner, and put water on for tea. While he ate the supper that his wife had fixed, he watched the late night news. Then, smoking a cigarette, he listened to the sports edition of "News Update." Then he got undressed and went to bed. Lyuba woke up and looked at him sullenly.

"They had me go out on patrol," Potapov said. "I tried to let you know, called several times, but the line was busy. Seems to be touch and go with that phone. Did you call to get it repaired?"

"Did you go to the school?" Lyuba asked.

"Yes. I talked with the vice-principal. Everything's going to be fine. Go to sleep."

Lyuba took one more sullen look at Potapov, then she turned to face the wall.

Potapov moved the alarm clock closer to him—it was 11:55. He wound the clock and set it for seven. For a few minutes he lay there with his eyes open, thinking about nothing in particular, then he turned over on his right side and closed his eyes.

Exactly at twelve midnight Potapov began to sleep.

The Dream

Early morning. I get up in a blissful mood. The sun is shining, birds are singing. I stretch, smile and merrily wink at my wife, "Good morning, how did you sleep?"

She: (gloomily) Lousy . . . I had a really stupid dream.

I: (lighting a cigarette) What kind of dream?

She: (angrily) Will you stop smoking on an empty stomach?

I obediently put out the cigarette. A pause.

She: It was a stupid dream. . . . You see I dreamed I was walking barefoot through this immense field. . . . It was cold and snowing, and the wind was blowing. Suddenly I saw a big crystal palace, sort of like a restaurant. You were sitting inside it. There was a huge table in front of you, set with all kinds of delicacies. I went up and knocked on the door, but you didn't turn around. Then I started to shout. You got up and took a bucket of water and poured it on my head.

I: (*concerned*) Unusual dream. Why should I have been so rude?

She: Who knows? That's not what's bothering me, anyway. What I want to know is where you got the money to go out to eat. Well, what do you have to say for yourself?

I: What is there to say?

She: I asked you where you got the money.

I: I don't have any idea. It's your dream, anyway. I probably borrowed it from somebody.

She: Who from?

I: How should I know? Whoever would give it to me.

She: And just how did you plan to pay it back? You were really living it up big.

I: Well, what did you expect? Was I supposed to order baloney sandwiches?

She: I didn't say a thing! It's perfectly all right! You could go ahead and drink our whole house away, for all I care, but why did you have to pour a bucket of water on my head?

I: You shouldn't make a nuisance of yourself when a guy's out having a good time. And anyway, what is it you're after? It's your dream and I'm not responsible for it.

Another pause.

She: (*lost in thought*) It was probably all because of that woman.

I: What woman?

She: It seemed to me that you weren't alone. There was some blonde sitting with you.

I: (*showing some interest*) Was she attractive?

She: Not bad. Her nose was a little crooked.

I: Yeah, well, it probably just seemed that way to you through the glass.

She: Who is she?

I: How should I know? I was about to ask you.

She: But you were the one sitting with her.

I: You dreamed all of this!

She: Where were you planning to go afterwards?

I: Were we going to go somewhere?

She: Of course you were. You'd left the restaurant and were headed for the car.

I: (*amazed*) I had a car?

She: Of course you did. Steel blue. You got behind the wheel and opened the door for her.

I: Yeah, and then what?

She: What do you mean, "then what?" Then I ran up and asked, "Just where do you think you're going?" And you answered, "The Carpathians." And I said, "You're out of your mind! Why don't you just go bring the laundry back from the cleaners instead? I've been asking you for a week now." But you just snorted and started the engine.

I: (*agitated*) You're a fine one to talk! A guy's trying to drive to the Carpathians and you bother him with all kinds of nonsense. . . . What happened next?

She: Then I set the car on fire.

I: (*losing my composure*) What do you mean?

She: I got some gasoline and set it on fire.

I: How could you? How dare you? Day after day I go to work, turn all my paychecks over to you. I work like a dog, and then just when I've got something to show for it—money, a car—you . . . you . . . set it all on fire!

She: (*maliciously*) So, you admit it! You were going to escape! You're grounded now, like it or not. I'll fix you, I'm going to come to work tomorrow, and report on you. I'll show you.

I: (*beside myself*) Shut up! Shut up! You've sapped all the life out of me!

My head begins to spin. Everything goes black and horrible before my eyes. I am suddenly holding a large, heavy chair. I pick it up and smash it over my wife's head. For a few seconds I look at her lifeless body, then I scream wildly, run to the window, throw it open, leap on the window sill, and jump.

The earth flies toward me like a black spot. . . .

I close my eyes and . . . wake up.

It's morning. The sun is shining and birds are singing.

I am lying in my own bed. My wife is asleep next to me.

I am shivering.

I sit up in bed, take a cigarette from the night table, and strike a match. My wife wakes up.

"I wish you'd stop smoking on an empty stomach," she says angrily, crawling out from under her blanket. "Why are you all bushy-tailed so early in the morning?"

"No reason," I answer. "I had a bad dream."

"Really?" she yawns. "I had a pretty silly dream, too. I dreamed that I was walking barefoot across this immense field. It was incredibly cold and it was snowing. Suddenly I saw this big crystal palace."

"Stop!" I shout. "Stop! Don't go any further!"

I quickly jump out of bed, remove all the chairs from the bedroom, and move the wardrobe in front of the window. I get back in bed and, lying down next to her, listlessly say, "All right, go ahead, dear."

Arkady Inin and Leonid Osadchuk

———————

———————

———————

———————

Arkady Yakovlevich Inin (b. 1938 in Kharkov, Ukraine) completed his studies at Kharkov Polytechnical Institute in 1960 and subsequently worked as an electrical engineer. In 1970 he received a degree from the National Institute of Cinematography. He has lived in Moscow since 1968, where he is a free-lance writer, the author of numerous books of satire and of screenplays. "The humor of the 1960s and 1970s was my start. Everything since then has been a sequel to that unforgettable beginning."

Leonid Viktorovich Osadchuk (b. 1940 in Kharkov) studied literature at Kharkov State University. Until 1973 he was a program editor for Kharkov TV. He lives in Kharkov as a free-lance writer. He has published several books in collaboration with Inin. "On the Same Day Every Month" appeared in 1978 in *Literary Gazette*.

On the Same Day Every Month

He had been waiting for this call.

"Did you call for a cab?" a tired female voice asked.

"Yes, I did."

"It'll be there in five minutes. Number 69–12."

"Thank you."

He set the receiver down, unhurriedly put on his coat, picked up his shallow suitcase, and went outside.

The taxi did, in fact, arrive in five minutes. There was a young fellow sitting at the wheel, and he had one of those open, garrulous faces. He liked that kind of cab driver. Riding with them was like riding with an old friend, and you didn't even notice the meter ticking.

"Got a flight to catch?" the driver smiled.

"That's right," he smiled back, taking a seat up front.

"Well, you're in luck. This evening's made for flying. It's gonna be just up, up and away. . . ."

Smiling again, he asked for permission to smoke and handed the driver a cigarette.

"Flying very far, if it's no secret?"

"Oh, no, not at all. I'm going to Kishinev. Business."

"Kishinev's mighty fine. Warm sun, cold wine! Fly very often?"

He relished the chance to tell him that he traveled on business every month, that just this year alone he had already been in Chita, Tallinn, Zaporozhe, Vladivostok, and Rostov.

The driver expressed admiration for his fare's unsedentary profession, though he was quick to praise his own carefree one: All the places you can be in the course of a day's shift, all the streets and back roads you get to drive down, all the different kinds of fares you get to meet.

The airport terminal appeared around a bend in the road. He glanced at his watch, thanked the driver, paid him, and gently shut the car door behind him.

"Enjoy your flight!" the guy called to him through the window.

"Have a good drive back," he smiled for the umpteenth time.

The cab driver's pleasant manner, the luminescent evening, the mysterious lights of the runway, all of these things were joyous and good. He knew this state of mind well; he even knew when to expect it, and he cherished every minute that it lasted.

He still had forty minutes till the flight to Kishinev. He went up to the bar on the mezzanine and ordered coffee and a shot of brandy. The bartender recognized him and gave a friendly nod.

He bought an evening paper at the newsstand, and then without stopping at the ticket counter, he went straight out the departure gate.

Out on the airfield it was life as usual. Airplanes disappeared into the sky or returned from the darkness, their mighty jets alternately straining toward maximum thrust or falling silent in exhaustion. The voice on the public address system announced in equally dispassionate tones departures of small commuter flights and of huge airliners destined for the ends of the earth.

He leaned his valise against the iron railing that divided romantic tarmac from prosaic asphalt. He looked at his watch; he lit a cigarette.

From this desolate spot at the end of the platform, he calmly and thoughtfully watched as the haut monde hurried off to someplace.

He had stopped looking at his watch, and he'd lost track of time. He was brought back to reality by the matter-of-fact voice announcing that the flight for Kishinev had begun boarding.

But he stayed put. He watched the passengers of his flight pass through the gate and climb into the shuttle bus as they hastily and absurdly tried to wave good-bye to the people seeing them off.

He waited for them to climb up the ramp, while trying to imagine who these passengers were, where they were going, and why.

He waited for the airplane to taxi out onto the runway, as he tried to picture the people referred to as the crew.

He waited for the jet to shoot up into the black sky, and he tried to imagine how he himself would feel if he were being torn from the surface of the earth.

He waved in the direction that the plane had vanished, then he picked up his valise, and at an unhurried pace went back inside the terminal. Here, at the bar—but a different one this time, on the second floor—he repeated his order: coffee and a shot of brandy. This second bartender also gave him a welcoming nod, as though they were old friends.

There was no line at the taxi stand.

"Evening," he said to the driver as he got in next to him. "Sub-development number 205, please."

The cab driver turned the meter on, but said nothing. They took off.

"So, how've things been in the old hometown? Any news? How's the weather been?" he asked and suddenly sensed that this driver was not the garrulous kind.

"You been away for long?" the driver answered his question with a question in such a bored tone that it seemed a forced conversation with passengers was part of the fare.

"Quite a while, actually. You see, I've been away on business. In Irkutsk."

The driver squinted in disbelief at his light overcoat, but said nothing.

He was on the verge of describing the splendors of Siberia to him, but seeing that the driver was profoundly indifferent to them, he fell silent.

When they drove up in front of his building, the driver accepted his fare and asked, "You make a lot on these business trips, don't you?"

He didn't reply. But he did bang the door shut just a bit louder than usual.

At home he unpacked his valise—took out the electric razor, the fresh shirt, the tie, two pairs of stockings, the house slippers, the soap dish, and the toothbrush. He carefully distributed these items to their assigned places, and he put the valise away in the closet.

Then, as usual, he put sheets on the couch, picked up a volume of Jules Verne, and climbed into bed. He always read Jules Verne before going to sleep.

He's no longer young, and he's lonely. The place where he works is just a block or two away from where he lives. He has never traveled anywhere—not on business, not to visit relatives—and he never will. He has the wrong kind of job for that, and the wrong kind of relatives.

Still, he makes his trips.

On the same day every month, on payday, he arranges a little holiday for himself. He creates his own haut monde, where someone is overjoyed and anxious to pick him up and see him off.

His payday falls on the twentieth. If you should happen to be in the airport on that day, walk all the way to the end of the boarding gate area and you'll see a middle-aged, shortish, rather unremarkable person. As a pretext for a conversation ask him to give you a light, then ask him, "Where are you headed?"

No one can say where he'll be headed this time, but one thing is certain, and that's that he'll be delighted to tell you all about it.

Dmitry Ivanov and Vladimir Trifonov

_____

_____

_____

_____

Dmitry Georgievich Ivanov (b. 1938 in Arkhangelsk, Russia) and Vladimir Ilich Trifonov (b. 1933 in Leningrad) both graduated in 1964 from the National Institute of Cinematography, Department of Script-writing. They have published together since 1960 as a free-lance writing team. They have to their credit collections of stories, over a dozen comedies, and screenplays. They write that "as we grow older and take all of the events in our country close to heart, we find we have lost our former boundless devotion to humor to a large extent, even though it is a wonderful remedy and often the only salvation in situations of stress." "Sugar, Sugar" appeared in 1972 and "My Second Self" in 1971, both in *Literary Gazette*.

Sugar, Sugar

My wife and I are having breakfast.

The white kitchen table cuts her in half. Over the table I can see half of my wife, and the same half of my wife is mirrored by the surface of the table. This way she resembles a queen of diamonds picked from a deck of cards. From her vantage point I must resemble a jack of clubs. But I don't suppose she has enough imagination to see that.

"That's all our trump cards."

There are at least two women I know to whom I wouldn't have had to explain why I said that. But my wife says, "What is it now?"

"Nothing," I answer, uncertain myself why I pronounced this reply in such a scathing tone.

"But it's obvious you're upset about something again. So tell me what's happened."

I don't answer. But in the meantime here's what happens: I move the butter dish so that it covers the mouth of the half of the queen of diamonds that's lying on the table. The queen of diamonds' upper half scoops up some butter with her knife and says, "Thank you."

"Can it possibly be," I think to myself, "that somewhere someone's breath is taken away when he sees her prancing up the stairs of an underpass? Is it possible that she's the one some guy who looks like England, the famous boxing referee, offered to carry a watermelon home for the other day? Walk in my shoes for five years," I think about Mr. Watermelon. "Just run to the bakery every morning for five years. Just try to listen to 'Do we have any cheese? I feel like a little cheese,' your jaws clenching all the while. As though cheese could appear out of the dust that she's been meaning to clean off her vanity mirror for a month. Then, Mr. Referee, I'd really like to see how you offer your services for transporting watermelons or heaving around all sorts of laundry bags. Finally, allow me to pose just one more question: 'What are we going to do tonight?'

"Let's say you get through the first year thanks to the good services of Mosfilm. We'll tack on another half year for Vysotsky playing Hamlet and that quaint restaurant in a historic mansion that serves bear steaks. But sooner or later, Mr. England, you'll come to regret your watermelon acquaintance."

I think about this and slowly peel an egg. And when I reach for the saltshaker, our hands meet.

"Oh, sorry," she says.

"Means a fight," I say, trying to collect the spilled salt with my knife.

She hastily tosses a pinch of salt over her left shoulder. "Sugar, sugar," she says superstitiously.

At this point our eyes meet. I can't say what she sees in mine, but I can see in hers complete and utter incredulity. It's clear that for the life of her she can't understand why she should be sitting here at 7:30 A.M., half-dressed, breaking bread and yoghurt with the stranger across the table. Why is this unshaved slob even here? She can't figure out why she should have to tell him when she'll be back from work and why this nonsense has been going on for five years. I suspect that many other obvious things are inaccessible to her as well, for instance, beer-drinking with the guys or the presence of a few old girlfriends' phone numbers in one's address book.

And this woman before me seems to have illegally usurped someone else's place. Somebody else should be sitting here: You know, one of those blue-eyed blondes with short hair, who could, if you wanted, turn into a green-eyed brunette; a boyish figure like a store window mannikin, provided everything else was in place; naive to the point of ecstasy, yet wise as the biblical snake; dressed in a print dress down to her heels, which might even turn out to be a short suede skirt; head over heels in love with me. Just as long as she doesn't get on my nerves with her "do this, don't do that."

Lost in these reveries, I peel a second egg and have a look at her, too. As I look, I understand that from her point of view I'm also taking up someone else's place, that someone else ought to be peeling this egg: Somebody a little younger than me, but who looks a little older; one of those chiseled bodies, but also with a brain in his head; something like a graphics designer or a theater manager; and so on . . . ; in a word, a real man, but a subtle one, with a nice touch. . . .

"Do you mean to say I don't have a nice touch?"

"You're okay," she says calmly, without missing a beat. "So what do you want to do tonight? . . ."

"Good question, what should we do?" Alex said.

This was on a Saturday, too. Only five years ago. The heat was unbearable in my bachelor flat, which faced south.

"It should cool down by eight," Alex reminded me. "But then it will be too late. All the girls with nice tans are taken by then."

I can't say any of this bothered me much. I just went to take a shower. Alex was already dialing the phone and leafing through his address book, beginning with the letter A.

"Hello, Anya?" he said, using the special velvet timbre that he reserved especially for these Saturday phone calls.

I hadn't turned on the faucet yet, so I heard Alex apologizing to Anya's aunt, assuring her that she had a very young voice. Then the water started pouring and I got into the shower.

"No go," Alex's cheerful voice resonated through the whole apartment. "She's in Koktebel. Back in ten days."

Several more times Alex called out "No go," but then he fell silent. He had made a connection.

And indeed, when I entered the room, Alex was lying on the sofa with his legs in the air, a sign of success.

"I'll just run right down and iron my pants," he assured her over the phone. "Be there at eight on the dot. . . ."

"She all right?" I asked when the phone call was over.

"No idea," Alex grinned. "Reached her by mistake. Shall we go?"

"Not me," I said. "I've had it with these blind dates. She'll turn out to be some lizard, and a complete idiot to boot. Probably covers her mouth when she laughs. . . ."

"So we lose a half hour," Alex said assuagingly. "What if it really is something special. You'll never forgive yourself."

The phone rang.

"It does look like the heat's subsiding," Alex said, picking up the receiver.

Now began the endless: "Yes, it's me. . . . No, I don't recognize it. . . . Well, how about it? Who told you you could reach me here? Of course. . . . I had a feeling we knew each other. . . ."

In short, toward eight it became evident that Alex's plans for tonight were changing; he was going to his girlfriend's. And it was probably out of idle curiosity that I went to the fountain outside the Arbat subway station shortly after eight. A wide assortment had already turned out, but naturally I had to size them all up. The three most impressive candidates were surprisingly quickly met by their boyfriends, or maybe husbands.

Suddenly my mouth went dry. I hadn't even noticed her approaching me. Legs, lips, eyes, everything special. She came up to me and asked in a husky voice, "Excuse me, you seem to have been here a long time."

"It's all right," I said, excusing all her future delays and, of course, the huskiness.

"You haven't seen a little boy in a white T-shirt with a toy machine gun, have you? Sorry to bother you. My son has disappeared. . . ."

"She's probably eaten ice cream, which would explain the voice," I thought in despair. "They just drop their kids off all over town, then sit around in coffee shops with God knows who. And I'm supposed to keep an eye on all the little boys with machine guns."

"How come you're late?" someone said from behind. "You said you'd be here on the dot."

I turned around. But the face with the hoarse voice had impressed itself on my eyes like a camera flash, and all I could see was a dark spot.

"Was that you talking to me on the phone?" the spot said, covering its mouth as it emitted a titter.

I had not yet recovered from shock, and I said, "That was me."

This is how it happened five years ago, when by some mistake of the phone company two totally unintroduced, but equally unsettled Saturday destinies crossed in a tangle of wires.

"So what are we going to do tonight?" she asks again.

It seems as though only now, in the sixth year of our marriage, have I gotten a good look at her. And just now it dawns on me that I really am sitting in the wrong place. And it's not some abstract character, not any Mr. England that should be sitting across from her, but my friend Alex. After all, he was the one who talked with her on the phone that time, he arranged the meeting on the Arbat, he got me mixed up in this business instead of himself.

"Marina, sweetheart," I want to shout to her. "There's been a terrible mistake. Call Alex, tell him to come over. I'll get my things together in twenty minutes and leave for my mother's in Davydkovo for good."

But at the very moment when my hand reaches for the phone, another, far more horrendous thought stops me. I remember the description of the girl who was supposed to show up on the Arbat five years ago just as Alex received it over the phone. Only now do I realize that instead of a tall brunette in a purple poncho, a short redhead in a white jacket showed up at the fountain. Now I have no doubt it wasn't the real one who showed up then, it was her friend. I wonder, could anything worthwhile have happened if two other people had met? I already know the answer, never in a lifetime! . . .

"So what are we going to do?" the queen of diamonds asks from across the table.

"Let's call Alex," I say. "Let him come and bring his girlfriend along."

"That's a good idea," the queen of diamonds says. "We'll have a good laugh. . . ."

My Second Self

I unlocked the door with my key and gave the Japanese pinup girl on the glossy calendar my habitual wink; she reciprocated with her studied smile. The tape player was flooding the whole apartment with

Engelbert Humperdinck's plaintive voice. But something was bothering me. I looked around.

Everything was in its place. There were the colored candles standing on the bookshelf, as usual, and the bottle collection and rows of blown-glass figurines holding their own next to them. Even the portrait of Hemingway wearing his thick sweater was hanging in its usual place. In a familiar gilt armchair (the work of Jean-Baptiste Lelarge the Younger) a horribly familiar blonde was sitting with some mohair knitting on her lap.

"My wife," I noted mechanically, applying a traditional kiss to her cheek, thick with facial cream. "Now she's going to ask about the tickets to the Volkonsky concert."

"I got them," I said.

"They promised they'd get me the Hieronymus Bosch album, in the Skir edition," she said.

"Remarkable artist," I said. "Fifteenth century."

". . . sure beats any of your Salvador Dalis," she finished without skipping a beat.

Everything was going smoothly, but still some worm of doubt was gnawing at me. Perhaps it was jealousy?

"Who promised to get you the Bosch?" I asked, and took a volume of Camus off the shelf without looking. "Was it the artist whose studio we visited?"

"The one where we had baked potatoes?" she asked.

Just then our red telephone emitted its familiar soft ring.

"I'm not here," she whispered, as usual.

"So, changed your mind about swapping your chignon for a velvet skirt again?" I said casually, out of habit. Something kept bothering me.

She didn't respond, which was typical.

"Did you hear?" a voice with a familiar lilt said in the receiver. "Ravenskikh is the new head director at the Maly Theater."

"Big deal," I answered. "You should see Bortnikov in 'Petersburg Reveries.'"

"Yeah. . . . We've really got to get together," the voice pronounced the usual farewell phrase.

"Let's keep in touch," I answered in kind.

As strange as it may seem, that habitual evening phone call soothed my nerves. As I stretched out in the flower-patterned bedsheets that I loved so much, I mechanically opened the latest issue of *Science and Life* to a half-read article about genetics. To my right, as usual, the pages of the latest issue of *Village Youth* were fluttering through the standard dose of Agatha Christie.

But precisely fifteen minutes later I heard for the thousandth time: "So, what will it be then. Are we getting a divorce or not? Or do you want a separation?"

I've always had a single answer to that one. I close my eyes and think how nice it would be to marry a movie star like Telichkina, or a girl from a chorus line. There would be all that shooting on location, road shows. . . . Every encounter would be like the first time! But then there's the kid.

"The kid," she read my thoughts. "The kid can live with grandmother, just like now."

I knew that was exactly what she would say.

"It's closer to the English-language school from there, music lessons, too," I went on by rote. "Yes, and figure-skating school, too."

"By the way, Dennis is interested in boxing."

Provided my wife and I aren't invited to the usual shish kabob cookout on some friends' balcony, I fall asleep like a log at eleven. But now I was jolted by a sudden realization.

"What Dennis?" I exclaimed.

"That happens to be our son's name," she said testily.

"But we have a daughter," I said, and I broke a sweat. "A daughter! I remember that very clearly."

We looked each other firmly in the eyes, something I had grown disused to in five years of married life. It became clear what had been bothering me.

"I beg your pardon," I said, knotting my tie. "These architects. . . . They're making all the units with balconies these days."

She broke into tears, just the way my wife would. Just the way hundreds of blondes would, faced with any of hundreds of brunets, if they were in our place.

The familiar sound of the doorbell could be heard in the doorway. Someone was at the door. I threw it open and had the feeling that somebody had set up a full-length mirror on the landing.

"I'm sorry," said my double, who was wearing a fur-lined suede coat and carrying a collapsible umbrella and a shallow attaché case. "Got the wrong floor. The doors are so similar."

I overtook him on the first flight down. I opened my door and winked at the Japanese pinup girl on the glossy calendar. Engelbert

Humperdinck was singing. My wife had laid her blue mohair knitting aside and was getting up out of the gilt armchair.

"They promised me Hieronymus Bosch," she said.

"Remarkable painter!" I said. "Fifteenth century."

"Sure beats any of your Salvador Dalis," she said.

Leonid Kaminsky

Leonid Davidovich Kaminsky (b. 1931, Kalinkovichi, Byelorussia) received degrees from the Leningrad Institute of Construction Engineering in 1954 and the Moscow Publishing Trade School in 1966. Kaminsky's talents are diverse. He has been a children's author, a graphic artist, and a writer of humorous short stories. "Hack Writer" was published in 1970 in *Literary Gazette*.

Hack Writer

There was a timid knock at the door.

"Come in," the editor said.

A bald man in a long, brown overcoat entered the room. His round-lensed spectacles were precariously perched on a pink nose. With one hand he self-consciously crumpled his green hat, and with the other he carefully pressed to his chest a dog-eared popular magazine that enfolded a bundle of papers. The man approached the editor's desk and cleared his throat.

"Good morning," he said quietly. "Permit me to introduce myself. I'm Afanasy Dmitrievich." He paused, then added, "Hack writer."

"Whaaaa?" said the editor, his eyebrows rising in astonishment. "Hack writer? I'm sorry, is that your last name, or what?"

"No, I told you, my last name is Dmitrievich. It looks like a patronymic, only the accent is on the 'e'. I admit, my patronymic is Dmitrievich, too, with the accent on the 'i'. Just a coincidence. So my full name is Afanasy Dmitrievich Dmitrievich. Hack writer is sort of a nickname. It's what they call me in various publishing houses. You see, I just love to write, and because of that. . . . It's okay, I've even gotten used to it."

The editor heaved a sigh and looked wearily out the window. Streetcar bells were ringing. It was snowing. It would be lunchtime soon.

"I understand," the hack writer said. "I'll go. I only have one request." He started to open the magazine and pull out a bundle of sheets of paper covered with dense handwriting. The editor's mouth went dry.

"Don't worry," Dmitrievich said affably and looked at the editor amicably. "I don't mean to hold you up. I only wanted to ask you to read the first page of my manuscript. If you find it doesn't interest you at all, I'll go. I'm really used to it."

The editor sighed, took up the sheet of paper and started to read it. It had been neatly headed in red ballpoint pen: "Hack Writer" (short story).

> There was a timid knock at the door.
> "Come in," the editor said.
> A bald man in a long, brown overcoat entered the room. His round-lensed spectacles were precariously perched on a pink nose. With one hand he self-consciously crumpled his green hat, and with the other he carefully pressed to his chest a dog-eared popular magazine that enfolded a bundle of papers. The man approached the editor's desk and cleared his throat.
> "Good morning," he said quietly. "Permit me to introduce myself. I'm Afanasy Dmitrievich." He paused, then added, "Hack writer."
> "Whaaaa?" said the editor, his eyebrows rising in astonishment.

The editor raised his eyebrows in astonishment. For a while he distractedly looked at the bald man. The latter nodded to him benignly and said, "Go ahead, read on."

> "Hack writer? I'm sorry, is that your last name, or what?"
> "No, I told you. my last name is Dmitrievich. It looks like a patronymic, only the accent is on the 'e'. I admit, my patronymic is Dmitrievich, too, with the accent on the 'i'. Just a coincidence. So my full name is Afanasy Dmitrievich Dmitrievich. Hack writer is sort of a nickname. It's what they call me in various publishing

houses. You see, I just love to write, and because of that. . . . It's
okay, I've even gotten used to it."

The editor looked wearily out the window. Streetcar bells were
ringing. It was snowing. It would be lunchtime soon.

The editor put the sheet of paper aside. He scratched his chin, then
drummed on the table with his fingers. He picked up the telephone
receiver, held it for a while, then put it back in the cradle. Then he
maneuvered the sheet of paper back in front of himself and continued
reading.

"I understand," the hack writer said. "I'll go. I only have one
request." He started to open the magazine and pull out a bundle of
sheets of paper covered with dense handwriting. The editor's
mouth went dry.

"Don't worry," Dmitrievich said affably, amicably looking at the
editor. "I don't mean to hold you up. I only wanted to ask you to
read the first page of my manuscript. If you find it doesn't interest
you at all, I'll go. I'm really used to it."

The editor sighed. . . .

The editor sighed.

"You know," he said, "why don't you leave this manuscript with
me? I think you've got something here. We might even be able to use it."

The bald man laid the dog-eared magazine with the manuscript on
the table, said good-bye, and vanished.

The editor paced about the room pensively and lit a cigarette. Then
he went over to his desk and picked up a page of the manuscript. Neatly
printed on it in red ballpoint pen, he read:

"You know," he said, "why don't you leave this manuscript with me?
I think you've got something here. We might even be able to use
it."

The bald man laid the dog-eared magazine with the manuscript on
the table, said good-bye, and vanished.

Felix Kamov

———————————
———————————
———————————
———————————

Felix Kamov (real name Felix Solomonovich Kandel, b. 1932 in Moscow) was a student at Moscow Aviation Institute and worked for a time as a design engineer. He published two books of stories and completed several scenarios for short animated films in the Soviet Union. In 1977 he emigrated to Israel, where he has published several books in Russian. "The Bald Angel" was published in 1971 in *Literary Gazette*.

The Bald Angel

He walked down the aisle between the tables. He was short, stooped, with a jutting stomach, and a gloss to his bald spot, the light fixtures on the ceiling creating a halo around his head.

"Are you an angel?" I asked.

He set his buttermilk on the table, then his plate of rice porridge with a pat of butter.

"No," he answered plainly. "I'm an accountant."

"Wrong. You're an angel."

"I assure you I'm an accountant."

"Angels can be accountants, too," I said with authority.

"Ah, but accountants can't be angels."

"Don't be so sure. I knew an accountant once. He was no ordinary human being. There was an angel for you."

"Really? What kind of accounting did he do?" he perked up faintly.

"Sins. He counted sins."

He smiled sadly, drank his buttermilk, and took a taste of the rice porridge.

"I'm old," he said, "old and bald. Angels aren't old and bald."

"Oh, yes they are. When angels have too many worries and not enough pleasures they look like you."

"I have a big family," he sighed. "I've heard tell angels are childless."

"Nonsense! They've got loads of children. Thousands of them."

"And are they angels, too?"

"Sure."

"My children are no angels. Far from it. . . ."

"Rubbish. They're just getting started."

"They are, maybe. But me. . . ." And with what was obviously tremendous effort he confessed, "I've got an ulcer; and kidney stones; and rheumatism; and my teeth are falling out."

"That's just the way it should be," I assured him. "All elderly angels have that: ulcers, kidney stones, and bad teeth."

"Why are you trying to convince me of this?" he implored. "What's in this for you?"

"Not a thing. But your ignorance does irritate me. Pardon me for saying this, but your naiveté is shocking, and a real waste. You should be flying, darting skyward, soaring through the mountain heights."

"You really think so?"

"What's to think? I know. Knew it the moment I saw you."

"To be real honest with you," he said quietly, "I once flew in a dream."

"There, you see? A sure sign."

"But that was long ago. Awfully long ago."

"Doesn't matter. You never lose a skill like that. You've just got to start again."

"You talk so convincingly," he smiled. "I'd like to believe you."

"So believe! Believe me. Finish your porridge, and then it's off with you. Onward and upward."

"Oh, to hell with this sop . . . I hate it." He pushed his plate away disdainfully, stood up, straightened his shoulders, and then asked with sudden suspicion, "So why don't you try?"

"I have, more than once. No luck. It's useless, really. I just don't have the knack. But with you it'll work. I'm sure it will. Come on, now, get going."

He paced up and down the aisle, spreading his arms a few times.

"There's not much room here," he said. "Let's go outside."

"Outside's no good. You'll just attract a lot of gawkers."

"But I can tell I'm going to need to get a good run at this."

"You could jump," I offered. "That'd be even more convenient."

"But where from? Where can I jump from?" he said anxiously, and just a shade willfully. "Where can I get any height? The cafeteria's on the ground floor."

"No, it's on the second."

"The second floor? That's still not nearly high enough," he said almost domineeringly. "That's just not high enough."

"There's a construction pit below. It should be enough."

"How do you know?" he said haughtily. "Have you ever flown?"

"No, but I checked it."

He was already standing on the window ledge.

"Hey!" he called out imperiously. "Hey, you! You tell the people at work that I've flown off."

"I'll tell them."

"And tell my wife there that I've got important business upstairs."

"I'll tell her."

"And you tell everyone else that I shall return to them."

"All right."

"So long, worm!"

And he stepped out. And off he flew. And. . . .

"No," I moaned. "He's not an angel. This one wasn't an angel, either."

And I wrung my hands, and held my head, and grew despondent over the dirty plates.

"Who is, then? Who?"

Who, indeed?

Nina Katerli

———————————
———————————
———————————
———————————

Nina Semyonovna Katerli (b. 1934 in Leningrad) graduated from Leningrad Technological Institute in 1958 with a degree in chemical engineering. Since 1976 she has been a free-lance writer. Katerli is a well-known prose writer with a number of collections of short stories to her credit. "Victory" appeared in 1977 in *Avrora*.

Victory

You've got to be quicker than they are. That's what I decided precisely at the moment when the soap popped out of my hands, flew across the room like a grasshopper, hit the tile floor, and streaked at top speed under the bathtub, its green belly gleaming maliciously. Now it's lodged in the farthest corner, and I know exactly what will happen if I try to get it. My garter will snap, twist fiendishly, and slide up my leg. The space beneath the tub will exhale its rotten breath in my face. And the bar of soap will be just far enough away to be unreachable. On the other hand, I'll manage to put a crick in my neck, and I'll sit on the floor a long time massaging it.

I stopped bothering with the soap. I went into the kitchen, but did not light the stove or set water on for coffee—the matches would have snapped, one after the other, and if I did manage to light the burner, the water would have boiled over and doused the flame. The wisest thing to do is not to get involved. So without even looking at the disappointed matches and kettle, I drank some water straight from the tap and went to get dressed.

A button on my skirt immediately tore off, but I had no intention of getting out a needle and thread. It's just what the thread was waiting for, so that it could tangle itself in a shaggy knot, and the needle could slip out of my fingers and get stuck in one of the cracks between the floor tiles, sharp end up. I calmly got out a safety pin and fastened my skirt with it, nicking my thumb on purpose so as not to give the safety pin the satisfaction of doing it on the sly.

Once I was out of the house, everything went by the book. A streetcar waited for me at my stop, then slowly rolled off just as I was pulling even with it. Even so I didn't try to catch up with it; I was sure it was headed for the garage. The next one would also be headed for the garage, then there would be no streetcars for twenty minutes. Then finally, a streetcar would appear and break down just around the first turn.

I walked and didn't even turn around when the streetcars started overtaking me, clanging loudly, and flashing their window panes. All of that was premeditated, too.

There were tangerines for sale at the stand on the corner, but I walked straight past them. I knew that all I had to do was stop there, and the saleswoman would immediately leave to help unload some incoming goods or faint dead away. The tangerines would turn out to be green tomatoes, which aren't available in January, but for me, even that could be arranged.

Trucks loaded high with bricks raced down the street, practically flush with the sidewalk. Somewhere, on some roof, there was some rusty iron sheeting that had come loose and now was waiting for a gust of wind. I had to get this over with.

I didn't manage to fall until a full block later, opposite a green-grocer's. I was forcing myself to stare at the store window, which displayed a huge pyramid of cabbage heads reminiscent of Vereshchagin's "Apotheosis of War," when I slipped and, with a sense of relief, banged my knee against the asphalt. My handbag, which I had dropped, lay sprawled next to me. Instead of having opened and spilled all my change and keys into the snow, it just lay there, stubbornly clenching its fastener.

A hideous tear should have appeared in the knee of my stocking, but when I checked, it was unblemished. I picked up my bag, stood up, and looked at my watch.

"Eleven," I said to the cabbage heads. "I've got my whole life ahead of me. Understood?"

The cabbage heads agreed, and I headed for the stand with tangerines. I had just enough money for a couple of pounds, to the cent. A streetcar approached the stop at precisely the same time as me, and it obsequiously opened its doors. It was empty. And when I discovered that I didn't have a single three-kopeck piece, I caught sight of a ticket next to my foot and realized that I had won.

Herbert Kemoklidze

Herbert Vasilevich Kemoklidze (b. 1939 in Tuapse, Russia) has lived in Yaroslavl, Russia, since 1963, when he graduated from Leningrad University in Slavic languages. He worked as a technical translator and as an editor in a Yaroslavl publishing house. Since 1986, he has been a free-lance writer, publishing numerous collections of stories. "The Truth" appeared in 1967 in *Literary Gazette*.

The Truth

Not everyone manages to find the truth, but I was lucky. The truth was lying in a box tied with a ribbon and was waiting for me to deliver it. But in order to deliver the truth, I had to get the approval of a board of five expert specialists.

THE COLOR SPECIALIST LOOKED at my truth and said, "Looks a little transparent to me. It needs a bit more blue and just a pinch of pink. Oh, now that's a different story!"

THE TASTE SPECIALIST LICKED my truth with his tongue and said, "Could use just a touch of sugar, otherwise it's too bitter. . . . Poor soul. Oh, now I understand, perfect!"

THE HEARING SPECIALIST BENT down to listen to my truth, shook it, and said, "It's not very resonant, now is it, friend? Let's hang a couple of bells on it. There. Now, admit it, that's really something!"

THE TOUCH SPECIALIST TOUCHED my truth, felt it, thumped it with his fingers, and said, "It's really not quite hard enough. No problem, we'll reinforce it with steel. Here, hold it. That's it. Now just look at it. Beautiful!"

"Can I really deliver it like that, finally?" I asked sadly, trying hard to recognize my discovery in this new, improved truth.

"Absolutely not!" the members of the board exclaimed. "We still have to check it for durability." And they began to kick my truth with their legs, bury their fists in it, throw it from corner to corner, trample it, and skewer it. "There, now you can deliver it." And I delivered a battered truth.

Alexander Khait

Alexander Iosifovich Khait (b. 1938 in Moscow) is a graduate of the Moscow Institute of Construction Engineering. Working at first as an engineer, he turned entirely to writing in 1965. He has authored collections of stories (two of them in collaboration with Aleksandr Kurlyandsky), plays, and screenplays for full-length and animated short films. "When I Look in the Mirror" appeared in 1976 in *Literary Gazette*.

When I Look in the Mirror

As far back as I can remember, people have always been taking me for someone else. Who exactly, I don't know, but it hasn't been me. Apparently there's something so banal and ordinary about my face that it's reminiscent of all the faces in the world. Even I get the feeling, when I look in the mirror, that I've seen this person someplace before. I just can't remember where—on the bus, at the bakery, or maybe at work?

Years ago, when I was still young and naive, I would argue, shout, even get out my driver's license, but as time passed I became resigned. That's when I finally understood that no matter what you do, you can't prove anything, you just alienate people. And so I walk the city streets looking like other people, sometimes concealing my stranger's face by pulling up my collar.

"Volodya!"

That's probably for me. Even though my name is really Petya. I look back. A short, hefty woman in a pants suit comes running down the street toward me. The woman is not my type, but that fact doesn't seem to inhibit her.

"Volodya, dear!" she calls from halfway down the street. "Where have you been? Shameless! You never call, you never come by."

"Oh, I lost track," I answer cautiously. "There's been so much work."

"Come on now," she wags her index finger at me. "I know all about your work. I've known you longer than that."

Longer than that. I see. So we've been carrying on like this for quite a while.

The woman takes up my hand and holds it.

"Say, wouldn't you like to come to my place, just for a minute?"

I can't refuse people who look at me with eyes like that. "Fine, but just for a minute."

I'm sitting with a strange woman in a strange apartment. We drink dry wine, which I can't stand, and we reminisce about the Crimea, where I've never been. Gradually our conversation spends itself. For a few minutes we sit in silence.

"Volodya, Volodya," my new acquaintance says. "I'm risking everything for you, cheating on my husband."

My sense of male solidarity is provoked. "That's not a good thing. Cheating on your husband is no good at all."

"Jerk," the woman says wearily. "How dare you lecture me after all this? You're just . . . You're just . . . Do you know what you are?"

I don't get a chance to find out, because just then the front door bangs shut.

"It's my husband," the woman says, frightened.

I glance around the room. There's the table with half-finished glasses of wine, the ashtray full of cigarette butts, the woman in her bathrobe. All we're missing is the husband returning from his business trip.

And here he is. A baldish man with woolly, poodle-like sideburns looks in through the doorway. He looks at me intently and says, "I see."

He heads toward me with deliberate step. I shut my eyes and sink down deeper into my chair. I don't like it when people hit me. It always seems to be a bad sign.

"I see," the husband repeats. "So you've finally deigned to come."

"This isn't me. There's a misunderstanding."

"Nonsense. You should be ashamed, Semyon Borisych. You borrowed the money for two weeks, and it's been half a year now already."

Out of the frying pan. . . . This one has me mixed up with somebody, too. Although it's far preferable to be caught a debtor than a lover.

"You know, I'd just come over to pay my debt to you. How much do I owe?"

"Forgotten that already, huh? Fifty on the nose."

"What!?" In shock, I look over at the woman, who doesn't speak. She can deal with that figure, as long as it's my money. Her honor is at stake.

"I've only got thirty on me," I smile pathetically. "If you don't mind, I'll bring the other twenty tomorrow."

The husband tears the notes out of my hand. "All right, then. And you'd better be sure I get the rest tomorrow."

I make a nimble exit from the apartment, forgetting to say good-bye to my dearest. In an effort to cover my tracks, I circle through a maze of back streets and inner courtyards. When I am confident no one is in pursuit, I venture out onto a through street, casually drawing on a cigarette.

There's a broad-shouldered type waiting for me out on the street.

"Valery?" he asks rhetorically.

I nod to him just in case.

"How long have I waited for this day," he says joyously, then slugs me full in the face.

"What's that for?" I shout. "What's that for?"

"That's what for. Don't tell me you've forgotten in just a month. Kulchitsky told me everything."

"Who's Kulchitsky? I don't know any Kulchitsky!"

"Really? Then maybe you don't know Tarasov either?" he says and moves toward me again.

I sense that it would be better not to raise a fuss.

"Tarasov I know. No use denying that."

"Then listen up. Tomorrow you're going to see Ivan Matveich and tell him everything just like it was."

"I'll tell him everything," I readily agree.

"You watch out, I'm gonna check up on you."

"Absolutely," I say. "'Trust but verify' is what I say."

For a few seconds he looks at me, apparently weighing whether or not to lay on some more. Then he turns and walks off down the street at a leisurely pace.

I wonder what that Valery got slugged for? What could he have done to deserve it?

As I walk down the avenue I get lost in thoughts of all these

Kulchitskys, Tarasovs, and many, many others whom I will never know anything about.

"Citizen," an old woman with a baby carriage calls out to me. "What happened to you? You said you'd be a minute, and now you've been gone for half an hour."

"I'm sorry," I say out of habit. "I got held up."

"Held up? As though I didn't have anything else to do but look after your baby."

And with a hefty shove she rolls the baby carriage over my way.

That was the limit, though. Even for me.

"Excuse me," I say, "but this is not my child."

"What do you mean not yours? You yourself asked me to keep an eye on him."

"You're mistaken. That was someone else who asked you."

The woman examines me closely. "That's strange. You look just alike, and the clothes are the same."

"The clothes, maybe, but not the baby. This is not my baby, do you hear? I don't have any children."

"That's strange. Very strange."

The child wakes up at the sound of our voices. He looks up out of the carriage, stretches his little arms out toward me, and says, "Da-da, da-da."

"Monster," the woman says. "Never heard of anyone renouncing their own child."

She turns away from me in disgust and vanishes down a dark path, swinging her shopping bag.

The two of us are left alone. Someone else's baby and I. Let's just wait, then. The real father is bound to come for him. Five minutes pass, then ten, and no one shows.

It begins to rain, a drizzly, piercing rain. People resembling me run past us, but the real father is not among them. The baby starts to whimper. He's probably cold, or hungry. I glance down into the buggy. Cute little boy, he even looks a little like me. Maybe I really should take him home. We could rest a while, warm up, then come back here.

I walk down the street, pushing a buggy with somebody else's baby in front of me. Cold raindrops roll down my collar, but I don't care. I'm in a fine mood. The streets are deserted now, and now at least, I can be myself for a few minutes. Which is something I need very much. You see, the day's not over yet, I still have to face my wife. I wonder who she'll take me for today.

Ruslan Kireev

Ruslan Timofeevich Kireev (b. 1941 in Kokand, Uzbekistan) graduated in 1967 from Gorky Literary Institute, Moscow, where he is now chairman of the creative writing program. He is a prolific author with several dozen novels and collections of stories. "My Strength of Character" appeared in 1972 in *Literary Gazette*.

My Strength of Character

I left the apartment to go buy some ravioli. A girl rode past on an orange bicycle. The sunlight played in its silvery spokes. In the rear basket there was an old-model Zil refrigerator. The girl was sniffing a white lily. With her other hand she held on to the handlebars.

"Shipment of refrigerators just in," said a woman in yellow house slippers as she walked past. She was eating an Eskimo pie. The Eskimo pie was melting and rhythmically dripping into her palm, which would extend intermittently to intercept each drop. A puddle was forming in her palm.

The girl raised the arm that was guiding the handlebars and signaled for me to come over. I stepped up to the curb.

"Do you mean me?" I asked.

Instead of answering, she tossed the lily at me. The lily landed on my shoulder. I turned my head and sniffed it. It smelled of violets. A speck of dust detached itself from the material covering my shoulder and flew into infinity.

"Thank you," I said.

The girl jumped off her bicycle and laughed an inaudible but dazzling laugh.

"Would you like me to sell you the refrigerator?" she asked.

I shook my head, carefully, so as not to dislodge the lily that smelled of violets.

"Why not?" the girl wondered.

The bicycle stood obediently at her side.

"I can't," I answered. "I only have a ruble. For two cans of ravioli."

"You can have it for a ruble," the girl said.

A passerby—the woman in yellow house slippers—stopped and stood next to us. She listened to our conversation while the Eskimo pie melted and filled up her palm.

"I can't," I said and blushed the color of her bicycle. "I have to buy ravioli."

Then the girl threw the refrigerator door open and the light inside it switched on, revealing a can of sardines.

"You can have the sardines," she said. "You'll have a refrigerator, too."

"I have to have ravioli," I grumbled uncertainly.

The lily on my shoulder was exuding scent and keeping me from being assertive.

"May I have it?" the woman in the yellow house slippers asked. "I live near here."

She had completely forgotten about her Eskimo pie. The drops running down into her palm had become a thin stream.

The girl did not dignify that with an answer.

"Think about it," she said to me. "You might be sorry."

"No," I said and shook my head—carefully, so as not to dislodge the lily. "I must fulfill my obligation."

"Oh, you!" the girl said, and laughed inaudibly but dazzlingly. She hopped back on her bicycle and raced off, steering with one hand.

"Take the flower!" I shouted after her, but she didn't turn back.

"Black marketeer for sure," the woman in yellow house slippers growled.

The Eskimo pie had flowed into her palm, where now an entire small lake was splashing. A boy was running past. He stopped, made a boat out of a newspaper, and launched it into the woman's palm.

I glanced cautiously at the lily.

"Shoo!" I whispered, and it disappeared.

And I was on my way to buy ravioli.

Vladimir Klimovich

Vladimir Vladimirovich Klimovich (b. 1935 in Moscow) was a student of the Moscow Regional School of Physical Education. He worked as a lathe operator and volleyball coach. From 1960 to 1990 he was a drummer in a number of jazz bands. "In the Nick of Time" appeared in 1970 in *Literary Gazette*.

In the Nick of Time

Disaster struck.

Our director, Fyodor Fyodorovich, took ill. Seriously ill, even terminally. Everyone in our office was upset and there was a good deal of crying. Fyodor Fyodorovich was a true leader and a decent person. He was well liked in our collective, and everyone made ready for his untimely demise.

His assistant, Ivan Stepanovich, prepared a eulogy, to the effect that he had passed on in his prime, and other things in that vein.

The union local set up a fund for an orchestra and a statue.

Each of us pitched in as much as he could for wreaths.

The central office made arrangements for burial at a special cemetery for dignitaries.

Fyodor Fyodorovich did not suffer long. He got better. He recuperated and left for a vacation at a resort.

At work everyone was thrown into a panic.

The sculptor had already been paid his advance.

The musicians had already brought their trumpets.

The cemetery called and demanded delivery. The burial was overdue and they had to meet the requirements of their plan.

Ivan Stepanovich's eulogy had been written for nothing.

All this gave me cause to reflect.

An opportunity like this comes once in a lifetime. You just couldn't pass it up. So I up and died.

Ivan Stepanovich delivered his eulogy, he just changed the initials and the last name.

My reprimand was officially revoked. Posthumously.

The sculptor made the statue's forehead a bit smaller and its ears a bit larger and turned out my spitting image.

An obituary appeared in the evening paper.

And here I lie beneath all my wreaths in the cemetery for dignitaries. My neighbor to the left is a famous actor, and there's a general to my left.

What bliss!

Nikolay Konyaev

Nikolay Mikhailovich Konyaev (b. 1949 in the village of Voznesene on Lake Onega, Russia), a graduate of Gorky Literary Institute, has been a free-lance writer since 1982. He has written a novel and collections of short stories. He continues to write ironic stories as a diversion from longer works. "Apparently there is something in me that fits only in these stories," Konyaev writes. "Nastenka the Tree" was published in 1976 in *Studencheskii meridian*.

Nastenka the Tree
(A Modern-Day Fairy Tale)

At twilight, when the pallid mist slowly crept along the garden paths, Nastenka would often leave the house and, standing beneath the windows, imagine that she was a tree. In this way she passed her earliest childhood, and when she started going to school a funny thing happened to her.

"What do you want to be when you grow up, children?" the teacher asked and, looking at her roster, called out a name, "Avdyukhin?"

A boy somewhat resembling a hippopotamus stood up at his desk and said in a forced bass, "I want to be a pilot."

"Very good," the teacher praised him and called out the next name, "Averkin?"

Everything went well. The children wanted to be policemen or doctors, sailors and salesmen, deep-sea divers and astronauts, until the teacher's finger hit on Nastya's name.

"I want to be a tree," Nastya said simply.

"Why a tree?" the teacher asked, perplexed, tearing her eyes from the roster to stare intently at Nastya.

"Because it's green," she answered smiling. "Bugs and all kinds of birds live in it."

"Now, now," the teacher interrupted her, "we all know what trees are. Please tell us what profession you're choosing. It's impossible to be a tree."

"I know," Nastenka said glumly, "but at least for a while I'd like to be . . ."

"What?" the teacher asked.

"A tree," Nastenka said and broke into tears.

At that point she was called in to the principal's office, but even there she wouldn't renounce the tree. "You're practically all grown up," they told her.

"I know," Nastenka answered, "but I want to be a tree."

"You ungrateful girl," her parents scolded her when they were summoned by the principal. "We do our best for you, try to raise you properly, and you refuse to become anything."

"But I do," Nastenka hurried to answer, swallowing parts of words, "I want to become a tree, with bran—so lots of bir—and bugs . . . can live in me."

Again they scolded and shamed her, and only her old, wrinkled grandmother asked, "What kind of tree do you want to be, sweetheart? A birch, or maybe a cherry tree?"

"Oh, grandma, you're so silly, I just want to be a tree."

Grandmother turned away, pressing a corner of her kerchief to her lips in grief.

But soon they quit bothering her. Years passed. Nastenka grew up, and so did the boys in her grade, and Avdyukhin looked less and less like a hippopotamus. Then school was over, and Nastenka started college. It turned out that she and Avdyukhin were in the same classes. She and Avdyukhin were thought to be on friendly terms, but they spoke only rarely, and mostly Nastenka only watched him from afar. It was from her friends that she learned that Avdyukhin was getting married. She cried all that day, burying her face in her pillow. In the evening she got up from bed and suddenly remembered that she was a tree. She quickly got her things together and hurried to catch the last commuter train to the country. It was already dark. Huge stars were shining above the train station. Dogs were drowsily barking at each other behind tall, obscure fences. When she reached her place she didn't enter the house, but headed straight for the overgrown orchard, where she threw off her overcoat and took her place among the trees.

That night was long and blissful. Rough bark gradually enveloped her, and buds languorously swelled up on the branches. Still conscious of herself, Nastenka tried to rearrange her feet so she would be facing the house, but her legs refused to obey her. They had taken root.

Her parents looked for her for a long time, but neither the police nor the feds could help them. All her parents could do was grow old in the bitter silence of the overgrown orchard.

Her father was eventually transferred to another city, and they sold their cabin. They sold it to Avdyukhin, the same young man with whom Nastenka had been so totally and hopelessly in love.

Avdyukhin had changed a great deal in the course of the years. He was fatter, balder, and very domesticated.

He wandered through the orchard a long time and sized things up. Here he would put in some strawberries, and there some cucumbers. He sighed. The orchard was old and dilapidated, and it had to be thinned out. He stood in front of Nastenka for a long time, but could not figure out what kind of tree she was. Then he gave up and decided it had to be cut down, too.

The tree was removed, but the shadow of its branches remained on the ground. And in this shadow neither strawberries nor cucumbers grew.

Before long Avdyukhin was asked to come to school. Apparently his son, a first grader, had said he wanted to become a lake.

"It's so bright and shiny and big," he said, and he cried. Avdyukhin gave his son a thorough beating with his belt.

Vitaly Korotich

Vitaly Alekseevich Korotich (b. 1936 in Kiev) completed his medical studies at Kiev Medical Institute in 1959 and practiced medicine until 1966, when he became a free-lance writer. He first established himself as a poet in Ukrainian, although he also wrote some prose in Russian. From 1978 to 1986 he was editor of the Ukrainian journal *Vsesvit*, and from 1986 to 1991 he was the editor-in-chief of the weekly magazine *Ogonek*, possibly the most influential forum of democratic reform in Russia during that period. He is the author of numerous books of poetry, fiction, and essays. "Something about Astronomy" was published in 1973 in *Literary Gazette*.

Something about Astronomy

Ivan Ivanovich Marchenko smoked cheap cigarettes and knew all there was to know about soccer and true love. Ivan Ivanovich Marchenko read about mob conspiracies in the evening paper and was incensed by the thought that such people were still walking on the face of the planet. There was no love lost between Marchenko and organized crime. Ivan Ivanovich Marchenko often went to the movies; he liked action-packed films with a minimum of songs. In the summer Ivan Ivanovich took a ferry to the beach, where with great relish he would consume cold beer in the shade. Then he would splash for a while in the river. (What else would you have him do, if he likes to swim and drink beer?)

Every day Ivan Ivanovich Marchenko went to work, where he composed various documents, for this was the essence of his job. All week long he would passionately look forward to the weekend, for he craved his rest like a bird does the sky (this of course is putting it very figuratively, because Marchenko had never flown, even in a plane). On Fridays, as he locked up his desk, Ivan Ivanovich never missed wishing everyone a pleasant weekend. And on his way home in the streetcar he thought of happiness—this thought was light and winged, for he was just that kind of happy person: after all, movies ran for his benefit, and the sun shone in his honor. Marchenko enjoyed living in the world.

Ivan Ivanovich Marchenko would have continued to live peacefully, if only he hadn't been caught up in a cleverly set snare. Someone remarked on television once that it was still unknown whether there was life on Venus and the other planets. That is, nobody knows yet exactly, and alas, it was impossible to hide from such a truth. And that is when Ivan Ivanovich suddenly got mad.

Until that day Ivan Ivanovich Marchenko had not had a single worry. And suddenly, it turned out that not everything in the world was certain. Ivan Ivanovich Marchenko silently sat in the park, paying no attention to the cold raindrops falling on his head through the branches of a drenched ash tree. "What now," he thought. "What have we come to?" Marchenko took ill with these complex, incomprehensible questions. Ivan Ivanovich Marchenko had always liked clarity in everything. He had gotten used to the fact that sparks come from stones and cold comes from wind and ice. . . . And he refused to understand why it was necessary to stand for all these mob conspiracies. Why was he forced to bear within him this question, cold and clammy like fear: "Is there life on Venus and all those other places?"

. . . At last Ivan Ivanovich Marchenko fell into a deep sleep. He had finally understood with piercing clarity that, in fact, everything had long been known, that the one who should know apparently already did, and that it would be revealed to him, Marchenko, at the appropriate time. And once again the world became peaceful and glorious. . . . Ivan Ivanovich Marchenko drinks cheap beer.

Felix Krivin

Felix Davidovich Krivin (b. 1928 in Mariupol, Ukraine) is a popular short story and fable writer. He received his degree in Russian from Kiev Pedagogical Institute in 1951, and for a while worked as a teacher and as an editor in a publishing house in Uzhhorod, Ukraine. He is the author of numerous collections of stories and several motion picture screenplays. He writes: "I have never made a special point of being humorous—things just tend to come out funny, because that's how life is." "If Such a Thing Should Happen" appeared in 1969 in *Iunost'*.

If Such a Thing Should Happen . . .

It has become something of a tradition to compare life to the theater. They say that in life, as in the theater, there are stars, extras and spectators. There is a stage one can enter onto, exit off of, or even step farther back from so that one can see the curtains.

And yet, when we compare life with the theater, we have to keep the differences in mind as well as the similarities. An actor gives a brilliant performance of a villain, and everyone applauds him. If a person takes that role on himself, he evokes sheer indignation, which becomes all the stronger, the better the role is played. If a person does a poor job portraying a king or minister of state, he would be hooted off the stage for it, while in life it's no big deal—people don't mind it, and even applaud it. For in life the main thing is what you portray, and how you do it is only secondary. In life it's better to do a poor job playing a volunteer patrolman than a good job playing a delinquent. (The best thing, of course, is to play a good role well.)

One more significant difference: in the theater an actor performs in different roles, while in life a person—premeditated frauds excluded—can't abandon a role once he assumes it, which is why it's so difficult for him to imagine himself as a participant in any other person's life dramas and collisions.

Even if only rarely, just once in a while. . . . If such a thing should happen. . . .

Gulliver Becomes Robinson Crusoe

The land of the Lilliputians is far behind, and the land of the giants is far away, and the land of Laputa and the land of the Houyhnhnms, all of them were somewhere in the midst of other seas. Lemuel Gulliver, a shipwrecked physician, found himself on an uninhabited island.

It all happened unexpectedly, spoiling the natural course of events. According to the natural course of events, it should have been Robinson Crusoe alighting on this island, but either his ship didn't wreck at the right time, or it wrecked in some unauthorized place. In any event, it was Gulliver who ended up on this uninhabited island, pursuing his independent course.

Middle-aged and medium height, this doctor, who had lived his life in the most average conditions, was hardly looking for the solitude that this uninhabited island could provide him. He was after Lilliputians, or at the very least after giants. He was looking for people of nonregulation size, among whom an average person could stand out in one way or the other. He could only live among the minute and the oversized. Their world fit good, old, average him just right.

And suddenly he wound up on a deserted island where there were no big or little people, where he would be alone, an average man. Gulliver was unaccustomed to being left to his own devices. He didn't know himself at all, didn't know how to behave himself in his presence, and he had no idea how to deal with himself.

And he said to himself, "Well."

And he answered, "What do you know."

He didn't even have a proper notion of how to talk to himself.

Back in his homeland, among other average people like himself, Gulliver did everything possible to avoid conformity. He scrupulously considered what he ought to say and how he should behave, because society closely scrutinized his every step. Sometimes he went against his own wishes, and sometimes he even opposed himself, because, as has been mentioned, he didn't know how to deal with himself. Secretly he dreamed about a land of Lilliputians or a land of giants where it would be easy for him to stand out while remaining himself.

And here was an uninhabited island. . . .

Gulliver crafted a shovel for himself. He dug up some dirt and planted something in it. He built a hut by weaving branches together. He wrapped himself in animal skins and waited for a passing ship, while gradually making his uninhabited island habitable.

And when they removed him from the island twenty years later, it was impossible to tell him from Robinson Crusoe. And they couldn't. They began writing that he was Robinson Crusoe, when he actually wasn't. He was Gulliver, an average man who never arrived in the land of Lilliputians or the land of giants.

Don Juan Becomes Quasimodo

Many books have been written about Don Juan. He is widely accused of having caused much unhappiness. Others defend him, saying that he was himself unhappy, seeking his ideal in vain.

One's ideal. You consider it your ideal up to the point where you find it. And when you look for it so intensively for so many years. . . .

Don Juan awoke and felt that he was Quasimodo. He looked in a mirror and was repulsed by what he saw. Nothing, but nothing was left of the former Don Juan.

He went outside. No one would look at him, not one timid smile, not a single furtive glance. If anyone did look at him, it was with pity rather than admiration. Something had changed, not only in him, but around him. Familiar faces became alien and unknown, homely women were transformed into unattainable beauties, and each of them resembled his ideal.

So one could find one's ideal after all, provided one only had patience. See how many there are? Just look at them. Go take your pick.

Don Juan did both. He looked and picked. He tried to say something, but they started away from him in fright. Even those who just yesterday had been drawn to him.

The world had been turned upside down and made totally different. Can it be that the entire world has to change just because one person does?

Don Juan was in pain. He was profoundly unhappy. Not the way a person is unhappy when he can't find his ideal, but the way he is unhappy when he himself cannot be the ideal, not for anyone in the whole world. This is suffering, a kind of suffering that had been foreign to Don Juan.

Poor Yorick Becomes the King of Denmark

Poor Yorick, the jester and eccentric, tugged the crown down on his naked skull, sat down on the throne, and said, as he embraced the kingdom of Denmark with a glance, "I am the king."

He said it in jest, because, after all, he was the jester. But everyone believed it at once, because once a jester sits down on the throne, what kind of joke can this be?

"Do you see this skull?" asked Yorick as he tapped a finger against his naked skull. "There may not be all that much brain in it, but who cares about that? After all, you put your crown on your noggin, not on your brain. And the noggin's the same for all of us. Just try and tell the difference."

Thus he entertained all assembled, but they did not laugh. And the prime minister said to the lesser prime minister, "Go try and tell the difference!" And the lesser prime minister hastened to fulfill this assignment.

"Do you see that skull? Some day it will be rotting in the ground, and no one will know whose skull it is—is it a jester's or the king of Denmark's? "

"The king of Denmark's," hastily confirmed the prime minister, who understood everything, which is why he was the prime minister.

And everyone agreed with him, "Of course, of course. The king of Denmark's."

Poor Yorick was bewildered. He had never had a joke flop quite so badly.

"Let's see what you say when it's lying in the ground," he chortled, not yet losing hope to amuse his audience.

"It won't be in the ground," said the lesser prime minister, who by now had understood everything. "It will never be in the ground."

Yorick grew pensive. Things were more serious than he had thought.

"Wouldn't you like to say that I'll live forever?"

"We would, we would!" both ministers replied.

"Are you sure you're not joking?" the jester asked, although he realized full well that the ministers weren't joking.

Then followed a long silence.

"I will never die," the jester said, now in total earnest. "And my skull will never lie in the ground. And there will be no problems on this account, none whatsoever."

Thus he spoke, grasping the arms of his throne with both hands, and for the first time he believed his every word. Nor did he laugh as he had been wont to do, neither did he joke. And he doubted nothing at all. . . . Poor Yorick.

Rosinante Becomes Bucephalus

There are horses that have distinguished themselves in the thunder of victories, and there are horses that have known nothing but defeat. Among the former is Bucephalus, the famous horse of Alexander the Great; and among the latter Rosinante, the horse of that sad knight Don Quixote.

All the windmills behind him, Rosinante wearily raised his long-suffering head to discover himself in the midst of a genuine battlefield. The field bristled with lances and glistened with swords; it rattled with threats and exploded with deafening laughter.

"Come on, you old nag."

Rosinante began to rattle his armor consisting of bulging ribs and bony legs. His tail, in which all too few hairs remained, could only tremble, but not flutter in the wind.

Old nag. . . . Easy to forget about it when there are just windmills and shacks fit only for firewood and battlements with holes and cracks. Then you'd like to throw your head back, beat the ground with your hooves and race to meet peril with your tail fluttering in the wind. Old nag. . . .

Rosinante sighed and took in as much of the chilly air as possible, which made his armor all the more pronounced. And he whinnied, at first quietly, but then more and more loudly, drowning out the rattle and thunder of the battle. And he advanced, stepping heavily, directly toward the lances and glistening swords. Old nag. . . . Which is perfectly true up to a point. But when that point is reached, Rosinante, if he really is Rosinante, becomes Bucephalus.

. . . If all these things happened. Yet such things occasionally do. Circumstances force the individual to renounce his former role.

Wouldn't it be better not to depend on roles? And if we're comparing life with the theater, isn't it better to relate to one's role conscientiously, like a real actor? And to perform your role so that everyone present freezes in delight and gratitude. To perform it in such a way as to justify your appearance onstage.

Andrey Kuchaev

Andrey Leonidovich Kuchaev (b. 1938 in Moscow) graduated from Moscow Electrotechnical Institute of Communications in 1964, with a major in radio engineering. In 1969 he became a free-lance writer and later enrolled in the Graduate Program of Directors and Screenwriters in Moscow. He has written collections of stories, stage plays, and screenplays. His first attempts at writing included poetry and short stories that the author himself characterizes as "black, tragic and lyrical"; however, his first published works were humorous stories. He still aspires to merge both currents into one genre. "Happiness" appeared in 1974 and "Nothing Special" in 1970, both in *Literary Gazette*; "What Happened to Sergeev" was published in 1975 in *Iunost'*.

What Happened to Sergeev

Let's return to our discussion of happiness.

Just think of all the things you hear on this topic. For instance, on the trolley I overheard a fairly young man say to a young woman: "By the end of the work day I'm so wrecked that just get me into my house slippers, and I'll figure out how to turn on the television somehow."

Or, as I overheard in a different setting: "I just need to stop by the donut shop on the corner, knock back a dozen donuts and some coffee, drop twenty kopecks in the concert piano, and I'm on ice."

As I understood it, the "concert piano" referred to a juke box in the donut shop, and "on ice" is the height of pleasure, nirvana.

A kettle drummer friend of mine once said to a meat cutter friend of mine: "There's no greater pleasure for me than sitting next to my kettle drum waiting for my turn to play. I may only get to hit it once, but it's from the heart, and suddenly life is worth living again."

The meat cutter thoughtfully replied: "Oh, Tolya, if you could see all the sawdust I've got in my apron pockets after a day's work, then you'd change your mind about your drum. Anybody can like music."

"Sawdust," as you've probably already deduced, is quite simply money.

The phrase "on ice" means something very specific for each person. But instead of getting into the extreme cases, let's meet Viktor Sergeev. He's a construction engineer, thirty-four years old, still unmarried, no children, college educated, nice job. Has his own room in a moderately crowded communal apartment. What's more, he has handsome nails, three business suits, a fashionable steel watchband, the freedom of a single man, a calm disposition, and no plans to marry, ever.

Adaptable, taller than average, wholesome, indulging only in champagne and only on very special occasions at that, indifferent to women, Sergeev never dreamed of becoming a writer or an explorer or an actor. He had always wanted to become a construction engineer, and he became one. He had never wanted to stop smoking, and he never did. His last x-rays had revealed pretty good lungs, and the blood tests were no cause for dismay, either.

Sergeev had never dreamed of buying a car, much less a motorcycle; he didn't understand and had no taste for hunting; he didn't overeat. He always crossed streets on the zebra stripes. In short, there was no way he could fall easy prey to risky circumstances. Let me repeat, femmes fatales had as much allure for him as cucumbers have for a cat.

So it was this sort of reinforced steel man that was sitting at work on the third of July, sharpening his number two pencil, thinking how nice it was to have his vacation behind him: back to well-ordered working days, an orderly life, and no interruptions to his schedule. No vacation resorts, no accidental friendships, no excruciating days of forced leisure, no boredom.

Sergeev worked on the eighteenth floor of a new building in the department of industrial construction, where he was supervised by knowledgeable, down-to-earth people. They never overloaded Sergeev with work, and Sergeev never missed his deadlines.

Presently his broken number two pencil would be sharpened and his neat, precise draft would be finished by lunch. There was time. Sergeev sharpened his pencil carefully, without hurrying. The lead had to be solid, long but not too long, and not too sharp. He set the sharp-ened pencil down, wrapped the shavings up in paper, threw the paper in the wastebasket, and headed for the men's room to wash his hands; there were traces of graphite on his fingers.

In the washroom, with its tiled walls and floor, Sergeev pains-takingly adjusted the faucet for a balanced flow of hot and cold water, holding his hands cupped above the blue porcelain basin. When the water reached the necessary temperature, he soaped up and rinsed his hands three times, then dried them under the blow drier, kept rubbing his palms together to massage the fingers, and turned to go back to his desk.

At just that moment the shining orb of day, completing its path through the sky, flashed across the washroom tiles so intensely that for a moment Sergeev thought that the floor and walls of the room were made not of tiles, but of ice—blinding, slick, and surprisingly unreli-able. In fright, our engineer lost his balance, slipped, started flailing his arms to regain his balance, tried to latch on to the aluminum window frame, missed, and wound up hanging halfway out the window, eigh-teen floors above the ground.

The funny thing is that he was afraid only for a second, and then he calmed down and thought, "Here goes. They're going to be scraping Sergeev off the sidewalk soon."

By some miracle he managed to catch on something with the toe of his shoe, he had no idea on what, but in any case he didn't fall. He held out, although his foot was already slipping little by little, and before long the inevitable would happen. "Oh, so what. The draft's almost finished. Anyone can put the final touches on it. Apparently by sharp-ening the pencil I've completed all my tasks on earth. Makes sense. Though of course it's unpleasant to think that someone else will finish my draft. They might wreck it or do a sloppy job. After all, it's got my signature on it. Wish I could finish it myself, take it to Alexander Fedotych, get his signature, send it to copying, then go home and feed Prokhor, my goldfinch."

Now, for some reason, the asphalt was above Sergeev, and beneath there was the warm summer sky, into which he could easily follow the birds, just like jumping into a pond.

"The neighbors can look after the bird just fine. I've straightened up the room. What else?"

Sergeev's foot slipped just a bit. His body slid into a more vertical position and it, or rather his pockets, poured out a passport, ID, address book, ballpoint pen, comb, change, pack of cigarettes, lighter, all of which streamed into the blue funnel, mingling with the martens flying low on this third of July.

"Don't really need my papers now," Sergeev consoled himself. "I've heard you can get there without them. Fine, forget about the draft. What can I say to make an appropriate exit?"

At this point more objects started falling out of Sergeev, out of secret pockets that even he wasn't aware of: some of Sergeev's free-lance jobs, blueprints with legends, a college diploma, a couple of somebody else's lecture notebooks, some average transcripts, a high school diploma, a fourth-grade honor roll certificate, counting sticks that spilled like matches, watercolors, and a pacifier with a plastic ring that had been hiding who knows where.

All of this vanished into the bottomless well, tiled with the windows of the surrounding high-rises, filled with the summer sky and poplar fluff.

Sergeev himself grew as light as the poplar fluff. Any second he would be caught up and transported, too. The last thing to fall out of Sergeev's coat pocket was a drafting set, hopelessly old-fashioned, useless for all professional purposes, with an inscription "To engineer Sergeev on his fiftieth birthday." "My father's. He left it to me," flashed through his mind. "I wonder who's going to get it now." And suddenly he felt a new surge of energy.

Performing a kind of pirouette with his legs, our construction engineer turned himself over like an hourglass and one second later was standing on the washroom floor. The sun had set behind the building opposite, and the tiles no longer bore the slightest resemblance to ice.

Sergeev straightened his tie in front of the mirror and ran out into the hallway toward the elevator. When he reached the first floor he ran outside and collected everything he had dropped—luckily the window faced the company's courtyard. Within a quarter of an hour he was sitting back at his drawing board. Carefully he set a straight edge on the sheet, posed his number two pencil over it, got ready, and pressed down, perhaps too hard, as he drew a line across the paper. The pencil point snapped and shot away.

"Oh, shoot, gosh darn." Sergeev tossed his pencil into the wastebasket.

All of his colleagues looked up in amazement. What could have happened to the engineer who never swore?

In conclusion I'd like to recall what one girl told her friend once within earshot of me on the subway.

"You know, yesterday I lost my keys, the whole ring. What a mess. My car keys, my apartment keys, my dacha keys—everything."

To which her friend replied, "I know just what you mean, I lost a library book yesterday, and it's awful."

And they began to console each other as hard as they could.

So you see what a slippery concept this "being on ice" can be. . . .

Nothing Special

Thirty-year-old engineer Malkin had gone with his wife to buy his first hat. There were only a few people in the store, and the haberdashery was completely deserted.

"Look at this," Malkin said to his wife, "what a great selection of hats they have."

"We'll see," his wife answered.

The salesman set out stacks of hats, covering the counter from one end to the other. Malkin started to try them on.

"Too small," he said, setting the first one aside.

"Too big." His wife took the second one off his head.

"Just right," the salesman said, jamming the third one on his head.

"I can't see a thing," Malkin said. The hat covered his eyes.

"We can drill holes for the eyes," the salesman suggested.

"How about this Tyrolean one?" His wife handed it to Malkin.

"It falls off," Malkin said. "Not deep enough, I'm afraid to bend my head."

"We can attach some strings to it," the salesman said.

"Try this one on, Peter," his wife said, handing him a straw hat.

"Just right," Malkin said, "except it's too tight."

"We can have it stretched out on a dummy," the salesman observed.

"Here, try this one on." His wife threw Malkin a hat with a wide, colored ribbon.

"Just right," Malkin enthused, "only my ears get in the way."

"We can take the ears and . . . ," the sullen salesman started to say.

"You see," his wife interrupted, "my husband's not quite like other people. He's different. It's really a shame. Let's go, Peter."

"Excuse me, just a minute," the salesman said. "Bend your head over, please."

Malkin did so.

The salesman took Malkin's head in his hands and squeezed it with his still powerful fingers.

Malkin's head gave way a bit and changed its shape. "Well, let's give it a try now," his wife said, handing Malkin a hat.

The hat fit Malkin just right.

"Thank you," Malkin said.

"That's what we're here for," the salesman said modestly. "And you said he's special. . . ."

Happiness

Morozov woke up from happiness.

He put off opening his eyes, prolonging his blissful state. But when Morozov's eyes finally did open, he was surprised to notice that the sense of happiness was still with him.

A tunnel of sunlight stretched from his window to the china cabinet, and a cool, summer luminescence circulated in it. Morozov slept behind the wardrobe. It was nice and shady behind the wardrobe; the sun didn't reach there.

"How's come it's so nice here?" Morozov wondered, pursing and savoring the stale butt of a cheap Belomor cigarette between his lips. "Why do I feel so light? How come I feel so great?" And Morozov began to reminisce.

. . . He'd had the usual three shots after the game. The usual two before the game. A pint during the match with a couple of his buddies. What was there to be happy about in that? The second string of his favorite team had lost their usual 4–0. . . .

Only now did Morozov notice that the pigeons were pacing about on the window ledge in anticipation of their usual feeding. Washed and squeaking as they tended to be on summer mornings, they scraped with their claws at the metal window guards.

"Go to blazes," Morozov said irritably. "What happened before the game? Why do I feel so light?"

. . . Before the game Morozov had quarreled with a friend. Next to the beer stand, on the sidewalk littered with the remains of smoked herring and processed-cheese wrappers, he had suffered to hear and himself said many an unjust and unpleasant word.

"Aw, jeez," Morozov groped for some matches and lit the butt. "He could have said that Lovchev's got a big head, or that Kolotov just runs around like a goose, but why did he have to touch Pilgui? Pilgui?! What a stupid guy."

Through the window the sunny day was getting off to a bright and brazen start. A streetcar loudly rattled around a curve. Somewhere a window went flying open with a bang and splashing water was heard all at once—someone washing windows. Morozov smiled and felt his eye throb. "You big dummy . . . unwashed ox."

Morozov sat down on his bed and scratched his bruised sides in anguished pleasure. He looked at his feet in their nylon socks and heaved an exasperated sigh, "It served him right. . . . And I shouldn't have stopped."

The sunny day was at its height in the city, glinting in the windows of far-off buildings. The still cool roofs clung to each other as far as the horizon, alternating with clumps of pristine tree crowns. All this Morozov saw from the perspective of his twelfth-floor apartment; all of this unmistakably evoked ecstasy in him.

"What did happen before that? What sort of pleasant stuff?" Morozov reached an arm out to the trousers that had been thrown on the floor (he had kept his t-shirt on), searched through them, and in the left pocket discovered not a five-ruble note as he had expected, but a crumpled one-ruble bill, along with his bus pass. "I must have spent that much before the fight," the thought flashed through his mind. "Who could have set me up like that? Yeah, Kurkov. That bloodsucker! He's never got any money. Shoot!" Morozov tossed the pants back on the floor, lay back in bed, and squinted his good eye. He grew morose, his contentment had passed.

"So why was I so happy just now? What kind of nonsense came over me?"

Morozov remembered the whole previous day, his work at the container warehouse, his lunch break, his assignments, and the book of receipts filled with purple ink. He remembered his co-workers Kramskoy and Dobuzhinsky, and at this his mood went completely sour, the last traces of his lightheartedness vanished.

In the meantime the pungent, humid air that marks the arrival of a thunderstorm had breezed in through the shutters. Just over the horizon, beneath a thunderhead, the sky darkened, and with it the white ceiling in the room. Heavy leaden thunder rumbled beyond the suburbs.

Morozov stubbed out his cigarette butt with a calloused finger and remembered, despite himself, that yesterday morning it had been summer too, that a storm had been gathering just like this, and that he had also awakened from happiness.

Alexander Kurlyandsky

——————————
——————————
——————————

Alexander Efimovich Kurlyandsky (b. 1938 in Moscow) graduated from the Moscow Institute of Construction Engineering in 1960. He has worked as a free-lance writer since the mid-1960s, publishing several collections of stories, as well as plays, screenplays, and scenarios for animated films. "Cheating" appeared in 1977 in *Literary Gazette*.

Cheating

I decided to cheat on my wife. We had lived together for twenty years. We had been through everything, good times and bad, but never anything like this. Once my wife and I saw a movie about a bank employee who slips it to his old lady. She thought he was going out bowling, but in fact he was having a fine time with some Luiza, and it certainly wasn't bowling balls they were playing with.

"You know, he was just like you," my wife said as we left the movie theater.

"How do you mean that?"

"Figuratively," she smiled. "I mean strictly his looks."

That's when the idea was planted. Fine, I thought, I'll show you. For a long time I thought about who would play my Luiza, and I finally settled on Nina Borisovna. A responsible woman, two kids, she would never blab.

During lunch break I took her aside and briefed her on the situation.

"Well," she said, "sure, I don't have any major objections. At least when it comes time to die I'll have something to remember. I just worry about my husband. What if he finds out?"

"We'll take care of it during work hours, that way your husband will never be the wiser."

At precisely ten o'clock the next day the doorbell rang. I opened the door to find Nina Borisovna there.

"Good morning. I'm not late, I hope."

"Not at all, right on time. My wife just left for work."

Nina Borisovna took off her coat and scarf and fixed her hair in front of the mirror.

"Could you take your shoes off, please?" I said. "We just had the floor varnished."

"But they're not dirty."

"Even so. House rules."

"I can't stay long," Nina Borisovna said. "I have to leave by one. I figured if the day was going to be shot I might as well get some wash done."

"Fine," I said. "In that case I'll have time to go pick up some wall-paper."

Nina Borisovna unclasped her purse and got out her cigarettes.

"Would you like a drink?"

"Thanks, never touch it."

"Why not?"

"Liver problems."

"It's the kidneys for me," I sighed. "All of a sudden I started passing these little granules last month."

"The granules aren't that bad. My husband had a stone. They had to smash it up with ultrasound treatments."

"Did he finally pass it?"

"Of course. Where else is it going to go?"

We sat in silence for a few minutes.

"Would you like some tea?"

"I wouldn't mind a cup. It is my expertise, you know," she joked.

We both had a big mug of tea.

"Would you like some more?"

"No, thank you."

I walked over and drew the curtains. The room was enveloped in twilight. Nina Borisovna asked from somewhere in the darkness, "Do you remember any poems?"

"Sure," I said. "I was just recently helping my son with one."

I recited Nekrasov's "Thoughts on the Fate of Russia on Seeing Peasants with a Petition at the Entrance of a High Official's Residence."

"Very good," Nina Borisovna said. "Too bad nothing ever came of you."

"If everyone was a success, who would be left to work in our office?"

"That's true," Nina Borisovna sighed. "You won't believe this, but I always dreamed of becoming a ballerina. I even took lessons. I did the best fouetté in my class. And you should have seen my arabesques . . . Would you like me to show you?"

She rose up on her toes and leaped into the air.

"Great, great, a regular Swan Lake, and without even having to watch TV."

But Nina Borisovna let out a yelp and fell back in her chair. "It's my back. Starting in again."

I helped her over to the couch and covered her with a wool comforter. The doorbell rang.

"Who is that?" Nina Borisovna asked.

"I don't know," I said. "Better cover yourself up to be on the safe side."

I opened the door. It was my wife. She kicked her shoes off and ran into the living room. "Just back for a second. I forgot to take the estimates."

Nina Borisovna was lying on the couch. One end of the comforter was tucked over her head, and her black-stockinged feet were sticking out at the other.

"Were you napping?" my wife asked, quickly scanning the room.

"Sweetheart. . . ."

"Have you seen a brown folder?"

"Look, sweetheart. . . ."

My wife stood up on the couch and reached toward the bookshelves.

"Ouch," Nina Borisovna yipped. "You're standing on my foot."

"Who's that?" my wife asked.

"Nina Borisovna. Remember when I told you about her?"

"What is she doing here?"

"She strained her back."

"I see," my wife said as she looked through the estimates. "Why don't you offer her some tea?"

"Thank you, we already had some."

My wife shut the folder. "I'm off." She flew out of the room, the door banging shut behind her.

"Your wife is nice," Nina Borisovna said. "You can tell right away that she's a good worker."

"You bet. She won us first place in the entire office this year."

Nina Borisovna got up off the couch and picked up her cigarettes. "I'll be going now. My back seems to be better."

"Maybe you should rest a while longer."

"No, time to go. My wash is soaking."

Alexander Kurlyandsky and Alexander Khait

"The Sixth Sense" was first published in 1968 in *Literary Gazette*. For information on the authors, see their separate entries.

The Sixth Sense

Pyotr Semyonovich Blinov started to perceive the abscyllochordia of the world around him. Just yesterday he had had only five senses, like any normal person. But today a sixth sense had been added to them—abscyllochordia. And all the objects that he had known since childhood—tables, chairs, slippers, trolleys—suddenly possessed a new and previously unknown quality. It would be hard to say just what that quality was, perhaps electromagnetic waves or some sort of special radiation still unknown to science. But known or not, Pyotr Semyonovich had acquired the sense of abscyllochordia.

The first person he told this startling news to was his wife.

"Abscyllochordia?" she asked. "What's that?"

"I don't know," Pyotr Semyonovich said. "I have no idea. There's just something unusual that I keep feeling all the time."

"How can that be?" his wife said. "How can you feel something and not know what it is?"

"No, you see, I know what it is, but I can't explain it."

"Then you can't feel it!"

"Try to understand," Pyotr Semyonovich said. "For instance, here's a chair. What is it like? It's soft, it's gray, and what else?"

"It's wooden," his wife said.

"Right, it's wooden. But I can sense that it has tremendous abscyllochordia. I can't even bear to sit on it."

"Then don't," said his wife and, offended, went to the kitchen.

Pyotr Semyonovich's wife had never understood him, and in situations like this he went to see his friends. That's what he did this time, too.

"Here's a bench. What is it like? It's wet, it's dirty. Everybody can see that. But I can sense that it has abscyllochordia."

His friends looked at each other.

"It's true, abscyllochordia. The bench has it, the air has it, the trees have it. . . ."

"Does that dog have it?"

"Yes."

"How about that cat?"

"Yes, it has it, too. Everything has it."

"Petya, don't you think you ought to go home?" his friends said. "Get a good rest, have a good night's sleep?"

"Oh, no . . . why can't you understand me? Abscyllochordia, it's like. . . ."

"Like what?"

"Oh, I can't explain it."

"No, go ahead, what is this abscyllochordia of yours like? Is it hot, is it cold, does it have some kind of smell?"

"No, none of that."

"Then what is it like?"

"Different."

His friends broke out laughing.

"Why are you laughing? I can feel it."

"Fascinating," his friends said. "He can feel this thing, and we're all a bunch of idiots."

"No, you're not idiots. You just can't feel it."

"Fine with us. Who needs it anyway?" his friends said. "We're perfectly all right without it."

To make a long story short, his friends didn't believe him either. But Pyotr Semyonovich really could feel it. How to explain the abscyllochordia that Pyotr Semyonovich was feeling? It's . . . oh well, it's impossible to explain, because it's impossible to explain to someone else something that he's never felt. You might as well try to explain to a deaf person how the birds are singing, or tell a blind person what color the sunset is. Similarly, everyone else was blind or deaf in relation to Pyotr Semyonovich, as far as abscyllochordia was concerned.

Soon Pyotr Semyonovich himself came to understand this. And he stopped trying to tell people what he felt when he looked at a simple ashtray or listened to a radio after it was turned off. Pyotr Semyonovich had come to the conclusion that he had acquired a sense that other people at this stage simply didn't yet have.

And then he turned inward. The world in which he lived from this point on not only had color, sound, and volume, but it was abscyllochordic, as well. He reveled in abscyllochordic dreams, smiled at abscyllochordic passersby and would go into childish raptures over a mere sheet of paper, if only it let off good abscyllochordia. Admittedly, he found it difficult to be in a room with excessively abscyllochordic walls or go outside during abscyllochordically bad weather, but if anyone had proposed that he forfeit this sense, he would have refused point-blank. Because thanks to it Pyotr Semyonovich's life had become unique and attractive.

Once Pyotr Semyonovich was sitting in a cafeteria—by now he rarely had lunch at home, because the food that his wife cooked, though delicious and nutritious, did not always have the right kind of abscyllochordia—dejectedly looking at the ravioli on his plate, not noticing the people around him or hearing the sound of knives and the banging of trays. He felt cold and depressed. He had already drunk his fruit juice and was getting ready to leave, when he suddenly felt something pleasant and delightful swathing him from head to foot. He raised his eyes. An elderly man was pushing his way toward his table. He was carrying a plastic tray, on which were set dishes perfectly selected in terms of abscyllochordia.

"May I join you?" the man asked.

"Help yourself," Pyotr Semyonovich said.

The man sat down. He was wearing a nicely abscyllochordic suit, a gray abscyllochordic tie, and a faintly scented abscyllochordic handkerchief was poking out of his breast pocket. The man looked at Pyotr Semyonovich observantly. Pyotr Semyonovich smiled, and so did the man.

"It's nice here," the other said.

It was as though springtime had burst forth for Pyotr Semyonovich. In fact, this place was dark and crowded, and they were serving lord knows what instead of food, but the abscyllochordia was outstanding.

"Of course it's nice," Pyotr Semyonovich said, "it's great. Well, not exactly great, but it's awfully pleasant as far as that's concerned."

"What precisely do you mean?" the stranger asked.

"Me? I mean what you mean."

"Don't tell me you feel it, too?"

"Of course I feel it. Rather strongly."

"I feel it, too," the stranger said. "And I've been feeling it for the last twenty years."

"Oh, good God," Pyotr Semyonovich exclaimed. "Then it exists. Abscyllochordia of the senses exists."

"Of course it exists."

They began talking nonstop. Each one told the other how hard it had been for him, how unpleasant that no one had understood him, and how wonderful it was to be able to pick up the abscyllochordia of the world around him.

"I insist," the stranger said, "that we celebrate this event. Trite as it may seem, I say we drink to this."

"Absolutely," said Pyotr Semyonovich.

He ran up to the serving line and brought back a bottle of port.

"Let's drink," Pyotr Semyonovich said, filling the glasses, "to it."

The stranger looked at the wine with amazement.

"What?" he asked. "Are you actually going to drink that?"

"What's wrong with it?" Pyotr Semyonovich asked apprehensively.

"But its lipotapia. . . ."

"What lipotapia?"

"It's low."

"I'm afraid I don't understand," Pyotr Semyonovich said. "What are you talking about?"

"About the lipotapia. You know, what you were just. . . ."

"Abscyllochordia?"

"No, the abscyllochordia's fine. But this lipotapia. . . ."

"I don't understand," Pyotr Semyonovich said. "What is this lipotapia?"

"What do you mean? But you can. . . ."

"What can I?"

"You can sense it, can't you?"

"No," Pyotr Semyonovich said. "You'll have to excuse me. Sight, hearing, abscyllochordia, that's all fine. But lipotapia? I'm sorry, I'm afraid I haven't reached any such stage of enlightenment."

The stranger lost his composure. "But it exists!"

"I doubt it," Pyotr Semyonovich said soberly.

"But I can sense it."

"Then explain it to me."

"Well, it's . . . How can I put it? No, it's just impossible!"

"You know, sir," Pyotr Semyonovich said, "I had thought that you were . . . could really . . . and now it turns out . . . Now I doubt that you can even sense abscyllochordia."

"How dare you!"

"Oh, please stop that. Just look at what you're saying. You're the only one who can sense it, and everybody else can't."

The stranger got up from the table.

"Good-bye. We have nothing more to talk about."

"See you later," Pyotr Semyonovich said. "My best to the Lipotatians!"

He watched the stranger leave, then he picked up his wine glass and contentedly squinted at it. No problems. Its abscyllochordia was fine.

Mikhail Mishin

Mikhail Anatolevich Mishin (b. 1947 in Tashkent, Uzbekistan) graduated from the Leningrad Electrotechnical Institute in 1971 and worked as an engineer until 1974, when he began writing full-time. He has published several collections of stories. "What Didn't Happen to Nenashev" was published in 1975 in *Avrora*.

What Didn't Happen to Nenashev

Nenashev didn't wake up in the morning in a good mood. He didn't have a thorough work-out, after which he didn't busy himself with his toilet. Not appreciating his breakfast as he should have, Nenashev didn't kiss his wife as he left the house. As he stepped outside, he didn't smile at the rays of the vernal sun. In the subway he did not yield his seat to an elderly woman.

Nenashev did not arrive at work on time, and immediately did not lose himself in a fascinating task. After a while, he didn't go to the library, where he didn't acquaint himself with the latest research in his field. Later, while attending a technical meeting, Nenashev, to the best of his ability, did not contribute to solving the matters on the agenda. Before lunch he managed not to make any comments to his employees about their overlong cigarette breaks.

"You all ought to be ashamed of yourselves, comrades," he didn't say.

Coming back after lunch, Nenashev didn't finish an urgent memo. At the trade union meeting at the end of the work day, Nenashev did not deliver a report and more than once did not take the floor during debate. During the voting on the first issue, Nenashev was not in favor, while on the second issue he was not opposed.

He did not leave work exhausted, but content, and on the street he immediately did not see a tough bothering a girl. Then he did not go up to a flower stand and did not buy his wife some violets. In the subway station Nenashev, as was his wont, did not inspect the theater announcements. When he read in the evening paper that the local soccer team had lost a game, he did not get upset. When he read that the hockey team had won, he was not overjoyed.

When he came home, Nenashev, as usual, did not go over his son's homework and did not help his wife with the household chores. Then he didn't write to his mother.

And it wasn't until late in the evening, right before he went to sleep, that Nenashev suddenly didn't become depressed, didn't become pensive, and didn't arrive at the firm conclusion that somehow he was not living as he should.

Lev Novozhenov

Lev Yurevich Novozhenov (b. 1946 in Moscow) studied history at the Moscow Pedagogical Institute and journalism at the Moscow Publishing Trade School; he works as a journalist. The author of numerous stories and two plays, his first book is forthcoming. "Humor has been my life-long occupation, my fate," he writes. "One Fifty Four" appeared in 1974 in *Literary Gazette*.

One Fifty Four

Ivan Petrovich Sidorov (no awards, no service record, no criminal record, never been abroad, knows no foreign languages) woke up in a good mood. The weather was also good (gentle to moderate wind, temperature fluctuating from 38 to 44 degrees, visibility two miles).

Neither had his spouse Sofya Antonovna (height five feet four inches, weight 154) changed from the day before.

Sidorov washed (Baby hand soap, Mary toothpaste, fights cavities) and then had breakfast (one poached egg for his diet, bologna, grade-A Georgian tea).

Sidorov smoked a cigarette (Yava brand, thirty kopecks for a pack of twenty) and left his apartment.

The elevator was working fine. There was a sign on the front door of the apartment building that said "Don't Slam Door." Sidorov did not slam it.

Outside, somebody asked Sidorov for a cigarette.

"I don't smoke," Sidorov answered.

Several paces later he was stopped and asked what time it was.

"I don't have a watch," Sidorov answered.

At the bus stop Sidorov was asked how to get to Kerosine Lane.

"I'm not from here," Sidorov answered.

Several people instantly accosted Sidorov on the bus. "Do you have change for the ticket machine?"

"I've got a bus pass," Sidorov cut them off.

He had barely entered his office when the phone rang.

"Ivan Petrovich, have you got a ruble?" the receiver droned.

"Sure do," Sidorov answered.

"Lend it to me till pay day."

"Can't. It's my last."

Five minutes later the phone rang again. "Sidorov, the director wants to see you."

"Have you ever been to France?" the director asked Sidorov as he was walking in.

"France?"

"That's right, France."

"I haven't been to France."

"We're sending you there. Lovely, incredible France," the director said longingly.

"I can't go to France just now," Sidorov said despondently.

"Why not?" the director said, nonplussed.

"My wife's caught cold," Sidorov said, still more despondently.

"I see, that changes things," the director said, disappointed. "Then we'll have to send Petrov."

Sidorov returned to his office. Seconds, then minutes, and whole hours went by.

At the end of the work day someone rushed into his office.

"Are you Sidorov?" the person asked.

"That's right," Sidorov answered.

"Ivan Petrovich Sidorov?"

"Yeah," Sidorov answered.

"Is your wallet black with a zipper?"

"What of it?" Sidorov said.

Sidorov picked it up, looked inside, counted the money.

"Nope, it's not mine," Sidorov said, returning the wallet.

"It's not yours?" the man asked.

"No, it's not."

"In that case, sorry," the man said and left.

After work Sidorov arrived home without incident. Just then his wife was weighing herself on the bathroom scales.

"Ivan Petrovich, guess how much I weigh," she shouted out to him.

"How much?" Sidorov asked cautiously.

"One fifty four," his wife shouted.

"Thank God," Sidorov sighed in relief.

Grigory Pruslin

Grigory Semyonovich Pruslin (b. 1936 in Leningrad) graduated from the Tula Polytechnical Institute in 1959, and later earned his Ph.D. He worked as an engineer in numerous scientific and research institutes until 1992. Currently he works as a journalist and continues to publish short stories. "Purple-Colored Camel" was published in 1971 in *Literary Gazette*.

Purple-Colored Camel

At 3:45 in the morning Evgeny Arkadevich dreamed of a purple-colored camel. Without switching on the light, the camel quietly entered his bedroom, walked up to Evgeny Arkadevich, sighed, closed its eyes, and kissed him on the forehead.

Evgeny Arkadevich shuddered and awoke. His forehead was wet, cold, and sticky.

Evgeny Arkadevich began to feel uneasy. He closed his eyes, and the camel was standing there next to him.

"Are you a camel?" Evgeny Arkadevich asked.

"That's right," the camel answered. "Why, does that shock you?"

This somewhat embarrassed Evgeny Arkadevich, and he said, "Oh, no, but what's the reason?"

"What do you mean? What's the reason I'm a camel? Well, I'll tell you, somehow it just worked out that way. Where I come from we're all camels. Myself included."

"No, no, don't misunderstand. I'll grant that you're a camel. But why a purple one?"

"What else? Were you expecting a light brown one?"

"More or less," Evgeny Arkadevich groped. "I had the impression camels were light brown. Well, maybe not exactly light brown, but sort of light-colored, you know. I'm sorry, won't you have a seat?"

"Thanks." The camel carefully folded back a corner of the sheet and sat down on the edge of the bed. "So what is it that bothers you?"

"The color. Your color bothers me," Evgeny Arkadevich babbled. "It just can't be."

"And why can't it?" the camel smacked its lips in displeasure. "Have you seen many camels?"

"Well, no, not so many."

"Then you're not in a position to judge. So," the camel crossed its legs, "mind if I smoke?"

An eerie feeling came over Evgeny Arkadevich. He sensed that it would be impossible for him to raise any objections.

"But I've read about this, and I've seen pictures," he gasped in despair.

"Now don't tell me you believe everything you read," the camel smiled perceptively. "Come now, you're a grown man."

"You're no kid, either. So prove it to me."

"Prove what? That I'm not a camel?"

"Not that. Why you're purple. Come on, let's hear it, explain it to me. I don't suppose you can."

"You're implying that you can explain everything?" his hump-backed interlocutor gibed again.

Evgeny Arkadevich lost all composure. His heart began to beat in violent, arrhythmic lurches. More than anything in the world, Evgeny Arkadevich valued clarity, always and in all things. He felt at ease on the job and at home only when everything could be readily understood. So far this had been possible. But now there was this purple camel sitting on his bed, with its legs crossed and a cigarette between its huge teeth.

"Maybe something happened to you," Evgeny Arkadevich tried to come to its aid.

"Like what?"

"Maybe you've been painted. I used to have a camel-hair blanket that was green," he blurted out tactlessly.

"Fortunately I'm not a rug, yet," the camel bristled. "Why are you getting so upset? Go to sleep."

"No, no, how can I. I get it! Maybe it's that you're foreign."

"No. I'm a local."

"Synthetic, maybe?"

"One hundred percent natural."

"Maybe you're the result of genetic engineering. . . ."

"No. I'm normal, unadulterated."

"I know, you're a mutant!" Evgeny Arkadevich suddenly guessed.

"And you're a loon. Leave me alone." The camel rose.

"Don't go!" Evgeny Arkadevich called out, tears choking his voice. "Don't go. If you go, I'll never find out, and it'll be the ruination of me."

There was so much genuine despair in his voice that the camel stopped.

"All right, I'll tell you." And he leaned right down over Evgeny Arkadevich's ear. "I'll tell you; that's the way it has to be. Do you read me? The way it has to be."

A huge load slipped off Evgeny Arkadevich's chest. The world once again became clear and rational. He fell back on his pillow and went to sleep.

He slept peacefully, breathing through his nose.

Nikolay Shakhbazov

———————
———————
———————
———————

Nikolay Grigorevich Shakhbazov (b. 1919 in Tbilisi, Georgia) gradu- ated from the Gorky Literary Institute in 1946. The free-lance author of several collections of stories, he also served as a literary censor under the Soviet regime. "An ironic turn of mind is second nature to me," he writes. "My Circle of Friends" appeared in 1968 in *Literary Gazette*.

My Circle of Friends

Someone said that somebody had died of cancer. Nobody present had known the deceased; still, they all nodded their heads and each of them mentioned somebody else that had died, and of cancer, too. The con- versation turned to the dead and someone recalled that cremation had been practiced even among the ancient Hindus. "Perfectly true," one young man said. "The ancient Hindus did not bury their dead; they committed them to fire." When it became clear that certain Hindu cus- toms had been preserved even to the present day, the suggestion was made that it would not be a bad idea to do some traveling, to see firsthand what was happening in the world. "Ancient Hindus aside," the young man said, "even Verrocchio and Leonard da Vinci can't really be appreciated from reproductions." Again everyone nodded as- sent, and each one said that appreciating Verrocchio and Leonardo da Vinci solely from reproductions of their work was simply out of the question.

About then the hostess served coffee, and the sugar bowl circulated among the guests. One of the women—an army wife who hadn't said a word all evening—suddenly said that she had found a real bargain on milk at the market that day. At this point everyone began talking at once, and nothing was really comprehensible, but it was at least clear that things couldn't go on like that. Someone remarked belatedly that some relative or other of one of his neighbors had died of cancer, but everyone shrugged him off. Somebody said that it would be nice to get together more often, preferably at the Smoliches' or at the Potapovs', as they used to. Incidentally, the Butkovskys were a good prospect, they had just gotten a new apartment, and Tatyana Pavlovna was rumored to have finally moved out.

"She's moved out? Tatyana Pavlovna has moved out?" was heard from every corner of the room. "It's hard to believe that Tatyana Pavlovna could have moved out," said the one who had bought milk at the market. "It just can't be, Tatyana Pavlovna can't have moved out," a young man said. "It positively can't be." "Beg your pardon," said the hostess's husband, "but I also heard that Tatyana Pavlovna had moved out." Everyone started talking at once and those present were split into two sides—a side that maintained that Tatyana Pavlovna had moved out, and a side that insisted that couldn't have happened.

"Where did Tatyana Pavlovna move to?" somebody asked. "What difference does it make?" the hostess said. "The main thing is that she's moved out." "She went back where she came from," said the hostess's husband. He didn't know where Tatyana Pavlovna had moved to, either. "It was either to Achinsk or Barnaul," said the one who had bought milk at the market. "It was Barnaul!" the hostess's husband confirmed. "Even so, we ought to get together at the Butkovskys'," a voice of reason said. "Whether or not Tatyana Pavlovna has moved out, we ought to get together at their place—they've got three rooms, and there are no kids."

"But they don't have a telephone," the hostess's husband said. "None of these new houses have telephones." "I envy anybody who doesn't have a telephone," came the voice that had recently discoursed on the ancient Hindus. "Nothing but trouble comes from telephones." "You know," exclaimed the hostess, recalling something, "someone has been calling us the last two nights. Alexander Vasilevich answers the phone, but whoever is on the other end just blows into the receiver." "A lot of my friends have had the same thing happen to them," said the young man. "You ought to call the police about it," said the voice of reason. "Better not, or they'll take your phone out," said the army wife who had bought milk at the market. "Then we'd better meet at the

Potapovs',” said the voice of reason. “Who would want to go all the way over to the Butkovskys' without knowing if they're home?”

The Potapovs lived downtown, but more importantly, they had a telephone, and it was always possible to get hold of them. The fact that they lived downtown and that it was always possible to get hold of them spoke most strongly for getting together at their place, and not at the Butkovskys' or even the Smoliches'. That had been obvious from the start, but for some reason nobody had mentioned it; still, when they had decided on the Potapovs', everyone said how amazed they were that it hadn't occurred to anyone earlier. From then on things were much simpler, and it happened that it occurred to everyone to get up to leave at precisely the same time. The conversation in the hallway concerned minutiae which there is no need to mention here, and as they were leaving, everyone felt particularly happy, having come to the conclusion that, whatever the others might have said to the contrary, life was in fact pretty curious.

Evgeny Shatko

Evgeny Ivanovich Shatko (b. 1931 in Engels, Russia) lived in Moscow from 1955 until his death in 1984. He graduated from the Saratov Art Institute in 1950 and the National Institute of Cinematography in 1955. Numerous collections of his stories have been published and four movies produced based on his screenplays. "The Wheel of Fortune" appeared in 1969 in *Literary Gazette*.

The Wheel of Fortune

When the guests started singing "The Last Train Home," Semyon Stepanovich picked up an empty salad bowl from the table and went into the kitchen for some more sauerkraut. He had just put the sauerkraut in his salad bowl when he noticed a soft light emanating from the corner. Semyon Stepanovich bent over and saw a hatch on the floor. There was a mossy stairway leading down from the hatch. An old man with a gold-trimmed velvet jacket draped over his shoulders was standing at the foot of the stairs. With a gnarled finger the old man was beckoning to the birthday boy.

"Come on down, Semyon Stepanovich."

Still holding on to the salad bowl, Semyon Stepanovich started down the stairs on legs like rubber, and found himself in a dimly lit chamber that seemed to go on forever. On all sides there were wheels arranged in endless rows. They emitted dreary squeaks as they turned, evoking the familiar sound of a dentist's drill. They were winding up some kind of ribbons. Above all of this, a huge wheel—apparently the main one—was turning.

"Don't worry, I'm alone here," the old man in the gold trim said and snatched the salad bowl out of Semyon Stepanovich's hands. "Just starting my shift."

"I don't smell any sulphur, and the old guy doesn't have any horns. What kind of trickery is this?" Semyon Stepanovich thought, and introduced himself to be on the safe side.

"Termidorov, D.D.S., tooth extractions are my specialty."

"I'm an immortal, sixth class," the old man said. "Division of personal destinies. I look after the turning of the wheels."

"Sorry, which wheels?"

"These wheels here," he said, pointing at the rows. "The wheel of fortune, what else? They call me Fortune Dweller, as a joke."

"Sure, it's a joke," Termidorov said faintly. "So they turn, they operate, huh?"

"Why shouldn't they?" the old man said. He took a pinch of sauerkraut out of the salad bowl. "They turn. Without ceasing. And without any stimulus."

"Do you have many of them under your supervision?"

"Figure one for each mortal."

Semyon Stepanovich asked jokingly, "Have you got a personalized one for me?"

"Why, sure. There it is, over there, in the third row. Go take a look."

The old man led his visitor up to an ordinary wheel, the kind attached to wagons. It was revolving in a void, without any visible axis. Emanating from no evident source—from some vague rustling up above—the pink ribbon of life was being wound up on it.

"Here it is, this is your life," the old man explained as he munched the sauerkraut. "Go ahead, touch it."

Semyon Stepanovich's teeth chattered, and he took hold of his own life as though it were ticker tape.

"Having a little get-together now," the old man ascertained enviously after he glanced at the tape. "Tippling just a bit. Quite a celebration. What's next?"

"Can you see if I get a raise?" Termidorov asked.

"According to the schedule, you'll have an unpleasant conversation tomorrow at your place of work, with consequences of the third class."

Termidorov went cold. At the union local tomorrow he was supposed to lodge official complaints on behalf of some patients against Zemfira Lvovna, the head dentist who astounded everyone with her rudeness.

"Stop the wheel, pops," Termidorov exclaimed in a gasp.

"Nein! Verboten!" the old man countered angrily. "I mean, not on your life!"

"Just what is it you do here?" Termidorov asked testily. "Injustice comes rolling, and you just confirm that it's going to happen! I'm making a formal complaint. Where's your . . . ? Who do I . . . ?"

"Don't even bother," the old man shouted. "No rewinds are permitted. If we stopped every little wheel, the main mechanism would collapse. Everything's synchronized: interconnected, deduction of resources, invariables, genes, plasma! You'll cause a complete disaster, and then what will we do?"

"But I'm going to suffer tomorrow," Semyon Stepanovich said plaintively.

"You'll be caught up in the course of history," the old man solemnly explained. "Behave yourself. Go on, citizen; go to bed."

When Semyon Stepanovich, crumpled and mussed, stepped back into his dining room, the guests were gone. His wife sighed. "Have a nice nap in the kitchen again? You're really slipping, Semyon."

"So all that nonsense was just a dream," an exultant Termidorov thought to himself as he crawled under the covers.

He closed his eyes, then suddenly shot upright, remembering that his salad bowl was still down there with Fortune Dweller. And the immortal old man had made short work of all the sauerkraut.

Semyon Stepanovich grabbed a pair of scissors, got out a bag of flour and mixed up some paste in a drinking glass. He approached the hatch.

The old man was asleep, lying suspended in emptiness, his jacket thrown over him. The empty salad bowl was silently revolving on a wooden stool beside him.

Semyon Stepanovich ran at a trot toward the third row. Blue from misfortune, the ribbon of his fate was creeping toward the wheel. Semyon Stepanovich seized the ribbon and neatly clipped off a piece of bad luck about five feet long. He thought for a second, and then cut off another foot and a half. Instantly something in the main wheel started to screech and snort.

His fingers shaking, Semyon Stepanovich pasted the ends of the ribbon together and bounded up the steps.

The next morning when he came to work Termidorov noticed a new announcement on the bulletin board—"Today's general meeting cancelled."

Just then a black service car pulled up outside. Old man Fortune jauntily entered the office wearing a uniform cap.

"You've been summoned, chop-chop," he said, and removed the salad bowl from his briefcase.

Termidorov had not even managed to get out of his lab coat before he found himself being seated in the back of the car.

The old man floored the gas pedal, then turned around, lifted his cap, and scratched his head. "You pretty near got me kicked off the lists of the immortal. Do you know they're still trying to fix the main wheel? You've been put under my supervision, and you're not to go to work for now. You're about to start an exceptionally trouble free blue period. We're putting you into complete anabiosis, to put it scientifically—on ice, for half a year."

"But what if they miss me at work?" Termidorov asked wearily. "What about the house, and my wife?"

"Your wife will also be quite content during the upcoming period of time. Not with you, though—the other way around.

"With who the other way around?" Termidorov shouted.

"You'll find that out later. Now don't fuss about this, you yourself clipped out your difficult mutual feelings with your wife."

"Tell me, what else did I clip out?" Termidorov cried.

The old man started to bend back his soot-smudged fingers one by one, "a knee sprain, and with that a new blossoming of your family happiness. A fine for jaywalking with pangs of conscience, and with that a free kitchen renovation and a bonus at work."

"Stop!" Termidorov cried out. "I don't want to go on ice. Please let me have the fine and the difficult mutual feelings and the pangs. Give me back everything!"

The old man stopped the car and said matter-of-factly, "Have you got the ribbon on you? Give it here."

Termidorov pulled the crumpled, tangled ribbon out of his back pocket and handed it to the old man.

"Please . . . everything . . . even the sprained ankle."

"Now you run straight back. History won't wait, you hear?" the old man commanded. "Run, you rascal, run right across the street and accept your fine."

Viktor Slavkin

Viktor Iosifovich Slavkin (b. 1935 in Moscow) was a student at the Moscow Institute of Railroad Engineering, from which he graduated in 1958. He worked for five years as an engineer and then became head of the humor department of the magazine *Iunost'*. He has been a free-lance writer since 1984. One of Russia's leading playwrights, he is also the author of numerous short stories. "Soyev's Masterpiece" was published in 1974 in *Literary Gazette*.

Soyev's Masterpiece

Soyev the writer is dead. Which is not to say that if you go to his apartment he won't open the door, because he will. You'll see a sad little figure in a bluish flannel jacket of indeterminate color and the same kind of sweat pants—flaring outrageously at the knees. The figure will snort and then whine, "What do you want?"

How am I, as a person of some refinement, supposed to relate to this figure on a daily basis, especially considering that several years ago, when I first met Soyev, he was a true gentleman—intelligent, learned, modest, and soft-spoken—qualities that I didn't at all appreciate in him then. As the two of us were leaving the Writers' Union restaurant on the first day of our acquaintance (Soyev had invited me there), I was unabashedly poking my finger through my mouth like a toothpick. Good God, it's horrifying to think just what kind of a person I was! And if Soyev the writer is dead today, then through his death he created a masterpiece of reincarnation, a miracle of transformation, a true case of metamorphosis. That masterpiece, that miracle, that metamorphosis is me.

As a way of paying my last respects to the deceased, I would like to tell my story.

I used to be a humble mechanic in a repair shop for Russian Fiats. My life was divided into days and evenings, and it usually began in the evening. Whatever a customer and I agreed on over dinner in a restaurant would become my production plan for the next day. I took no money for my services. I did accept payment in kind, though, especially scarce goods, a trade which these days is better than any currency, Western or otherwise. Scarce goods can get you all the money you want, but even for all the money in the world you couldn't get scarce goods. The Marxist maxim "goods—money—goods" was reduced in my book to the minimum: "scarce goods—scarce goods—scarce goods."

He was brought to me just before the end of the workday, and since I was free that evening, I agreed to join him for dinner at the Writers' Union, in accordance with my new client's profession.

We sat at a little table in the corner. Soyev, pinning me to the wall, busily poured French cognac down me, which I chased with a deep sniff of my unappetizing Soviet-made jacket sleeve, ignoring the elaborate hors d'oeuvres.

"So, chief," I said to him when we were catching our breath after the first round, "what sort of goods are you dealing?"

"What?" Soyev seemed not to understand.

"What, what?" I hiccuped facetiously. "What do you propose to give me in exchange for putting your car in tip-top shape again? Hm? What do you have that nobody else does?"

"I have a book," Soyev said uncomfortably.

"Doesn't count," I cut him off. "I'll ask you again, what kind of goods are you dealing?"

Soyev thought for a while and said, "I can deal two tickets to the Taganka."

"Is that a bathhouse?"

"Theater. I get free tickets to all the openings. If you want, here, take this, tomorrow there's a preview." And Soyev extended a white piece of paper to me.

"Pretty lousy merchandise," I said, frowning at the piece of paper. "I can tell I'm not going to get anything worthwhile out of you. I'll take Klava along. It'll give her a chance to get dolled up."

And so I went to the theater.

"Well, how was it?" Soyev asked me several days later when he drove into the shop with his banged-up Fiat.

"Pretty good. There was some shooting, and one gal that cried like for real."

"That shouldn't be hard for an actress to do," Soyev said to keep the conversation going.

"Not in the theater. During intermission, at the buffet. They'd run out of oranges, and she wanted to take some to a sick friend in the hospital."

Soyev frowned, but tactfully, as though he were simply reacting to the objectionable odor of the imported window cleaner that I had accidentally spilled on the floor at his feet.

I straightened out his door for him, installed new yellow fog lights and said, "Well, partner, how about that merchandise now? Or is it back to the theater?"

Soyev shrank. "I don't have anything else. That's all I know how to get."

"I guess that'll have to do," I spat. That same evening, with no great enthusiasm, I set out for the Bolshoi to see the ballet of "Anna Karenina."

And from that time on my life started to change.

Soyev was a mess. He kept smashing up his Fiat, he often had his windshield wipers or his headlights stolen. Sometimes they'd even make off with the tires. I had to obtain hard-to-get spare parts for him nearly every day, and in return, he offered me his endless tickets and passes. I was powerless to refuse another person's scarce commodities, and bit by bit I became a habitué of play openings and art exhibits. I practically lived in clubs for artists and writers.

People soon began to notice me, to nod to me during intermissions, and sometimes they invited me to discussions of plays, exhibits, or new books. I even contributed at some of these gatherings.

More and more I was taken for Soyev himself. The fact is that his car had been so badly damaged in an accident that after the repairs Soyev's entire wardrobe passed into my hands. His brown leather jacket, baggy pleated trousers, and deck shoes made me practically indistinguishable amidst the crowd of other original and creative spirits.

At first Soyev mourned the loss of his former life. He kept coming to me with his auto mishaps, and while I fiddled with his motor he would pump me with questions about the plays, exhibits, and readings I had attended, and about the new books I had gotten with his pass to the Writer's Union bookstore. At first I would grumble something incoherent in reply, but as time progressed I began to relish these synopses. I learned how to explain the meaning of works of art cogently; how to give an original interpretation of them; how to analyze them, identifying their strengths, but also pointing out their weaknesses. But the more thoroughly I assimilated such skills, the less Soyev seemed interested in these signals from the world of beauty and intellect. And only after all our business was finished, he would typically say just two words: "How much?" I would answer "two" or "three," depending on the difficulty of the repair and the cost of the spare parts, and Soyev would hand me two or three green volumes from the "Literary Monuments" series. As you can probably guess, Soyev's entire library eventually made its way into my hands, complete with the bookcases that by then were of no use whatever to him. Soyev did, however, keep his last remaining book under the pillow on his perpetually unmade bed; it was *Your Fiat: Operation and Maintenance.*

As for me, as an employee of a service industry who has become a refined intellectual, practically a bohemian, without having to give up my profession—indeed, thanks to it—I owe it all to Soyev, and I pledge to remain faithful to his memory as a writer. Of course he can always count on my services as a mechanic, even if he doesn't have an album of Botticelli reproductions in the Skir edition or an autographed copy of Andrey Voznesensky's latest book to offer me in return.

Speaking of which, I used to have both of those items in my collection, but I recently had to give them to a fellow who has been helping me get a condominium in an actors' cooperative. He didn't seem interested in my services as a mechanic, and he insisted on getting some scarce item from me. I am comforted by the thought that if he and I continue to do business (and getting a condominium is time-consuming and complex), then by the time I move into my new home he will have become a thoroughly cultured person.

Viktoria Tokareva

Viktoria Samoilovna Tokareva (b. 1937 in Leningrad) graduated from the National Institute of Cinematography in 1969 and has lived in Moscow since then. A well-known author, she has published several books and written a number of screenplays. She says, "I continue to write with humor to this day, although I don't consider myself a humorist in the strict sense." "One, Two, Three . . ." appeared in 1969 and "A Ruble Sixty Isn't Much" in 1968, both in *Literary Gazette*.

One, Two, Three . . .

My wife resembles Rembrandt's wife, Saskia. Imagine Saskia with short hair, with a leather skirt, and with a shopping net in her hand, and you'll have my wife.

I'm as used to her face as I am to the view from our window. That landscape is a mixture of genres—there is a village of about a dozen farmsteads, squeezed together by prefab apartment buildings. The apartment buildings are modern and look as though they've been glued together at the seams. But the village is old-fashioned, with luxuriant flower beds, arrogant cows, chickens beside a well, and mud in spring-time. I stand at the window and look at the construction cranes, huge herons lost in thought above this tiny village.

I know everything that will happen an hour, a day, ten years from now. In an hour the door will open, and my wife will come in with her shopping net and ask, "Do you love me?"

"No," I'll say.

"What do you mean 'no'?" my wife will say, at a loss.

"It's quite simple. I don't love you, period."

"But you promised to love me forever. Does that mean you lied?"

"No, I didn't lie."

"Then are you lying now?"

"No, I'm not lying now, either."

"I don't understand a thing."

I will have to explain to my wife what she doesn't understand. If I manage to explain it to her well, then she will be offended. She will tell me about her friend, a hideous and immoral woman who lives downtown and is loved to distraction by an incredible number of men, while my beautiful and moral wife lives here, among the chickens, and even a non-entity like myself doesn't love her. No one needs beauty and moral character these days. People want only external and internal deformity. Then my wife will turn from her own qualities to mine and will comment on how I stand in front of the window for days on end, how my face looks as though I had slept on it, and how it no longer reflects even the slightest interest in life.

I will take offense and we will argue. And then, of course, we'll make up. So why argue if we're going to have to make up anyway? This is why I propose a different dialogue:

"Do you love me?" my wife will ask.

"Yes, I do."

"A lot?"

"Mhm."

"How much?"

"Lots and lots."

"Good lord, the way you say that!" my wife will sigh disappointedly and carry her shopping net to the kitchen.

An unmarried man is unlike a married one in that he doesn't know what will happen an hour, or a day, or ten years from now. When a man doesn't know what will be, he fantasizes. Fantasy is creation, and creation is a flight from mundane reality. An unmarried man can occasionally rise above mundane reality.

And why can't a married man do that, even for little while?

There's a children's rhyme that goes: one, two, three, now you're free.

One: I put on my white shirt.

Two: I get out the phone book and sit down next to the telephone.

Three: I dial a number and listen to the rings.

What a marvelous invention, the telephone! The earth is covered with a network of phone cables, which are like nerves. And all the people are linked with each other. And it's so uncomplicated: just go up to the telephone, dial the right code, a series of digits as inexplicable and random as fate itself.

"Hello, Ira?"

"Who is this?" Ira asks, confused.

I tell her my first name, last name, and middle name, as though responding to a questionnaire. Then my date of birth and distinguishing marks. Then she remembers.

"Where in the world have you been?" she asks in amazement.

"On Franz Joseph Island, digging for diamonds. Let's get together."

"What do you want to do?"

"Let's rise above mundane reality."

"You go alone, I'm busy."

"What with?"

"I've got my dissertation."

"What dissertation?"

"The effect of electromagnetism on germanium crystals."

While I'd been on Franz Joseph Island, Ira hadn't lost any time. "What do you need those electromagnetic effects for?"

"I don't. Mankind does."

"Well, it's up to you," I say.

When a person is preoccupied with the fate of mankind, it's injudicious to disturb her. For it's a very rare quality to think of somebody besides yourself.

I leaf through my address book in alphabetical order and read the names. An address book is a token of life itself, with its major routes and detours, its holidays, its cemetery. The names in my address book stand in formation like the crosses in the New Riga cemetery. Something hovers over certain names, but others are just dumb and stony. The people that have these names continue to exist somewhere, but they are no longer in your life, which is to say that they don't exist. And calling a number like that is the same as summoning a voice from the beyond.

"Hello, Galya?" I jauntily shout.

"Who is this?" Galya asks.

"Guess."

"Borya?"

"No, I'm not Borya."

"Sasha?"

"I'm not Sasha, either."

"Alya?"

"What, do I sound like a woman to you?"

"No, you sound like a man."

"Then let's get together."

"I can't. I have to go pick the baby up at mother's."

"Send your husband."

"You're right. I'll send my husband to pick up the baby so that I can go out with God knows who."

All perfectly logical. People go out with people they know. So I'll go out with someone I've known since kindergarten.

I don't need my address book for this one, because I know the number by heart.

"Andrey," I shout, "how are you doing?"

My wife thinks that Andrey looks like Kirillov, the television announcer. If Kirillov lost all his hair, had a pug nose and a round face, then he would look just like my friend Andrey.

"Hi," Andrey answers.

"Let's escape from everyday reality."

"You mean go drinking?" Andrey asks.

"We'll see," I say uncertainly.

"I can't today. A relative of mine is having a birthday party."

"You can't possibly really want to go!"

"It's a tradition."

"To hell with traditions."

"That's easy for you to say. If you don't have any traditions you might as well not have any clothes."

So that's how it is. One person has his life's work, another has a family, still another has traditions. The earth is covered with telephone cables, like nerves. You can dial any combination of digits and call any apartment you want. That is, you can call, but you can't get through to anybody. Is there a number you can call to actually reach another human being?

The lines are busy, and people are busy, each one with his own work and traditions. By the way, I also have relatives. And I have a wife who resembles Rembrandt's wife. Perhaps she would also like to go soaring, but she's gone to the store instead. She'll be back soon.

The two of us can leave our building and soar together. But why should we escape from everyday reality if, sooner or later, we'll just have to return to it?

One: I take off my white shirt.

Two: I go back to the window and watch my landscape.

Three: The door opens and my wife appears, shopping net in hand.

"Do you love me?" she asks with apprehension in her eyes, as though that question was her reason for coming.

"Yes, I do."

"A lot?"

"Mhm."

"How much?"

"Lots and lots."

"Good lord, how you say that!" my wife sighs and carries her shopping net into the kitchen.

A Ruble Sixty Isn't Much

At a kiosk outside Novaya Cheremushka subway station there were some invisible caps for sale. They had little pompons at the crown and looked like ski caps. Nobody was buying them. I stopped at the kiosk, examined one of the caps, and asked the saleswoman, "Why isn't anyone buying these?"

"They're polyester," she explained indifferently.

I felt the cap. It really was something other than wool and was probably cold.

"Well, what do you say?" The saleswoman was young with a beehive hairdo which she carried proudly, like a deer carries its antlers.

"What do they cost?" I asked guiltily.

"A ruble sixty," she said. "You'd waste more getting drunk. Here at least you'd have the cap."

A ruble sixty isn't that much, and at least I'd have a cap.

"Wrap it up for me," I asked.

The saleswoman took down the cap I had pointed to, put it on her head, and disappeared. I was at a loss. By and large it's almost impossible to surprise me. I am in intimate touch with the roots of life. I am capable of understanding and explaining anything. But here, I understood nothing.

In the meantime the saleswoman had taken the cap off and reappeared.

"Is it working?" she asked indifferently. Apparently this piece of merchandise was like any other for her. "It can be a problem when it's cold, you know. They tend to run down. Some of them don't start at all, and some just start half-way. . . . Shall I wrap it for you?"

"Oh, you don't have to." I took the cap and walked away from the kiosk. I pulled it snugly over my head and set out for work.

The main thing in this life is to know how to set your priorities. To be able to distinguish the important things from the not so important. For example, in the subway if somebody jabs you in the back and steps on your feet, you have to understand that this is a temporary inconvenience. Here I stand in my invisible cap, squeezed in on all sides. Beside me, virtually at negative distance from me, there is a farmer's wife in a plush jacket and with a kerchief on her head. She has a string of pretzels around her neck, like an ancient Olympic wreath.

"Grandma," I hear an offended voice say behind my back. "You think maybe you could move?"

My cap is on, and there is an empty space where I am standing. The woman moves toward that space, but it's filled with me.

"Just where am I supposed to move to?" she snaps back. She is so stunned by the city, by civilization, and by her various bags that nothing surprises her anymore.

"You hick," the voice behind my back says angrily. I could turn around and with two fingers take this urbanite by the nose, at its very tip, and teach him how to set his priorities straight. Then on the other hand, is it really worth it to grab people by the nose if they don't know how to set their priorities and are obviously suffering because of it? They're miserable enough as it is.

Our institute is huge, practically its own city. Kopylov is our director. Kopylov is a genius. It costs him no effort to invent a new airplane or discover a new law. And when he does, he doesn't shout eureka like Archimedes, he just leans back in his chair and does isometric exercises with his arms. I envy Kopylov as Salieri envied Mozart. I envy him because he's a genius, and I'm just a talented person. I probably could invent an airplane, but it would take a lot of time, because I would get distracted. But nothing distracts Kopylov. Everything else is a matter of indifference to him. Which is not to say that he's absent-minded and nearsighted like the stereotypical scientist in literature— the kind that knocks chairs over when he walks in his mismatched shoes. Kopylov is punctilious. He is never late for anything. He wears super-elegant cuff links with rubies, and his hair is always fashionably cut. Occasionally I run into him and say hello, and he answers and goes on.

In V. Tereshchenko's article "Proper Behavior for Managers," there is this passage: "Any employee will work better if he knows that his supervisor notices him." I have a single fond dream in life. My dream is that on some beautiful, sunny day (the season is irrelevant) Kopylov will notice me, approach, and extend his hand. "Hello, Slava," Kopylov the genius will say. "Hello, Igor Rostislavovich," I'll answer politely. We will smile at each other and then each go his way.

Today is February 22. It's a beautiful, sunny day. Right now, for instance, I could very well head over to Kopylov's, sit down in the chair at his desk, and take off my cap. Kopylov would look at me, then quietly ask, "When did you come in?"

"Just now."

"And who let you in?"

"Nobody. I came on my own, in my invisible cap."

I'll hand him the cap. Kopylov will scrupulously examine it and say, "Semiconductors?" And hand it back. Then he'll look at me. Not just look in my direction, but at me. But I'm not going to see Kopylov.

I approach my building. I try to imagine how I'm going to appear in a minute, how I'll switch on and then off again. Irina will have a fit. Her natural reflexes tend to dominate. Elemental reactions. Zheleznov will say, "Anything to avoid work, eh?" Zheleznov places work above all else. Grisha Garin's reaction will be quick, "How much did you pay for it?"

"A ruble sixty," I'll answer as quickly.

"Take three for it?" Grishka will say.

But my friend Sasha will say nothing. He won't even look at it. He's skeptical about me, and tends to write off anything I say. He thinks I'm just a show-off, that that's my mission in life. I defended my master's thesis (which my advisors, in view of its merits, wanted to count as a dissertation) not because I'm bright and worked hard, but just to show everyone. I had the best looking girlfriend not because I liked her, but because it was a way to get everyone jealous. And now I've come to work in an invisible cap so that everybody will drop whatever they're doing and pay attention to me alone. There is no way I could convince Sasha that I bought it at a stand for a ruble sixty.

Occasionally, and particularly when I've had a few to drink, I feel like calling Sasha up and saying, "You and I were classmates for five years, we played on the same team, we were even friends once. How is it now that you don't know me anymore at all?" But I'll never call him, and I'll never say that.

When I walked into the office everyone was at his desk. They were heatedly arguing about something. Since I'd missed the beginning of the conversation I wasn't interested in what they were saying.

"Neither fish nor fowl," Irina countered.

"What does that have to do with anything?" Sasha puzzled.

"Character has everything to do with talent."

"And just how do you know about Slava's firmness of character?"

I never would have expected him to be interested in such a topic. I always thought he was strictly business.

"I have absolutely no desire to embrace him," Irina said disdainfully.

"What makes you think he wants you to?" Grisha Garin asked.

I tacitly thanked Grisha for that remark.

"That's not the point," Irina took offense.

I know. Now she'll deliver a speech and write me off in the eyes of my colleagues once and for all. I had decided to whisk the cap off while there was still time, but before I could Zheleznov asked, "Say, why isn't Slava at his desk? Do you suppose he's sick?"

"He's here," Sasha said without turning around.

"Have you seen him?" Zheleznov tried to ascertain. He was concerned with discipline in the workplace.

Sasha turned around and looked me straight in the face. "Yes, I have," he said not to Zheleznov, but to me. And judging from the way he was fixedly looking at me, I realized that he could see me. No one else saw me, but he could.

I had lost all desire to make a show of it. I moved toward the door, carefully navigating past the chairs and tables. As I passed Sasha's desk he and I exchanged glances. "See you," Sasha said to me.

I walk down the street in my invisible cap, looking right and left. I can see everybody else, but no one can see me. I could do anything I want. I could walk into a jewelry store and steal their biggest diamond. But I don't, because I don't need diamonds. If I were a glazier I might need one to cut glass, but I'm not. I'm an engineer. My means of production are a pencil and talent. I've got more than enough pencils, and talent isn't available for the stealing. It would be nice if they sold talent, love, hope, and the like in a stand near Gorky Park. Limit one pound to a customer. I could go there and pick up a whole shopping bag full for my friends and myself without even standing in line.

But they don't sell happiness on street corners. They sell oranges. If worse comes to worst you could buy oranges and pass them out to passersby instead of happiness. Imagine some tired, disillusioned type walking down the street, the kind who's lost all his great expectations. Out of the blue an orange comes flying at him, round and glowing like the sun at evening. On the other hand, a flying orange could lead a person to believe that he's lost the battle with life's contradictions and quietly lost his mind. In that case the orange would cause him more grief than pleasure. Consequently I refrain from any such actions one way or the other.

One day Grisha Garin brought to work a questionnaire out of some foreign magazine. The questionnaire included questions like: Do you feel sorry for drunks? How do you feel about children under one year old? Would you ever consider cheating on your wife? You were supposed to answer yes or no and mark the answers plus or minus. Depending on the balance of pluses and minuses you were supposed to be able to determine your personality. Our personalities turned out as follows: Irina—childlike with undeveloped tastes; Zheleznov—gloomy despot; Sasha—fighter for right with philistine tendencies; Grisha— Moorish by nature, no philistinism; and me—embittered petit bourgeois. Besides these there was one more category: well-bred individual. I was just one plus short of being that.

If the invisible cap had wound up on Grisha Garin's head, he would have embroiled three or four governments in a squabble, traveled to Paris, robbed the Banque nationale, married Brigitte Bardot with the money, and come back home to brag about it. Grisha is Moorish by nature, with no philistinism, but I am almost a well-bred person. The most I am capable of is sneaking away from work and going to the movies.

The movie had just been released. It was impossible to get tickets for the evening showings, as well as for the matinees. Grisha could probably have gotten in without a ticket and sat in the best seat in the house. While I, like a good citizen, took my place at the very end of the line. When my turn finally came at the box office I took off my cap and stuck my head in through the cashier's window. But just then someone tugged at my sleeve. I retracted my head from the window, looked around, and saw a woman about sixty or seventy years old. With people that age I can't tell the difference anymore.

"How's it goin'?" she said with unexpected fashionableness. "Where did you come from? Just sprout out of the ground?"

"I was in line," I said with dignity.

"Just like in the song, isn't it? Doors open to the young, hats off to the old."

"Don't give him a ticket," the entire line, consisting mainly of old people, proclaimed in unison.

I opened my mouth, but then closed it again. I am helpless to argue when I don't feel any link with my audience. To be sure, I think more highly of humanity than it thinks of me. I choose Grisha's solution—I walk through the doors ticketless and take the best seat in the tenth row. I sit and wait for it to happen. And here's what it will be: a nervous spectator will appear and take the seat corresponding to his ticket. Unsuspectingly he'll sit down on my lap, then jump up, fill his lungs with air, and scream. I'll scream, too, and run over a succession of feet to the end of the row. The entire row will freeze in horror at first, then the panic will start.

I crane my neck to find my spectator, but he hasn't arrived. The lights go out. I take off my cap, stretch out my legs and start watching the screen. Someone behind me starts to thump me on the back. I look around and see a boy.

"Mister," he whispers, "you're blocking the screen."

I pull the cap out of my pocket and put it on my head.

"Mister," the boy taps me again, "you're blurring the screen."

My wife's name is Masha, and I have a daughter named Vitka. Vitka is different from other children by virtue of the fact that she's my daughter. Masha is different from other wives by virtue of the fact that she loves me. In her eyes I am the brightest, proudest, most important man alive, just like in the Edita Pyekha song. Masha works as a typist for a movie studio. She started working there four years ago with hopes of marrying a movie director and becoming a star. She didn't get her director, though, and got me instead. When we first met, Masha started writing me letters every day, typing them on her typewriter, and she would give them to me at night so I could read them in her company. Now she's stopped writing me letters, simply doesn't have time for them—at work she thinks about work, after work she runs to the store, and then to pick up the kid. I have no idea what she composes en route.

Once she's back home she stops thinking altogether, because there's no time for it. And when everybody has gone to bed and there's finally time to concentrate and write a proper letter, Masha goes into the kitchen, sets a pillow on one of the chairs, and types some rush job.

As I listen to the typewriter rattling away, I think of a quiet, shady street twenty minutes from my apartment. That street is part of my past, and I never go there, since according to the laws of the dialectic it is impossible to return to one's past. There is a handsome, old-fashioned building there, with old-fashioned secrets. Its staircase is broad and the steps are low.

I prefer not to think about that, so I crawl out from under my blanket and go to the kitchen. "That's enough," I say. "Let's go to bed."

As a rule we both get home from work at the same time, or at most I'll get back a little earlier, Masha and Vitka a little later. Today is like any other. First me, then them. Their entrance begins on a very high note.

Outside on the landing I hear the elevator door slam, then my wife starts shouting angrily. Then it all bursts into our apartment—my wife, Vitka, and the shouting. Vitka runs into the room, flops tummy-first onto the couch, clumps of half-melted snow flying off her galoshes in all directions. If it were permissible to jump on the sofa with your feet, if that were considered normal behavior, Vitka would never do it. The whole point is in engendering conflict, the collision of opposed interests. Then there's some drama to it. Masha couldn't care less about drama. She shouts loud enough for them to hear it at the subway station, by turns addressing first Vitka ("What's wrong, can't you hear?") and then me ("What's wrong, can't you see?").

I do see, but not at all what Masha does. I understand Vitka and sympathize with her. But I understand my wife, too. In the course of a day she has to overcome a myriad of petty details that consume just as much energy as the major ones do.

I go over to Vitka and pick her up.

"What did you bring me?" Vitka asks and looks straight into my pupils. Love is fine, but there have to be presents. Vitka doesn't confuse the two. I fetch the invisible cap from the hallway. "One," I start counting mysteriously, "two. . . ."

"Three!" Vitka finishes. She still doesn't know why, but she's already intrigued. At the count of three I put the cap on and vanish. Vitka is confused for a second. She didn't expect me to disappear. It frustrated her and she burst into tears.

"One," I started counting out of nowhere, "two, three." And I reappeared. Vitka was overjoyed and instantly started laughing. I kept disappearing and reappearing, while she gasped and breathlessly waited for me to reappear.

I wanted to give Masha a surprise, to abduct her from the kitchen into a fairy tale. I put the cap on and walked over to her. "Masha," I called out. She turned around and looked straight through me at the bare wall. Then I whipped the cap off and appeared before her. Nothing in her face changed. She looked at me just as she had been looking at the wall, at the bare space. Then she turned away, gingerly took the milk off the burner, and started peeling potatoes.

I was perplexed, but didn't say anything. I watched her elbows moving. "Masha," I called out to her, upset. She turned around again. I took the cap off and put it back on. For a second her eyes were fixed on me. She was recollecting something, perhaps the time when she wanted to be a movie star. I realized she wasn't looking at me, just in my direction. Like Kopylov. It's one thing when your boss doesn't notice you, but quite another when it's your own wife.

I understand that she's more or less indifferent to my presence. I don't know myself whether I live here or not. I eat, sleep, play with my daughter, and talk with my wife. We say all the necessary words to each other—hello, how are you, change the channel, don't spoil her she'll take advantage of it. But in point of fact I'm not here. She's gotten used to that and stopped noticing me.

I always thought that I gave meaning to her life. By being faithful to her I strengthened my own sense of identity. And now it turns out that I don't exist as far as she's concerned. Just as I don't exist for Kopylov. Do I exist at all? If I suddenly vanished no one would notice. Except for Zheleznov.

Why did I buy the cap? To find out all about myself? Is it that important to know all about yourself? No wonder those caps were lying in big stacks with nobody buying them.

That evening Masha didn't do any typing. She probably didn't have any rush jobs. A faint cracking sound came from the hallway—the wallpaper was peeling off. Vitka quickly mumbled something to herself in her sleep. She had grown up in the last few days and had started having dreams. Masha slept blissfully ignorant of the existence of invisible caps. I sat looking up at the ceiling and wondering why I had bought it. Surely not just so I could get in to see movies for free. I realized I wasn't going to get much sleep. I quietly dressed and went outside.

A car pulled up beside me and the driver asked, "Where are you headed?"

"To a quiet, shady street."

I climbed into the back and rode into my past. To Vika, whom I had left four years ago because she had left me. She'd traded me in for someone better. I'd known her for ten months—three hundred days. During that time I was happy for nine days and unhappy for the other 291. My love for her was a feeling of unending frustration. Still, I had never been so happy and so thoroughly unhappy with anyone else.

I used to wait for her on the sidewalk, beneath a tree. She would appear to me out of the darkness of an entryway. No, I don't mean she walked out of the entryway, she actually appeared from it (hair flowing freely to her shoulder blades, aloof and full of well being), moving toward me with a gait, lissome like a model's. Each time I would lose heart, feeling a quiet delight and wishing she could be less pretty, less glamorous, and a little shorter.

I tried to imagine myself invisibly entering her apartment and finding them together, her and the guy she traded me for. I won't take the cap off yet. I'll wait until he leaves the room, then I'll close the door and appear before her like the ghost of Spessart Castle. "Say what you will," she'll say calmly, "it won't change anything." "Let's start all over again," I plead. "That's impossible." "But why?" "Because you can't step into the same stream twice. . . ."

Vika lived in the handsome, old-fashioned building. Next to her entry-way there was a sign identifying the pay phone that should have been beneath it. The sign was hanging just as it had been four years ago, and the house was in the same spot. The same broad staircase with shallow steps. Nothing in the world changes, only we ourselves do. I put the cap on.

Vika was asleep. Her bedroom window had been left ajar. It was cool and smelled like snow. I cautiously walked up to her desk and sat down in the armchair. Everything was as it had been—the same book-shelves ranged one next to the other, the same ritual mask from Easter Island hanging on the wall. The whole undertaking suddenly seemed ludicrous to me, the attempt to step into the same stream twice. I realized I ought to get up and leave before she woke up, but I couldn't force myself to. I suddenly felt how exhausted I'd gotten in the course of the day, most likely from loneliness, from being able to see everyone else while no one could see me.

Vika woke up abruptly. She sat up on the couch and pulled the tassel on the floor lamp. She was looking straight at the chair in which I was sitting. Her hair was woven into two tiny braids, probably so it wouldn't get in her face while she slept. She was wearing a child's flannel shirt with three buttons at the top. Taken altogether, with her braids and her shirt, she resembled a schoolgirl. I had expected to see her as anything but a schoolgirl.

Slowly I pulled the cap off my head.

"Slavka!" Vika said calmly, as though I had been sitting there all four years. "How did you get in? Through the window?"

"No." I handed her the cap. "In my invisible cap."

"Did you design it yourself?" She tugged at the pompon.

"I bought it for a ruble sixty."

She didn't believe it.

"I knew you'd think of something. And that you'd come back. But why did you take so long?"

"Were you waiting?"

"Of course."

"Why didn't you say anything?"

"You didn't ask."

She had dumped me, and though everyone pretended not to notice, they all knew. And now it turned out that I had been expected to call and ask. Maybe in fact I should have.

"Because you left me."

"I regretted it soon enough. . . ."

"Why didn't you tell me?"

"I didn't think you needed that."

I had been able to think and talk only about her. Day and night. I could never bear to be left alone and became so crazed that at one point I broke into tears at a taxi stand in broad daylight.

"I loved you."

"Why didn't you say anything?"

"I was afraid of looking ridiculous."

I was afraid of looking ridiculous. As though I'm not ridiculous now. In the twentieth century when heart transplants are a common-place and an astronaut can leave his capsule for the sky, two people who need each other still cannot simply come to each other and simply tell each other about it. We need some kind of miracle, an invisible cap no less, so that two people living in the same time and the same city, twenty minutes from each other by foot, can meet. I was seething with resentment, but I held my tongue. Apparently the embittered petit bourgeois in me was struggling with the well-bred individual.

"So, how's it going?" I asked.

"The usual. Creative pangs. Bad when there are too many of them. Bad when there aren't any."

Vika's speech was wooden, lacking emotion. Obviously she wasn't thinking about creativity just then.

"Are you working for Kopylov?" she asked.

"Yeah, so is Sasha."

"He idolizes you, you know."

"Who?"

"Kopylov. You're a very talented engineer."

"That may be how it looks to you," I answered evasively. I didn't want to disillusion her.

"Looks nothing, it is," Vika objected. "Do you remember your thesis? They wanted to count it as a dissertation."

Oh, sure, but that was way back when, I thought.

"What's your daughter's name?"

"Viktoria."

Neither of us said anything for a while.

"Your wife probably adores you."

"She gets tired a lot," I said vaguely.

"Well, sure, but she sees you every day."

"Do you think that's such a gift?"

"I most certainly do," she said with conviction.

I went up to her and saw that she was crying. That's why her speech was so flat and wooden. She was crying and tried to hide her tears. I didn't try to comfort her. At some level I couldn't forgive her for these four years and the fact that Vitka was not our daughter. Vika sat hunched over—submissive, dependent, and consequently seeming less glamorous and shorter. I felt neither bashfulness nor quiet delight, and I understood that it had been easier for me to leave the former Vika than it would be to leave this one.

"Would you like the cap as a present?" I rested my hand on her neck. It was frail and warm.

"That's all right," she shook her head.

"Why not?"

"It'll ruin my hair. I wear kerchiefs."

No. She hadn't changed the slightest during these four years. And just generally, nothing in life changes as long as we stay the same.

I returned home, from my former life to the present one. I had the cap in my pocket, and now I knew why I had bought it. To find out all about myself. And I do. I'm a talented engineer and it's a gift for others to see me every day. Kopylov will surely notice me. And the finest woman in the world, who looks like a schoolgirl, is waiting for me in an old-fashioned building. I've found out all about myself and now I don't need the cap anymore. I can leave it on the railing of the Crimea Bridge, which I'm walking across now. But what if the bridge suddenly vanishes and I'm left walking through the air like Christ? Some poor insomniac will walk up to his window, open the curtains, and see a happy man walking over the city.

A ruble sixty isn't that much. I leaned over the railing and threw the cap into the water. Now it will be ruined by the cold, it won't switch on, and it will become an ordinary cap, not quite a ski cap and not quite a child's.

I made my way up to Sadovoye Ring, walked from October Square to Zubovskaya Street and didn't encounter a soul the entire way. Maybe it was the hour, and everyone was still sleeping. Or maybe invisible caps had come into fashion. Maybe the streets were full of people, but I just couldn't see any of them.

They can all see me, but I can't see anyone.

Mikhail Zadornov

Mikhail Nikolaevich Zadornov (b. 1948 in Jurmala, Latvia) is a graduate of the Moscow Aviation Institute and worked for a short time as an engineer. Since then he has been writing, publishing, and giving stage performances of his humorous short stories. "Still Young" was published in 1979 in *Literary Gazette*.

Still Young

She woke him up. He had been sleeping with his head on her shoulder.

"Do you hear, Avtozavodskaya," she yelled in his ear. "Will you wake up?"

"What, are we there already?" he asked as he came to.

It was pleasant in the subway. Everyone was dressed in their Sunday best, and everyone seemed to be in a good mood.

"How about if we ride all the way to Kakhovskaya?" he suggested.

"What's gotten into you?" she asked in amazement.

"Nothing," he said. "Can't we ride to Kakhovskaya just once in our lives?"

"What for?" she asked, still not understanding.

"What do you mean what for?" he fidgeted. "How many years have we been living here, and we haven't once ridden to the end of the line."

"Oh, come on!" she grew indignant. "Has it occurred to you that we both have to get up early tomorrow morning?"

"To hell with that! So what if you oversleep for once in your life? So what if you're late for work? So what if you miss work tomorrow altogether? We're still young! Can't we afford to say to hell with it all and just drop everything and ride to Kakhovskaya?"

She thought for a while, then said, "No, we'd better not. Maybe next time. I have to get some things ready for tomorrow and wash out your shirt. You got it stained somehow at Dimka's. You can't go to work tomorrow in a dirty shirt. As for Kakhovskaya, you and I will go some other time when we don't have quite so much to do. We'll work things out in advance and then take off."

"Oh, come on, let's go today," he argued. "Think about it, life is trickling away and we never get to see anything. At this rate we won't have anything to reminisce about in our old age. Just imagine, they say that after Avtozavodskaya the subway runs above ground. We'll see Moscow by night! And then we'll reach Warsaw station, and after that Kakhovskaya! We'll get off, take a walk around, it'll be neat! After all, people go there for some reason."

"Oh, all right, you've convinced me," she suddenly said. "Really, who needs all that stuff? We're still young, why not go all the way to Kakhovskaya?"

But at that moment the train stopped and a pleasant recorded female voice announced, "Avtozavodskaya! Last stop for this train, all passengers please get off."

They got off the train together with all the other passengers and went to the bus stop.

"It wasn't meant to be," he sighed.

"Don't worry, next time we'll arrange things in advance and then just take off," she started to comfort him.

"I'm not particularly upset," he said, shrugging his shoulders. "After all, we had a pretty good day as it was. Spartak won the soccer game, we had some beer and smoked fish. And I really can't go to work tomorrow with this spot on my shirt. Have to get up early tomorrow, too. So, overall, I think we were right to hold back. But next time we'll really say to hell with it all and just take off, how about it?"

"It's a deal," she answered.

Mark Zakharov

Mark Anatolevich Zakharov (b. 1933 in Moscow) is a prominent Russian theater director. Currently he is artistic director of the Moscow "Lenkom" Theater. "One Life to Live . . . or a Tavern Story" was published in 1967 in *Literary Gazette*.

One Life to Live . . . or a Tavern Story

I walked into the Georgian restaurant as a good-looking young guy. I showed off my biceps. I was young. The blood ran hot in my veins. I radiated energy, personality, and intellect. All this brought instant dividends. As I was finishing my lula-kebab, a nice-looking blonde sitting at the next table noticed me. I tossed her some salad and a few quips. Before long we were both sitting at my table and chewing on lobio together. When they brought us the chicken à la Tbilisi she told me about her rough childhood and I knew that I had found my destiny. We ordered a bottle of Gurdzhaani, two bottles of Borzhomi mineral water, and a chocolate bar. The maître d' himself proposed the first toast, we exchanged rings, the hat check clerk threw a handful of rice, and the whole restaurant applauded. Those were wonderful moments. We had chicken satsiri garnished with cabbage à la Guri. My sweetheart was munching salted peanuts and drinking fruit punch. Before long she started to get a little nauseous.

"We'll name him Viktor," I said. "After his grandfather."

Just then her parents joined us at the table, and to celebrate we had to order yet another bottle, this time Tsinandali. Then we had kupaty in a spicy sauce.

"Here we go again. Little Vitya has crawled under the next table again," my wife threw up her hands and drew back the tablecloth. "You never lift a finger to discipline him."

I was about to order some more chakhokhbili, but then I felt my heart beating irregularly. "Viktor," I said to my son when he turned up, "if you keep upsetting your father with bad grades, I'll lose my appetite."

"Aw, come on, Dad," he said in a melancholy bass and held out a high school diploma marked "with distinction."

"Good job," I said loudly and ordered two portions of kharcho soup.

After the kharcho Vitya returned, this time hand in hand with a snub-nosed girl.

"Dad, this is her," he said blushing. "This is the one I was telling you about. This summer we went on a field trip close to Kiev together, then to the Irtysh River. Remember, I was. . . ."

"Kiev," I thought, "sounds so familiar, where did I hear about that recently?" And then I remembered that it was because of the chicken Kiev I had just ordered. But this Irtysh, what the heck was that? It didn't sound like anything.

I was just about to bite off some chicken, but applied myself to a glass of mineral water instead. My heart began racing desperately.

"Well, I'm not the man I used to be," I sighed. "Time to settle up."

"Bring me the check, please," I asked and sat back in my chair once and for all.

Alexander Zhitinsky

Alexander Nikolaevich Zhitinsky (b. 1941 in Simferopol, Ukraine) was a student at the Leningrad Polytechnical Institute, from which he graduated in 1965. Until 1978 he worked as a research associate at various engineering institutes; since then he has been a free-lance writer. Zhitinsky has published short stories, novels, and poetry, and he has written plays for stage and screen. The vignettes in "Fantastic Miniatures" appeared separately in *Avrora* and *Studencheskii meridian* in the early 1970s and as a group in the anthology *Molodoi Leningrad 1973*.

Fantastic Miniatures

Temptation

I threw the balcony door open. A mass of frigid air enveloped me from head to foot. I was about to step back, but three yards away I noticed a man flying past in the direction of the park. The expression on his face was intent, and his eyes were teary, probably from the wind. He was not very seasonally dressed.

"Let's go flying!" he called out to me.

"It's too cold," I said and shivered, so that he would see that I really was cold.

"Put something on," he said. "I'll wait."

"I don't know how to fly," I confessed.

"Have you ever tried?" he asked as he made a smooth turn to the left. To all appearances he was enjoying his flight.

"No. But it looks like something I don't know how to do." He shook his head. His body swayed, too.

"I'm not going to waste time trying to convince you," he said. "I've got an easy route today. You could give it a try. You can't imagine how nice it is!"

"I think I can," I answered. "It's a pretty useful thing to do, I suppose."

"Nothing more useless!" he exclaimed. It appeared that this had angered him, and in order to calm down he did a forward somersault.

"Well, what do you say?"

I hesitated. It was indeed too cold to go flying in my shirtsleeves, and it seemed downright indecent to go flying in a coat. Who ever goes flying in a coat?

"So you don't want to?" He put his hands together over his head and shot up about five yards. "You really are strange."

"Shut the balcony door!" my wife called out from the kitchen. "There's a draft."

I closed the door and, with my forehead pressed against the pane, I watched him fly for a good long time. He flew slowly, bent slightly forward, and nothing seemed to be obstructing his flight. His feet were turned out like a gymnast's, and he seemed to be navigating with his arms. He was probably a nice person. I don't know if he ever found a traveling companion. The window fogged over, and I lost him from sight.

The House

I awoke to some mysterious sound. Somewhere down below there was an intermittent rustling, as though someone were grating cabbage. I looked out the window and saw two men sawing at the foundation of our nine-story high-rise apartment building. The saw made a slight ringing sound and shone in the light of a lantern.

"Hey! What's this for?" I shouted.

"Don't worry!" one of them answered. "Go back to sleep. Contractor made a slight mistake. These were supposed to be townhouses, but they put up a high-rise instead."

"We'll be done and out of here by morning," the other promised.

"No problem," I told my wife. "There was a mix-up with the blueprints. It'll be fixed by morning."

And we fell back asleep to the rhythmic sounds of the saw. During the night they dropped the building on its side and we woke up on the wall. I ran over to our neighbors to find out what they were planning to do. They had already moved their furniture onto their former wall and were frantically putting wallpaper on their former ceiling.

"No," I told my wife when I returned. "We're going to keep things the way they were before. Who knows what they might do next—turn the building upside down? We'd just have to redecorate all over again."

And so life goes on, horizontal as it may be now. Unfortunately, when we go outside we have to realign ourselves vertically, to make riding on the streetcar more convenient.

The Tree

There was a tree on which money grew. Rubles on the lower branches, green three-ruble notes a bit higher, then five-ruble notes, and the very top was lilac-colored. That's where the twenty-five-ruble notes grew.

I tore off a ruble and ran to the store for some pasta. Then I came back, jumped up, and tore off a three-ruble note, which I owed a friend.

The next day I came to take a ruble for lunch. All of the lower branches had already been picked clean, and up at the top, in the thick foliage of the twenty-five-ruble notes, a man in a nice suit was sitting neatly clipping the bills off with a pair of scissors. As he did so, he carefully checked each one against the light. He tied the stacks of bills together with a rubber band and put them away in his backpack.

Judging by the amount of money, he probably had enough work there for a lifetime.

The Airplane Crash

An airplane was flying high up in the sky, and for some reason it cracked open. And all of the passengers spilled out of it.

It was a long way to the ground and they dropped like tea leaves to the bottom of a cup. They had time to talk and reminisce.

The weather was pleasant; not a cloud in the sky. All of the continents and oceans were spread out before them.

"Look over there," said one of them. "There's the Crimea. I spent my vacation there last year."

"What resort did you stay in?" another asked. It was an idle question asked for lack of anything better to do.

"At the Seagull."

"The food's bad there," the other said. "Incredibly bad."

"Oh, come on," a woman intruded. She was heavier than the others and dropped faster. Consequently she was in a hurry to have her say. "Of course, the Seagull's not for anyone who's used to spicy food. But it's ideal for ulcer patients: cottage cheese, sour cream, buttermilk. . . ."

And she flew on.

"Women amaze me," the first man grumbled. "They don't know anything and still they just babble on. It's got nothing to do with ulcer patients. They stay at the Surf."

"Nice," the other said, taking in the landscape. "I wonder what the water temperature is."

"At least seventy-five degrees, I'd say."

"It's probably awfully hard to get a room there."

"Who can afford a room when just a cot goes for a ruble a day?"

They had run out of things to talk about. They sighed and flew on in silence, approaching the earth at the speed of an express train.

The Taxi Driver

"Admiralty spire," I said as I got into the taxi.

"Very top?" the driver asked.

"If you can get me there."

"Three rubles over the meter fare," the driver said after a pause.

"That seems like a lot. I'm not moving a refrigerator, you know," I said.

"Nonlicensed drivers would ask for five," the driver warned me.

"Do they even go there?"

"For the most part, no," the driver admitted. "They're afraid of the police."

"Look, I don't have three rubles. I've got one ruble," I said.

"What a nerve! Admiralty spire! Admiralty spire!" the driver shouted. "I've never even driven there; even so, this is a discount."

"I don't need a discount. Either we go by the rules or I'm getting out."

"Oh, screw you!" he said. He slammed the door shut and we took off. To the very top of the Admiralty spire, where the little ship is.

Little Girl

A little girl with a white bow in her hair ran down the street, looking like a tiny helicopter. She cried as she ran—a tiny, crying, radio-controlled helicopter.

It was clear even to the unaided eye that the helicopter was over-loaded with hurt, which was preventing it from taking off. When the girl came even with me, I took the hurt away from her. I wadded it up, tied it with some twine, and stuffed it deep down into my briefcase. There were lots of them there. One more or less wouldn't make any difference.

The most surprising thing was that the girl wasn't particularly eager to part with the hurt. She cried for a while when she realized she wouldn't see it again, but all the same, she gave her ribbon a good spin and took off, leaving me in the hot, windy wake of her propeller.

I went on down the street with the hurt, watching as the girl swayed to and fro in the sky, like a daisy with silently rotating petals.

The Pedestrian

A man in a black overcoat was slowly walking along the streetcar cables with his hands behind his back. Streetcars would roll past beneath him, crackling like a match struck against his heels, and fountains of sparks would go flying from under his feet.

But he paid no attention to this and just kept walking, his head lowered pensively.

As always, the passersby reacted to the man in all sorts of ways. Some applauded him, trying to show that they understood what was going on. Others were outraged by the man's behavior, but the majority didn't even look up, focused as they were on tiny puddles along the asphalt.

When the fire department arrived in a screeching red truck and got the man down, he couldn't give a reasonable explanation for his actions. He said that he had been preoccupied and didn't notice taking a wrong turn.

At any rate, he apologized for the inconvenience he had caused and went on more cautiously, carefully lifting his feet each time a streetcar passed below him.

The Loafer

You could always find him in the corridor, smoking and holding the wall up with his shoulder. There was a calm serenity in his pose, and this, of course, was a source of displeasure for his colleagues running past.

He stood and smoked, and his gaze glided down the wall to infinity. There was always a chalky powder from that same wall on the shoulder of his sport coat.

Finally he was fired, and on the next day the wall collapsed.

Glasses

My friends gave me an unusual pair of glasses as a present. One lens magnified, the other reduced what you looked at. If you looked at something with both eyes at the same time, the results could be pretty strange.

Let's say a very large and very handsome man comes up to me, and on his stomach a diminutive double of himself is flopping around like a necktie—only it has the small features of a pigmy and the manners of an ape.

The big man spreads out his massive arms and approaches me with a broad smile on his face, but I can see the little one mimicking his gestures, jerking his little arms around, and distorting his tiny mouth in a grotesque, forced smile.

The tall man slaps me on the back and guffaws, while the little one punches me in the pit of the stomach and titters.

The big man looks me square in the face, but I can't figure out where the little one is looking.

Of course, I could shut one eye. But which?

The Microbe

I was once looking through a microscope and at the other end of the barrel I saw a fat, fluffy, little microbe that looked like a teddy bear. We looked at each other in silence for a minute, each fearing infection.

"Which one are you?" I finally shouted down the barrel.

"Cholera," the microbe answered plainly. "And which are you?"

"Do you mean age?" I said, not understanding.

"No, no. Just in general. . . ."

"Well, I'm alive," I said uncertainly.

"So am I," said the microbe. "Can you be a little more precise?"

I thought about it for a long time, but couldn't come up with an answer.

"There, you see?" the microbe said reproachfully. "And here you come nosing into my life with your microscope. Figure yourself out first."

And he was absolutely right.

Cabbage

We were driven to the collective farm our office sponsors and shown a huge field of cabbage. The cabbage heads stuck out of the ground in nice, even rows. We were supposed to look for children among the cabbage. The quota was twenty-five children per worker.

I moved slowly down my row, checking under the damp, crisp leaves. No one was under the first cabbage head, but under the second there was a peasant in a jacket, smoking a cigarette.

"Oh, it's them," he gloomily ascertained.

I didn't pick him because he was overgrown. In the same row I came across a group of five people drinking vodka and munching on cabbage leaves. They didn't meet our specifications, either.

Only one child was found in the entire field. I complained to our work brigade leader.

"It's your own fault," the brigade leader said. "In the time it takes to round all you people up, they grow up. Go ahead and pick them; we'll take them as seconds."

When we had dragged all of them out and marked them as seconds, it turned out there were about a hundred of them. They sang us a folk song and went home to the village. So we stayed to harvest the cabbage.

The Fishing Pole

A line was dropped down to us from above. The pole itself wasn't visible; only the line reached up into the clouds, piercing them like a knitting needle. It was as thick as an arm and was made of stainless steel. At our end of the line a hook had been soldered on, like those on construction cranes. There was an informational brochure about heaven attached to it and a poster with the words: "Be our guests!"

People instantly began latching onto the hook. Many of them brought their belongings. They swarmed around the hook like ants and shouted, "Oh God, pull us up, will you?"

The line jerked tight and the candidates for heaven, resembling a bunch of grapes, slowly started to inch upward. When they floated past my balcony I managed to pass one of the bottom candidates a note to give to whatever authorities he found when he got there. The note said: "Cannot come. Sinful."

As soon as my messenger had shoved the note into his pocket, the line burst with a horrendous din. Everyone was scattered onto the pavement. They got up, shook the dust off their clothes, and for a long time after that cursed me for overloading the line.

INDEX